ULSTER ALIEN

GAY MEN'S PRESS

Ulster Alien

by Stephen Birkett

First published 1999 by Millivres Ltd,
part of the Millivres Prowler Group,
3 Broadbent Close, London N6 5GG

A CIP catalogue record for this book is available
from the British Library

ISBN 1 902852 01 X

Distributed in Europe by Central Books,
99 Wallis Rd, London E9 5LN

Distributed in North America by InBook/LPC Group,
1436 West Randolph, Chicago, IL 60607

Distributed in Australia by Bulldog Books,
P O Box 300, Beaconsfield, NSW 2014

Printed and bound in the EU by WSOY, Juva, Finland

This book is dedicated to all the volunteers with whom I've worked in Foyle Friend and Derry Cara-Friend, to all the people they've helped over the years and especially to those people they have yet to help.

I would like to thank Patti Christie and Veronique Gauthier for reading and correcting my manuscript and persuading me that it could be worth publishing. Also thanks to Jeff Dudgeon for checking the details of the events which led up to him taking the UK government to Strasbourg.

Part One
INNOCENCE

1: Matthew, Alexander and Daniel

The old school-house with its tall, narrow windows stood by the main road into Londonderry. On a bright May morning in 1962 a small boy gripped his mother's hand at the high, iron gate. As he gaped at the melée before him, it began to dawn upon him that his safe, cosy little world was about to be violated. Matthew wasn't Ulster born: his father's family had farmed the Westmorland hills for generations. The youngest son had married a wartime Land Girl who had immediately presented him with twins. Matthew arrived on the scene nearly ten years later. When his father-in-law fell ill in 1960, Richard agreed to move to Northern Ireland to run his farm. The twins were halfway through Grammar School so they remained in Kendal to do their O-levels, while four-year-old Matthew arrived in his new home with the status of an only child. Matthew's ash-blond fringe shaded deep blue eyes. He would have been the quintessential English cherub if it weren't for his button-like nose; it was just too snub to be cute.

Mrs Wilson relished the idea of having her new grandson at home; she hadn't seen nearly enough of the twins and wasn't at all impressed when her son-in-law announced that they were going to stay in 'that Godless country'. If she had been expecting a doting grandson, she was soon to be disappointed. He was a strangely distant child who drifted through his early years in a solitary dreamy trance. Matthew never had much opportunity to mix with other children. The neighbours had no children of his age and, suspicious of Ulster fundamentalism, Richard refused to allow his son to go to Sunday school. Worried for her grandson's immortal soul, Mrs Wilson took responsibility for his spiritual education but, being a busy woman, all this amounted to was periodically taking him to the local Church of Ireland services. She needn't have bothered. His body may have physically been on the hard, austere pew but his mind was in a world of his own; a world of fields, ponds swarming with newts, and an imaginary friend with whom he ranged over the rolling fields of Strathbeg chasing space monsters or stalking lions.

Now the fateful day had come. His mummy had put him into a crisp, blue Trutex shirt and grey shorts. She tied a blue and grey tie around his neck with a knot which dwarfed his little chin. A brand new pair of long grey socks with two broad blue bands at their tops were tugged onto his legs and pinioned to his calves with elasticated garters which cut off the circulation to his feet. His face was washed for the second time that morning and he was directed to climb into the old green Wolsley to wait for his daddy. He had been vaguely aware for some time that he had to go to school but, until he arrived at those railings, the horrible significance of this hadn't impinged on his consciousness. The first bit wasn't too bad. The teacher was nice and she gave him lots of interesting things to do. She said that he was very late starting school and that the other children of his age had been there a year already but she was sure he would soon catch up. And then it was 'playtime'. For the first time in his life he was expected to mix with other boys and he didn't like it. They played games like slaps, Chinese burns, fights and, worst of all, football.

Matthew's instinct was to avoid the rough and tumble of the playground but a dark-haired ruffian called Alexander wouldn't countenance this. After a couple of days he strutted over to where Matthew was lurking and demanded that he should join the other boys. Matthew told him thank you but he didn't want to play with them, thank you very much. At this Alexander pushed him roughly against the wall and said, "You've got to. All the boys in our class play with us." He screwed up his nose: "You're a cissy if you don't!" Matthew still declined so Alexander launched himself at him, wrestled him to the ground and pinned him to the concrete. "Will you play now?" he demanded, his face so close that Matthew could see the tiny flecks of sleep on his eyelashes. He tried to struggle but he couldn't squirm out from under his bony knees and unyielding body. He couldn't free his hands from his assailant's iron grip and, worst of all, he could smell what Alexander had just been eating, mingled with a dirty, sweaty smell that lingered on his clothes. He wasn't really hurting Matthew but the sensation of being helpless under this strong, smelly creature unnerved him. So he gave in and pretend to play for a while until he could slope off to stare longingly through the school railings.

School itself was alright though. He enjoyed learning and Miss McCormac was very kind but the end of each day was a blessed release for him. Strathbeg was about half an hour's walk from school. Once he'd left the main road, he could amble along the narrow country lane lined with towering hawthorn hedges, heavy with drifts of sweet, white blossom. It could take hours to get home and his mother wasn't in the least bit alarmed when he dawdled in at five o'clock with muddy feet and handfuls of squirming red and black, hairy caterpillars or armfuls of mayflowers. Back at the farm he could lose himself in his private world free from bullying boys and giggling girls and their nasty games.

10

And then his saviour appeared. Daniel had been off school with chickenpox when Matthew had started. As soon as he came back Matthew noticed him. He couldn't help it, he was so striking. Matthew had never seen anyone who looked quite so extraordinary before. He had a kind, freckled face with sparkling, pale blue eyes and furry, almost white eyebrows which contrasted with his shock of red hair that shone like burnished copper. Daniel liked playing with the other boys but he wasn't part of their gang. He was always getting winded and, when he did, he would abandon the game and join Matthew for a while. Daniel didn't try to force Matthew to play but told him things and asked him things. He was as tough as any of the other mini-thugs in the playground and before long he made Matthew's protection his duty. For the first time in his life Matthew had a friend who wasn't a figment of his imagination.

Keen to show Daniel around his safe little domain, Matthew asked his mother if he could invite him to the farm. Mrs Woodhead was delighted and said that she would ring Mrs McDaid to see if Daniel could stay for tea.

"No," Matthew yelped, "I haven't asked him if he wants to come yet!"

"Alright dear, but be sure to tell him to ask his mummy to telephone me if he can come."

"I'll ask him tomorrow," Matthew promised and wandered off to his den having conversations in his head with his new friend. He went through all the things he would show him, what Daniel would say and how he would admire his secret den and the flax dam where you could get frog and newt tadpoles in spring.

The next morning Matthew got to school early and was waiting for Daniel to arrive. He popped the momentous question; would he come or wouldn't he?

To Matthew's amazement Daniel didn't give it a second thought: "Yeah, if you like."

"But Mummy says that you have to ask your mummy first."

"Why?"

"To see if she'll let you come."

"Course she will."

Matthew worried that Daniel's mummy wouldn't let him come but he didn't want to push him in case he changed his mind.

Daniel's visit didn't turn out to be anything like Matthew imagined it would be. As soon as they got to the farm they ran out into the long meadow where they played tig for a bit. Then Matthew took him to the hay barn and showed him how to make tunnels and dens from the few remaining bales. They hadn't even

11

got as far as the flax dam when Mrs Woodhead called them in for tea.

Matthew had revelled in the luxury of having the wondrous boy to himself for a whole two and a half hours and felt curiously empty when Daniel had gone. The next day Daniel gave him a neat little letter inviting him to his house for tea and an envelope for him to give his mummy with an even neater thank-you note from Mrs McDaid.

And so it was that on the following Friday afternoon he walked with Daniel to his house at the edge of the rough Carson estate. Matthew was surprised at the McDaid's suburban semi; it was *so* small! Subconsciously he had expected Daniel's house to have a den and a newt pond but evidently such things weren't possible there with so many other houses around. Daniel guided him into the living room where he was left to wait whilst Daniel got changed. Matthew thought it was very cramped! Three easy chairs and a big sofa were crammed into the small room and one end was dominated by an enormous sideboard chock-a-block with an amazing clutter of photographs, shiny trinkets and an enormous statue of Virgin Mary carrying The Little Baby Jesus. There were loads of pictures on the wall too but one struck him as being rather gruesome. It was of Lord Jesus; his hands were in the air and his crown of thorns was sticking into his head, making it bleed. The worst thing was that you could see his heart; it was poking out of his chest and blood was dripping from it. It was horrible! Matthew couldn't imagine why anyone would want a picture like that in their house. He was staring at it in fascination when the door opened. He spun round fearing they could read his thoughts. Daniel came in with three small children, two with the same coppery hair as Daniel and one as blond as Matthew. Daniel put his arm around the diminutive version of himself: "This is Patrick, he's two," he said. Then he turned to the little blond boy: "Christopher's three and Soibhan" (he pronounced it *she-vaun*) "is four."

Matthew had never heard of such a name and said, "Is that foreign?"

"What?"

"Your sister's name, is it foreign?"

"Soibhan?"

"Yes," Matthew said, "That's not a proper name is it?"

Daniel laughed. "Course it is. It's Irish; like Sinead or Sean or Seamus. Do you know nothin'?"

Matthew had never heard of names like those: "Why do you call her that anyway?"

"'Cos she's Irish."

Matthew wasn't accepting that. "Well why haven't you *all* got Irish names then?" he demanded.

"We have."

"Daniel's not Irish."

Daniel frowned at him: "'Tis. Look at 'Danny Boy'. Danny's short for Daniel you know. And Patrick's our saint!" he said in a tone that told Matthew not to argue.

Daniel dismissed his siblings and took Matthew upstairs where he showed him his 'inventions'; things made out of lolly sticks and elastic bands that did things. He had a wonderful book called *Three Hundred and Sixty-Five Things to Make and Do* which gave him all his ideas. He wanted to make a formarium, a place for keeping ants, but he needed to get a queen and some workers and didn't know where to look for them. Matthew was sure they could get them on the farm and, with his heart in his mouth, told him he could come to look for them any time. Daniel eagerly accepted and his frequent visits to the farm began.

The Woodheads were delighted to accommodate Daniel and he spent practically all his free time at Strathbeg. That summer Roger was, as usual, working on the farm. At six and sixteen the two sons had little in common and Roger generally ignored his little brother, but with Daniel he was very different. Here was what a little brother should have been like; tough and sporty; a game little lad although Matthew noticed that Roger often got his friend's name wrong and called him Paddy or Mick. Matthew knew that Daniel much preferred playing boys' games and mending things with Roger but he always made sure that Matthew got most of his attention. Daniel was invited into Matthew's fantasy world. They would spend hours talking each other through adventures they could never have. Sometimes they became so involved that they tumbled into Mrs Woodhead's kitchen so full of their fantasies it was as if they really had been fighting pirates or hunting dinosaurs in the woods and fields of County Londonderry. In return Daniel taught Matthew the skills he thought all boys should have, and gradually the isolated child became averagely competent at kicking and catching the variously sized spherical objects which Daniel considered so important. The boy had an instinct around Matthew; he knew when to tease and when to relent and would initiate wrestling bouts as a ploy to improve Matthew's underdeveloped fighting skills. With his superior strength Daniel could have beaten Matthew, no problem, but he held back in the hope that his friend would discover some thus far undiscovered fighting spirit. However aggression was a totally alien emotion to Matthew and he invariably ended up pinned to the floor by his muscular friend. He didn't mind though. Daniel didn't want to hurt him and he didn't smell like Alexander did.

Alexander dominated the school with his brains and his brawn and all the tough boys were in his gang. Sometimes he tried to get Daniel into his gang despite the sectarian wishes of the other boys but Daniel was a loner. Matthew was his only friend and he would not be recruited. When Alexander wasn't courting Daniel he was warring with him. He was determined to beat him in every way. In class he wanted to be top; in sport he had to be the captain and when he fought Daniel he tried to give him a pasting. Alexander thought that there was something wrong with Matthew being Daniel's friend; he ought to be in his gang and he became another prize in the ongoing playground power struggle. Not that things were always sweetness and light between Matthew and Daniel. Daniel would sometimes push his protégé too far and then Matthew would be seduced to Alexander's side. But it was never for long. Alexander tried keep Matthew on his side through fear but Daniel invariably regained Matthew's trust and they were soon friends again. Alexander, Daniel and Matthew; three boys with little in common and yet there was an unfathomable bond which, it seemed, would never allow them to escape from each other despite their rivalries and squabbles.

Matthew began to realise that Daniel was special. He was intelligent, strong and self-confident. Boys always wanted him on their team, girls teased him flirtatiously and, best of all, he was his friend. He was so perfect that Matthew felt he could never be as good as him in real life, but in his dreams it was all so different! In one dream, which he had over and over again, he won his friend's eternal gratitude by rescuing him. Daniel was being swept down a river towards a deadly waterfall but Matthew could fly and he scooped him up in his arms and carried him to safety. Dreams like these made Matthew's tummy feel nice but they never went on long enough and he always awoke sure that he'd missed something important.

No matter how brutal he was, Alexander could never ruffle Daniel and Matthew believed that he hadn't a care in the world; it was all part of his magic. This all changed one hot Saturday in July 1966. The friends were going to build a pen in Daniel's back garden for one of Flopsy's babies. Flopsy was Matthew's Dutch rabbit and she had been mated with a buck that his daddy had brought over from Donemana. As the boys walked to Daniel's house, several youths passed them going into the estate. They were all dressed in the same, smart, pale blue uniform trimmed with red tartan.

Bright red lanyards were looped over their shoulders, they wore matching hats and some of them were carrying musical instruments. Matthew thought they were very smart but Daniel sullenly declared that they looked stupid.

The thud, thud of what must have been an enormous drum, beat time to the afternoon as they worked.

"Let's go and see them," Matthew suggested.

Daniel was unusually rude. "You want your blooming head examined!" he growled.

Matthew didn't like being told off by his normally tolerant friend but he supposed Daniel wanted to finish the job so he sulked quietly and got on with the work.

The sun was parching so they were glad when Mrs McDaid crept up and meekly suggested they might like to come in for a glass of milk and a biscuit. Sitting in the tiny kitchen they could hear the crash of the great drum getting nearer and nearer; the parade was coming out of the estate. Matthew wanted to go out onto the road to watch but Mrs McDaid wouldn't let him and told the children to go and watch from the living-room window.

They were coming. At their head was an enormous banner in scarlet, bearing a picture of a dashing, old-fashioned man waving a sword from the back of a rearing, white horse. The drum was so loud now that it seemed to be controlling Matthew's heartbeat. Chirpy pipes and snappy snare drums were playing a jaunty tune that forced his feet to tap as he pressed his snub nose to the cool glass. The music was so wonderfully exciting that it made him want to jig along and follow the band. As the marchers drew level with the house, the parade stopped. The drum was crashing inside his skull but instead of the jolly, cheering throng he expected to see beyond the garden wall, hard, hostile faces glared past him. He suddenly wondered what they were looking at and spun round. The tableau behind him was forever etched on his memory. Mrs McDaid, face pinched and white, was hugging her four frightened children. Soibhan and Christopher were whimpering although Christopher was trying not to show it. Every beat of that great drum sent in another wave of hatred breaking over them in a foam of fear.

Matthew had no idea how long they stopped outside the house; it was probably only minutes but it seemed like years. Like gutter dogs, the marchers were marking out their territory; each heart-stopping crash was another squirt of piss on the McDaid's gatepost. As the march moved on and Matthew watched them disappear down the road he began to realise that his friendship with Daniel might not always be easy.

2: Willy-John McIntyre

Only three boys passed the eleven plus. Alexander and Matthew got in to Londonderry Grammar School but, to Matthew's dismay, Daniel was to go the Christian Brothers' School. On his first morning Matthew boarded the bus resplendent in his scarlet blazer and matching cap trimmed in white and blue braid. The back seats were occupied by youths in dishevelled versions of Matthew's uniform and girls immaculate in royal blue. Near the front sat some boys in black blazers and green ties. Matthew found an empty seat near the front and waited excitedly for Daniel's stop. The bus drew up at the road into the estate and he scanned the waiting forest of blue and red blazers for Daniel's coppery head. Alexander and he were the last aboard, his hair glowing against his black blazer. Matthew pounded the seat next to him, sending up a cloud of dust and Daniel sat next to him before Alexander could take the seat. Daniel was unusually quiet and withdrawn so Matthew tried to make conversation. "What class will you be in?"

"Don't know," he mumbled.

He tried again. "Are there girls at your school?"

"No," he snapped. "It's a boys' school."

Matthew wondered why he was being so unfriendly. "What bus are you catching home?"

"Don't know," Daniel retorted, in his don't-bother-me tone.

Matthew gave up and they completed the journey in an awkward silence.

Matthew met his first new friend in the astonishing hubbub of dinner time. A boy with mousy hair, a freckled face and an impish grin was sitting next to him. Matthew had noticed him in class that morning. He seemed to know all the answers; Matthew thought he must be the cleverest boy in 1A.

"You were on the bus this morning; sitting with that ginger-headed being. I'm McIntyre, who're you?"

"Woodhead."

"Where d'you live?"

"Just outside Londonderry; Daddy has a farm at Strathbeg – where do you live?"

"Just outside Claudy. Old man's a solicitor; he's an office in Dungiven." The conversation switched to teachers. "What about Philson! Did you smell him? He's really poncy! Smyth says he wears perfume!"

A boy called Miller butted in. "It's not perfume, it's aftershave, my brother uses it."

"Which one's Philson?" Matthew wanted to know.

"French teacher; little one with short black hair and a big nose, you know he talks like this." McIntyre pinched his nose to deliver the last phrase. The others imitated his nasal voice and chortled hysterically.

"Aftershave's puffy anyway," McIntyre announced; and *that* was definitive. He turned to Matthew: "Are you catching the same bus home?"

"Yes, the quarter past four."

"You can sit with me on the way home then."

"Thanks, but I'll be sitting with Daniel."

"The ginger-knob?"

"Yes; he's my best friend."

"Well if you want to sit with him you can, but you'd be better sitting with us at the back."

"Why?"

"Just!"

"Just?"

"Just, just!"

After school there were plenty of black blazers at the bus station but there was no sign of Daniel so Matthew ended up sitting with McIntyre after all. Daniel wasn't on the bus the next morning, nor was he there that evening, so Matthew hopped on his bike and headed up to his friend's house. Daniel explained that it was better for him to get an earlier bus in the morning and after school he caught a town bus. It didn't go as far as the Carson estate but it got there earlier and it wasn't all that far for Daniel to walk home. Explanations dispensed with, the two boys compared notes on their respective schools. Matthew thought that his own school was full of extraordinary people but Daniel's was obviously much stranger. How Daniel had learned so much in two days, Matthew couldn't imagine. He told of 'brothers' who concealed weapons of torture about their persons and who were ready to use them at the slightest provocation. He described senior boys who routinely, and apparently with the sanction of the teachers, tortured the new boys. But the thing which had scared Daniel most was someone called Father Kearnan who would 'touch you up' if he thought he could get away with it. Daniel's school sounded dreadful; Matthew cycled home glad he was Protestant and wondering what touching up was.

Matthew and McIntyre teamed up with two other boys, Miller and Smyth. Like McIntyre, they were round-faced with sandy, straight hair. McIntyre's given name was William, William John actually so inevitably he was called Willy-John. William Miller was known as Billy and Crispin Smyth was soon nick-named Snotty. Willy-John's talents astonished Matthew; he knew something about everything and was constantly bringing new ideas to the group. Willy-John invariably had the first copy of the latest hit single. It was Willy-John who discovered a little shop in Londonderry where the boys could buy illicit copies of *Playboy* and he always regaled the others with what was what in the current news. At school Willy-John was too busy to give Matthew much attention but on the way home it was very different. Willy-John bounced his ideas off Matthew on the bus so he often knew of Willy-John's inspirations before the rest. That's how the normally staid Matthew gained kudos when he and Willy-John arrived in one day with their ties fixed outside their jumpers with flashy tie-pins filched from their fathers. The fashion caught on and for a brief moment his light flickered up there with Willy-John's as a style guru.

Matthew's initial disappointment at not seeing Daniel on the bus had soon become relief when he saw what a hard time his schoolfriends gave the Catholic kids on the bus. The Fenians, as the boys called the Catholics, always sat on the front seats for a quick get-away. One morning a girl sat on a first year from the Christian Brothers' School who had the temerity to occupy a seat near the back. The bus was nearly in Cloony before Matthew heard a whimper and saw a small shoe sticking out from under a rather big fourth-former. As usual the CBS boys were first off the bus at Foyle Street with the Grammar School boys hot on their heels. Matthew hung back to see if the CBS kid was OK. The terrified child scuttled about retrieving the contents of his school-bag, like a frightened squirrel collecting nuts. Matthew tried to help him but the kid told him to fuck off, gathered his things together and stalked away trying hide his tears.

The first year at the Grammar School flew by for Matthew. As the year wore on he saw less and less of Daniel as he developed new friendships at his school. Willy-John filled the vacuum but Matthew secretly pined for his ginger-headed pal. Willy-John simply wasn't the same. He admired Willy-John but never felt he wanted to be close to him. He didn't want to fight or wrestle with Willy-John and always had a vague, uneasy feeling that Willy-John didn't actually *like* him but was his friend for some other reason. For the first summer he had no regrets when he was packed off to Kendal for the holiday. He wouldn't miss Willy-John like he used to miss Daniel.

Nineteen sixty-eight was a year of international turmoil but Matthew and his friends were oblivious to it all. Civil rights was becoming an increasingly important issue in Northern Ireland; not that they would have known a civil right if it landed in the school quadrangle and flapped its wings! They simply had no inkling of the sense of injustice and frustration that was growing in the neighbouring Catholic community. Willy-John wasn't untypical in his attitude: "Never trust a Fenian," he once warned Matthew, "they'd rob their own granny for a few bob. They're bone idle too. They cry about not having jobs but you can't get a decent day's work out of them. And they're filthy too. They never wash – have you ever smelt one of them?"

Matthew didn't feel he could contradict Willy-John. Other than Daniel, he didn't know any Catholics but he'd seen some really unkempt people in Londonderry and he was pretty sure they weren't Protestants. Nevertheless he felt he had to protest on Daniel's behalf. "But they're not all like that," he objected. "I've known Daniel since he was six and he's honest and he's always clean; so is his house."

"There's always some that look alright but deep down they're all the same. It's the Celtic blood; they can't help it."

Matthew was sure he was wrong but he hadn't the confidence to argue with the fount of all knowledge.

When the bus drew up at Matthew's bus stop on the first Monday of 1969 it sounded like a motorised Orange parade. Dozens of feet stamped out a rhythm as the massed chorus pounded out 'The Sash'. He boarded as the song reached its crescendo. "THE SASH MY FATHER WORE," the pupils roared. Matthew edged past the cowed kids at the front to join his elated schoolmates; he had never seen them quite so boisterous and he soon discovered what was electrifying them.

"Thrashed the bastards."

"That'll teach them."

"Civil fucking rights! They want to learn to be a bit more civil!"

They were talking about what became known as the Battle of Burntollet Bridge. The bridge, only a couple of miles from Strathbeg, is still there but the main road to Belfast bypasses it now. There had been a march from Belfast to Londonderry under the banner of People's Democracy. It was to draw public attention to civil injustice. At that time there was a considerable body, both Protestant and Catholic, who believed that the march could achieve something. The opposition was evidently worried that it would.

So, as the weary marchers approached the end of their seventy-five mile trek, the reactionaries gathered at Burntollet armed with staves and worse. When the marchers arrived there was a fearful fracas and, according to some observers, there were plenty of policemen there who didn't intervene too enthusiastically. It would have been all too easy for Matthew to have been drawn into the general anti-Catholic euphoria. The surge of popular feeling and the thrill of being comrades in adversity seduced many of the boys into expressing sentiments they didn't really harbour. Matthew could have made many a cheap quip to be seen as less of an outsider but he couldn't forget that Danny might be one of the 'papists' to whom they would like to give a kicking.

All that year nasty things kept happening. They heard about riots, buses being burnt and water and electricity works being bombed but it just seemed to be the work of a handful of agitators. The seriousness of the deteriorating political situation didn't impinge upon Matthew until the twelfth of August that year when there was a parade by the Apprentice Boys of Derry – a confusing name for a passionately Unionist organisation. They went provocatively near the Catholic Bogside and a two-day riot ensued. The Woodheads stopped shopping in Derry and started going to Coleraine instead, and they wondered if it was going to be safe for Matthew go back to school the next term. From then on, things got worse and worse although it all seemed somehow remote. The family sat in the safety of their cosy kitchen and watched the nightly horrors unfold on their television screen. The British government sent the army in to protect Catholics from Protestant rioters but the honeymoon was short and soon the new 'Provisional' IRA was attacking soldiers and policemen. When internment was introduced there were even more bombs, hijackings, riots, shootings and – worst of all in Matthew's eyes – people's homes being burnt as Catholics were forced out of Protestant areas and vice versa. Ulster seemed on the verge of civil war.

One night, late, the phone rang. After a brief conversation Mr Woodhead came back grim-faced, said something to his wife and left hurriedly. Matthew looked at his worried mother. "What's wrong, Mummy?"

She swept a strained look from her face. "Nothing, dear."

"Where's Daddy gone?"

"Business. Now come on, it's time you were in bed."

"Night-night, Mummy."

"Goodnight my love," she said softly and looked at him with a funny smile. He had reached the kitchen door when he turned back. He wanted to ask her what was wrong but he knew he shouldn't so he just stood and looked back at her. She glided over and gave him a big hug, kissing his forehead. "Off you go now, sleep tight."

"G'night," he mumbled and crept up the stairs, puzzling.

On the bus the next morning he heard the news that the few Catholic families had been burned out of the Carson estate but it took Willy-John to spell it out for him: "I see your Fenian friend got it last night," he said with barely disguised relish.

Then Matthew felt sure that he had lost Daniel for ever.

3: 'Juliet'

Matthew had been enjoying the Grammar School but in third year things began to go wrong. He decided he wanted his friends to call him Matt which sounded more manly to him but Woodhead was just too redolent of meaning to be left alone. Blockhead, Woodentop and Tree-brain were some of the names tried out on him by inventive juvenile minds in his first two years there. Unfortunately for Matthew, juvenile minds aren't confined to schoolboys. There was one Mr Banks who taught, or was supposed to teach, English. In fact he spent most of his lessons discussing rugby with the few privileged boys who had already made it onto the under-fifteens. Mr Banks seemed incapable of using the boys' real names and Woodhead caused him no problems.

"Ena" – this unfortunate boy's name was Sharples – "You read Romeo, and bear in mind that he's an Italian noble's son and not a yobbo from the Fountain!. Chippy" – that was the name he had given Matthew – "you're Juliet; if your hair gets any longer you won't have to pretend!" He smirked.

3A sniggered.

"Juliet is fifteen and innocent. So, Chippy, use your imagination and think like a maiden – that shouldn't be too hard for you!"

There were roars of approval from the class.

Matthew took Mr Banks at his word and tried his utmost to sound like a girl. He was doing very well but 3A could barely control its mirth.

The teacher intervened. "All right Juliet – SILENCE 3A! Chippy, you had better carry on as a Londonderry boy... you seem to need more practice at that!" he said archly.

3A erupted with delight. Matthew tried to make his voice sound masculinely deep but the embarrassing squeaks that escaped added to 3A's amusement. He ground to a halt.

"CHIPPPEY!" He dragged his nickname out ominously.

"Obviously you *are* better as a girl than a boy; I'm beginning to *wonder* about you." He paused to grin conspiratorially with the sniggering class. "King," he barked, "Stop talking, boy! Can you do any better?"

Alexander King, Matthew's tormentor from primary school, had developed precociously. The biggest kid in the year, he was as useful as any fourth-former, and even some fifth-formers, on the rugby pitch. A martyr to rampant puberty, his face was a hormonal battleground. The sight of an embryonic moustache of black hairs vying for prominence with weeping yellow acne turned Matthew's stomach but Alex was one of Banks's favourites.

"As a boy or a girl, sir?" he replied cheekily; 3A thoroughly enjoyed that one.

"SILENCE," Banks roared. "As a HUMAN BEING, boy, if that's possible!"

"Yes, sir."

So Alexander lisped and verbally minced through Juliet without any danger of compromising his masculinity. It just didn't seem fair to Matthew.

Alan Beattie was the first to get a dig in. He was a smug little hard case in 3B who was renown for his vicious slagging. Matthew was in the cloakrooms one morning when Alan came up behind him. "Hey, Juliet, show us your tits," he roared.

Matthew blushed. "Bugger off," he sneered at the obnoxious face gloating at the embarrassment he had caused.

But once started the teasing gained a momentum of its own. The next incident was a few days later in the changing rooms after P.T. Matthew had just removed his sweaty vest when a pair of hands came round from behind and clamped onto his breasts. "Let's feel your boobs then, Juliet," Alan declared to his amused friends.

"Get off," Matthew whined trying to shake Alan loose.

"Come on then, give us a kiss," Alan demanded. "I hear you are a bit of a go-er, Juliet."

Matthew squirmed and clawed at Alan's hands. "Get off, you queer," he growled.

Angered, Alan kneed Matthew in the balls and sneered. "It's not me that's the queer – Juliet!"

Matthew gasped with pain and scowled at his attacker. "Bastard," he said to himself. "Bloody little bastard."

But Alan had found Matthew's weak point. All the boys in his class were galloping into puberty and they seemed to get more masculine every day. Matthew felt he was being left behind and his Beatle-cut, blonde hair, his fine features and his sylph-like physique did give him an androgynous quality.

22

He was paranoid about his lack of masculinity and every jibe about him being girlish hit home. Mocking Matthew became a class pastime and even his so-called friends weren't averse to joining in.

He loved his long hair, it was the longest in the class but he got a short back and sides in an attempt to dispel the feminine image. It was all to no avail. One rainy playtime 3A were all in their classroom. They were supposed to be supervised but the prefects were holed up in their study and the kids were going wild. Someone started singing 'Juliette' and soon the whole class was joining in the Four Pennys' hit ballad in falsetto voices: "Ju-li-e-e-ette, dooon't foor-ge-e-et. Visions of yooo, in shades of blue, Joo-leee, Joo-leee, Joo-leee-ette..." Matthew was mortified but he thought it better to ignore them and pretended to get on with his maths homework.

Every morning Matthew got ready for school dreading the humiliation that might be heaped upon him that day. He began to find excuses for staying off school; a headache was passed off as a migraine; a tummy ache became a grumbling appendix and a head cold was crippling flu. His school work declined but no one seemed to realise there was anything wrong with him. On his school report there were comments like 'More work needed' and 'Unsatisfactory progress', which meant that his teachers assumed he had turned into a lazy boy like so many others of his age.

Just after Easter he woke up in the middle of the night feeling marvellous. He felt relaxed and happier than he'd been for ages. It was several seconds before he realised that there was something wrong; his pyjama pants were warm, wet and slippery. Anxiously his hand explored the bedclothes and soon found a wet patch on the bottom sheet. It was obvious to him that he hadn't simply pissed himself. For a start it had been so nice and having a wee was never so delicious. His schoolfriends were always going on about 'wet dreams'. At first he had though that they *were* wetting their beds and he couldn't understand why they were so proud about it. However, cautious questioning had cleared up that misconception. Now he had had one at last. Now he knew what they were talking about. He could join in their banter and the others would realise he *was* a young man like the rest of them.

But at that moment his immediate concern was to get rid of the mess. He crept to the toilet praying that he wouldn't bump into anyone on the landing because then he would have to explain the wet patch on his jym-jams and he couldn't think how to. Luckily no such encounter occurred and he wrenched handfuls of toilet paper off the roll. It wasn't as easy to get the stuff off as he expected; it seemed to have insinuated itself into the very weave of the fabric. Soon he had reduced it to a tacky damp patch then he grabbed more paper, shoved it down his pyjama pants and made his way back to clean up the bed.

By next morning the heat of his body had dried it up but there was a distressingly stiff patch on his pyjamas and in the cold light of day there was a visible discolouration of the sheet around a similarly hardened patch.

The pyjamas were easy to deal with. "Mummy," he said as he wandered into the kitchen for breakfast, "Can I have some clean pyjamas?"

"Those were clean on yesterday!" she said distractedly.

"They're soakin'," he apologised, holding out the dripping garment, "I dropped them in the toilet."

His mother looked at him in exasperation. "You are the clumsiest child I know!" she exclaimed. "There's a clean pair in the hot-press, give them to me." She took the pyjama bottoms between her forefinger and thumb and dropped them into a washing basket.

He bounced onto the bus and plonked himself down next to Willy-John. How could he bring it up? He decided on the direct approach: "Had a wet dream last night."

"Good one?" his friend asked.

"Yeah."

"What was it about?"

That threw Matthew. He didn't recall it being *about* any thing; it just *was*. "Can't remember," he admitted.

"Can't have been that good, then," Willy-John scoffed.

"Suppose," Matthew admitted. "What're yours about?"

"Fit birds, of course," he grinned impishly. "Everybody's dreaming about gorgeous wimmin when they have 'em!" He jabbed Matthew in the ribs with his elbow. "Bet *you* were really. You're just too goody-goody to admit it," he cajoled.

"Aye," Matthew conformed, forcing his face into what he hoped Willy-John would interpret as a sexually interested leer, "it must have been about a woman." Next time, he thought, he would have to try to pay more attention to its content.

His bed wasn't due for changing until Monday so that night he sneaked the sheet into the bathroom and scrubbed at the semen stain with a soap-loaded nailbrush before rinsing it clean. There was now a huge damp patch but at least it was only water. He dried it as best as he could with a towel and smuggled the sheet back to his room. He spent an uncomfortable night on a wet sheet but by the morning it was dry and, thankfully, stain-free. Partly to his relief and partly to his disappointment he didn't have another wet dream that night.

He'd almost forgotten about wet dreams when the next one came. It was weeks later and he was having a marvellous dream. He was underwater but it was warm and dry and he was floating free and relaxed. The water was caressing his naked body and sucking at his groin. Streams of pleasure rushed from his lungs, from his sides, from his legs, all coursing towards his groin and suddenly he felt as if his whole being was surging out of his penis. It was wonderful and he woke up knowing it had happened again. This time he knew exactly what to do. He washed his pyjama pants in the bathroom and mopped up the mess on the sheet with a wet face-flannel. It would dry overnight and his mum would never know anything.

"Willy-John." Matthew asked quietly as they waited in the dinner queue.

"Yeah?"

"I had another wet dream last night."

"Aye?"

"There wasn't anyone in it."

"No birds?"

"No."

"You're weird, Chippy. You should be dreaming about birds you know," he whispered.

"I was swimming," Matthew explained. "In the nude. And I just came and came and came!"

"You perve!" Willy-John giggled.

Aaron was behind them in the queue. "What's up with you two?" he demanded.

Willy John started, "Matthew's been having..." but Matthew put his hand over his friend's mouth.

"Shut up!" he ordered.

Willy-John fought free: "Matthew's been having sexy dreams," he shouted before Matthew gagged him again.

Mr Banks was on duty. He overheard Willy-John and rushed over to stop them tussling.

"Come here McIntyre, you disgusting boy," he demanded. "If I hear that sort of language from you again, it will be cold showers for you every day!" He turned to Matthew and put on a falsely gentle voice. "I'm sure Woodhead's not like that, are you, Chippy?"

"No sir," he said shamefacedly.

"She probably has periods," Aaron said snidely.

Banks tried to suppress a smirk: "I heard that, Lindsay. Shut up or you'll be having cold showers along with them."

Aaron glanced at Matthew and his face fell.

"Don't worry, I won't make Chippy go in with you!" Banks laughed.

Matthew couldn't believe he had said that. He looked desperately at Willy-John but he was grinning from ear to ear so he slunk back into the dinner queue hoping it would swallow him up.

On the bus home he tackled Willy-John. "Why did you tell Aaron?" he demanded.

"What?"

"About my dream."

"It was only a joke," he said limply.

"That wasn't fair. You *know* what Aaron's like! Never misses a chance for a slagging." Matthew complained. "You set me up!"

"You don't want to listen to him! Anyway it serves you right for going on about your wet dreams; what do you expect?"

Matthew looked crestfallen.

Willy-John took pity on him. "Come on Matthew, Cheer up. It's only nine days to the holidays. Nine more days to go, nine more days of sorrow," he began to sing.

Matthew joined in, "Nine more days of work, no rest. Eight more days tomorrow..."

4: Tommy Jennings

As usual, Matthew was sent to Kendal for most of the summer. He always enjoyed his visits to Birkholm where he spent the blissful, innocent weeks with his cousin playing and generally drinking in the beauty of south Westmorland.

"Do you have a girlfriend, Matthew?" Amanda asked as they sat by the tarn above Birkholm.

He lobbed a few pebbles into the still water. "No," he replied cautiously, "I'm not ready for that sort of thing yet. Do you have a boyfriend?"

"Not at the moment... but there *is* a boy in my class."

"What's he called?"

"Tommy Jennings. He's so nice. Not as nice as you Matthew," she added quickly, "but he's so handsome. He's got curly black hair and the loveliest blue eyes you ever did see. He's *such* a dreamboat."

Matthew was intrigued. "What *is* it about a boy that makes you like him?"

She thought a moment and said, "It's hard to say exactly. He's got to be good-looking but it's more than that. He's got to be kind to me and he's got to stand up for me when I need him to.

He's got to be clever and he's got to have a good sense of humour. Tommy's a right laugh you know. He can say things to the teachers and they never tell him off because he's so nice and clever. He's good at games too. He plays footy for the school team."

"I'd like to meet him," Matthew said without really knowing why.

Amanda beamed, this was the excuse she'd been waiting for – 'my cousin is lonely and doesn't know any boys round here' – it was perfect. "I could invite him over for tea. If you would *really* like to meet him," she suggested.

Matthew was suddenly scared and he didn't know why. "Yeah, okay," he said nonchalantly propelling stones as far as he could into the lake.

Tommy came over two days later. Amanda was right, he was a charming, effervescent boy and he soon had captivated Matthew, much as Daniel had done nine years before.

Matthew's Auntie Mary took the three youngsters to Windermere for the day. They had lunch at the Swan Hotel in Newby Bridge then took a rowing boat out. The two boys took the bow end and rowed Amanda and her mother along the reed-lined river as far as the lake.

Tommy was a year younger than Matthew but he was stronger and Matthew had to struggle to keep pace with him. When he slackened off the boat started going in circles and once, in an attempt to keep up with Tommy he splashed him. Tommy wasn't cross though but simply giggled and started to splash Matthew back. Matthew responded and a hysterical water fight ensued with Auntie Mary vainly trying to warn them about capsizing the boat and Amanda screeching that they were soaking her.

At last they stopped and, drenched to the skin, the two boys collapsed back onto one another, laughing uncontrollably.

Tommy's body was warm through his cold, wet shirt. For a few magical moments Matthew's head cradled on Tommy's chest. He could hear Tommy's strong little heart thumping under his heaving ribs. He closed his eyes and a warm familiarity impinged upon his consciousness. This was the first time he'd been physically close to another person since he had lost Daniel, and it felt good.

"Come on boys," Auntie Mary chortled. "We'd better get back or they'll be charging us for another hour!"

After he'd gone home the cousins talked about Tommy.

"He's lovely, isn't he," Amanda sighed.

Matthew wanted to agree but he knew that wasn't the right response so he said, "Yeah. He's a good laugh."

"He liked you," she said, "er, do you think he liked me?"

Matthew's heart skipped a beat. He did like me, he thought. Not like Willy-John. Not feeling sorry for me. He *liked* me! Why, he thought, couldn't I have met him at the beginning of the holiday?

He had been thinking long enough; he had to answer his cousin: "He didn't *say* anything but I *think* he did, you know."

"Well he's coming back next week, so I'll find out then," she grinned.

"I won't be here," Matthew objected. "I'm going back on Friday."

"I know that," Amanda smiled, "but he doesn't!"

Matthew was impressed by his little cousin's deviousness but a bit peeved that she would have him all to herself. "You crafty thing!" he exclaimed.

"I'll write and tell you all about it," she grinned as he went up to bed.

That night he had his best erotic dream to date. He knew how to deal with its consequences by then but this one puzzled him because for the first time it *was* about *somebody* and it was *so* vivid. His naked body was touching another. He couldn't be sure in what way they were touching or who he was touching but there was an image in the dream. An disturbingly attractive image of someone with black curly locks and sparkling blue eyes. It could have been a girl but, equally, it could have been Tommy.

Matthew prayed that the teasing wouldn't continue into fourth form but his prayers were not answered; to many in his class he *was* Juliet.

Willy-John and the others didn't take it seriously. They told Matthew he was being pathetic and that if he would wise up it would stop. It didn't, in fact the intensity and frequency increased and by Christmas Matthew was at his wits' end. He had to get away from that hell-hole. Anywhere would do but there was one perfect solution. He would ask his parents to send him to school in Kendal like his brother and sister before him and if he went there he would be able to be friends with Tommy too. He would leave it until Christmas though. Jenny and Roger would be home and everyone would be in a good mood and by then his mummy and daddy would have had time to digest what he *knew* was going to be a scathing school report.

The prefects' Christmas review was coming up and every junior pupil was anxiously watching the prefects' notice-board to see if they had been selected to perform. Matthew's heart jumped when Mark Christie bustled into the classroom and said, "It's up! And Matthew's been chosen!"

"What am I doing?" he cried.

Mark made sure that as many of the class were listening before delivering his coup de grâce. "Juliet's going to be the head boy's floozy, of course!"

The whole class erupted in cat-calls and wolf-whistles. Chrissie Gilmore stuck his face in Matthew's. "You're going to get screwed by Billy Brown on stage. Lucky old Juliet!"

That was the final straw. Matthew lost it, grabbed his wooden pencil case and slammed it into the side of Chrissie's head. Chrissie reeled and Matthew thumped him in the ribs before he had recovered. As Chrissie jumped up and lunged at his assailant the class closed in and formed a ragged, cheering semicircle around the now struggling pair.

A stentorian voice broke though the clamour and 4A disappeared as if by magic leaving a trembling Matthew to face Billy Brown; the huge, rugby-playing head boy.

"What was going on?" he roared.

"Nothin'," Matthew snivelled.

"Well get out then," the head boy ordered.

To his amazement Matthew found himself saying, "No, I'm not your girlfriend yet. You can't tell me what to do!"

Billy stared at the little fourth-former in astonishment. "What are you talking about? What's your name, anyway?"

"Matthew Woodhead," Matthew admitted. "I'm not going out. I hate them all and I hate this bloody school. I hate everyone in this place and they all hate me," he screamed.

Billy put a friendly hand on Matthew's shoulder. "I don't hate you, Matthew," he reassured.

Matthew looked at the huge man in terror. "I'm not going to be your girlfriend, am I?" he asked weakly.

Billy started. His immediate response was to lash out, thinking that this was some bizzare slur on his sexuality, but Matthew was so obviously miserable that he felt he had to find out what was going on and help him if he could. "Sit down, Matthew, and tell me what you're talking about."

Matthew explained and Billy laughed in relief. "No, Matthew. I'm sorry. You aren't in the review. Your friends were having you on."

"They're no friends of mine," Matthew grumbled.

"Forget it. They're just immature wee brats. You don't want to be taking any notice of them. They'll grow out of it you know. Look. You stay here for a while and pull yourself together. If anyone comes, tell them you have my permission to stay in, okay?"

Matthew sniffed and nodded and the head boy left him in peace. He buried his face in his folded arms and sobbed quietly. I can't stand this any more, he said to himself. If I killed myself then they would see. Then they would know how much they've hurt me.

He tried to imagine the most dramatic way to finish himself. It would have to be at school to make the right impact and his thoughts wandered to the chemistry lab; lots of deadly things in there, he thought. He revelled in the idea of punishing the other boys for their persecution of him but the picture of his distraught parents rather spoiled the anticipated pleasure.

He heard a sound and sensed a shadow falling over him. At first he thought that Billy was back but instead Alexander was towering over him.

"Are you alright, Matthew?" he grunted.

Matthew nodded unconvincingly.

"This is really getting at you, isn't it?" he said softly. "You're getting near the end of your tether, aren't you?"

Matthew swallowed: "What is it to you? You started it!"

"Aw come on, Matthew. That was ages ago and I didn't mean anything!"

"I know, I know. It's my own fault, if I was more like a bloke..." He stopped, appalled at what he had admitted to his enemy.

"Don't be dopey, Matthew. Of course you're a bloke. I've seen you in the showers, remember."

Matthew blushed violently. He was acutely embarrassed by his few pale pubic hairs next to his classmates' burgeoning bushes and he was convinced he had the smallest dick ever.

"Look Matthew," Alex continued, "I would stick up for you if I thought it would help but I can't always be there for you. You have to fight your own fights. Giving Chrissie a belt was the best thing you could have done. He'll think twice before slagging you again and maybe some of the others will too. And I'd stop talking about my wet dreams if I was you," he added gently. "The others think you're twisted going on about it so much. Why not stop yourself having them?"

"How?" Matthew whimpered.

"Like everyone else does. Toss yourself off! If you get rid of it, you won't come in your sleep. It's obvious, isn't it?"

"Everyone else tosses off?" he said in disbelief.

Alex chuckled and his face lit up.

Matthew realised for the first time that Alex was actually

quite good looking. Just as the rest of the class were erupting in spots, his acne had cleared. Now he had shaved all those indecent black hairs from his cheeks and chin he looked a little bit like a younger Paul McCartney.

"Matthew. You're wild innocent you know. Beattie and his gang have a tossing-off club every lunchtime behind the rhododendrons. Why don't you join them?"

Matthew was repelled by the thought, though he was intrigued as to exactly what they got up to. "What do they do?"

"*I* don't know! I wouldn't want to join that lot. I do it on my own!"

"How *do* you do it?"

"You've never done it?" Alexander asked incredulously.

Matthew shook his head. "Never."

"You're not a Fenian, are you?"

Matthew was astonished: "You know I'm not. Why did you say that?"

"They don't toss off, you know. They're terrified of having a wet dream because they think they'll go to hell if they come. Their dads check their sheets in the morning to make sure, you know."

That sounded scary to Matthew. "But it's not like that for us Protestants, is it?"

"Nah. I wouldn't go telling your minister you're tossing though," he grinned. "Our lot think any sex is wrong but it's different. They think it's immoral but not, er... you know?"

Matthew hadn't a clue what he was talking about but said he did.

"Look," Alex said confidentially. "I've this really sexy girly mag. I just take it into the toilet and get my dick out and Bob's your uncle."

Matthew realised he was getting a hard-on. "You mean you look at dirty pictures and that does it to you?"

Alex sniggered. "No, you dim-wit! I pull myself off." He made a wanking gesture with his semi-closed hand in his groin, then waved his hand in Matthew's face. "With my hand."

As the rest of the class began to stream into the classroom, without warning, Alex violently fell back from Matthew, crashing into the next desk and clutching his balls. Before Matthew had a chance to ask him what was wrong he began too make profuse apologies. "Sorry Matthew, I won't call you that again. I promise."

Alex rose slowly from the desk and limped over to his own desk at a crouch. Chrissie joined him and they commiserated with each other for getting on the wrong side of Matthew's temper.

During the lesson Matthew glanced across at Alex who gave him a big wink and made the wanking gesture from under his desk. Matthew winked back and returned the sign.

Matthew got hold of a copy of *Playboy* and tried to do like Alex had suggested but the busty girls posed behind judiciously placed potted palms and tastefully draped flimsy material did nothing for him. He guessed he wasn't doing it right and, in desperation, asked Alex for advice.

"You could join the tossers," he smirked, "or go for the real thing!"

"What do you mean?"

"Get a bird and you can have it off with her."

"Have you... done it?"

"Course! Loads of times," Alex boasted.

Matthew felt pathetic next to such a stud. "I'm too young yet, I'm not ready," he whimpered.

"You'll do it in time," his new friend assured him. "It takes longer for some than others, that's all. Anyway, you know my mag? I don't need it any more so you can have it if you like."

The following Saturday Alex turned up at the farm with a duffel bag. "I've brought it," he said, patting the bag. The two youngsters pounded up to Matthew's bedroom.

"Let's have a geek," Matthew asked breathlessly.

"Patience, Matthew, patience," Alex joked as he drew the dog-eared magazine out of the bag. He spread the magazine on the floor and the boys lay side by side as Alex turned the pages. "She's gorgeous, isn't she," Alex breathed, nudging Matthew."

"Aye," Matthew agreed.

"She really turns me on. This is the one I usually use, you can tell by the sticky bits!" Alex sniggered.

"Yeah," Matthew said excitedly, "she is really sexy." To his delight he really was turned on and he could feel his penis hard against the carpet.

"Well," Alex said. "Better go before we get too horny, eh? Enjoy them." And with that he was gone. Matthew rushed to the toilet and had his first wank. It was so easy. He used Alex's magazines for a while. Most of the pictures didn't work but that one, the one with the sticky bits, always did the trick. Eventually he realised he didn't need the magazine and burnt it in case his parents found it, but he had learnt how to masturbate and it did cut down the wet dreams. Not only that but the other boys had stopped teasing him and he started fifth form feeling that things might not be too bad after all.

5: Being Grown-Up

By the time Matthew came to do his O-levels the civil unrest had escalated. On the last Sunday in January everyone had been stunned by the events at the Rossville flats, a 1960s concrete development just by Derry's old city walls. A hostile crowd which had assembled to demonstrate against army harassment had been fired upon by the Parachute Regiment. Thirteen of the demonstrators were killed and another died later. Bloody Sunday, as it came to be known, was officially justified by claiming that the victims were all armed; Matthew and his friends believed it because the alternative was unthinkable. Nevertheless he anxiously scanned the list of victims in the *Derry Journal*. The name leapt out of the page; there it was, McDaid, but to his relief it wasn't Daniel nor any of his family, as far as he could tell.

The nationalist backlash to Bloody Sunday was dramatic; parts of Londonderry became 'no go areas' and bombs ripped out its very heart. Things were bad elsewhere too; in Belfast the Abercorn Cafe was bombed killing two and horrifically injuring scores of others; it was the first time the Provisional IRA had deliberately targeted civilians and Ulster reeled. Hope came in the guise of a cease-fire but the IRA demanded a total British withdrawal and when this was rejected the violence started again with increased ferocity. Now civilians had definitely become the targets.

As soon as his exams were over he went to his uncle's for summer. Ostensibly it was to help on the farm but Matthew was fully aware that this annual visit was to get him away from Ulster's troubles for a couple of months. On his arrival Amanda introduced him to Michael, her new boyfriend; to Matthew's quiet satisfaction she had never managed to get off with Tommy.

Michael was a year older than Matthew and very keen on hiking. He had quickly got Amanda hooked and they were both keen to introduce Matthew to the Lake District hills.

He took to hill-walking immediately and spent many happy days on the fells. He would have been even happier if Tommy had wanted to come along but he was too busy with his current girlfriend.

The last walk of the holiday was the most ambitious. It was up Pavey Arc, a dramatic buttress in the Langdales. At first glance a novice would think that only an experienced rock-climber could possibly attempt the ascent but there was a walkers' path up.

A short walk brought them to the far side of Stickle Tarn and the bottom of a steep scree which spewed from the base of the cliff. As they scrambled up the scree they passed rugged rock-climbers sorting out their ropes and karibiners. The path followed a cleft diagonally up the face. Most of the way there was a banister of rock up one side and the rock face at the other so he felt safe but there were two hairy bits. The first was about three-quarters of the way up where the fault line folded back on itself. For a short distance he was on an exposed ledge and looking down the giddying drop he saw the helmets of the real men climbing below him. The second dodgy bit was near the top; it was known as the Bad Step. There was a huge block lodged in the gully; Amanda and Michael swarmed over it but Matthew held back, terrified.

If it had been at ground level it wouldn't have created any difficulty whatsoever, but he looked back down the gully and realised that if he slipped he would slither down the chute and be catapulted out into thin air. It wasn't the air that worried him!

He took his life in his hands and scrambled over it like a clumsy puppy. As soon as he was in reach, Michael grabbed his hand and hauled him up. He had done it; he was inordinately proud of himself.

Another of Michael's passions was a radio programme called 'I'm Sorry I'll Read That Again'. He was delighted when Matthew took to it and by the end of the holiday they had listened to every show he had on tape. Matthew could join in extended renditions, revelling in the surrealistic banter as they made their way over the hills. The cracked voice which had given 3A so much amusement was perfect for Lady Constance DeCoverlet, the monstrous dowager created by Tim Brooke-Taylor.

Shortly after Matthew left Northern Ireland there had been a horrendous car bomb in Claudy. It had gone off without warning in the main street of the sleepy little village a few miles from Strathbeg. His mother told him about friends who had been going about their everyday business one minute and who were shredded by the blast the next. Six locals were lost that day. In comfortable Kendal it sounded so awful; he couldn't imagine life at home could ever be the same again and he was dreading going back. And yet, when he returned, the outrage had been absorbed as just one more atrocity that had to be endured. At school it was topical for a while but soon its currency was supplanted by fresher horrors.

The two summer months had wrought great changes on Matthew and his friends; they left as fifth-formers in grubby junior uniforms and returned transformed into smart young men in immaculate sixth-form outfits. Michael had transferred some of the best I.S.I.R.T.A. shows onto audio-cassettes which Matthew took to school with a forbidden portable cassette player. For nearly two weeks he was the person it was in to be with and boys pushed close to him to hear the precious tapes. Then, to his dismay, Billy Miller discovered 'Round The Horne' and Matthew's standing waned. Matthew had to admit that 'Round The Horne' was brilliant though; there were two characters called Julian and Sandy and they talked like two old women. It was even funnier when Willy-John explained that they were supposed to be fruits. If anyone wanted to get a guaranteed laugh, all he had to say was, "Hello, my name's Julian and this is my friend Sandy," in a simpering, nasal tone. It was Willy-John who first christened a pair of quiet boys in the class Julian and Sandy, and started a pernicious persecution of the two hapless creatures next to which Matthew's experiences paled into insignificance.

Being sixth-formers, getting a woman became a priority. Alexander, Willy-John and Crispin had been going to dances since fourth form but the rest of them were innocents. Their first opportunity to try their hands came at Christmas. The Girls' High School was having a dance and the sixth form was invited – the men would be there.

"What are you wearing?" Matthew asked Willy-John on the bus home.

"Standard pullin' gear," he replied casually.

"Oh, aye," he tried to sneer. "What like?"

"Smooth, sexy; usual style."

Matthew's bravado evaporated: "I don't think I've got anything like that. All I've got's my suit."

"Colour is it?"

"Charcoal grey. You know the one; I wore it at your granny's funeral."

Willy-John raised his eyes heavenwards: "Got any decent shirts?"

"I've a new one," he enthused. "It's white but it's a penny round!"

"Fuck, Matthew! Have you nothin' even a bit with it?"

"You know I've never really been interested in clothes," he said weakly. "I don't go out much really."

"Well it's about time you did! You're never going to pull in your Sunday best. Is that what you want?"

Matthew reddened. "Course not. It's just that I've no money to get any clothes, leastways not till after Christmas. I'd better not go. You'll enjoy it better without me hanging around."

"You're just looking for sympathy, tosser. If you don't come to this dance you can forget coming anywhere with me again. You can just sit on your bloody farm and play with yourself. Christ, Matthew! You've got to wake up and stop being such a pathetic weed. Women aren't going to queue up at your door waiting for you to take your pick! You've gotta go out an' get 'em man; you're only young once!"

Matthew sat on the shuddering bus staring at his feet.

Willy-John softened. "I'll tell you what, some of my stuff would fit you."

"But you're twice my size!"

"Aye, I am, but I was your size not that long ago. I reckon I could fix you up with a jacket and a pair of trousers and I've loads of shirts. They were dead on when I bought them," he smirked, "so you'll only look a wee bit culchie!" He thumped Matthew and grinned the smile that had melted a thousand girls' hearts. "Come round tonight and we'll get you fixed up, okay?"

The bus was pulling up at Matthew's stop.

"Dead on," Matthew beamed. "See you after supper then. See-ya!"

As Matthew dashed to the front of the bus his school bag bounced off a few Fenian heads. The driver had just shut the doors and opened them again with bad grace. "Hi boy!" he snarled, "wake up. You'll go to the next stop next time."

He would too, the bastard, Matthew thought as he jumped off the moving bus and swung down the lane. He was on a high; Willy-John had taken him in hand and everything would be alright.

Willy-John and his father picked Matthew up at a quarter to eight. As he left, his mother gave him three quid. It would easily pay him in and there would be enough left over to buy pop and crisps.

Willy-John turned to him in the car. "Your mum gave you some dough?"

"Aye, three quid."

"Irish?"

He delved into his pocket; they were Southern Irish bank notes – punts.

"Darn! I never thought. What do you think?"

In border areas British and Irish pound notes were interchangeable but some loyalists were beginning to refuse the Irish currency. It would only need there to be an awkward so-and-so on the door to put him in an embarrassing situation. Fortunately Mr McIntyre was able to change the notes.

The dance was being held in a church hall in the Waterside, the mostly Protestant east side of the River Foyle. They couldn't have it in the school as no one would risk going to the city side at night. Matthew felt sorry for Billy. He lived near the school and his parents wouldn't let him out at all so he couldn't go to the dance. The rest of them lived on the east side of the river but it was still a bit of a novelty to go out at all. Everyone had heard about IRA roadblocks and hijackings on the dark, country roads around Londonderry so most people didn't venture out much at night.

They paid and went into the dimly lit hall. At the far end, on a small stage, a band was churning out 'Jambalaya'. A few girls were jiving on the dance floor but most people were in single-sex clusters just inside the door. Matthew thought his schoolmates looked really grown-up now they were dressed up; some fellers who were nothing in school uniform looked really handsome. Aaron and Crispin were already there. On seeing Matthew and Willy-John a delighted Crispin steered them to a dark corner.

"Keep a watch," he ordered Aaron.

Aaron turned his back on the little group and nonchalantly watched the hall.

Crispin pulled something out of his jacket; it was a half bottle of vodka. With a quick twist he removed the cap, took a surreptitious slug and passed it to Willy-John who wiped the neck with his sleeve; as he drank, bubbles glooped up through the clear liquid. He handed the bottle to Matthew, who hesitated.

"Go on, Matthew," Crispy urged. "It'll help you relax."

Aaron was getting impatient. "Come on, hurry up."

It's the Big Step all over again, Matthew thought, don't think about the pros and cons, just do it. He put the bottle to his lips and gulped. The fiery liquor burned on its way down, making him cough and splutter. Crispin grabbed the bottle, resealed it and whipped it into his pocket with one swift, smooth action as Willy-John pounded Matthew's back and gave him some Coke to sip.

"What the buck're you doin'? Come on, hurry up," Aaron complained.

No one else had noticed Matthew's distress so Willy-John kept an eye open for teachers whilst Aaron had his share.

Aaron quizzed Matthew. "Never drunk vodka before?"

"No," he admitted shamefacedly.

"Just beer, I suppose."

"Actually I've never taken drink; unless you count wine on special occasions."

"I might've known! Typical middle-class English. All very *nice*," he emphasised, making it sound distasteful in the extreme.

"Doesn't drink, doesn't go with wimmin, what a poof! What did you come for?" Crispin sneered.

"Piss off," Matthew said, acutely embarrassed.

"Okay, Romeo," Crispin challenged, "show us what you're made of. See the one in the blue dress? You ask her; I'll tackle her friend."

Matthew was dizzy and his heart was thumping as he went over to the girl in blue. She had long, blonde hair and a fine, porcelain face; she was dauntingly good looking.

"Excuse me," he stuttered. She half turned towards him. "Would you like the next dance?"

Crispin was negotiating the same manoeuvre with her friend but in a more accomplished style. The girls looked at each other and smirked. "All right then," the girl in blue conceded, "but only if it's a fast one."

The next set started with 'Popcorn'; a bouncy tune with the tempo of a demented fairground organ. They bobbed and jerked to the music, arms flailing, skirts swirling and jackets flapping. To his surprise he enjoyed dancing with her and was quite peeved when the girls said thank you at the end of the set and fled into the toilets.

"You're in there," Crispin nudged. "Mine's a bit of a slag. Ask yours up again when she comes out of the bog."

The two lads found a table opposite the toilets and kept watch. When their targets finally emerged they made a bee-line for some other girls at a table and merged with them but Matthew hadn't the nerve to approach such a coven. Willy-John joined them with three Coca-Colas.

Matthew sipped his – it tasted peculiar: "What's this?"

"Vodka and Coke."

Matthew was taken aback but he wasn't about to let the others know. "Oh. Great! It's dead on."

"He's improving," Willy-John grinned. "Might not be a virgin much longer!"

Matthew was trying to think what he would say to the blue-dressed girl if he did manage to get her up for a dance. He asked Willy-John for advice.

"Just chat her up," his friend reassured.

"What should I say?"

Willy-John was deadpan: "Ask what university she wants to

go to. Where she lives. What music she likes. Does she screw?"

The last one worried Matthew. What if she said yes?

Willy-John produced more vodka and Matthew bought some Cokes. He watched, waited and drank. Eventually the cabal fragmented leaving his subject exposed. He weaved over to her. "Want another dance?"

"Sure," she said as if he had asked her for a light.

"Do you like this one?" he ventured.

She glanced at her friends, said "It's alright," and led him onto the dance floor.

As they bopped to 'Jumping Jack Flash' Matthew realised that the Coke was churning uncomfortably in his stomach. Oh my God! he panicked; it was coming up! Hand over mouth, he fled to the toilets; black liquid squirting out between his fingers. He retched into a hand basin and suddenly the men were all there, cleaning him up with toilet roll and paper towels. They made him drink water, tidied him up and escorted him back to the table where a High School teacher bore down upon them. "What's wrong with you, boy?" he demanded imperiously.

"Too much Coke, sir," Willy-John answered, "Fizzed up in him when he was dancing, sir."

"Can't he speak for himself?" the teacher said sternly. "Have – you – been drinking, boy?" he demanded, sniffing in Matthew's direction.

"No sir," Matthew said confidently. "Just not feeling very well, sir."

He scrutinised Matthew's pale face as if making up his mind whether or not to accept his story. "If I find you've been drinking," he threatened, "your headmaster will know of it first thing Monday morning."

"Yessir," they all said in contrite unison.

As soon as the teacher was out of the way Matthew was applauded: "Brill Matthew, you carried it off."

"Yeah, fooled the stupid old cunt. Can't beat the men, eh!"

The girl in blue came over: "Is he alright?"

"I'm okay, just a bit too much Coke, you know."

"Yes I *know*," she said meaningfully.

Matthew smiled conspiratorially.

"Do you still want to dance then?" she asked.

"I'd better not just yet, thanks very much, I'd better let my stomach settle down a bit," he replied weakly.

Willy-John broke in: "I'll dance," he smiled.

She accepted and they melted into the jigging throng leaving Aaron and Crispin to berate him for being slow on the uptake.

Aaron said, "Come on Crispy, let's tackle those two." And, turning to Matthew, "You'll be alright on your own, won't you?"

Matthew watched glumly as they insinuated themselves between two girls in Laura Ashley print dresses who were bopping around their handbags.

His preoccupation was interrupted: "Hi!" It was the other girl, the one Crispin had called a slag. "Are you okay?"

"Aye," he said, trying to smile but failing miserably.

"You don't sound it." She sat down opposite him. She had long, mousey blonde hair, a round face, glasses and a lot of make-up. Her dress was a long, straight black shiny thing with red flowers all over. It was hanging off her shoulders by thin straps. "I'm Sandra."

"Hi, I'm Matthew." Now what did Willy-John say? he thought. University, home, music, screwing. No – better forget the screwing. "What A-levels are you doing?"

"Home economics and English."

That was easy, he thought: "I'm doing biology, geography and maths. What do you want to do when you finish?"

"Nursing at the Royal, what about you?"

"Dunno yet, I'll have to wait and see how they go. What do you need for nursing?"

"Just O-levels actually but if you have A-levels you can get in easier."

Before he knew it they were deep in conversation. She was very nice, really easy to talk to but he didn't want to kiss her or anything. He supposed that would come in time.

After the disaster of the High School dance his mates slagged him mercilessly for totally failing to get off with a woman who was, as they so delicately put it, dying for it. He probably wouldn't have gone out with them again had he not been the first of the gang to get his driving test. He became instantly popular because his father let him have the farm Landrover. Not only was it the only vehicle at the clique's disposal but it could carry ten quite comfortably. His father reasoned the vehicle was so decrepit that if he did hit something, he couldn't do himself much harm. It took Willy-John to show him how wrong he was. Nine months later Willy-John wrote off his father's expensive car in a slight contretemps with a 'pig', one of the Saracen armoured cars the army were driving around in. It came at him on the wrong side of the road and neatly removed the car's near-side along with the – fortunately empty – passenger seat. For some unfathomable reason he was wearing his seat belt and came out with a broken collar bone, a few cuts and some bad bruises.

Once mobile the friends were out on the tear every weekend. Their evening would start in the Regal, a tiny pub on the Waterside. After that they headed to a dance somewhere. Often it was the City of Derry Rugby Club or the Drummond Hotel in Ballykelly. If they were feeling more adventurous they might stray as far afield as Omagh or Portrush. Sandra, Helen (the girl in blue) and another High School girl called Jean became part of the clique. Sandra was nominally Matthew's girlfriend for a while but they never actually went together, the others drifted in and out of various permutations.

Billy had been excluded from the clique's nocturnal ramblings by virtue of where he lived. He complained bitterly all the time but was at his most miserable on Monday mornings. Ten-thirty would find the clique lounging in their corner of the sixth-form study. Willy-John was in history but the rest of them were free and this was their first opportunity to mull over the events of the weekend. One particular Monday Aaron started the ball rolling. "Some craic Saturday night, Billy; should've seen Alex."

Until sixth form Alex had been considered a bit too plebeian for the clique. His friends had been the hard Orangemen from the rough housing estates. Although Matthew was beginning to like Alex he was wary of his friends with their intimidating attitudes and language and their hopelessly myopic view of the world. However most of the extreme hard men had left after failing their GCEs and those that had stayed on seemed to have mellowed. Alex, Willy-John, Crispy and Aaron were only lower-sixth boys in the first XV rugby team so Alex had become one of the clique and an occasional occupant of Matthew's Landrover.

Aaron continued to gloat about Alex's adventure. "Yeah, spent all night chatting up this woman from Limavady and when she went to the bogs d'you know what he did?"

Knowing Alex as he did, it wasn't difficult for Billy to guess. "I can't imagine," he said disinterestedly.

"Took her friend outside for a court and got back before the other one came out of the bog. And after about ten minutes, didn't he take the first one outside too! Some neck on that boy!"

"He's a fly bastard," complained Crispy. "If I tried it on like that I'd get a slap round the beak!"

"Just a smooth operator, aren't you Alex?" Aaron grinned, hoping for a reciprocal compliment.

But Alex didn't oblige: "You either have it or you don't; and you don't," he said coolly. Then, rising to his full six foot one, he strolled out of the study room leaving Aaron to try to salvage his credibility.

Billy watched as Alex brazenly walked past the staff room a full seven minutes before the bell would make such a traverse legal. "I don't know how he does it. He's an ignorant gulpin and yet he gets away with blue murder. If *we* got up to *half* the things he does we'd be up in front of the boss like a shot but the teachers bloody well love him! And he treats women like shit and they flock about him like flies round a midden."

"You'll have to see him in action to understand," Matthew said. "Then you'll know how he does it. It's his savoir-faire."

"Is that aftershave?" Billy quipped.

"No it's know-how, what you and me ain't got, isn't that right Crispy?"

"Speak for yourself," he sneered.

"I was meaning me and Billy."

"There isn't much chance of me ever seeing him in action," Billy responded, "not with my dad being like he is about going out. There's no way he'll let me across the city at night. The way he goes on you'd think the Provos were waiting at the front gate every night – the house is like Fort Knox!"

Matthew felt a dangerous wave of pity and before he had time to check it, it was out. "Would he let you stay at our place overnight?"

The suppressed joy in Billy's voice was pathetic. "I dunno, I could ask."

Later Aaron cornered Matthew. "You've done it now, Chippy. You know what he's like; you'll never get rid of him."

"It's only one night, you know."

"Wait and see if I'm right. He's like NSU."

"What?"

"Non-specific urethritis, it's a sort of VD, pick it up in a moment's weakness and you'll never get rid of it!"

6: Matthew's Eyes Are Opened

Tall, thin and bespectacled; Alistair was one half of the 'Julian and Sandy' duo; the other guy was called John. Alistair was an evangelical Baptist; Matthew worked with him in biology. Five years of scrupulously non-denominational divinity classes had left Matthew with little understanding of religion but, on the very few occasions when he darkened the local church's doors, Matthew had heard a lot about God punishing the wicked. He didn't think that God sounded very nice but Alistair disagreed. "In a perfect

42

world there would be no sin or misery because everyone would be living in virtue as God wants them to."

"If he's so powerful, why doesn't he make everyone do what he wants them to?"

"He's given us free will so that when we come to love and obey Him, it's *us*, not God, that has achieved that goodness."

"But what's the point? Surely he isn't so petty that he needs us to grovel to him to make him feel good."

"You don't understand Him. We can only think in our own human terms and they are totally inadequate. God *is* love; He *is* everything; and only when you come to live His word can you know the true happiness of God's love."

"Why do so many people in the world suffer then? In Biafra, for example, why did all those chilldren starve? They can't all be evil; I'm sure that in their own ways they believe in God, even if it doesn't happen to be your version of him."

Alistair responded with a cool confidence: "That was man's fault, not God's. Heathens caused that disaster. There is only one God and He sent His son, Jesus Christ into the world to save mankind. It's through human imperfection that the gospel hasn't spread to all for their salvation. That's why missionaries have to take God's word to all corners of the earth."

"But what about Hindus, Jews, Moslems and so on? They believe in God, don't they? Couldn't they be right too?"

Matthew expected some sort of compromise but Alistair's answer stunned him. "No. Only Christ has the truth for all mankind."

After a moment Matthew said, "So God is making them suffer because they had the misfortune to be born in a Third World country and not in good Christian Europe!"

"Not exactly. If the whole world was Christian they wouldn't suffer but as it isn't, they do. So we have to do our best to bring God's word to them."

"That's so arrogant!" Matthew spat. Then, seeing Mr Forbes peering over his spectacles, he continued in a lower voice, "What *right* have you to say that you're right and the rest of the world is wrong?"

Alistair smiled beatifically: "You may find it hard to accept but it *is* God's word."

"We'll never agree you know. I'm sure I'm right but, as a scientist, I have to accept that I could be wrong. On the other hand you can only believe that you are right. So we can never have a balanced discussion because you can never concede anything to me!"

"Of course I can! I'm not perfect and I may learn from talking to you. God works through many agents. He might be using you to tell me something."

"Shit! I don't fancy being one of God's tools."

"Ah!" he beamed. "You can't thwart God's plans that easily."

Matthew grimaced. "Okay, then. What about you?" He was about to venture onto dangerous territory. "If you're so good why do you get tormented by the other guys; why does God let you go through all that crap when us shits don't suffer at all?"

"But you *are* suffering. Every time you use those obscene words the devil is twisting his knife into your soul."

"You'd have great difficulty convincing the others of that. How do you feel though? You must get really fed up being teased like that all the time. Remember when they used to call me Juliet? I was miserable."

"It's a burden I have to bear, it might be God's way of teaching me. But my love of God makes the burden a pleasure."

"How does John feel about it? Is he a Christian too?"

"Yes he is, but I can't speak for him. I do know that he finds it difficult being branded a sodomite."

"A what?"

Alistair reddened: "A sodomite. You know, a man who lieth with man. I sometimes think he feels that if enough people say it enough times it might somehow... become true."

Matthew stopped filtering the enzyme extract and stared at him. "You mean he thinks that us calling you Julian and Sandy will make you poofs? That's ridiculous!"

Alistair was absorbed with filling test tubes with dilute iodine solution. Matthew glanced at the clock: "Christ, Alistair! We'd better get a move on."

"Don't blaspheme, Matthew!" he reprimanded mildly.

In the flurry that followed the conversation was dropped but Matthew was left with a sense of unease. Could Alistair really *believe* all that stuff? And were the clique *really* having that effect on John?

In March a new boy joined the biology class. The son of an Asian family expelled from Uganda, Vijay sat next to Matthew in class and ruined his concentration. Matthew thought Vijay had a wonderful smell; a sort of sweet pungency that insinuated its way into his nostrils and caught the top of his throat. Then there was Vijay's skin; it intrigued Matthew; it had the texture of satin and looked as smooth as cigarette paper. Matthew couldn't help thinking about it; he was intrigued to know what it felt like. Sometimes Vijay's crisp, white cuff rode up his wrist and exposed a luxuriance of silky, black hair which only reinforced the disturbing urge to touch his skin. Often, as Mr Forbes droned on, Matthew's mind drifted from biology to that skin. When contact came, it was genuinely accidental. Mr Forbes was showing them slides of nerve tissues. Matthew's fingers, groping for his pencil, met Vijay's hand. He let them linger for a fraction of a second longer than they should have done. That beautiful skin was no different from anyone else's and yet it was charged with... well, with an electricity. A superb sensation shot up his arm and down his spine to explode in his loins. He was thrilled and shocked. He determined to get to know Vijay better.

At first Vijay was very reluctant to mix with the other boys but Matthew kept up the effort and gradually he began to say more and more about his life in East Africa. As Vijay talked Matthew watched his mobile, brown lips and liquid brown eyes. His lilting accent and his outrageous exaggeration exerted a powerful influence on Matthew; so much so that several years later, when he visited Roger in Kenya, he ignored common sense and journeyed across strife-torn Uganda to see the location of Vijay's wonderful stories. Matthew longed to be friends with him. He remembered the long nights of his childhood when Danny and he talked until they drifted into innocent sleep and wondered if Vijay would come to stay at Strathbeg so they, too, could talk all night.

Willy-John and Crispy clattered in from English and slumped down next to Vijay and Matthew. "Shit! Banks is a fucking prat! You'd think he'd have wised up since we were in third form! He still calls Alex 'Romeo' you know."

"Not too far out there," Matthew laughed.

"It wouldn't be too bad if he knew that Alex was poking every bit of skirt around. But its from that time you made such an arse of yourself doing Juliet!"

"He mustn't have much to occupy his tiny mind," Matthew sneered, then switched to a jaunty tone. "Vijay's been telling me all about the Queen Elizabeth Park in Uganda."

"Oh goodness gracious me!" sang Willy-John, mimicking Peter Sellers's catch-phrase.

Matthew reddened at his friend's tactlessness but Vijay didn't seem to notice. Matthew tried to make amends. "I thought Vijay might like to come out with us some night."

Willy-John turned to Vijay. "You wouldn't like it. Very rough you know; hard-drinking men and noisy music."

"For God's sake, Willy-John!" Matthew exploded, "Don't

tell him what he does and doesn't like. Do you fancy coming out with us, Vijay?"

"No, really Matthew. You are most kind but I don't drink alcohol and I never go out at night."

"Why not just come out for the craic?"

"Crack? What *is* this crack I am always hearing about?"

Matthew grinned. "You know, craic! Good fun; a bit of a laugh! Good craic!"

"I understand, but no. You are very thoughtful, but I really don't want to."

Matthew was disappointed but he tried not to show it. "Oh well. If you want to come anytime, just say, won't you."

Willy-John followed Matthew out of the study. As soon as they were out of Vijay's hearing he rounded on him. "What the fuck did you ask him for?"

"What have you got against him? He's a nice guy."

"He may be... but he's... you know!"

"What!" Matthew demanded

Eyes wide, he mouthed, "He's black!" as if Matthew was a half-wit.

"So what? He's dead on, for Christ's sake!"

"But you don't know what he's *really* like. You never know what he's thinking." He looked furtively from side to side, lowered his voice and said in disgust, "*and* he smells."

Matthew was embarrassed. He knew he should stick up for his new friend but didn't know how to. "What do you mean, he smells?" he said with as much indignation as he could muster.

"You know fucking well what I mean," Willy-John growled. "You've smelt him! He reeks; it's revolting and he tries to cover it up with perfume. He's probably a poof too!"

Matthew's heart kicked at the thought. The idea that Vijay might be queer made him feel decidedly strange; he had to make Willy-John see that Vijay had his good points. "He's a really interesting guy. You should try talking to him some time. He had some amazing experiences when he lived in Africa. He smells different because of the food he eats; all those Indian spices and curries and stuff; you know." The perfume had puzzled Matthew too: it had a disconcerting effect on his penis but he couldn't admit that. He bluffed: "And the perfume is as natural to a Hindu as aftershave is to us."

Willy-John wasn't impressed. "Look. You can do what you want, but I don't want him around *me*; okay?" and with that he stomped off to his next class, leaving Matthew angry and bewildered.

Matthew waited a couple of weeks, hoping that Vijay would have forgotten Willy-John's ignorance, then gently quizzed him. "Do you find that people here treat you differently? You know, because you're Indian?"

"Naturally, like you, people are curious because I am from a different country."

"But are people actually rude to you because," he hesitated, "well... because of your skin?"

"You mean your friend Willy-John?"

He nodded in embarrassment. "Aye, do things like that happen much?"

"As you know, Matthew, I do not mix socially here. Sometimes the young schoolchildren call me wog or coon but this is from children who know no better; to whom it is a convenient label. At the market it is different. They are envious of our success so they do things to hurt us."

"What sort of things do they do?"

"Before I came to Ireland my uncle's van was interfered with."

"How?"

"Knives were put into the tyres and on the side was written 'Pakkies go home'."

"Who did it?"

"He does not know. It could have been ragamuffins, but he suspects that some of the other stallholders were involved."

"Doesn't it frighten you? It would me."

Vijay smiled and fixed Matthew with his hypnotic eyes. "In Kampala we were blamed for Idi Amin's bankrupt economy. The hatred was coming from the government; they passed laws which made us inferior citizens and eventually they threw us out of the country and stole our possessions. That couldn't happen here; there will always be stupid and ignorant people but the British law will protect us. There will never be laws in Britain to remove the rights of some people but not others."

Matthew shook his head. "You can't pass laws to alter the way people think."

"No. But as long as they know that the law is against them, they dare not go too far in their actions against us." Vijay's blind faith in British justice was heart-warming and at that stage it was still possible for Matthew to believe he was right.

Matthew's persistence eventually paid off and quite out of the blue Vijay invited him to come to his home for a meal. Matthew was excited and could think of little else. He pretended to himself that it was the food he was looking forward to but really it was the chance of being alone with Vijay.

Vijay's mother picked the two boys up after school and took them to Culmore. Matthew's first surprise was how big the house was; he'd had the impression that the family was penniless but the house didn't support that idea at all.

His second surprise altered his view of Vijay for ever, for the first person he was introduced to was – Vijay's wife! Matthew couldn't understand why meeting her made him feel so bad but once he knew Vijay was a married man he understood why he never hung out with the gang. He stopped trying to persuade Vijay to come out and, although they remained friends, he never again felt the same need to be with him.

The moment Willy-John and Matthew slouched into the sixth-form study room they could tell that something was wrong. Faces, normally jolly or Monday-morning bored, wore serious expressions. Little clusters of boys were engaged in animated conversations. Aaron spotted them, swooped and landed next to the friends.

"Did you hear about John Russell?"

"Who?"

"That poof that left at Easter." It was Alistair's friend they were talking about.

"No, what about him?"

"Only gone and topped himself; that's all!"

"Jesus fuckin' Christ!" Willy-John exclaimed. "Stupid bastard. How? Why? When?"

"Some say he shot himself but I've a mate, Trevor, lives near him and he says hung."

Willy-John was wide-eyed: "Why did he do it?"

Aaron had a novel angle and made the best of it. "Trev says drugs, he was a weirdo anyway; I reckon he was mental. He'd been in Gransha already; slashed his wrists about the time he left school; no one found out at the time. "What's wrong with you Matthew?"

He was standing in open-mouthed disgust: "You're bastards – both of you. The poor guy's dead... and we could have done it!"

Willy-John stared at him in disbelief. "What the fuck are you on about?"

"Nothing," Matthew scowled.

"Yeah well... course we're sorry for him but you must admit that he really was a bit weird; where's Julian?" Willy-John went on.

"Not in yet?" Aaron replied.

Willy-John scanned the room. "I wonder does he know yet?"

"Maybe they've both done it together," Aaron sniggered, "like

Romeo and Juliet; a lovers' tryst."

That was too much for Matthew. "For God's sake you two," he yelled. "Shut up! It's a bloody tragedy and you're making a joke out of it!"

Willy-John put his hand on Matthew's shoulder. "Okay, okay, you know we don't mean it. Perhaps we're joking to cover up our shock or something," he said gently. "Come on," he continued excitedly, "we're late for assembly, I want to hear what the boss says about it."

Alistair stayed off until after the funeral. When he came back he looked terrible. Matthew knew it was tactless but he had to know what had happened so he collared Alistair at break. "Can I have a word with you? Somewhere private."

"Certainly, what is it about?"

"I'd rather not say until we're alone."

So Matthew risked his reputation and punishment for being out of the study and went with Alistair to the benches hidden from the main school by a bank of rhododendrons. "I hope you don't mind me asking – it's about John."

"I thought it might be."

"Look. I'm not being morbid or anything. It's... well... I suppose it's being selfish really. But," he paused, looking at Alistair's drawn face, "I've got to know if it was our fault."

"What are you talking about?"

"Was it us calling you two Julian and Sandy?"

Alistair smiled sadly, his lower lip was trembling. Matthew started to panic; he thought Alistair was going to cry but he didn't. "No it wasn't you. Oh, you may have contributed, but so did everyone else in this wicked world – me included."

"What do you mean?" Matthew said gently.

"I'm sorry, I can't talk about it. John's soul is in a better place and everything else is between God and my conscience. I didn't heed God's word and now this has befallen John. God, in his wisdom, will guide me and I must take more care not to stray from his chosen path in the future."

What on earth could Alistair mean? Matthew puzzled. This opened up more questions than it answered but he didn't dare delve any further.

"I wanted to say how sorry I am about it all. We were all really horrified. None of us wanted this to happen." After an embarrassed silence, he declared, "Hey! We'd better get back before the period's over or we'll be in trouble."

7: More than Rugby

Willy-John's brush with the Saracen opened up a new world for Matthew. Although not seriously hurt, Willy-John was effectively excluded from rugby until long after Christmas. For a variety of reasons other more eligible players were unavailable too so, when the first XV team list went up there it was: left back, Woodhead. The regular back was to play prop.

Rugby was practically mandatory at the Grammar School and the boys had been immersed in its delights since first form. They took it for granted that Saturday meant pulling on clean strip in a smelly changing-room in some backwater of Northern Ireland and it became second nature to spend an hour and thirty-five minutes running about on a rain-lashed, muddy pitch getting kicked and strangled. The first fifteen, the pick of the senior school, could hold their own against any of the local schools but the seconds were the indulgence of an over-ambitious P.E. teacher. If you could walk you were on the seconds and that description fitted Matthew to a T. He may have participated but he never entered into the spirit of the game. Before each match they were supposed to work themselves into a bellicose fervour with ritual chants of mindless banality. Kenny, their captain, wasn't very good at this; he tried his best, but they simply couldn't take him seriously. Nevertheless, like the others, Matthew went through the motions and, until Willy-John's accident, he drifted through match after match faring well enough against the second-rate teams they met. When he was selected for the firsts he naively assumed that he had been underestimating his own abilities

Alex was captain of the firsts; and very popular he was. His savoir-faire with girls extended to the first XV. On the field he never used Christian names and when he barked out a surname it was in a tone that made the player feel like a competent man – one of the team. Off the field he exuded bonhomie, always quick to joke, never malicious. His size made him an indomitable player. Over six feet tall, he had the shoulders of his sturdy Ulster-Scot farming stock, hands like spades and powerful, tree-trunk legs. When he got the ball he was as unstoppable as Willy-John's Saracen. Matthew was slightly afraid of Alex's wild, dangerous streak. He was also envious of him because he oozed masculinity; Alex was everything he wasn't. Matthew had long, fine, blond hair whereas Alex's was short-cropped, thick and jet black. His dense eyebrows, dark brown eyes and wide nose and mouth were framed in a strong square face that always needed a shave. In fourth form, Alex had been the only boy in the class with hair on his chest; by sixth it had proliferated into a silky torrent which welled up from dark nipples and flowed gently towards his sternum before cascading from his rapidly expanding pectorals. The hirsute chute narrowed until reaching his navel where it eddied into a dense black pool which lapped at a large, sullen penis. Fine rivulets trickled down his legs to his ankles. Matthew thought it so unfair; he hadn't even started shaving yet!

Alex encouraged Matthew on the field and he began to enjoy the camaraderie but dreaded the team's changing-room antics after the game. The boys' boisterous language intimidated him. Each lad had to fight their way up the pecking order, and aggressive language was the means. Matthew was astonished at the quick-fired inventiveness of their incessant putting down and slagging of each other and he dreaded being on its receiving end. Even worse was the first XV league table. The movable ladder appeared on the wall of the sixth-form study in September each year and stayed there for the whole season. Billy and Matthew were the only clique members not on it. They had guessed endlessly what it was about but the mystery had remained. After Matthew's second match they were trooping muddily into the changing rooms when Alex said, "Now Matt, time to put you on the league table."

"Where do I come?" he asked eagerly.

This caused great hilarity.

"*Come*, and find out," roared Crispy.

The team howled with delight at this witticism.

Aaron joined in. "*Come* on, Matty. Let's see what's in you."

Matthew was confused; he was missing something here but he didn't like to sound stupid so he smiled and joked along to cover up his ignorance. Alex ordered Chrissy to watch the door and called John McAnnet over. Matthew knew that he was always top of the league table.

"Right, *come* on, Jerker, show him how to do it."

John crossed to the showers, rolled his underpants to his feet, stepped out of them, positioned his toes on the edge of the tiled floor and started to pull on his penis. He soon had an erection and, watched by the cheering team, began to masturbate. John's face tightened and he drew short sharp breaths as, keeping his toes firmly planted on the edge of the tiles, he thrust his thighs forwards sending little spurts of semen onto the tiling. A tape measure was produced and the distance from the tile edge to the furthest drop was measured.

"Ninety-eight centimetres!" someone shouted.

"Pathetic," Alex chided. "You're lucky you can't be demoted

for a poor performance."

The showers were turned on and the tiles hurriedly sluiced down. All eyes turned on Matthew; he thought that his willy was going to crawl up inside him. He stood on the prescribed spot and tried to copy John but he couldn't get his little scrap to harden at all. A barrage of lascivious yells of encouragement and abuse assaulted him. "Come on, think of Marianne Faithful," someone hooted.

"Come on, wank, you wanker!" Russell said with ill-disguised scorn.

"Imagine you're putting one up Helen Hall!" another cried.

"Crispy doesn't need to imagine," Aaron jeered.

Matthew was trying, but nothing would happen.

"Who do you think about when you wank, Matt?" Aaron insinuated snidely, "Alistair?"

Just as he thought all was lost he felt a hard arm coil around his shoulder. A sandpaper chin scratched the soft skin of his shoulder and Alex whispered in his ear, "Think of screwing Sandra." That did more for his libido that all the other boys' shouts, and his penis began to swell. The image of Alex's muscular, hairy, naked body on Sandra swam into his head. The chemistry worked and, to his great relief, he managed to ejaculate.

Matthew was glad to retire from the firsts when Willy-John was well enough to play again but he had learned one thing from his time on the rugby team. Up to then masturbation had been a purely mechanical activity but thereafter a climax came so much more easily if he closed his eyes and imagined that he wasn't weedy old Matthew but big, strong, virile Alex.

It was Alex who initiated the clique into the joys of Orange Hall dances. They were all in a lounge bar in Newtownstewart, a small town about thirty miles south of Derry. Billy, who didn't drink, was driving Mr Woodhead's Landrover, so Matthew was getting quietly pissed whilst the others were chatting up women. Other than a group of loud, drunken squaddies, the lounge was pretty dead. At half twelve Alex said, "Anyone want to see what the culchies get up to of a Friday night? There's a dance at Cavnaleck Orange Hall. Fancy it?"

"Where the fuck's Cavna-fuckin-leck?" Willy-John squeaked.

"Up behind Sion Mills. Come on. For the craic."

They drove for what seemed like miles along narrow, dark lanes until they came to a cluster of houses. The Orange Hall stood by a bridge. Both sides of the road were lined with parked vehicles; cars, some good but most in various states of decay, mini-vans, pickups and even a scattering of tractors. After a quick reminder from Alex to say they came from Londonderry, not Derry, they went in.

In the foyer a big farmer with tousled, straw-like hair was collecting money in his massive, callused hands. Youths of various ages lurked at his shoulder. They paid, pushed through the reinforced glass-panelled doors and stepped straight back into the 1950s. Not the flashing lights and psychedelic oil projection of the disco for Cavnaleck but a single row of fluorescent lights hanging from the rafters. At the far end a show band played unenthusiastically on a stage. Matthew had seen the same group at the Rugby Club but there they had played eminently danceable numbers whereas here it was dreary country and western with the occasional waltz thrown in. They were churning out 'Goodnight Irene' when the clique made their entrance. Pairs of women in print dresses were shuffling around the near-deserted dance floor. More women, staring blankly ahead, were scattered along tubular steel stacking chairs lining each side of the hall. Just inside the door the local men were surveying the scene as if at a cattle auction – an impression reinforced by a distinct aroma of livestock lingering under the Brut. Willy-John nudged Matthew and pointed to a thickset man of about thirty. His hair was in the pudding basin style and his emotionless, stodgy face was transfixed by the waltzing couples. He wore a floral shirt with a tie of identical material, but what had excited Willy-John's attention was a line of cow dung spattered up the leg of his sagging grey-flannel suit. "Christ!" he sniggered. "Someone's going to take a sheep out for a smooch next."

"Come on," Matthew chided. "This is all there is here. If you lived here you would be first here, wellies an' all!"

"Like fuck I would! I'd top myself if I thought that this was all there was to life."

"Any of them with any sense have done already," Aaron sneered.

"Right enough! Some of this lot look the living dead!" Willy-John grimaced, pointing to a gaunt creature with a parchment face. "See that guy over there! They dug him up specially for tonight; needed him to swell the numbers!"

"Has to be back before sunrise," Matthew giggled, "or ARGHHH....!" He did a passable imitation of Dracula being exposed to the sun.

"Needs his nightly fix. The blood... of a virgin... *sheep!*" Willy-John warned. "So you had better watch out, Matty."

"How dare you insinuate that I'm a sheep!" he yelped.

The band struck up a marginally more lively tune. "Come

on," Willy-John shouted. "Let's show the culchies how to dance."
At that the gang flooded onto the floor and freaked out as best they
could to a country and western number.

Over the next few Friday nights, Cavnaleck Orange Hall was
subjected to their drunken schoolboy misbehaviour and inevitably feathers were ruffled. They were standing for the national
anthem when Crispy whispered something to Willy-John and the
two of them dissolved into a fit of giggles. After the last 'God Save
The Queen', a Neanderthal stalked up to Crispy, drawled, "S'bout
time you learned some respect for your Queen," and punched
Crispy in the stomach. As Crispy folded, Willy-John launched in
to intercept the huge knee about to smash into Crispy's face. Someone pulled Willy-John off, but by then Aaron and Alex were there
and all Matthew could see was a struggling melée until the police
arrived.

The clique regrouped by the door, Crispy dabbing his lip
with Helen's hanky. Two of the officers came over. "Right boys,
what's the story?"

Crispy pouted, "That great ape there just went for me!"

"I've already spoken to him. He says you've been coming
here for weeks, making a nuisance of yourselves."

"We haven't," Willy-John objected weakly. "We've just been
enjoying ourselves."

"You may call it that but Mr Millar over there," he indicated
a respectable looking middle-aged man, "says that you leap about
and generally annoy people." He surveyed the little gang. "Where
are you boys from?"

"Londonderry," they mumbled, not quite in unison.

"Well, if you'll take my advice you will stick to Londonderry and stop upsetting people here. Next time we might not be
about to save your skins. Now boys, take yourselves back to Londonderry... and don't come back."

They left muttering empty words of defiance and Matthew
never stepped inside an Orange Hall again.

8: Off to University

The A-levels were imminent and the friends started on revision
programmes with varying degrees of commitment and success.
Matthew submerged himself so completely that he hardly noticed
Ulster tearing out its own heart, but by May even he couldn't ignore the United Ulster Unionist Council's strike. Half the time
there was no electricity, there was talk of food rationing and there

were appalling stories of what was happening to strikebreakers. Somehow Matthew could accept that Republicans could behave so viciously but when it was his own sort, Protestants, well, it disturbed him, to say the least.

Being largely Nationalist, Derry City was more normal than usual; most shops were open and most buses were running. But in the countryside roads were blocked and, with no milk collections possible, some farmers had to tip gallons of milk down the drains. Fortunately Matthew's father didn't lose much but he was disgusted by some of his neighbours; men who would normally moan about the slightest drop in yield were happy to sacrifice their profits in the name of the UUUC. The school stayed open although some days there were hardly any boys there. Whether this was due to lack of transport, solidarity with the strike or just taking a few days off, wasn't clear. It began to look like the GCE exams would be disrupted and all sorts of contingency plans were made but the strike collapsed before they had to be implemented.

As soon as his last exam was over Matthew dashed across the water to Birkholm. Michael was going to India and Matthew desperately wanted to see him before he went. To Matthew's delight Amanda had acquired a crowd of friends with whom she went out rather as Matthew's clique did back in Derry. However life in Kendal was so much more relaxed than Matthew was used to. The young friends could drive about without having to worry about military checkpoints or hijackings and Matthew found himself stopping at shop doorways for body-checks by non-existent security guards. There was an air of freedom and the strangest thing was that Matthew hadn't realised that it was missing at home. English pubs were a revelation; relaxed people talked freely and he didn't have to worry whether they were Protestant or Catholic. Even in Protestant pubs at home he had to watch what he said. It was axiomatic that you never discussed politics or religion in Ulster pubs but to express *any* opinion other than the accepted norm was to venture beyond the pale. The Protestant community was under siege and any dissent was dangerous.

The days when he could spend two months in Kendal were long past and all too soon he had to go home to help on the farm. Every morning he thanked his lucky stars that Roger would take over when his dad retired. He loathed getting up at five-thirty, pulling on mucky jeans and tee-shirt prickly from the previous day's chaff and going to find the cows for milking. Only when he had the milking done could he have breakfast. By then his father would be out harvesting with Roger and Rick but Matthew had to turn the herd out, then feed the hens, pigs and calves. Finally he had to muck out the milking parlour. This done, he was available for other jobs and that usually meant helping Rick.

Rick was about five years older than Matthew. The son of a local farm worker, he had left school at fourteen to work for the Woodheads. He had a wisdom beyond his years. Not classically handsome; Rick had a round, red, jolly miller face and his strong, functional body worked like a well-oiled machine. Watching him work gave Matthew the satisfaction others got from ballet dancers or highly tuned athletes. Matthew felt like a shambling, gangling foal next to him. Rick's world was firmly rooted in rural Ulster. He had never been to Belfast, and Londonderry was to be avoided if at all possible. Where the urban Derry accent grated on the ear, Rick's gentle lilt was like the wind in the corn. His humour sprang from the land he loved and he entertained Matthew with tales which would have left a towny cold. His love for his country was blind and absolute as was his hatred for the Republican movement. As far as Rick was concerned the IRA threatened everything he held dear, so he became a part-time member of the new Ulster Defence Regiment. Some mornings he would turn up exhausted after manning checkpoints on lonely country roads all night. Rick couldn't understand why Matthew wouldn't join the UDR too. "Don't you want to defend your country? Protect your Mammy?" he drawled.

"I can't very well, can I? You know I'm going across the water in October," Matthew explained.

That in itself bewildered Rick: "You don't want to be going to yon university. You've a brave lot of learning already. You should stay here and help your daddy."

"If I did that you would be out of a job, wouldn't you?" Matthew teased.

Rick took him absolutely seriously: "I would soon get a job round here. A man should work his father's land."

"But what about Roger? He'll be taking over. You can't expect me to work for him for the rest of my life."

"You could work Strathbeg between you."

"Come on! Roger's got an HND in agriculture – he's really keen on farming. You know I'm not!"

"Pfwaw!" – that was Rick's sceptical sound – "book learning! You can't farm with a book in one hand."

Even had Rick been prepared to listen, Matthew couldn't have given him a reason for the way he felt. He knew that he didn't want to join the Regiment, but why? Was it cowardice? UDR men were easy targets for the IRA and this was a source of constant worry for him. He sickened at the thought of flying shards of searing metal ripping into Rick but that wasn't his principal worry. Rick was kind and gentle, undoubtedly many of the other part-time soldiers were equally decent, but he had no delusions about the rest. They would be the drum-banging bullies that had driven Daniel from his house, the boys at school without a good word for Catholics, and the Orange Hall men that punched you for giggling during the national anthem. He couldn't survive in that environment and he had no intention of trying to.

By mid September Crispy had already gone to Sandhurst, Sandra had started her nurse's training in Belfast and Alex had joined the police. Willy-John and Aaron were soon to start at Queen's University in Belfast, Helen at Trinity in Dublin and Billy had succumbed to a fate worse than death; he was going to the New University of Ulster in Coleraine. Matthew had been accepted to read biology at the University of Lancaster. The last few days before they dispersed were the best Matthew could remember. The impending students headed off to Willy-John's family's cottage in Downings and were out on the tear every night. It was as if they knew they weren't going to see the friends they had grown up with again. Sure, they would all meet again, but by then they would have been through different experiences; they would all be different people.

Matthew saw university as his opportunity to change; he could be himself and not a bit-player in the Willy-John and Alex show. He would express his own opinions and do what *he* wanted to do!

At 7:15 a.m. on the 30th September 1974 Matthew disembarked from the Belfast ferry at Heysham. Bleary-eyed and slightly sticky, he stepped out of the stuffy atmosphere of stale cigarette smoke and beer, into the sharp morning air tainted by the ICI plant down the road. He scanned the terminal for his Uncle John but his eyes lit upon a tanned face with glasses perched upon a beaky nose.

"Michael! Mandy! Hi, great! What are you doing here?"

Mike grinned. "Got back the day before yesterday. Thought we'd better make sure you got to Lancaster in one piece."

"Great to see you; God, you're really, really brown. How was India and how come I didn't get a postcard?"

"I sent one! It was amazing; I'll tell you all about it on the way. Where's your stuff?"

They spent most of the day in Kendal talking about India and it was tea-time by the time they delivered Matthew to Lancaster. The two boys manhandled Matthew's trunk up concrete stairs and along brick corridors to a room about the size of Strathbeg's upstairs toilet. At the far end there was an enormous window over-looking a modern quadrangle. Along one wall was a functional bed with an orange candlewick bedspread. A wardrobe occupied the space between the bed and the door end of the room. The other wall had a simple, large desk and an orange, wooden-armed chair. The lino-tiled floor was softened by an orange tumble-twist rug. Matthew wondered if the Catholics got green decor in their rooms.

They heard the student bar before seeing it. Pushing through the door they entered a sea of denim jeans, tee-shirts and baggy jump-ers. The floor swilled with spilt beer and the din of shouting youth, and jukebox music electrified the smoky atmosphere. Matthew surveyed the scene; this was it! Mike found an unoccupied square foot and staked his claim amongst cigarette stubs and crisp packets. Soon it was pints of McEwans Export all round. There was more to hear about India but Matthew found it difficult to concentrate with all that was going on around him. When it was his turn to go to the bar he edged his way through the throng and managed to push in next to a huge pair of shoulders clad in blue denim and topped with a mane of red hair. Matthew couldn't see the bar for the enormous arm so he said, "Excuse me." The arm didn't move so he tapped on the shoulder. "Excuse me, can I get to the bar please?"

A gruff Derry accent responded, "Sure, mate." The big man turned and they were face to face.

Matthew looked at a ruddy round face with pale blue eyes and recognition dawned. "DANIEL!" he cried.

"Fucking hell... Matthew! Jesus, Mary and Joseph you bas-tard! What are you doing here?"

"Biological sciences, what about you?"

"Chemical engineering. Holy Christ, I never thought I'd see you again! When did you get here?"

"Just now. I'm here with my cousin Amanda and her boy-friend."

"Oh yeah; you said about them in your letter," he said defen-sively.

"You got it then? I thought you hadn't."

"Yeah, meant to reply but... you know."

Matthew didn't, but he said he did.

Danny and Matthew were in the same college but in differ-ent 'parishes', as they were called. All the others on Matthew's corridor were English. Art, an uncouth farmer's son from near Selby was the person Matthew felt most familiar with but the in-habitant he found most exotic was Tony, a small, swarthy Londoner of Italian extraction. Tony seemed to have come to university for the sole purpose of satisfying his prodigious sexual appetite at least once a day, and preferably more. Smouldering dark eyes, classically arrogant features, glossy hair and an irrepressible Latin charm ensured his success. Matthew was impressed by his sexual prowess and Tony soon replaced Alex in Matthew's wank fantasies.

Life at Lancaster was one long round of parties and boozing sessions, and Danny and Matthew were soon as firm friends as they had ever been. The ten weeks flew by and all too soon it was Christmas. Danny promised to visit Strathbeg during the vacs and, just to make sure, Matthew got his mother to give Danny a lift home from the railway station. He lived in a tall Victorian, terraced house near Rosemount barracks. Never having been there before, Matthew was surprised to find such a pleasant, normal-looking street so close to the dreaded Bogside. Matthew hardly recognised Soibhan because her hair was black instead of bronze and baby Patrick was much as Danny had been last time he'd seen him. But it was Christopher who made the most impression on Matthew. When Matthew walked in he was slumped in an armchair, his head buried in a book.

Matthew nodded to him. "Hello Christopher, remember me?"

Chris looked him over. Matthew found Chris's gaze unsettling; it was as if the brooding adolescent was weighing him up. Chris wasn't as big as Danny and he was having problems with acne, but this only added to the impression of his mind working in mysterious ways behind his glowering blue eyes.

Matthew tried smiling at him. "It's me, Matthew, remember? I was at Dungiven Road with Danny."

Chris merely nodded, got up and left.

"Don't take any notice of him," his old friend said, with evident embarrassment. "He's a weirdo."

"It's okay, I know what kids are like."

"He's sixteen! Not exactly a child any more, he should have more manners."

"Och, don't worry about it Danny, it doesn't worry me in the least."

"It worries *me*. You're my friend, and he's no business being so bloody ignorant."

Chris's behaviour dismissed, they parted with a firm agreement to meet up as soon as they had done their 'dutiful son' acts.

Matthew was looking forward to impressing his old schoolfriends with tales of Lancaster and the extraordinarily interesting people he'd met there. He phoned Willy-John and they arranged to meet up with the others in the Regal. Willy-John was having a great time in Belfast and Matthew thought that his own stories seemed flat compared to Willy-John's tales of drunken debauchery and Helen's account of balls, cocktail parties and esoteric college traditions, redolent of J. P. Donleavy novels. Matthew's only consolation was that Billy was evidently having a really dull time at Coleraine. One curious aspect of Willy-John's tales was the complete absence of Aaron; Matthew wanted to know why. "Do you see much of Aaron?"

"Aye, he's on the second XV but he's becoming a real deadbeat. He has a pint or two after training then pisses off home – never comes out on the tear with the rest of us. Heading for a first, that boy – boring old fart."

"No craic at all from him?"

"Nah, he's his own friends now; aspiring middle-class farts who don't approve of going out on the rampage – not like us, eh Matt?"

He glowed with the inclusion. "You should have been there the night they had a wine-tasting in the junior common room. Danny... Do you remember Danny? Went to primary school with me."

"Aye I do, your little red-headed Fenian friend."

"That's him. He's not so little now, though!"

"Still free is he? Not in Long Kesh yet?"

"Come on! He's an okay guy. He's in the same college as me! Anyway, there was a wine-tasting in the JCR and he managed to make a stash of about ten bottles of the old vino plonko. He told Niall..."

"More Fenians," Willy-John interrupted, "we'll have to watch you!"

"Piss off! Anyway, Niall went outside and Danny passed them to me behind the curtains, then I passed them out through the window. We were pretty pissed when we left then we all got really slaughtered in his room after and all for free! Danny fell asleep on the bog and we hadn't a notion where he was – spent the whole night there!"

Willy-John wagged an admonishing finger, "You want to watch them, Matt; nicking wine! They'll get you into trouble."

"Come off it Willy-John," Helen objected. "If you'd been there you would have been first to reallocate the wine."

"Nonsense, I'd have gone for champagne or nothing. Nah, Matty knows I'm only kidding, don't you Matt?"

"Aye, of course," he said. But he wasn't sure.

Danny's visit to Strathbeg had an inauspicious start. When Matthew suggested going out for a drink Danny pointed out that there was no way he could go to any of Matthew's usual haunts and he was sure that Matthew wouldn't want to go drinking in the city. Matthew disagreed. "There's loads of Catholics at the Rugby Club; there's no problem there."

"Aye. But they're middle-class Catholics – Protestants that cross themselves. They're not from the Bog or the Creggan."

"You know what you are!" Matthew chided, "You're an inverted snob! We're not all bigots. Look at Willy-John," and immediately wished he hadn't started that line of argument. "He doesn't have anything against Catholics," he ended lamely.

"He may be alright but there are plenty who aren't."

They couldn't agree on anywhere to go and ended up sitting in Matthew's kitchen, drinking coffee, scoffing Mrs Woodhead's home-made biscuits and mulling over their past exploits until Danny said it was time he was getting along. Matthew drove him home, vowing that he would get some tins in for next time Danny came, but he didn't see him again that Christmas.

Despite having worked in Belfast since graduating from Queen's, Matthew's sister had a prodigious number of friends locally and a little brother just back from his first term at university was an asset to flaunt. One evening at dinner Jenny casually dropped a suggestion: "Wouldn't it be lovely if we could all three go out for an evening together – you know, two brothers and sister together. With Matthew being so young we've never been able to go out as three adults."

Roger was startled by the suggestion. "What's come over you sis? You never wanted to go anywhere with me before. Why start now?"

"Now, now, Roger," their mother reprimanded, "It's a lovely idea, all my three going out together. I've always regretted that you didn't grow up together. You two were like one family and little Matthew was another."

"Don't be silly, Mummy," Jenny wheedled. "You've always done the best for us and we haven't turned out too badly, have we?"

"Of course not, dear. There can't be many mothers can boast that all their children have done so well at college."

"Don't speak too soon, Mum," Matthew warned through a mouthful of spuds.

"Oh, you'll get your degree. And a jolly good one too."

He waved crossed fingers at her.

Jenny continued, turning to Roger: "You could bring Iris along, after all she's practically family. That would balance it up, two boys and two girls."

It sounded harmless enough so the two brothers agreed to go to the new hotel in Londonderry.

Matthew had thought that they were just going for a drink but the next thing he knew a table had been booked for a meal; a table for six!

"I hope you don't mind the intrusion," Jenny flapped that night. "Gerry's going back to Brussels soon and if I don't see him tonight I'll not see him for ages... Matthew! You're not wearing that shirt, it hasn't been ironed. Go and get a decent one – this is a respectable place."

He lifted his eyes to the ceiling. "If I had known that it was going to be all this bother, I wouldn't have agreed. I would much prefer to go down the pub for a jar with you two than have all this faff!"

"You've no sense of occasion, that's your trouble," Jenny shouted to his retreating back. "If you had gone to a *proper* university you would know what it means to get dressed up and go out for a meal."

Fortunately Matthew didn't hear that last jibe; otherwise it would have started a row.

Matthew was amazed at the Everglades. As they padded over the plush carpets of a huge reception area he admired the unfaced brickwork and flower beds burgeoning with tropical plants. In the bar, the jungle had encroached even further. One wall was all glass and, peering through the vegetation, he could see a swimming pool beyond, complete with a very well-proportioned male swimmer. The two brothers wanted beer but Jenny insisted on an aperitif. They settled on gin and tonics, something that Matthew had never tried before but to which he took an immediate shine. Gerry soon joined them. An affable, bearded chap about Jenny's age, the signs of the good life in Belgium bulged over his waistband. He was escorting an attractive young lady; his wife, Matthew assumed.

"Matthew, this is Gerrard and this is his sister, Tara."

Matthew remembered to stand up to be introduced and shook their hands. Tara was nice enough but her conversation was mind-numbingly superficial. Matthew could not give a damn about the 'relevance' of *Gulliver's Travels* and although he liked going to the pictures, he certainly wasn't prepared to dissect every film that he had seen. The swimmer didn't help either, he was distracting him every time he crossed his line of sight behind her.

At the dinner table, Jenny arranged the party into neat little couples. Rodge and Iris were engrossed in conversation about some Young Farmers business and Jenny monopolised Gerry, leaving Tara and Matthew to entertain each other once more. He was becoming increasingly annoyed; what had started off as a night out with his sibs had developed into a formal occasion with him trying to make polite conversation with a woman in whom he had no interest whatsoever. He wanted to get back to the bar; perhaps he could talk to his brother. Failing that he could always watch the swimmer.

Once in the bar (the swimmer had gone), the conversation was easier. Unlike his sister, Gerry was really quite interesting but Jenny wanted him to herself. At long last the bar closed and it was time to go home, but Matthew's torture had not come to an end.

"Gerry has invited us back for coffee. Isn't that nice?" his sister twittered.

"I hope we won't be too long," said his wonderful brother. "I have to do the milking tomorrow!"

Gerry spoke. "Look, if you two want to go on, I'll run Jenny and Matthew home later."

Roger escaped.

Sitting in that house in Prehen with the beautiful furniture and the immaculate toilet Matthew thought the night would never end. He had nothing to say to Tara and Jenny wasn't going to let him get a word in edgeways with Gerry.

Jenny was furious when they finally got home. "What's the matter with you? Didn't you like Tara?"

"She's alright, not the sort of girl that I would choose to go out with."

"You could at least have been pleasant to her, you practically ignored her all evening. I was *so* embarrassed."

"Look, I'm tired... and I want to go to bed," Matthew snapped. "And I don't *have* to like somebody just because you happen to have the hots for her brother!" With that he slammed the door and stormed up to bed leaving his raging sister in the kitchen.

Lesser mortals would have given up there and then, but not Jenny. Over the next two weeks Matthew was paraded before a whole range of eligible young women. The fact that he wasn't interested never seemed to daunt her. Matthew was sure that girls didn't like him anyway. His pallid face sprouted a swathe of freckles every summer and his nose was still ridiculous, the little button variety you see on whimsical dolls, but the worst thing was his spots. His face wasn't too bad but his back and chest were covered with angry, red blotches and his long hair hid a worse mess on the back of his neck. His only compensation for this overdue pubescent spurt was that his beard had started growing at long last. He was actually having to shave once every other week. He was even getting hair on his chest although it was only a wispy tangle of pale filaments around each nipple.

9: A Moment of Truth

Danny was a serial boyfriend. Matthew admired the way he breezed through one casual relationship after another but most of all he envied the fact that Danny got sex on a regular basis. Matthew was still a virgin and was becoming increasingly embarrassed about it, but it was more than that. He was desperate for the intimacy that having a girlfriend brought but had singularly failed to get a woman all year. He put it down to him being ugly but Danny tried to wise him up.

"You're no pin-up," he said gently, " but neither am I and I get a shag regularly."

"But you are!" Matthew complained. "You're much better looking than me."

"Thanks Matt, but it's not true you know. It's all a matter of confidence. If you tackle a woman thinking you'll fail, you will. Go out believing you'll score and Bob's your mother's brother. You get laid!"

If that was Danny's philosophy it certainly was working for him; he got some gorgeous women. Matthew was sure he couldn't get a really good-looking girl but thought he would give Danny's approach a try. He was crap at dancing and knew he wouldn't have a chance of picking up a woman at a disco so he thought he would try it out in safer territory. He turned his attention to Lisa, a girl on his biology course. She had a serious, angular face and straight, sensible hair. She usually wore a blouse and corduroy jeans and as far as he knew she had never had a boyfriend. He found it surprisingly easy to strike up a friendship with her and by the summer term they were a regular pair at lectures. Yet he never quite had the nerve to ask her out. Once she became a friend he was worried that if he tried and she blew him out their friendship would be ruined. His dilemma was removed when she took the initiative. "I'm going to see 'The Exorcist' tomorrow night, would you like to come?"

That was probably the very last film he would have chosen; horror films gave him nightmares but he kept that to himself. "I'd love to. If you'll promise to hold my hand if it gets too scary!" That was daring; Danny would be proud of him.

"It's not that bad!" she scoffed, "but you can always close your eyes if it gets too much for you," she grinned.

He rushed back to tell Danny that he'd invited Lisa to the pictures.

On the momentous night he went to her room twenty minutes before they were due to leave. "I'm not ready yet," came the muffled call from her door. "Wait in the kitchen."

Matthew had noticed that women's residences always smelt different. There was a sort of pungent smell that couldn't be masked by feminine toiletries. That odour, loaded with pheromones, sent the blood racing through most boys' veins, but Matthew never got that buzz. However, that evening he could believe it would grow on him.

When Lisa appeared her hair glowed, her lips shone and a skimpy dress showed off a figure he hadn't even suspected existed; he actually found her attractive and, for the first time in his life, his heart fluttered at being with a woman. As they walked down the spine to the bus stop he prayed that someone he knew would see them together. To his relief, she paid her own bus fare which boded well for the cinema. Had he asked her out he would have had to pay for her ticket but she had asked him, so he wondered if he should offer to pay for her ticket or not. She resolved his dilemma by paying for both of them with a fiver then asking him for his share.

The film started. The small-talk subsided and his spine tingled at the strains of 'Tubular Bells'. He thought he ought to have put his arm round her but he wasn't sure how this tricky manoeuvre was to be achieved. He had rehearsed it in his head the previous night but the film was so gripping that it was over before he got round to trying anything. He was glad that he hadn't tried after all. He reasoned that a clumsy pass would have wrecked their friendship.

When they got back to campus he invited her up to his room for coffee. As he made it in the communal kitchen she gazed down at the dimly lit quadrangle from where the roars of drunken students rose. Suddenly the kitchen door practically burst off its hinges as Danny crashed in, followed by Niall and Kevin. They had been playing soccer that afternoon and had evidently been in the bar since. "Makin' coffee Matt?" Danny slurred, "geeus a cup."

"Okay, Danny; want one Niall?"

"Aye."

"Kev?"

"Wha'?"

"Coffee; want a cup?"

"Taa, milk an' lotsa sugar."

Danny had lurched over to Lisa, "Good film then?"

"Yes. It was an interesting exploration of contemporary attitudes to religion; and in particular to the concept of the power of good over evil. Wasn't it, Matthew?"

"Fuck!" Danny exclaimed, "I thought it w's an 'orror wi'

lots'f blood an' boke an' everyfin'."

Matthew hurried over with the coffee, shooting apologetic glances at Lisa.

"Here you are, milk and three sugars... careful, it's hot."

Coffee clutched in one hand, Danny flung his arm round Matthew and fixed his gaze on Lisa. The arm was meant as an affectionate gesture, but it rapidly became his main means of support: "Bes' mate a guy could have, 'im." He looked at Matthew blearily and patted him clumsily on the cheek with his free hand: "Aren't you, Matt?"

"Course, but I won't be for long if you spill your coffee down my best jumper."

Lisa prised the slopping cup from Danny's hand and put it on the table. Matthew thought he spotted a smirk on her face.

"Fffuck your jumper, you're me mate an' I know you'd do anyfin f'r your mate." He turned to address Niall, Kevin and a few others who had drifted in.

"When I wa' wee, I wa' the only Taig in a shitty wee Prod school an' none of the wee Orange shits would have nuffin' to do with me. An' along comes wee Matty here an' you know what he does? You know?"

No one, including Matthew, did know.

"The stupid wee fucker makes frien's wi' me. An' the wee shits gi'im a hard time 'cos he's my mate an' he doesn't care, he sticks by me. "

At this point his bottom lip was quivering dangerously. Matthew felt he had to put the record straight: "But you were the toughest kid in the class and no one ever came near you because they knew that if they did, you would give them a kicking."

He turned to the others. "I didn't even know that he was Catholic at first and when I did find out, I didn't really know what it meant."

Danny picked up his coffee and tried to slurp it but this upset his equilibrium and he started pirouetting into Matthew. He managed to catch him and lower him into a chair. Danny's confession continued. "You never knew why I stopped catchin' the same bus as you, did y' Matty?"

"You had to get the earlier bus. You explained that at the time."

"Fuck! An' you believed me, didn't y'? Shit! You never knew did y'? You're so fuckin' innocent Matt! Those fuckin' Orange fuckin' bastards from the estate gave me such a hard time. I caught the earlier bus to miss the fuckin' Orange bastards. An' you never knew... you never even knew."

Danny started to sob. Matthew shot a glance at Lisa, kneeled down and put his arm round Danny's heaving shoulders.

"Shush, shush, it's all right now, you're not in Derry now. It's alright Danny, you're okay, shush."

Lisa was in the chair next to him but everyone else had lost interest. She took Danny's huge red hand and gave it a squeeze. He smiled at her and put his head on Matthew's shoulder.

Calmer, and more lucid now, he was talking to Lisa. "You know they came and burned our house. I was in bed an' I heard 'em shouting FENIAN BASTARDS an' GET BACK WHERE YOU CAME FROM then there was this crash – it were more'v a thud really – it was a petrol bomb in the front room. Mammy and Daddy got us out the back door an' we had to go past them. They was jeering and spitting at us. It was pishin' down and we was standing on the Dungiven road in our pyjamas wi' nowhere to go and then Matty's dad came and he took us to Uncle Liam's in Dungiven. They shouted FENIAN LOVER an' things like that at him but he's like Matt, he didn't take no notice of 'em." He fixed Matthew with his pale, blue eyes; they were remarkably clear. "Won't lose each other again Matty; won't lose each other again."

By then Matthew was close to tears too. "No Danny, we'll always be mates."

"Yeah, f'rever an' ever." Danny's head nodded onto his chest.

Matthew put on a cheerful face. "Come on Danny, beddy-byes for you."

The big Gaelic player was too heavy for Matthew to lift but he moved to Matthew's room on auto-pilot. Matthew knew he ought to undress him but didn't dare so he left him snoring peacefully on the bed, fully clothed, whilst Matthew kipped on his own floor.

Just before Christmas Danny's sister had an interview at Lancaster. Soibhan and her school-friend were to stay in Danny's room and he was to sleep in Matthew's. The night followed the usual routine: meal, bar, kitchen for coffee, bed. Danny saw the girls to his room and then joined Matthew.

"You have the bed; I'll doss on the floor," Matthew said nobly.

"Get stuffed, why should you? It's your room," Danny objected. "There's room for two in the bed anyway; I've done it often enough," he grinned as he casually stripped down to his underpants and climbed into Matthew's bed. Dry lipped, Matthew switched off the light and followed suit.

Danny was a big man and, even though he slid right over to

the wall, there wasn't a lot of room in the bed for Matthew, small as he was. "Don't move or you'll have me on the floor," he warned.

"We can't have that," Danny chuckled, "come here." And he put a big, warm arm under Matthew's neck and drew him to him until Matthew's shoulder was nestling in Danny's humid armpit. His huge hand secured Matthew's thigh. Lying on his side, Matthew's head was resting on Danny's shoulder. His knees were gripping Danny's hairy leg and his bum was hanging over the edge of the bed. Matthew's heart was thumping like a drum as he realised that he was getting an erection. He was terrified that his bulging underpants would touch his friend.

"I hope you've locked the door," Danny joked, "if anyone comes in now, they'll think we're a couple of queers!"

"You've no worries there," Matthew assured him. "Everyone knows how many women you've had!"

"I wish you were a woman not a feller."

Matthew smiled inwardly. "So do I," he said wistfully.

"What?" Danny coughed.

"I mean, I wish for your sake that I was a girl."

"Would you like to be a girl," he said slowly, "my girlfriend?"

"NO!" Matthew exclaimed in alarm, "I don't mean THAT... I wish that you had a girl in bed now... instead of me."

"Oh. Aye... Ah well, maybe tomorrow night, eh Matt? I might get lucky with Mary."

"That's all very well for you but I'll end up alone... as usual."

Matthew rested his head on Danny's heaving chest, breathing in the wafts of aftershave and whisky fumes. Soon Danny shifted onto his side with his back to the wall so Matthew was able to turn over and, by turning his back on Danny, lie more comfortably. In his sleep Danny drew Matthew to him, curling round him and clutching him like a teddy bear until the two lay like spoons in a drawer. Danny's great arm was coiled around Matthew with his hand dangling limply at his chest. Matthew covered Danny's arm with his and risked gently fingering the hairs on his wrists. Lightly clasping his idol's hand Matthew drifted into the wonderful semi-conscious state between sleep and wakefulness.

Things, strange things, intensely exciting things, flitted through his mind and dissident feelings flowed without check. In the drowsy warmth of the bed it was easy to forget whose sleeping form enfolded him. He imagined the man burying his mouth into his neck; he wanted him to caress him. He was willing Danny's rough hand into his underpants where his erection was straining against wet, slippery cotton. Cautiously he shifted backwards until he could feel the warm bulk of Daniel's penis on his buttocks. If

68

he wished hard enough, maybe Danny would get an erection, maybe he would enter him in his sleep. He didn't of course.

In his half-conscious state, with adrenaline and testosterone coursing recklessly through his veins, the significance of his fantasies didn't impinge on Matthew but in the cold light of the next day, with Daniel sitting opposite him, fully compos mentis, chatting to Soibhan and Mary, he could hardly credit what he had been thinking only hours before. He felt sick at what Danny would think if he knew. What if he had given in to his urges? It didn't bear thinking about. He agonised for weeks, trying to rationalise his feelings. He told himself that loads of fellers had experiences like that but he wasn't convincing himself. Worse still, he began to have exquisite erotic dreams of a previously unexperienced intensity and he couldn't get away from the fact that they centred on Danny. He gradually accepted that he was strongly attracted to Danny, emotionally and sexually, although he didn't think that he was actually a homosexual; it was doubtless a pasing phase.

Willy-John's parents were having a party to greet 1977 and had invited all the old clique. With the understandable exception of Crispy and Jean who were over at Sandhurst, everyone accepted. Matthew's invitation was by phone on Boxing Day. "Should be good craic; we've not really been all together since school." He hesitated, "Er, listen Matt, do you want to bring your mate along, the one from Lancaster, Daniel isn't it?"

"I'll ask him but I don't know what he will be doing. He might have been invited somewhere else. Thanks anyway."

"Okay then. Great. I'll look forward to meeting him. I've heard that much about him, I probably know him better than he knows himself. Just keep him away from Aaron, that's all!"

Matthew phoned Danny: "Willy-John's having a Hogmanay Party, are you doing owt?"

"When is it?"

"Geek! When do you expect a Hogmanay party to be?"

"Dunno?"

"Are you serious? It's Scottish for New Year's Eve; do you really not know what it is?"

"Nah! How would I know that? I'm not an Ulster Scot!"

"Anyway, what are you doing?"

"Nothin'. Probably go into town and get full."

"Like to come then? You can stay at our house that night?"

"I'd like to see the New Year in with you but I'm not so sure about your Proddy friends."

"Dad'll be there and he doesn't drink, so he can run us home anytime. Fair enough?"

"Yeah; great."

"I'll pick you up about five on Friday. What did you get for Christmas?"

The party was going well. There was stacks of booze and food and Danny wasn't the only Catholic there although the rest, as Danny had so succinctly put it, were Protestants who crossed themselves. Willy-John went out of his way to make Danny feel welcome and, after a few Bushes, Danny and Alex were deep in conversation. They were all being so amazingly chummy with Danny that Matthew began to wonder what was going on.

In complete contrast to the rest of the old clique, Aaron was wearing a neat, dove-grey, three-piece suit. The image was deliberate and he left just after midnight without having said more than a few polite words to any of his revelling former friends.

At midnight Danny soon got the hang of 'Auld Lang Syne', nearly ripping Matthew's arm out of its socket in his enthusiasm. Then Alex macerated Matthew's hand in his great paw as he pumped his arm in a New Year's greeting and then nearly crushed his ribs with a bear hug. Alex's current girlfriend, Sue, gave Matthew a great sloppy kiss, as did Sandra. Matthew proffered his hand to Danny but he threw his arms round him and, burying his lips near Matthew's ear, mumbled, "Happy New Year, mate."

"Happy New Year," he responded, slightly confused.

Danny gripped Matthew's shoulders and held him in front of him, fixing him with bleary blue eyes. "This is it Matty, this year is the one when we make it or blow it. This," he gesticulated to the hubbub around them, "gives me a bit of hope for the six counties. But I'm not coming back here ever again and you'd better do the same."

"What? To Willy-John's?"

"No, to Ireland. I'm getting out." He lowered his voice and shook Matthew gently, stroking his neck with his thumbs. "I'm getting out and you should too."

"Is that your New Year's resolution?" Matthew said shakily.

"If you like, yeah. What's yours?"

"I'm going to make a determined effort to get a girlfriend this year. I'm really going to try with the women."

Danny let go of Matthew's shoulders. "Go for it Matt, if you would just forget yourself you would breeze through the women. You just don't have faith in yourself. You haven't the nerve to put yourself forward and you should."

At that moment Mr Woodhead edged his way through the

throng. "Happy New Year, son," he bellowed as they shook hands.

"Happy New Year, Dad."

"Well Daniel, Happy New Year, Good to see you here. Enjoying yourself?"

"Yes thanks. Happy New Year and Mr Woodhead... thanks... for *everything*."

Matthew's father turned to him. "I told your mother that I would be back as soon after midnight as I could but don't worry, just give me a ring when you want a lift back."

"Are you sure, Dad? We could come with you now if you like."

"No boys, you enjoy yourselves, I'll see you later, bye."

Laying in bed that night Matthew recalled Danny's affectionate behaviour and cursed himself for saying he wanted to get a woman. He did, of course, but at that moment he wanted Daniel. Had Danny been giving him the come-on? Had he blown it? Drunk and tired as he was he couldn't sleep for thinking about Danny. Would he come to him? Should he go to Danny's room? He even got out of bed and tip-toed across the landing but Danny's door was closed. Had it been ajar he could have pushed it open but to turn the handle was too much of an admission of what he wanted so he returned to his lonely bed.

The first surprise of 1977 came in the form of a letter from Aaron, of all people:

17, Prehen View,
LONDONDERRY,

Dear Matthew,
You will probably have already heard the news
about Billy Miller's father but, just in case you haven't,
I thought I'd better tell you that Mr Miller was murdered by Republican terrorists on the twelfth of
January. The funeral will be at the Lawrence Road
Methodist Church on the sixteenth of January at 2 p.m.
I know that Billy would want you to be at the
funeral but he will also understand that it will be
impractical for you to try to get here for the service.
Yours sincerely,

Aaron Lindsay

He had heard, of course. His mother had rung him immediately in a dreadful state. Mr Miller had been a victim of a 'tit for tat' killing. Day after day ordinary people were being gunned down; one day a Catholic the next a Protestant; no one was safe. Billy's father was in his shop when they rang the doorbell. As he reached for the security lock, bullets ripped through the wood and tore his insides out. Matthew wrote a letter of condolence to Billy but what could he say?

Matthew was curious as to exactly why Aaron had taken it upon himself to do the letter writing. He had never been particularly nice to Billy; Matthew supposed himself Billy's best friend and that was by default! He couldn't help wondering what Aaron was up to.

The threat of finals loomed and then Daniel abruptly disappeared. He spent all his time in his room and never surfaced, even for coffee. Initially, Matthew admired him for his dedication but after two days of total exclusion he began to feel peeved. He was his best friend; he had a duty to be with him sometimes! After fruitlessly combing every bar looking for company he bought a bottle of red wine and went to his room to revise. Why be mean? he thought, and went to pound on Danny's door.

"Fuck off," he growled through the door.

"Danny, it's me, Matt. Let me in."

"Go away."

"Please, Danny," he wheedled, "I need to talk to you," he lied; the wine would be a nice surprise. "Please Danny, it's important."

The door opened. Danny looked terrible, he obviously hadn't shaved for days. He stood before Matthew, barefoot, with a crumpled and dirty orange shirt half in and half out of his unzipped jeans. The room stank of dirty socks and farts.

"Wha'?" he demanded.

"Can I come in?"

He looked at the floor swaying slightly and nodded.

"Are you alright?"

"Aye," then, "nah! I'm fucking not alright."

Matthew realised that he was drunk. He waved the wine at him, "I bought some vin rouge."

"You're a fuckin' wonder Matt, just what I need. Get it open."

Two half-pint glasses were filled with the blood-red poison. Among the chaos of his desk was an empty Bushmills bottle and half a bottle of flat-looking white lemonade.

"Having trouble with revision are you?"

"No," Danny snapped, examining the floor.

"Daniel, look at me."

The familiar bleary, porcelain blue eyes peered out of his puffed-up pale face.

"Something's wrong. I'm supposed to be your best mate, you can tell me, nothing's going to freak me out, you know that."

Danny bit his bottom lip and stared at his belly. "You don't want to know. It's bad. Bloody bad!"

"Daniel, you know how much I care for you. Tell me what's eating you."

"It's Patrick."

Matthew was suddenly alarmed. "What's happened to him, is he alright?"

"No he's not fuckin' alright... He's fuckin' dead, that's what he is."

Matthew was stunned into a moment's silence. "My God, Daniel, what happened?... I'm so, so sorry!" he sat on the bed next to Danny and put his arm round his shoulder but Danny shook it off.

"You won't be so sorry when you hear what happened," he said ominously.

"Try me."

"Paddy was a volunteer."

"A volunteer what?"

Danny gave Matthew a sardonic smile: "Some fuckin' Derry man you, hey! A volunteer of the Irish Republican Army; a Provi." He waited for Matthew's reaction but, shocked as he was, he was determined to give none.

He was as nonchalant as possible: "Go on."

"Shot by the Brits on active service."

"I'm sorry, I'm really very sorry, that's terrible."

Danny glared at Matthew. "You shouldn't be fuckin' sorry," he spat. "He was your enemy. The Provies shot your mate's dad. You should be glad that there's one more Taig underground."

Something snapped inside Matthew: "How... how dare you!" he choked. "How could you think that I would want to see anyone die; especially your brother! It hurts me right there," he thumped his heart, "to see you so upset!"

Danny doubled up and began to sob; silently at first then with great shuddering heaves. This time he didn't shrug Matthew off so he held his shaking frame, tears coursing down his own cheeks. When he composed himself he mumbled, "Sorry, I should have known. I dunno what I was thinking about. I s'pose I was too wrapped up in my own problems."

"There's no need to apologise... God, you've been through so much and now you're sitting here alone. Oh Danny, you poor bastard. Do you want to talk about it?... Don't if you don't want to."

He did want to and the story tumbled out. Essentially Paddy, embittered by experiences like being burnt out of their home, had developed a venomous hatred for 'the enemy'. Nationalist feelings flourished in the school environment and by fifteen he was thoroughly steeped in radical Republicanism. That wasn't unusual for a young Derryman so Paddy's political views didn't raise any suspicions in the McDaid household. Then, whilst rooting for Christmas decorations in the loft, Danny had come across a cache of ammunition in a cardboard box. At first he wasn't a hundred percent sure which of his brothers, or indeed his sister, was responsible but it didn't take long to find out. Danny and Paddy had a furious row which ended with Danny telling Paddy to get the gear out of his mother's house. This Paddy agreed to do, but he declared that he was absolutely committed to the armed struggle. Danny knew little more about Paddy's activities until his death at the age of twenty years and two months. He was in a derelict house overlooking the Bogside, sniping on an army patrol. Sadly for Paddy, another patrol reached the house before he could get away. They burst into the room and riddled him with bullets. He was given a hero's funeral. An honour guard of his fellow volunteers fired a volley of shots over his tricolour-draped coffin. Danny was glad he'd missed it.

11: Matthew Spreads His Wings

Danny threw himself into his work and looked like sailing through with a 'two one' or even first-class honours. They settled into a routine of working until ten, then going down to the bar to get smashed. What Matthew had taken for lemonade in Danny's room was pure ethanol nicked from the labs. The two friends would go down to the bar and buy Coke all night, perking it up with a dash of ethanol, and Danny used to have a whiskey and ethanol each night to help him sleep too.

Tony had booked a cheap flight to Rome and was sickening all his friends with his plans of a sun-drenched summer populated with willing Italian women. Danny and Matthew were of one mind so Matthew reserved two seats for the fourth of July, two days after their graduation. Matthew rang his mother with his plans and asked her to work on his father. Not only did he sanction the trip but he promised to help finance the expedition, the actual amount being proportional to the quality of his final degree. Matthew gritted his teeth, hid his distaste for bribes and promised to get back in August for harvesting.

Danny and Lisa were spending more and more time together. He would work at the desk with her stretched out on his bed, buried in a sea of physiology notes. Sometimes they didn't even come down to the bar. Matthew knew he should have discussed the holiday with Danny sooner but he didn't want to hassle him and before he knew it, the date for confirming the reservations was upon him. He had a three-hour animal physiology paper in the morning so he was going into town to confirm that afternoon. Coming out of the exam he found Danny lying on the grass outside his room, revising. His stereo was on full blast and his window was rattling to the strains of 'Tubular Bells'.

"What about Rome then?" Matthew asked casually, flopping down next to his friend.

"Rome?"

"Aye. We've got to confirm today."

"What's that got to do with me?"

"Don't you want to go?"

"Love to, but I'm going to Scotland with Lisa."

Matthew hadn't expected that. "Oh!" – he couldn't hide the disappointment in his voice.

"Jesus, Mary and Joseph, Matt! You didn't still think... ?"

"Well yes, actually. I've reserved two seats. We've got to confirm today."

"I'm really sorry Matt, I thought you knew we were going to Scotland, I told you ages ago."

"When?"

"Dunno, in the bar sometime."

"I don't remember, but then I haven't seen much of you lately." He paused to emphasise the next phrase. "You two are always in your room."

If Danny picked up his innuendo, he ignored it. "Matt, I'm sorry, really I am. What'll you do?"

"It doesn't matter. I'm sure I'll find someone who wants a cheap flight to Italy."

"What about Tony?"

"He's already got his."

"Ach, you'll find someone to go with you, Matt. You'll have a great time and you might even find a nice Italian bint eh! Nudge, nudge!"

It was like being told on December 24th that Christmas has been cancelled. He slunk off to his room, flung himself onto his bed and sobbed as Mike Oldfield's voice reverberated round the block: "and tu-bu-lar... bells".

There was a tap on the door. It was Danny looking uncharacteristically serious. "Matthew, I'm dead, dead sorry, I've been a prat."

"No you haven't; it's okay."

"It's not, and you know bloody well it's not. I shouldn't have said what I said about a bird."

"Why not, I might get a bird, you never know – she may be blind *and* stupid."

Danny sat on the bed and patted the space next to him. Matthew obeyed and Danny put his arm round his shoulder. Matthew tensed. "Why can't you accept what's staring you in the face?" Danny said gently.

"I don't know what you mean."

"Do I have to spell it out to you?"

"Looks like it," Matthew muttered.

"You can't cling to me for ever. We've our own lives to live. I don't know where we're going but it's not the same place."

Matthew was looking straight ahead. All he saw was a tearful blur.

"Matt," Danny whispered, "It's not a woman you want, is it?"

"No," he sniffled.

"I wish," he paused, "I wish that I *could* give you what you want... what you need." He drew Matthew gently to him, stroking his long hair. Matthew relaxed, the sensation was wonderful. "If I could... If it was in me to do it... there is no one I would rather do it with than you. I suppose I love you but I'm not, I'm just not..." Danny's voice was breaking up and very, very quiet. "I'm sorry, I'm... not... gay... Are you?"

"Sorry or gay," Matthew quipped with a sniffle.

"You know what I mean," he whispered with feigned impatience.

"I don't know... I don't fancy you – not sexually. It's just that I love being with you." The moment Matthew had denied it, he realised it was true. He was totally obsessed with him. He clung to Danny and wept uncontrollably. When he stopped, Danny kissed him gently on the forehead and stroked his hair. Matthew looked at him longingly, his face got closer and closer and then Danny kissed him on the lips; not passionately, but gently and intimately.

Danny smiled. "You're the first man I've ever kissed."

"You're my first too."

"Aye, but I reckon you'll kiss loads more. And I'm fuckin' sure I won't!"

Matthew laughed a smile at him.

"Matt. I know you fancy me but I can't do it. I would if I could but it's not in me. Don't torture yourself mate. We all need someone to love... Jees! that sounds clichéd," he grimaced. "I don't care who you need to love, boy, girl or bloody sheep. It doesn't matter a toss, as long as you're happy, just go for it!"

They sat in silence listening to his alarm clock ticking, then Danny said, "Come on, let's go and get rat-arsed!"

American Independence Day saw Matthew descending the aircraft steps at Rome airport. The heat slammed up at him from the tarmac. In the city he booked into a cheapo hotel for four nights and then he had nearly a month to thumb home. Matthew fell in love with Rome; never in his life had he seen such a beautiful city. He filled the sweltering days by wandering from monument to monument, wondering at Renaissance splendour or ancient extravagance. His favourite spot was the Palatine hill where he sat on a shady bench watching long-legged, American boys doing the sights. But it was the Italians that gave him most pleasure; never in his life had he seen so many beautiful men. Every youth had the physique of a Greek god with a spot-free, olive complexion. What was more, they dressed so erotically; no baggy jeans and sloppy jumpers for the youths of Rome! They wore skin-tight slacks and figure-hugging, neatly ironed shirts which showed every contour of their fine bodies. They strolled in cosy little groups, often arm in arm; they lolled about the piazzas, idly smoking strong cigarettes; they chugged around on Vespas and they chatted animatedly to gaudy females. In the dim hotel room, with the background of hooting cars and the sounds and smells of the trattoria fighting their way up through the stifling air, he liberated his fantasy and, imagining their warm, willowy bodies, he masturbated unrestrainedly; he finally *knew* he *was* gay.

From Rome he took a train to the coast and started to hitch north, ending up on a campsite on the Isle of Elba. He had become quite ruthless in his voyeurism, deliberately positioning his tent near those of attractive men. On Elba all the small tents were near the beach so that was the spot to be. As he sat in front of his little tent the occupant of a tiny, green, light-weight emerged. He watched a pair of long, thin, honey-brown legs, then a neat bum in cut-down jeans, followed by a sinewy, tanned body and finally a mop of curly, ash-blond hair. The Adonis leapt to his feet, flung a towel over his shoulder and strolled to the sea with the grace of a giraffe. Matthew could only dream; he was thin and insipid with straggly hair half-way down his spotty back. The beauty was hardly likely to give him a second glance and, in any case, he was sure to have an equally beautiful Nordic girl somewhere not too far away.

However when the boy came back alone Matthew took his courage in his hands and used the oldest ruse in the book: "Excuse me."

The blond looked up. His eyes were clear; deep blue; Matthew nearly faltered. "Do you speak English?"

"Ja, a little."

"Oh good. Do you have any matches I could borrow?"

"Ja I haf, just one moment pliss." His gorgeous head and arms were hidden for a long moment as he searched his tent.

"Here, you can keep these box, I am not needing them." He flashed Matthew a brilliant smile. "When are you arriving here?"

"I came over on this morning's ferry. The man from the Piccadilly restaurant brought me here in his car; I think he owns the campsite."

"I think Roberto is owning half of the island. He tells me that he is being top man in Portoferraio."

"I think he's top bull-shitter but..."

"Als u blief? I'm sorry – if you please?"

"Bull-shitter, teller of tall tales, you can't believe all he says. Do you know what I mean?"

"Ja, ja." The delicious boy held out his hand; he had a hard, firm grip. "I am Henk and I come from Holland."

"Hi. I'm Matt, I'm from Northern Ireland." Unfortunately he said this with the Ulster accent so it came out as Norn-Irand.

"Iran?"

"No, I'm from Northern Ireland, you know, the island west of Britain."

"Ja, ja, Belfast, Dublin, the IRA."

"Yeah," he smiled, "but we don't like to talk about that."

"Tell me, what is it really like in Northern Ireland?"

So followed the draft version of the Woodhead history of the Ulster problem which, over the years, he refined into a veritable lecture.

Henk wasn't classically handsome but there was something appealing about him. His lower jaw jutted slightly beyond the upper, giving him a vaguely pugnacious air, but it was his gentle personality which attracted Matthew. They talked for hours about life in their respective countries. Henk was both interested and interesting; moreover, he didn't mention girls once. The two boys fell in with three Italian boys and two German girls. Henk drew Matthew's attention to one of the girls, Margareet. He said that she had taken a liking to Matthew but if he wasn't quick, Giorgio would get in before him. Matthew's heart sank as he was thrust back into the pretence of being interested and he slipped back into the nightmare as if he had never escaped. On the other hand perhaps this was what he needed; a kick-start into heterosexuality. If he could make it with Margareet he might discover the normal part of his sexuality and even if nothing happened, it would give him credibility with Henk. He had the brain-wave of buying a bottle of wine and inviting her to join him on the headland to watch the Mediterranean sunset. Dead romantic! But Giorgio was no dozer; he had some bread and cheese if she liked – the battle lines were drawn.

The pretty fraulein perched on the rocks being wooed from both sides. It didn't take Matthew long to realise that he would have preferred to be seducing Giorgio. He had hardly been able to keep his eyes off him. Giorgio was so slim that when he was sunbathing his pelvis, projecting above his flat abdomen, stretched his taut trunks from ilium to ilium so that by manoeuvring into the right position Matthew could glimpse his thick, brown penis glowering in the dark recesses of his trunks.

As the wine bottle emptied and the sun sank into a clichéd sunset, the conversation degenerated into a slanging match which culminated in Giorgio saying, "My country and your country were allies in the last war against Britain." To Matthew's disgust she welcomed this; game, set and match to Giorgio! Matthew stomped off in mock anger, glad to leave Giorgio to do what he wanted with her.

Henk was hitching north so they decided to travel together. He was nineteen, from Rotterdam and had just done his first year at university in Delft. As they journeyed Matthew grew more fond of him; he was the most unflappable person he'd ever met. They spent their last night in Italy on a campsite just outside Bellano. In the gloaming, the elegant, black, spear-like cypresses were mirrored in the luminous waters of a serene Lake Como. But it was the hills that excited Henk; the rugged peaks, black against the gentle night sky, were giving him a foretaste of what was to come.

The following morning found the two boys standing by the roadside in Colico. They took it in turn to hold a strip of card bearing the legend Chiavenna. Henk was on duty when a tiny, black Fiat with matching woman slithered to a halt. Matthew squeezed into the back with the two rucksacks and Henk folded his six-foot frame into the front seat.

One thing that amazed Matthew was Henk's ear for language. When Matthew had met him, his English was fair, now it was excellent and he had picked up enough Italian to get by on. The lady rattled on, apparently oblivious of Matthew's inability and Henk's limited facility to understand. At one interchange Henk roared, said something in his Italian and she shrieked, turning round to blast Matthew with a string of hysterical words. Henk twisted in his seat and grinned broadly. "The lady tells me that she would not, in normal circumstances, give lifts but she thought that I looked like a nice man," he paused for a stunning grin, "and my girlfriend looked nice too!"

That was it, Matthew decided. His long hair was coming off the moment he got home.

The black-clad woman was going to see her son who worked in an hotel in Splugen. They had intended to cross into Switzerland via St Moritz but with hitching as it was they decided to go over the Splugen pass with the signora. The road to Chiavenna forged its way through a fertile valley between shattered peaks. Chiavenna itself was a jumble of elderly, dilapidated houses, the tall, square, shuttered type seen all over northern Italy. Just after crossing the river, the lady turned into what looked like a cobbled side street. This was the start of the spectacular road to Splugen. At first it picked its way up a steep valley scattered with great boulders. Her driving was astonishing! Where a Brit wouldn't dream of overtaking for fear of meeting oncoming traffic, she trusted in God and flew past. At one point she nipped past a wheezing, fuming truck on the inside of a hairpin bend. Matthew couldn't see Henk's face but his own was white.

The road to Pianazzo quite literally clawed its way up a sheer rock face in a series of tunnels and sharp hairpins. Looking up Matthew could see bits of road sticking out of the rock face. Then they were at the top, well above the tree line and shooting past alpine meadows studded with stunning arrays of brightly coloured flowers. The higher they got the bleaker it became and soon they reached a dammed lake, at the far end of which was an untidy scattering of decaying houses. This was the village of Monte Spluga. The lady screeched to a halt and jabbered at Henk who had become remarkably quiet. "Are we there?" Matthew asked.

"No, it is a coffee break," Henk replied brusquely.

They eased themselves out of the car and followed the lady to a cafe. The air was bracing. All around them glistening white, snowcapped crags stabbed the brilliant blue sky; Henk was green.

Matthew insisted on paying for the coffee, it still gave him a kick to hand out notes with so many zeros on. Henk was very quiet so when the lady went to the toilet Matthew quizzed him. "Are you okay?"

"I thought we would never get out of that car alife. I cannot get in again."

Matthew was amazed, the unperturbable Henk was definitely fazed.

"I'll walk down if I cannot get a different lift," he concluded.

"Don't be daft! We're here, aren't we?"

"If she drives uphill at that great speed, at what speed will she go downhill? And what is the road into Switzerland like?"

On the map the road looked far worse. "It looks better," Matthew lied. "I'll go in the front. You can tell her that I want to see the view... Shush, she's coming back."

The Swiss side was *nothing* in comparison. The road surface was better, it zig-zagged down a comparatively gentle grassy slope into a forest and thereafter it was an ordinary road into Splugen. It took them ages to get a lift out of Splugen but eventually a Swiss teacher picked them up. He spoke wonderful English and they were soon into the standard hitch-hiker's conversation; where they were from; what they did; where they had been; where they were going. As it was far easier than trying to explain all about Northern Ireland, Matthew usually told people he was English but Werner got the truth. He was most offended that the boys didn't intend to stay in Switzerland. They explained that they could hardly afford to do so.

"Graubunden," Werner said, "is undoubtedly the finest canton of Switzerland. I would propose that you stay at my home for two nights so that I can show you my beautiful canton."

Matthew tried not to sound too eager, but Henk voiced his thoughts. "That is very good. Now we can pass another day together."

In Chur Matthew noticed tram lines. "I see there are trams here."

Werner didn't catch what he said. "I beg your pardon."

"Trams, I see you have trams, you know, like buses but running on rails in the road."

"Ah! *Strassenbahn!* Trams, yes, I see. No, this is not a *Strassenbahn*, it is the Arosabahn. It is a railway but in Chur it runs in the street." Right on cue a bright red, electric railcoach with a train of goods wagons rumbled up the street causing traffic chaos for a few minutes. "Tomorrow we will take the Arosabahn to Arosa, it is a very beautiful place. Then you can see what the Arosabahn is like from the inside," promised Werner.

Henk laughed: "Now you must come to visit Rotterdam, the city is full of trams – they are great crawling snakes."

"I would love to," Matthew replied happily, "and you must

come to Ireland." But he was troubled. It was Danny all over again. He had become infatuated with Henk. He would love to visit him in Holland but was it right to when Henk had no idea about how he felt about him? He had to tell him before they parted.

That evening they all sat in a pavement cafe and drank a few beers in the balmy heat of the city before returning to Werner's to retire at the alarmingly early hour of nine-thirty. Matthew's spirits rose when they were shown a giant double bed in the guest room. He fantasised that their bodies might touch in the night then chemistry would do the rest. But a vast plain of cold sheets stretched between them. He tried contorting his body until the sole of his foot rested on Henk's knee but lost his nerve and withdrew to a night in isolation.

The Arosabahn ground its way up through forests, along steep valley edges and through picturesque villages to the resort. Arosa itself was a bit dull but was surrounded by the most wonderful mountains. They ate sausage and drank beer on a sun-drenched terrace at the top of the Weisshorn, eight thousand feet above sea level. All around them was the panorama of great peaks flecked with snow. They walked back down into Arosa past rocks sprinkled with a kaleidoscopic carpet of tiny alpine flowers. The spring gentians were such an intense shade of blue that Matthew's eyes could hardly accommodate it. As they dropped back into the valley their conversation ranged far and wide but all the time, at the back of his mind, was the certainty that he had to tell Henk how he was feeling about him. If Henk *was* gay, the next night could be one of unrestrained passion. But if he wasn't – and on balance that seemed more likely – it would be a terrible thing to tell him before sharing a bed with him. Discretion won and he didn't get round to telling him. The next day Matthew was to head towards Zurich and Henk to Innsbruck . Time was getting on and he had promised his father to be back for harvest, so, thumb well-oiled, he prepared for a dash across France.

12: Too Near the Sun

The morning they were to depart found Matthew in Werner's well-appointed bathroom where he took advantage of the ample supply of hot water to have a shave and ponder his future. Who would want a spotty, snub-nosed, overgrown schoolboy? he mused. But when he appraised his naked self in the full-length mirror he was pleasantly surprised. Whether it was the diet, the sun, the fresh air or the effects of his mental liberation, he hadn't a clue, but he was delighted. The striking contrast between his tan and the white skin at his waist pleased him and his hair was fairer too. But what delighted him most was his spots – they had nearly all gone. I'm not *that* bad looking after all! he thought.

Four p.m., two days later, found Matthew stuck outside Châlons-sur-Marne. He had hoped to reach Reims before nightfall but he'd been waiting in the same spot for well over two hours. He was hot, sticky and demoralised by the time an old, grey, Citroën 2CV van rattled to a halt and a farmer in work-worn clothes offered him a lift.

Marcel was returning from market in Châlons. He wasn't going far but Matthew was glad of the ride. Despite Matthew's sketchy command of French and his limited interest in farming matters they were soon deep in conversation. After half an hour Marcel pulled in at a roadside cafe. Matthew reached for his rucksack but Marcel patted him on the hand and indicated that he should leave it in the van. He pointed the thumb of his clenched fist down his open throat and pointed to the cafe.

Shabby formica-topped tables completed the distinctly fifties atmosphere of the functional French bar. Before they had entered, the only activity was a clumsy youth locked in mortal combat with a fruit machine. Four silent figures perched on bar stools wore drab jackets, shabby grey boots, trousers of indefinable material and colourless, collarless shirts. Their skin resembled old, supple leather.

Matthew and Marcel's entrance animated the tableau. They were greeted warmly and drinks were ordered from a woman who appeared, as if by magic. Her blonde, bouffant hair and rouged cheeks delighted Matthew. Great jangling ornaments dangled from her distended earlobes. She produced two cognacs in honour of Marcel's birthday. Two became four and four, six. Marcel was a double hero for reaching forty-two and for finding the curious English boy who stammered a few juvenile phrases for their delight. Marcel disappeared into the back room and returned to inform Matthew that his daughter was preparing a meal and he was to stay at his home that night.

Several brandies later, the 2CV wove its uncertain way up a narrow, wooded road through the dappled evening sun. It found its way down a rutted lane to a low, modern bungalow in a clearing; a field devoid of fencing of any sort. Someone had started to cut the long grass from the inside but this enterprise had been abandoned uncompleted and a tiny tractor lay where work had ground to a halt. The car was likewise abandoned as the two were welcomed by a little girl with short, dark hair and a face the shape and colour of an olive. She was about eight and wore a shabby print frock. Maria let herself be swept up in Marcel's arms for a kiss before skipping back to the kitchen. They made their way round to the sunny side of the house where a long-haired youth in shorts and a grubby Black Sabbath tee-shirt lounged with his guitar. This was Pascal and Matthew was informed that there was also an older son who was doing his military service. Luc had phoned earlier to say that he was on leave and was trying to get home.

Pascal was instructed to entertain Matthew whilst Marcel went in to clean up. At first, he wouldn't attempt to speak English but, being fanatical about rock music, he capitulated in frustration at Matthew's inability to communicate in French. He soon discovered that Matthew knew little about his passion but by then it was too late to retreat into French.

There was a tantalising animal quality about Pascal. Visions of him naked, bounding gazelle-like through the dusky grass, flitted through Matthew's brandy-flushed mind but his fantasies were grounded with Pascal's first conversational gambit: "The girls of Ireland, they are beautiful, yes?"

"Of course," Matthew replied churlishly.

His eyes lit up. "Do they?" he made a lewd gesture, the finger of one hand through the pinched finger and thumb of the other, and whistled – in, out, in, out.

Matthew decided to steer clear of dangerous territory by telling him that Irish girls didn't until they were married. This caused great hilarity; the youth goggled at him: "So you are a virgin?"

He ploughed a deeper rut for himself. "Yes, in Ireland all unmarried men and women are virgins." It was a quite ridiculous thing to have said, but, once he'd started, he felt he had to keep it up.

"It's true?" the wide-eyed boy asked.

Matthew nodded seriously.

Pascal looked at him with the sincere masculinity that only a sixteen-year-old can affect. "In France no man of your age is still a virgin."

Matthew searched desperately for a witty retort but all he could dredge up was a rather prissy, "Love is more important than sex."

The topic, Matthew hoped, was closed and they walked back to the house in silence.

A large, rough, wooden table set for five had appeared on the stubble and Marcel was already enjoying an aperitif. It was a delicious, balmy evening, with a gentle hum of insects in the air. Matthew thought he was in the most beautiful and peaceful place in the world and wished that he could capture its essence. Pascal and he were given generous glasses of calvados as Maria served tender pieces of beefsteak fried in garlic and onion. They ate with hunks of fresh bread and lashings of the local red wine. To finish the leisurely meal there was a green salad, bitter with endives.

In the cool blue of the evening Matthew luxuriated in the glow of the wine, trying to imagine such a scene at Strathbeg. He was mellow and the calvados was flowing as freely as his French. He entertained his hosts who listened intently, despite him being repeatedly distracted by strange, antediluvian cries from the encircling forest. Marcel spoke to him and Matthew realised he was telling him to come inside. He followed into the sparsely-furnished living room but once there he could hardly keep his eyes open and he was directed to a bed.

Luc's bedroom had practically no furniture and yet there was an impression of clutter. On every wall, arrays of posters defined his character; the predominant themes were motorbikes, war and women but Matthew was soon unconscious, so they didn't offend him long.

Matthew's next experience was a dream come true. A pair of strong, masculine lips were kissing his. Better still, they were attached to a stubbly cheek and accompanied by a firm caressing hand. In those delectable, waking moments it didn't occur to him to wonder why a man should be doing this. Then Pascal's screeches of laughter jerked him into full consciousness. The kisser stopped abruptly and growled at Pascal who was chanting, "Pédé, pédé, pédé, c'est un homme!"

In the early dawn light filtering through the shutters the kisser peered at Matthew and then, with a roar, he lunged for his hysterical brother who deftly dodged him. Pascal fled, taunting the young soldier until, infuriated, Marcel silenced them. Luc, muttering venom for his sibling, returned to his bedroom and slammed the door.

With the light on, Matthew saw his assailant for the first time. Like the rest of his family, he was compact. His black hair was cropped into a functional military crew-cut. The stubble that had excited Matthew cast a dark shadow on his hollow cheeks. His face had few soft contours and its slight asymmetry made him sneer, even when he smiled.

Matthew tried to make apologies for being in Luc's bed but Luc insisted on explaining his behaviour. He started far too quickly for Matthew's comprehension then, at Matthew's request to slow down, he spoke as if to a half-wit. He sat close to Matthew on the edge of the bed, his eyes boring into him as he told his tale. He had taken the train with some friends as far as Reims intending to hitch home but he had stayed with them, drinking. On getting home he found his brother strumming his guitar. Pascal had greeted him with 'guess who's in your bed?' or something of the sort, and Luc had joked, 'a beautiful, blonde virgin'. It was too good an opportunity to miss and Pascal spun him a yarn about inviting a woman home for the night, only to find that she had always had the hots for Luc. He came to Matthew with a notion of playing Prince Charming to his Sleeping Beauty.

Luc's act of innocent stupidity and raw sensuality drew Matthew in; he found Luc indescribably desirable and fought to conceal his lust. He told Luc that there was no problem and he would sleep in the lounge but Luc wouldn't hear of it; the bed was big enough for two. As Luc spoke, he was slowly peeling off his crumpled uniform to reveal his taut body. Clad only in flimsy briefs, he sat on the bed next to Matthew. Languidly, delectably, gracefully, he reached over Matthew to pull the light cord and as he did, his dense underarm hair passed so near Matthew's face that he could have stuck out his tongue and licked it. The musky smell of Luc's body made Matthew's head spin. The light went out and with a single, lithe movement Luc shed his briefs and slid his body under the sheet next to Matthew's.

Luc said, "Dors bien," turned from him and began to emit deep, regular breaths.

Matthew could feel the heat from Luc's back only inches from him. He moved his hand close to feel its glow and as he did Luc shifted closer so that Matthew's hand made contact with his hot, tight skin.

Matthew held his breath but Luc didn't flinch. He risked gently running his finger along Luc's knobbly spine. Matthew was so tense he hardly dared breathe; his whole body was quivering. His fingers crept up Luc's shoulder blade and down the firm muscles of his arm. The soldier rolled onto his back and lay motionless letting Matthew 's fingers rove over his hard, damp chest. The hair was silky; his nipples hot and erect. Matthew froze as a hand closed on his wrist but Luc's firm, gentle grip guided Matthew's willing hand towards his hot groin. For the first time in his life Matthew had another man's penis in his hand. He wanted to lie all night caressing the engorged column and fingering the coarse, damp pubic hairs but Luc turned to face him. He could feel Luc's alcohol-laden breath on his face then a hairy leg pinned his to the mattress. Matthew stroked the prickly skin of Luc's jaw, then his chin and then the soft, warm lips which drew his fingers in.

Luc curled a hard hand round Matthew's neck and drew his

face to him. Matthew submitted as Luc's mouth and tongue probed and sucked at his. He wanted to be touching every bit of his wonderful flesh at once and as he tried they writhed together, slippery with sweat and saliva. Abruptly, Luc pulled away from him. Please don't stop, he prayed, but Luc wasn't stopping. He rolled Matthew onto his face, dragging clumsily at his underpants and for a few sweating seconds poked his hard penis urgently at the gap between Matthew's buttocks. Failing to penetrate, he searched with his fingers; his nails scratched and tore until he found Matthew's anus and, with a triumphal thrust, entered him.

Matthew hadn't expected it to hurt so much. "Aghh! *No!*" he begged. "No. Stop, please don't! Arrêt, arrêt," he cried out, "*Aoww!*" but Luc clamped his hand over his mouth and fucked him mercilessly until, with a shudder and an ecstatic gasp, he came inside him.

Satisfied, he rolled off and lay panting. Matthew languished next to him, feeling totally subjugated. He reached a shaking hand towards Luc but he pushed him away. Then, saying he was to tell no one, Luc left and didn't return.

Matthew needed to go to the loo but didn't dare, his bum was agony and he was sure that if anyone saw him trying to walk they would know what had just happened. But after lying uncomfortably for an age, needs drove and he waddled to the bathroom where he tried to clean himself up. He had to remove every trace of sweat, spunk and saliva. He felt disgusting; filthy.

Luc was gone when Matthew got up. He had slept in the living room telling his father that he didn't want to disturb Matthew. That was a joke; nothing was ever to have such a profound affect on Matthew's life as that one desperate fuck. Matthew couldn't look his host or his family in the face, excusing himself with a dreadful hangover. Marcel drove him to the main road and he was on his way to the coast, Britain and safety.

The journey home gave him ample opportunity to worry at his leisure. Luc had used him; he had used him as a superior form of masturbation. Matthew decided that it was his own fault; he had started it; in Luc's position he might have done the same sort of thing. He had found being fucked exceptionally unpleasant which was most worrying. He loved the touching and kissing but he would never, ever let anyone do that to him again! He couldn't understand it; surely that was what homosexuals did but why did they let each other do it? With a glimmer of guilty hope he thought, maybe I'm not really gay. But, if that was so, he reasoned, how come men turn me on and women don't?

These confusions were to plague him much longer but his most immediate concerns were physical. Not only had Luc hurt him at the time but he seemed to have damaged him inside. He kept messing his underpants with blood and slime and this really frightened him. Was he permanently injured? Had Luc given him VD? He hadn't a clue. He wouldn't be able to tell his family doctor what had happened so he decided to go to see the student medical officer at Lancaster. But by the time he got to Lancaster the physical effects had diminished, so he didn't bother and hoped he was alright.

Part Two
EXPERIMENT

13: Belfast

In a desperate attempt to put off having to go out into the real world, Matthew applied to do teacher training. Not that he had any intention of being a teacher! He would have liked to stay in Lancaster but he could only get a grant to go to Stranmillis College in Belfast.

Willy-John arrived at Strathbeg: "Hi Matt, good summer?"

"Yeah, great thanks. I flew to Rome then hitched back."

"On your tod?"

"Aye... well, I started off on my own but I met loads of interesting people. There was this Dutch man called Henk – he was really nice."

"Oh aye," Willy-John said, implying all sorts by his tone.

Matthew reddened: "No, no, not like that," he said a little too quickly. "He was just dead easy to get on with, you know? Good craic."

Willy-John listened enthusiastically to a sanitised account of Matthew's adventures. After quizzing him on various details he enquired, "What're you going to do now?"

"I'm joining you."

"Eh?"

"I'm coming to Belfast; Stran'."

Willy-John goggled and choked theatrically. "You? Jesus! I can't imagine you teaching, even with your new haircut!"

"What else is there? I only got a two-two and I want to stay a student as long as I can."

"But Stranmillis! It's like going back to school. Students there have to get notes from their mummies if they want to stay out after nine-thirty. Most don't want to anyway!"

"That's crap," Matthew laughed. "It's just a college like any other."

"Do you *know* any Stran students?" Willy-John queried.

"Not actually, but students are students anywhere, aren't they?"

"I wish someone would tell them."

"Thanks a lot!"

"No, not you. But most of them have chips on their shoulders because they didn't get into university."

"You're not exactly whetting my appetite," Matthew grinned. "I was quite looking forward to another year of student life."

"Never mind, me old mucker. I'll still be there; you can always come out on the tear with us."

But when Matthew moved to Belfast it wasn't quite as he expected. Willy-John worked late all week and played rugby every Saturday, which only left Friday nights for Matthew. And having to get up early for rugby the next day, he never wanted to be out late. Feeling let down by Willy-John, Matthew looked up Sandra, his nearly girlfriend from their schooldays. She and some of the other nurses went out every Thursday night and she suggested he should join them. As she said, they would love to have 'such a wee dote' along.

He was to meet them in the Eglinton Inn on the Malone Road. The Egg, as it was affectionately known, had a large, well-appointed lounge downstairs and a slightly less salubrious bar upstairs where the students tended to congregate. He found the overwhelmingly female company a bit intimidating at first but as the evening wore on he started to relax. He didn't have to pretend to fancy any woman; he didn't have to care whether or not Ireland got the Triple Crown and he could safely mention that the Russian roulette game in *The Deer Hunter* had given him nightmares for weeks; it was almost like being with Henk again! By the end of the evening, Matthew was discussing the merits of various male pop stars with the nurses; and they weren't talking about their vocal attributes.

The next Thursday found him in the Egg, as did the next, and then disaster struck. Matthew's nemesis came in the form of Dierdre. She wasn't conventionally good-looking but she oozed something; probably pheromones. Matthew envisaged her fisting foaming tankards of ale in a nineteenth-century Whitechapel tavern. She soon annexed him and as the kitty dwindled so did Dierdre's sobriety. She became over-familiar with Matthew; fiddling with his collar and fingering the little strands of hair straying over it. When she started to play with the button at his throat he got nervous and tried to edge away but she merely slumped closer and tried to kiss him.

"What's the matter?" she asked as he recoiled, "I thought you liked me!"

"I do, I do. It's just that... I don't... I don't want to kiss! I'm sorry."

She was evidently hurt. "Am I that ugly?"

"Don't be silly. Of course not. You're very nice... really. But everyone can't fancy everyone, can they?"

"What's wrong with me?" she whined.

"Nothing! I like you. I like talking to you but... I don't fancy you, I'm sorry."

"Just my luck," she pouted, "typical of my bloody life," and she began to sniffle. He felt a real shit and, not knowing what to do for the best, put his arm round her sobbing shoulders, praying she wouldn't think she'd changed his mind. He was saved by the bell; it was drinking-up time. He walked with her to the parting of the ways, pecked her on the cheek and fled to the safety of his flat, never to go out with the nurses again.

Aaron was the only other one of Matthew's old friends in Belfast. He had tried to contact him on arriving but every time he called at his Ulsterville Avenue flat he stood in vain at the door. Matthew didn't like going there because Willy-John had told him there was a prostitute in the flat below and the vice squad had her under surveillance. Willy-John told Matthew they would have him on their computer as one of her regulars. He strung Matthew along for weeks but being Willy-John, took it too far.

Aaron's flat was in a dilapidated Georgian house in the Crescent, Belfast's answer to Bath's elegant terraces. One dreary November afternoon Willy-John greeted Matthew with, "Been for your special massage?" as he negotiated the dangerous staircase.

"I just waited for a minute," Matthew said nervously. "Are you sure he still lives there?" he queried, skirting an avalanche of soiled laundry on the second flight.

"Vice squad'll know the colour of your underkecks by now!"

"Get lost," Matthew blustered, "I bet it's just an ordinary massage parlour."

He reached the landing despite the daunting odds. "They wouldn't allow a place like that there anyway, the local residents would be up in arms! They'd be onto their MP like a shot if anything like that was going on. Who is their MP anyway, Robert Bradford?"

"He's one of Gertie's best customers... along with the Big Man himself!"

"Paisley!" Matthew asked in astonishment.

The huge grin on Willy-John's face told Matthew how he'd been had. "You bastard, you made the whole thing up!"

"Who? Me?" he said in mock innocence. "Would I do that?"

"I believed you, you sod. You'll make a great lawyer – you lie with absolute conviction."

"There really is a sexy masseuse there. She's not called Gertie though, she's called Helga."

"I'm not as green as I'm cabbage looking!" Matthew exploded.

"Honest Matt, she is. I've a mate used to live in Aaron's flat

93

and he said there was a stream of men. And the bin was always full of fetid tissues."

Matthew gagged. "You're disgusting, you. And you're the biggest slabber I know."

"I don't give a toss whether or not you believe me – I don't know why you want to see him anyway. He's fallen in with Paisley's lot, you know. He doesn't want to have anything to do with the likes of us any more."

"Come off it," Matthew objected, "Aaron's as much of a header as the rest of us."

"Nah! He was never the mad dog he made out. All bluff; trying to keep in with us."

"I know his folks were Free Presbyterians but I thought he'd rebelled."

"Not Aaron. Blood's thicker and all that. I wouldn't bother with him if I was you."

After the debacle with Dierdre, Matthew had been going home most weekends and then, one Thursday evening before Christmas, Willy-John called round to Ridgeway Street. "Goin' home this weekend?" he asked as he sat down on Matthew's unmade bed.

"Yeah, why?"

"Match's been cancelled, so I'll be free all weekend. Fancy going out on the tear?"

"Great stuff!" Matthew enthused. "I'll stay up. What's the drill?"

"When's your last lecture?"

"Finishes about half three."

"Fine!" Willy-John said, then he grimaced. "Shit! I've got to get to the Linnenhall library before the weekend. I won't be around till half five, six... Tell you what, I'll meet you in Robinson's at six, OK?"

"Dead on. What're you doing now? Time for a pint?"

"Love to but I've got work to do, sorry."

"No prob," Matthew said, with evident disappointment, "see you tomorrow at six then."

"Aye, must go now, see you."

"Cheers."

After his last lecture, Matthew trotted up Stranmillis Road to his flat, flung his notes on the bed, ripped the infernal tie from his neck and had a quick wash. Pulling on his jeans and sweatshirt, he grabbed his parka and headed to the shops to stock up for the weekend. That done, he wandered into town.

Belfast was having a pretty rough time in the late seventies but the city was trying to carry on as normal. The only reminders of the troubles in the university area were the occasional army or police Landrovers cautiously patrolling the respectable Victorian streets. It was dank and cold, with the threat of drizzle on the wind, and by the time Matthew got to Crane's bookshop he felt the mist had penetrated every fibre of his clothing. He spent half an hour browsing through coffee-table books before wending his way through the homeward throng to their rendezvous point.

Robinson's was a typical Belfast city pub with glass-panelled, wooden partitions along the bar and similarly partitioned stalls along the facing wall. The dingy, smoky atmosphere was alive with damp celebrants of the weekend. Matthew found a stool at the bar and waited the age it takes to pour a proper pint of Guinness. He was watching a guy playing Space Invaders when a man in a tired, grey suit spoke. "They should be banned from bars."

Matthew wasn't paying much attention; he turned to the speaker: "I'm sorry?"

"Space Invaders, they make intelligent conversation impossible."

"Aye."

"Fruit machines are the worst. People get hooked on them, you know – like drugs – can't help themselves – need their fix. I've a wee girl working for me and her man's addicted – spends every penny on them. She has to support the family on what I pay her."

Matthew tried to get a word in when the man paused for breath but he was off again: "It all goes to the IRA you know, or the UDA. Ninety-five percent of slot machines in Belfast belong to the paramilitaries. That's why they should be banned. Do you want a drink?"

"Er, no thank you," he said. He was peering round the bar for any sign of Willy-John.

"Excuse me if I have one," the man said as he signalled to the knowing barman.

Matthew escaped to the toilets and by the time he got back the bore had buttonholed some other unlucky punter, so he was able to lift his pint and sneak off as the tale of the unfortunate wee girl was unfolding.

Willy-John arrived with four friends. They were all built like the proverbial brick shithouses and two of them sported rugger shirts; they were evidently some of the first XV. The little group occupied a stall and a fiver from each of them went into a kitty; the session had started. Crude jokes and tales of signal victories both on the rugger field and in the seemingly not dissimilar field of female conquest were the order of the evening. It was exactly as it had been at school but that was nearly four years ago and Matthew was out of practice.

After Robinson's, they rolled down to Lavery's Gin Palace in Shaftsbury Square, then on to the Club Bar and ended up in the Students' Union. Basic low tables, scarred with years of careless fag-ends, were covered in soggy stubs and pink or yellow sheets of paper announcing this or that union event or protest. Like the tables, the floor was slippery with beer and the cacophony of rock music was drowned out by the roar of happy students. After a couple of pints, Willy-John leaned over and shouted into Matthew's ear, "Wanna go to a disco?"

"Aye, where is it?"

"Downstairs."

In a dreadful, mock American accent someone yelled, "Great, let's get going then man!"

"Bring your pint," Willy-John shouted and one-third of the university first fifteen plus Matthew went down the wide, concrete stairs to the basement whence came the thud of disco music. A table guarded by two unstudent-like men in their late twenties blocked the entrance.

Willy-John led the assault. "How much is it?"

The taller of the two men spoke in a soft Belfast accent. "D'you know this is a gay disco?"

Ever confident, Willy-John ploughed on. "Course, how much?"

Matthew didn't know it was a gay disco and panic welled up in him. He pulled Willy-John to one side. "Come on Willy-John, we don't want to go in that much, do we?" he whispered, "Let's go."

Willy-John quietly cajoled him. "Nah, it'll be a good laugh. Come on, they're supposed to be the best discos in the uni. Don't worry, we'll look after you." He indicated the four brutes with them: "They won't *dare* touch us."

He led Matthew back to the table and the taller man quietly asked, "*Are* you gay?"

Willy-John put his arm round Matthew. "Course, this is my boyfriend, aren't you, Matty darling?"

He shrugged his friend's arm off. "Fuck off, no, we're not... Come on, let's go."

"What's up Matt? Come on – it'll be good craic."

"You can go in if you like but if you do, I'm going home."

The tall man looked into Matthew's mind and smiled sadly. "I think it would be better if you all went," he said. He shot a quick glance at Matthew. "Come back if you decide you really are gay, though." Matthew found it profoundly disturbing.

Highly amused by all this, the others had been hanging back but now Symie stepped in. "There's an extension at the Botanic. I'd much rather get queer and pissed in the Bot, than risk a queer pissing in my bot!"

The first-fifteen men roared at this glittering show of wit but Matthew was affronted. They were being so ignorant to the door-man, who seemed to be really nice, but it did break the deadlock and they made their way back upstairs. Matthew turned to see the doorman disdainfully watching their retreating backs.

He hadn't realised there *were* gay people in Belfast and now he wanted to meet them, to talk to them about the way he felt and possibly to find the sort of love he craved. On the other hand, he had a vision of them all being like Luc and he couldn't face that. But his overriding reason for not doing anything was the dread of discovery. He could never look Willy-John or the others in the face if they ever found out – him, their friend, one of *them*! And if they found out at Stranmillis he was sure he would get thrown out and he knew would never get a teaching job, for sure. Then there was the family; his Mum and Dad would die if they knew. Although his parents had hardly ever mentioned homosexuality there had been enough signals for him to know they wouldn't approve, and more particularly they obviously expected him to be hetero-sexual. Even as a toddler his friendship with Amanda was met with comments like, "Matthew's got a new girlfriend – haven't you Matthew?" He quickly learned not to tell his mother about Willy-John's girlfriends because she would ask him when he was going to bring a nice girl home. But the most crucial incident was when he was eleven.

He was staying at his Uncle John's in Kendal. A lad called Barry worked on the farm and, despite being five years older than Matthew, Barry liked having little Matthew around. Matthew liked being with Barry too and one afternoon he had skipped up to him and begged him to take him to the tarn. A few days before they had swum there together. It had been an idyllic day which had finished blissfully with them walking home chatting happily, Matthew's little paw in Barry's big, warm hand.

"No," the farm-hand snapped.

"Why not?" he whined.

"'Cos your uncle was dead mad at me after last time," Barry almost shouted. He sounded so angry and Matthew was confused. His Uncle John had seen them coming home the last time and hadn't said anything to him, so it must have been allowed. Matthew grabbed Barry's hand and demanded to know why but he shook the little boy off as if he had leprosy.

Matthew's hurt eyes questioned him.

"And you mustn't do that," he growled, "people'll think you're *soft* if you hold another boy's hand!" He said 'soft' with a sneer. "And if your uncle sees you holding my hand again, he'll tell your dad and then you'll be in real trouble!"

There was something in his voice that scared Matthew. He had never heard anyone speak like that before. After that Barry avoided Matthew and the following summer he wasn't working on the farm. Matthew was sure it was because of him; the seeds of guilt and fear were thoroughly sown.

But now Matthew *knew* he was homosexual and the shadow of the consequences cast a grey miasma over his whole existence. They scared him so much that he couldn't even focus on them to think about them rationally; no wife, no children, no grandchildren, no friends, no job, just a bleak, black, cold, empty future. Surely that couldn't be what life had in store for him.

14: The RUC Man

He was sitting at home one Saturday evening in March when Alex appeared. He was more muscular than ever and sported an impressive beard. Matthew jumped out of his chair, beaming from ear to ear. "Alex, how are you? Great to see you. You're looking really well!"

That wasn't entirely true. The skin round his eyes was wrinkled and puffy which made him look old and tired.

"Sit down, sit down. Tell me all about life in the Royal Ulster Constabulary." He deliberately mispronounced constabulary by saying the *bul* part with an *e* as in mule.

This seemed to amuse Alex and a broad smile momentarily swept the tiredness from his eyes. "Don't you want to go out for a drink?"

"Sure, the Regal?"

"Can't really; not that safe."

"Suppose not, there can't be anywhere safe in Derry, is there?"

"There's a few, but Ballykelly's OK – full of squaddies. They'll think you're one with your haircut and your English accent."

"Thanks a lot," Matthew laughed, "I'd prefer not to think people could mistake me for an English soldier, thank you very much!"

Alex pulled a reproachful face at him then grinned.

"Hang on, I'll just go and get changed," Matthew said, flinging himself out of the door. He had worshipped Alex from afar but he'd never been particularly friendly with him and Alex had never sought out his company before. Moments later Matthew floated downstairs, his heart thumping.

Alex clapped him on the back. "You're even more like a soldier now. You'll go down a bomb in Ballykelly. Might have trouble getting you out again though!"

"Do they have soldiers as weedy as me?" Matthew asked pathetically.

Alex shook his head slowly. "You don't change, do you? Come on, shift your arse. I'm dying for a pint."

They shot down the narrow lanes to the main Limavady road in Alex's sleek, red Triumph TR7. There he opened her up; Matthew had never been so fast before in his life.

"What speed are we doing?" he enquired nervously.

"Ninety. Wanna go faster?"

"No thank you. Em... aren't you breaking the speed limit rather?"

"Yep."

"What if you get caught? Won't you get into terrible trouble? Aren't you supposed to set an example or something?"

"Aye," he replied and his foot went to the floor sending the needle past the one hundred mark; Matthew gripped the seat.

It was early and the lounge bar was quiet; a few off-duty soldiers leaned against the bar chatting up the waitresses and at the far side of the dance floor some roadies were setting up the PA for a band. Alex brought a couple of pints over to the low table.

"Well, Matt, how's life abusing you? What's Stran like?"

"OK, well... a bit boring really. I haven't made any friends and none of the gang are around much."

"Who's there now? Just Willy-John and Sandra? Don't you see them?"

"There's Aaron, don't forget."

"Watch him, Matt. I'd steer clear of him if I was you."

"I don't know what you're talking about. What do you mean, watch him?"

"Forget it. He's changed, he's no craic any more."

"I haven't seen him for nearly a year. Willy-John's New Year party was the last time and I wasn't speaking to him there really. I keep going round to his flat but I'm always missing him."

"You've been lucky."

Matthew stared in disbelief at the policeman. "What's wrong with you Alex? He's your mate. I don't know what's going on; Willy-John's the same."

"He's got more sense than I credited him with then."

"Alex! Willy-John too?"

"No. He's OK. More money than sense but basically sound."

He looked at Alex in a new light. "You surprise me. I always thought of you three as being thick as thieves and now I hear you all stabbing each other in the back."

"Why, what's Willy-John been saying about me?" Alex demanded sharply.

"Nothing, honestly, but you've both been having a go at poor old Aaron, what's he done to upset you so much?"

"You know what it's like; you get in with a different crowd and you change. Except Willy-John that is, he's exactly the same as he was in fifth form. Well, Aaron's changed and I don't think you would like the way he's gone. We've all changed. You have, you know; so have I."

"For the better, I'm sure," Matthew blurted, but it didn't quite come out as he intended it to.

"I see," Alex pretended to huff, "you didn't like me before then?"

Matthew was flustered, "Course I did. But you seem more relaxed now somehow; easier to be with."

"I'm growing older, more mature, so are you."

"No," Matthew insisted, "it's not like that. You really seem different; calmer perhaps. Nah, that's not right either."

Alex was embarrassed and he downed the half pint in his glass in one gulp. "Want another?"

"It's my shout," Matthew said, "hold on while I finish this. How have I changed?"

"Shorter hair."

"No. Seriously!"

"Very short hair."

"Aw, come on," Matthew wheedled.

Alex paused to think then said, "You seem more sure of yourself – more independent."

Matthew was intrigued. "What do you mean?"

Alex wrinkled his brow. "Hard to explain. At school you were a bit of a sheep."

"What?"

"A very nice sheep Matty, but you did follow everyone else – you weren't exactly the first to suggest anything, were you?"

"Not really, no. Everyone else seemed to have the best ideas."

"Well, now you do what *you* want to do."

"I'd like to think so, but if there was any of the crowd left I'd probably follow them still."

"Shut up!" Alex growled. "You're at it again!"

Embarrassed, Matthew stood up to go to the bar. "Bass or Smithwicks? – At what, anyway?"

"You'll only get Bass here. Putting yourself down."

"I'm not, it's just that at school all the others seemed to know what it was all about. You and Willy-John particularly. You knew where to go, and what to wear. You knew exactly how to chat up the birds and the right way to dance. You even knew which music was the best. I knew nothing. Anything I was into was boring!"

Alex was sprawling in the seat, listening with a knowing smile which had expanded into a broad grin by the time Matthew finished. The disco lights picked out the laughter lines. "I'm right though, aren't I? You always were different and now you've discovered that it's good to be yourself."

"Maybe," Matthew conceded. "But what about you? How is life in the RUC?"

"Great – love it."

"Aren't you scared though? I'd always be worrying about someone taking a pot-shot at me."

"You've got to mind that, right enough, but you sort'a grow to accept that and it doesn't worry you so much after a while." He wasn't convincing Matthew. "There's more to being in the police that fighting terrorism you know. There's traffic branch," he smirked. "Then there's CID and the drugs squad. I've done a bit of community relations work around Enniskillen and if I get posted to South Down I could get into the mountain rescue team. You'd like to do that, wouldn't you?"

"I couldn't see me in the police somehow. Where do you actually live?"

"In barracks, it's not too bad really. You've got your own room or sometimes you share with another guy. There's everything you want in the compound – there's a good bar, really cheap and no fucking around with closing times. I play rugby, there's cricket in summer and I'm top of the pool league."

"Nothing like the first XV league, I hope!" Matthew joked.

"Right enough," he grinned, "though there's plenty of wankers about. No Matt, you'd love it in the barracks, loads of fit, young men all locked up together with nothing to do but jar and craic."

Matthew reddened. "What do you mean by that?" he asked indignantly.

"You know! Loads of good-lookin', single fellers."

Matthew was getting flustered; was Alex getting at what he thought he was or was he being hypersensitive? "Alex. What are you trying to say?"

"Come on Matt – everyone knows."

"Knows what?"

"You know, about you being," he paused looking a bit uncomfortable, "you know!"

Matthew fixed him in his big brown eyes. "Alex. Say what you mean."

"You're... er... gay, aren't you?" he blurted out.

A hole opened up in the floor and Matthew's stomach fell through it. The colour drained from his face.

Alex ploughed on. "Look, I don't mind... as long as you leave *my* arse alone."

Matthew had to compose himself. He had to put on a brave face. "Where the fuck did you get that idea from?"

"It's true, isn't it?"

"No... well... sort off."

That was going too far, Matthew thought; it was an admission! How did Alex know anyway? Had Danny told him? How could he? Danny hadn't been home since he told him.

"Look, I'm not actually gay you know. I just got a bit hung up about another guy once, that's all. I might be a bit bisexual."

"Stop giving me crap, Matt. I've known you long enough. It was obvious at school. We all knew and if we were worried about it, why do you think we hung round with you? Answer me that!"

Matthew hung his head in confusion.

Alex shook him gently. "Look, this isn't a great place to talk; let's go and sit in the car."

Alex threw his car into gear and they shot out of the car park spraying gravel in their wake. They sped up the road until they got to Ballykelly forest where Alex slid the car into a clearing. Normally cars there would conceal courting couples. Matthew chuckled at the idea. "What's up?" Alex asked as he turned the ignition off.

"Nothing... except this is the last situation I expected to be in tonight..." Matthew went to light a cigarette but Alex asked him not to. "I hate the smell of smoke," he confided.

They sat for a couple of minutes in an embarrassed silence before Alex spoke. "Look, if you don't want to talk, that's OK. I've no right to nose into your business." He paused and, turning to face the slight figure in the passenger seat, said, "You say you're not queer, er, gay or not really gay, but what about Danny?"

"He's not gay! He's doing a really steady line with a woman in London."

Alex sounded disappointed. "Sorry. I thought you two were... you know?"

Matthew sat there as if poleaxed; he was having difficulty articulating. "But... at school... you all hated poofs! You never missed a chance to slag a fruit and yet you thought I was one."

"You were *different* – one of us. You weren't a pansy like that creep Alistair. Anyway you never actually *did* anything, did you?"

Matthew should have been mortally offended by Alex's denial of his sexuality but he was turning his charm on full blast and Matthew basked in its glow. His defences dissolved and suddenly he was telling Alex things about himself that even he didn't know. He started haltingly: "At school I didn't really fancy girls but I assumed that no one else did and that it would come in time. Do you remember going to the library to look at the *National Geographic* magazine?" Alex shook his head and Matthew scoffed at himself. "Well we did – in second form. We used to look for articles with pictures of naked natives. The others were looking for tits, of course, but it was the dicks that caught my attention! Even then I must have fancied other fellers but I didn't know I fancied them – can you understand that?"

"Go on," Alex said gently.

"Well," Matthew hesitated, "like... I hope you don't mind me saying this – it's about you."

"You used to fancy me, didn't you?" Alex said softly.

"How did you know?"

"Not sure; just knew. Maybe it was the way you used to look at me; no one else looked at me like that – leastways, not boys."

Matthew flushed and tried to peer at his feet. "Sorry."

"Don't apologise for fuck's sake. I'm not queer but it used to flatter me that I had fellers falling for me as well as women!"

Matthew smiled shyly. "You can't blame me though... sorry, I shouldn't have said that." He looked at Alex's smirking face. "I didn't know what it was then. I used to fantasise about you – that I was you. I didn't understand how I was feeling; I didn't know I fancied you." Matthew couldn't believe what he was saying. Deep down there was a faint hope that Alex would say, 'Matthew, come to me'.

Alex shifted uneasily. "You poor bastard. You must have been scared shitless. What's the scene now? Do you have a... em.. friend?"

Matthew shook his head. "You're the first person I've ever talked to about the way I feel. I was still a virgin, if that's what you would call it, until this summer. I had a..."

Alex interrupted, "Stop, please. I don't want to hear about that stuff, I'm sorry. It's illegal anyway."

Matthew was seized by panic; he'd gone too far; he'd assumed that Alex was more tolerant than he was.

Alex reached forward and twisted the key in the ignition, mumbling, "I'd better get you home."

The car roared into life.

At the farm Alex declined an invitation for coffee. "Nah, I've got to get up early tomorrow."

Matthew was climbing out of the car when a gentle, iron grip drew him back in again.

Alex looked sadly into Matthew's eyes. "I'm sorry if I've ever done anything to lead you on or anything. I didn't ever mean to screw you up, you know that. Of all the crowd you're the one I always liked the best. Did you know that?"

Matthew shook his head.

"Well I did. The others had money and never missed an opportunity to show it."

"I don't think that's true."

"Well that's how I felt anyway." He paused, looking fondly at Matthew. "I don't want to see you hurt, Matt. Be careful. You do know it's illegal don't you?"

"What is?"

"Homosexuality."

"It's OK if you're over twenty-one."

"Not here it isn't, and if I had to arrest you I would, you know. Even though you're a friend you can't be above the law."

Matthew thought that sounded a bit pompous, especially considering the number of traffic offences he had committed that night.

"Be careful at the college too," Alex continued, "you'll never get a job if it gets out. You'll have to keep it quiet, but don't worry, I won't tell anyone. Your secret's safe with me."

"Thanks."

"OK, look after yourself. I'm sorry tonight got so heavy. Next time I'm home at the weekend we'll go out and get blutered, OK?"

"Dead on, g'night."

The door slammed and the little red car screeched out of the yard.

He sneaked in and shot up the stairs without calling in at the kitchen. In one part of his mind was the horrible feeling he had done something irrevocable but also there was a joy; a feeling of freedom he had never known before. Alex knew and he didn't mind; perhaps there was still hope.

15: 'Save Ulster From Sodomy'

It was a bright spring afternoon and the pocket-handkerchief gardens along the Stranmillis Road were bursting with colour. Yet as Matthew passed the imposing mock-Elizabethan frontage of Queens University, a foreboding crept upon him. Alex was sure to have told Willy-John everything he'd revealed on Saturday and he was uncertain how Willy-John would take it.

The brass knocker had been painted with the same peeling, yellow paint as the ruinous Georgian door. Noisy feet clattered down the stairs and someone wrestled the door open. It was Symie, one of Willy-John's rugger friends.

"He's upstairs," he called distractedly, wandering into the kitchen.

"Taa," Matthew muttered, trying to force the door back into its warped frame. He hopped over the hole in the hall floor and picked his way up the stairs taking his usual sly glance at the full-length male nude the rugger lads found so amusing.

Willy-John was in his room, stereo blaring. Without turning, he said, "Just a mo, let me get this finished," and waved Matthew towards the bed.

He watched his friend's back. His sandy hair had never been very long but now it was neatly cut, tapered to a point. His broad shoulders gave the pale, green and white striped rugby shirt a pleasing shape – an effect accentuated by slight movements under the tight cotton as he wrote.

Suddenly Willy-John slammed the book closed and swivelled round on his chair beaming at Matthew. His angular face was plain, but open and honest; typically Ulster Protestant, Matthew thought.

"Sorry 'bout that. I was in mid-flow; would've lost it if I'd stopped. What can I do you for?"

Matthew suddenly realised that he didn't know. "Nowt really," he replied, "I was just passing and I thought I would pop in to hear the bars."

"Ain't got none! 'Bout you?"

"Same here. Except I was out with Alex on Saturday."

Willy-John sounded surprised: "How is he? Still in Enniskillen?"

"He's dead on. Playing hard, driving hard and drinking hard

– surprise, surprise!"

They both laughed, then Willy-John said, "I haven't seen him for ages, I suppose he can't move around too freely now. I couldn't stand that, hey!"

Matthew demurred. "He seems to be having a great time and he's on bloody good money. You should see the car he's driving; it's dead flash."

"What's he got?"

"Dunno; it's red."

"Prat."

"Nah. It's an XR7, I think."

Willy-John wrinkled his nose: "Not bad for starters. Still pullin' the women, is he?"

"We didn't talk about women," Matthew said thoughtfully, "but I suppose so."

"What the heck did you talk about? I'm damn sure it wasn't sport."

"Nowt really," Matthew said lamely, "just about life here and what it's like in the RUC."

Willy-John stood up and moved for the door. "Look Matt, I'd love to chat but I've really got to get this finished. How about going for a pint later?"

"Sure."

"OK then; ten at the Bot?"

"Ten then," Matthew said cheerily, "see you."

Aaron's flat was in an unassuming, red brick, Victorian town house in Ulsterville Avenue. Matthew rang the bell and waited, staring at the dank patch of balding lawn edged with a grimy privet hedge. Nothing had much chance of growing there; the trees may have raised the street to avenue status, but they did nothing for photo-synthesis in the dismal little gardens.

Aaron greeted him with a restrained smile and invited him in. Matthew was only mildly surprised to find him in immaculate grey slacks, white shirt and a sober tie but his pristine living room still came as a shock. Matthew couldn't imagine that a student could live in a flat without unwashed coffee mugs, ashtrays full of fag butts and dismembered newspapers scattered over the floor.

"Can I take your coat?" Aaron asked.

He gave him his grubby parka.

"Would you like a cup of tea, Matthew?"

He sat on the neat settee as Aaron busied himself in the kitchen; Matthew imagined that it would be as perfect as in any detergent commercial. Net curtains hid the neat sitting room from prying eyes. Each wall boasted a framed print of an Ulster view. The only sign that someone actually lived in the flat was a bureau in the far corner with its lid down supporting a single writing pad, an open textbook and a fountain pen placed with geometrical precision.

Aaron returned with a tray bearing two cups and saucers, a milk jug, a teapot, a sugar bowl and a plate of cakes and biscuits.

"Nice flat, Aaron," Matthew commented, "how on earth did you land such a luxurious pad?"

"It belongs to a friend of my father."

"Whole house?" He was thinking of Helga, if she existed.

"No, just this flat and the one upstairs. What brings you here; are you working in Belfast?"

"Didn't you hear? I'm at Stran, going to swell the ranks of the teaching profession."

"I presume you're going to teach biology."

"Aye. What else?"

"You'll be teaching evolution then?"

Matthew nodded.

"Doesn't it worry you... telling all those lies?"

"What lies?"

"You don't actually believe all that about monkeys becoming men, do you?"

"You mean human evolution? Don't you believe in it?"

"I CERTAINLY DO NOT!" His venom took Matthew aback. "It's a blasphemy," he ranted. "The Bible tells us that He made the world in six days. It's a sin to claim otherwise."

"I didn't know you felt like that about it," Matthew said hesitantly, "I don't recall you thinking like that at school."

"That Godless place!" Aaron spat, "I didn't know my own mind there. I was influenced by the others; they made me think I wanted to behave like that! We were being influenced by the agents of Satan. I'm lucky. I was strong enough to shake him off but all over Ulster the minds of our youth are being corrupted in schools like that."

"I suppose you have a point," Matthew conceded, "look at what we did to Alistair and John." He hesitated, "I seem to remember that you were pretty hard on them."

"If that school had any morality at all, those two would have been dealt with," Aaron snapped.

He was taken aback. "What do you mean, dealt with?"

"They would have been told in no uncertain terms that their sodomite tendencies would not be tolerated. Our schools have gone soft on morals. Parents are entitled to expect their children to be educated in a Christian environment by teachers who set a good example."

"I think you're going a bit far, Aaron. We all got through school without our moral fibre being too badly eroded, didn't we?"

"Do you think so Matthew, do you really think so?"

"Aye, of course, look at us all, we're OK."

Aaron's features hardened as he said darkly, "I look at Willy-John and I am disgusted by his depravity. He drinks to excess, he fornicates, he swears and I can tell you Matthew, that he has not darkened the doors of a church since he came to Belfast."

Matthew suppressed a smirk. "And you blame that on the school?"

"I most certainly do."

"Well it doesn't seem to have harmed you. I don't think school has that much effect on us."

"You are wrong Matthew. School is the foremost formative influence in a young life. Why do you think the Papists insist on their children being taught in Roman Catholic schools? They know that by controlling what the children hear at school they control their minds... We believe..."

Matthew interrupted. "Who is we?"

"The Free Presbyterian Church. We know how important the school is in the moral development of young people. A school with sloppy morals irreparably damages young minds. That's why we are setting up our own schools where all the teachers will be Christians who know the importance of God in their lives. Our children will not be taught the lies of evolution. Our children will get a good, solid, moral education based on the Bible and not so-called liberal sex education. Have you seen the sort of things schools are giving our youngsters to study? They call it English literature; it's filth and pornography! I had to study *A Passage to India* for A-level." Disgust crept into his tone, "Banks actually admitted that E. M. Forster was a homosexual!" It was as if that word burnt his mouth as he spoke it. "He implied that we couldn't understand the book unless we had read his perverted writings on sodomy!" Aaron glared at Matthew as if he held him personally responsible for this insult. "Dalzell obtained a copy of *Maurice*, a book about his sodomistic activities, and quoted it in an essay." Aaron's face soured. "Banks complimented him for his initiative and asked us why we couldn't have sought out our own sources." His voice hit an apocalyptic pitch. "There will be none of that sort of deviance in our schools. English books will be carefully chosen so that pupils read no perversion or foul language."

"Do you think they will catch on?" Matthew asked in a small

voice; the thought appalled him.

"The first ones are well advanced and others are planned. The state system will have to take itself in hand. They will soon revise their liberal ideas when the parents start to vote with their feet and they lose pupils, then teachers. The godless ones will be the first to go."

By this point Matthew was beginning to wish he had taken Alex's advice. He was desperate to get him off the topic but Aaron's fanaticism sapped all Matthew's inventiveness. Eventually he managed to ask, "How's the course going?"

Aaron was quietly confident. "Very well, I'm down for a first or upper second."

"Hmm. I got a two-two you know."

"So I heard – I was disappointed, I thought you were capable of at least a two-one."

"I think I did very well all things considered. It was pretty hectic!"

"Not womanising and drinking your grant away, I hope."

Matthew shook his head and tried to steer the conversation through to safer waters but he soon dried up.

He made his excuses and left, resolving to steer clear of Aaron in future and buy a copy of *Maurice*.

On Wednesday, he came home to find a note in his letter-box. It read:

Matt,
In Belfast on a course this week. Let's meet for a drink.
Ring 69125 between 6pm and 10pm.
Alex.

Alex arranged to pick Matthew up the next evening and they headed to Bangor for a pint in a pub Alex's friends had said was OK. Alex joined him with two brimming glasses. "Can't drink much – got to present a respectable face tomorrow!"

"And you're driving," Matthew added, half seriously.

Alex grimaced. "Aye, and that too."

Neither of them mentioned the previous weekend's conversation but Matthew filled Alex in about his strange visit to Aaron. Alex kept Matthew entertained with stories of police work in County Fermanagh and the good life of a young recruit; the boozing, the womanising, the camaraderie, the money. To Matthew, it sounded just like student life; young, active minds in an enclosed environment with an infinite capacity for invention, but he got the sneaking feeling that, in telling him how wonderful it all was, Alex was really trying to convince himself.

In the RUC Alex had been thrown into sustained, intimate contact with other men for the first time in his life. Every moment they were on duty they were aware one of them could be the next terrorist victim. Alex had dismissed this as one of the facts of life but the strain had to tell. One safety valve was to vent their frustrations on 'the enemy'. Nationalist youths habitually wound up the RUC patrols and some policemen reacted predictably by using their authority to make life unpleasant for them. But that was only one outcome; the tension was also turned inwards. There was a self-destructive tendency which variously manifested itself amongst the young constables. They played boisterous pranks on each other – but with a vicious streak. Alex's jokey narrative was tainted with relief that he hadn't been a victim yet.

This unsuspected vein of vulnerability made Matthew feel even more warmly towards Alex and he began to wonder if his sudden reappearance had a reason. After his revelations Matthew had convinced himself that Alex would avoid him. Then, when he got the note, he worried that Alex was feeling sorry for him or felt he had a duty to him. Now his trust dispelled Matthew's paranoia and he suspected that Alex feared his colleagues finding a chink in his macho armour and saw Matthew as a safe person to be with.

Alex was in the throes of a yarn about a riot in Ballycol, a border town in north Fermanagh, when Matthew interrupted his flow. "I've applied for a job there, you know."

"You're mad," Alex retorted, "it's a Fenian hole. What's the job?"

"Teaching."

"Smart-arse. Teaching where and what?"

"Biology; in the High School."

"That's the Protestant school anyway! Knowing you, you'd apply to a Fenian school as a statement of your non-sectarian principles."

Matthew laughed. "Even I'm not that naïve."

"What? Is our Matt actually showing... turagh, turaghgh," he gave him a mock fanfare, "sectarian bias?"

Matthew smiled witheringly at him. "No, it's just that one of *us* wouldn't have a cat-in-hell's chance of getting a job in one. There are some Catholic students at Stran and even *they* have bother because they didn't go to a Catholic teacher training college! I tell you Alex, the Catholic church has it sewn up; Aaron's right on that count anyway."

"Bloody Fenians," Alex's eyes narrowed, "they whinge when

they don't get equal job opportunities but they wouldn't give us a chance."

"I wouldn't *want* to work in a Catholic school," Matthew said incredulously.

Alex nodded. "When's the interview anyway?"

"Dunno, I might not even get one you know."

"Look. Let me know if you do. St. Angelo's only about twenty miles from Ballycol. We can meet up."

Matthew got an interview and Alex insisted on picking him up in Belfast. He was grateful because the bus journey to Ballycol was terrible; it could take hours.

He was offered the job on the spot; the headmaster told him there had only been two applicants for the job and the other one didn't have a degree. Alex was waiting for him in the school's car park.

"Well, how did it go?" he demanded as Matthew slid into his smoothmobile.

Matthew gave the clenched fist salute.

"Congratulations," he smiled.

"Could hardly fail," Matthew sneered, "no other qualified candidates."

Alex looked puzzled. "None?"

"None worth speaking of."

Alex wrinkled his nose. "What's wrong with the place – other than being in Ballycol?"

Matthew shook his head: "Dunno. Seems really nice; kids're well behaved and the buildings are in good nick – which speaks volumes. Oh, and you'll never guess what?"

"Go on."

"Guess who's working here already."

"I haven't a fucking clue, how would I?"

"Someone you didn't like at school."

"I didn't like most of them at our school! Who is it?"

"Alistair McDowell, you know, Julian of Julian and Sandy."

"Oh fuck!" the policeman ejaculated, "God in person!"

"Aye! But there are bound to a few piss artists on the staff, I'll be OK."

Alex left him to Ballygawley where he caught the Derry Express bus.

Ballycol had a bad reputation and Matthew guessed that his parents weren't too happy about him living there, but his father was very encouraging and promised to take him flat hunting in August.

At Strathbeg there was a letter from Henk tactfully wondering if his last letter had got lost in the post. He reiterated his invitation for that summer. Matthew had to lay his cards on the table with Henk if he was to accept. He sat down and wrote a long, rambling letter detailing all his adventures since they parted. But once on paper it didn't seem right, so the last three pages ended up on the fire to be substituted by a limp acceptance of his invitation which made no mention of his sexuality.

He was slobbing around the flat one afternoon in May when Aaron, smiling like an insurance salesman, appeared on his doorstep. He had to invite him in, dreading what he would think of his slovenly lifestyle.

"Would you like a cup of coffee?" Matthew asked.

"No, thank you Matthew, I haven't long," he replied looking disdainfully at the filthy room and the coffee cup with cigarette butts in it.

There was an awkward silence. He couldn't exactly say, "What do you want?" but he couldn't think of anything constructive either.

Aaron broke the silence. "Well," he said, "how has your course gone?"

"Fine, I've got a job – Ballycol High – biology."

"Very good," was his guarded response, "it's a bad area but I'm sure you will be fine. I was going to ask you for help around Londonderry but you might be more use in Ballycol."

"Help. In what way?" Matthew asked nervously.

"You remember our conversation last time we met?"

"Yes," he said slowly.

"The moral decline that we were bemoaning has reached a new low and we must do all in our power to resist it. You may not know this Matthew, but there are evil forces at work to corrupt the youth of this country."

"The IRA?" Matthew nodded.

"They destroy the body but it's the soul, the very fibre of our youth that is in danger."

Matthew didn't need to ask Aaron why. After a suitable dramatic pause he continued: "Sodomites. They want our children!"

"What for?" Matthew quipped. It was meant as a joke but Aaron glared at him.

"They want their perverted ways legalised so that they can get their disgusting hands on our children with impunity. The sodomite-dominated Westminister government is trying to legalise sodomy here. We have to stop them."

Matthew smirked inwardly. Aaron had adopted Ian Paisley's habit of mis-pronouncing Westminster as 'West-minister'. "How do you intend to do that?" he asked, "and what has it to do with me?"

"Dr Paisley has started the Save Ulster From Sodomy campaign. It is up to us, the God-fearing, ordinary Ulstermen, to stand up and be counted. We cannot stand by and allow our country to be polluted by these perverts." He pulled a sheaf of papers out of his briefcase and flourished them at Matthew.

"What's that?"

"The petition," he said in mild surprise. "We are taking this to every corner of Ulster and when we have the names of every Christian man and woman in Ulster we will take this to Westminister and we will demand that they drop this evil legislation."

"And you want me to sign it?"

"I want you to sign it, Matthew. I want you to sign it and take it into Stranmillis and get your fellow students to sign it – the very people who will soon be there helping to protect our youth from the corruption that is upon us. And when you have done that you can help us to take it out into the streets and get the ordinary Ulster men and women who are ignorant of what is about to be visited on their children, to add their names to the growing opposition to this... this abomination."

Aaron sat there, glowing with a frightening fervour. Matthew tried to imagine what was going on in his mind. Why was he so full of venom for them... for Matthew's own kind? He couldn't possibly sign his piece of paper, never mind take it into college, but how could he tell him?

"I'm sorry Aaron, I don't know where you got the idea that I might help; you know me and you know what I believe in."

"As far as I remember you believe in decency and morality," Aaron snapped.

"I do, but it seems that my idea of decency is different from yours. You want to force your version of decency onto everyone. I happen to believe that each one of us has the right to make our own choice and that includes your so-called sodomites." Matthew drew a deep breath: "No Aaron, I'm sorry but I won't sign your petition – I certainly will not be taking it into college and, to be honest, I hope it fails, and fails miserably."

Aaron stood up, his face like death. "I'm very disappointed in you Matthew; I had expected better of you. I was sure that you had been awakened to the corruption of our society, but it is obvious that you are as bad as all the rest; worse in fact because you are going into teaching carrying your perverted version of morality with you. It is people like you who are responsible for the moral decline."

He stood up, dominating Matthew's little slum like some avenging angel. "It's you and your ilk that we are up against. I'm giving you fair warning Matthew, you and your kind will be the first to suffer when our schools get established."

With that he stalked to the door and left; Matthew hoped for ever.

Ian Paisley and his Democratic Unionist Party did as Aaron had predicted. His minions swamped every Ulster town with their squalid petition collecting signatures of hatred and ignorance. Matthew came across two of them in Derry – dreary, middle-aged farmers. How they had the nerve to stand in the heart of Catholic Derry with their sordid bit of paper he couldn't understand, but there they were. What was more, a good number of people were signing it. As he approached, a group of youths was reading the preamble in approbation. Matthew took his courage in his hands and walked over to them.

The dreary man said, " Would you like to help Save Ulster From Sodomy?"

"No I would not," Matthew replied churlishly, turning to the young men. "You know that this is Ian Paisley's campaign? They're the DUP!"

This caused a stir. "Fuck aff," the lads sneered, "fucking Orange bastards." And to Matthew's delight they moved off shouting republican slogans as they went.

The subject was widely debated on radio, TV and in the press. It was the first time the subject of homosexuality had been discussed openly in Ulster and it began to feel as if Ulster's people were implacably opposed to homosexuals. Catholics and Protestants seemed united in their condemnation.

16: Dutch Leave

Danny was working in London so Matthew arranged to visit him on his way to Harwich. On arriving he was dragged in, hugged and given a can of beer.

"Eaten?" Danny asked.

"No, well, I made an attempt at a British Rail sandwich! Fortunately I could only afford one."

"We'll go and get a chinkie then."

"Aye, dead on."

"Come on," Danny said affably, grabbing his anorak.

Matthew held back. "Where's Lisa?"

"She'll be in later. Come on, there's a place just around the corner."

As they waited, Danny offered him a fag. Matthew was surprised; unless you counted dope, Danny hadn't smoked at University.

"Smoking straights, Daniel?"

"Aye. Don't know why – Lisa hates it; probably that's why."

"I never thought I'd see Mr Fit smoking. Not them anyway."

"Smoked at school, you know. Gave 'em up in sixth form; I think it's the dope that's got me back on 'em again."

"Much around here?"

"Aye and good stuff too. I thought Lancaster was coming down with the stuff but it's ubiquitous here."

"What about the law?"

"Pigs don't worry about a bit of blow. It's the hard stuff they're death on."

After a quick pint at the local they headed back to the flat, arms laden with warm, fragrant, aluminium containers. Lisa welcomed Matthew then rounded on Danny. "You knew I was making a lasagne. I told you I was going to get the stuff on the way home," she said with a mixture of anger and frustration.

"Aye, but I thought a chinkie would be quicker, more time for jarring. We can have it tomorrow."

Her cheeks were flushed; there was an hysterical edge to her voice: "Fine."

They ate the Chinese meal in an uncomfortable mixture of polite conversation and silence. As soon as they'd finished Danny was ready for the pub. Lisa balked: "The lasagne's not cooked yet."

At Danny's blank look she glowered and stalked out of the room.

"Come on then," he said throwing Matthew his coat.

He faltered. "What about Lisa?"

"She won't want to come. She knows we want to have a good old yarn together."

Matthew worried about leaving Lisa but after a few pints he forgot all about her. The two friends drifted from pub to pub, ending up in an Irish club, its walls plastered with Republican posters. Under normal circumstances this would have freaked Matthew out but by the time they arrived there he was in no state to worry about digging with the wrong foot. Matthew's night ended with a dimly recollected taxi ride to Danny's flat and the vague memory of struggling into his sleeping bag on the settee.

When Matthew awoke, Danny was sprawled out under a blanket on the floor. His big hand was clutching a mug, half-full of cold coffee. Matthew padded to the kitchen, put the kettle on and started making toast. At the sound of the boiling kettle, Danny stirred and staggered into the kitchen looking awful. He clapped Matthew on the back, smiled benignly, wished him a cheery good morning, then grimaced and clutched his forehead.

Lisa had already gone to work but it didn't occur to Matthew to ask Danny why he hadn't done likewise. Not wanting to enquire too closely about the events of the previous night, and in particular as to the state of their relationship, he made small talk about Holland. It was soon time to go and they parted with promises of longer together on his way back.

Matthew rang Henk on disembarkation and arranged to meet him at Delft station. The sight of Henk filled him with a warm feeling; he had forgotten just how beautiful he was. He stood there cool yet warm. Resisting the urge to give him a big hug, Matthew offered him a restrained hand.

After affectionate, but suitably masculine greetings Henk whisked Matthew's rucksack onto his broad back and led the way out. They went under the railway and were soon in a leafy, cobbled street with neat houses in tiny, dark red bricks. Henk's flat was in a narrow side street where a narrow door led them onto a narrow, steep flight of stairs from which came a lingering smell of old cabbages.

His room spanned the depth of the building. At the far end was a single bed, a washing area and a tiny shower cubicle; the rest was the living area. On one wall was an enormous bookcase and the narrow windows were almost obscured by a screen of plants supported by tiers of hanging shelves.

"Where's the kitchen?" Matthew asked.

"I cook here," Henk replied, lifting the lid off a cupboard to reveal a neat, little, two-burner cooker. There was neither oven nor grill. "Are you hungry?"

He was, so Henk produced some bread and hard cheese and put a pan of water on to boil. He indicated the couch. "I am afraid you will have to sleep here."

"Suits me fine," he replied cheerfully.

"What do you want to do when you are here?" the Dutchman asked.

"I'm not sure really. I'd like to visit Amsterdam, if it's not too far away, and I would like to see a little of the countryside too if that's possible."

"Can you ride a bicycle?"

Matthew laughed. "Yes, although I haven't ridden one for ages. You need a car to get anywhere in Northern Ireland you know."

"Good, I can borrow a bicycle from a friend and then we can go cycling. This is good," he nodded seriously.

"Will we cycle to Amsterdam?" Matthew asked; it looked to be miles away on the map.

Henk bent over and felt Matthew's calves. "You may cycle there, my friend. But you must be very strong. For myself, I will take the train."

The next day found them bowling along a brick road atop a dyke. Matthew was surprised to see tiny farms so near the great conurbations of Rotterdam and Den Haag. Moored along the river were wonderful old barges with paddle-like stabilisers; the older ones had masts and a few were under sail on the summer flow. At lunchtime they found a little cafe where they munched ham sandwiches and sipped Heineken as they watched boats negotiating a lock. Matthew took a deep breath, sighed with satisfaction and relaxed back into his seat.

Henk spoke. "Tell me more about your new job."

"Not a lot to tell really," he said. "It's a controlled school in a small border town."

"What is a controlled school?" Henk asked as if he was speaking to his English teacher.

"Well," he started, "it's all rather complicated. You have to know a bit about the history and politics of Northern Ireland to understand what it's all about. Can you stand a Woodhead history lesson?" Henk grinned at him. Thus Matthew explained how the Northern Irish segregated school system had evolved and that, despite it being a state school, Ballycol High was essentially Protestant. He moved on to explain about Ballycol. "It's not a big town, about twenty thousand inhabitants, I think – mostly Catholic. It's right on the border with the Republic of Ireland, in County Fermanagh. Do you know where that is?" he checked.

"No, where is it?"

Matthew wrinkled his nose in thought. "I'll show you on a map," he smiled.

"What is the town like?"

"I've only been there once," he explained. "It's quite pretty really. There's a lake on the border, called Lough Coll. The town has grown on its Northern Ireland shore. It's a typical Ulster plantation town." He looked at Henk's puzzled face. "You don't know what a plantation town is, do you?"

Henk shook his head. "I'm sorry."

"This is turning into an intensive history lesson, isn't it?"

"I enjoy it," he responded, so Matthew continued. Their friendship was probably based on Henk's seemingly limitless capacity for listening to Matthew's long rambling explanations of Northern Ireland issues.

After his potted history of Ballycol Henk said, "It sounds an interesting place. I would like to visit."

"I hope you do," Matthew replied. "You know you are welcome anytime, don't you?"

"You must be looking forward to going there."

"Well yes," he hesitated, "and no."

Henk cocked his head on one side.

Matthew slowed down and spoke falteringly. "I am looking forward to having a job, with my own money, and all that. But, to be honest, I find it all a bit frightening."

Henk leaned over the table towards him, his lovely face creased with concern. "Why is that?"

Matthew stared at his crumb-strewn plate. Was this the time to break it to Henk?

"I'm not sure how well I will manage as a teacher."

Henk clapped him on the shoulder, shook him and laughed. "If you tell the children stories like those you tell me, you will be a wonderful teacher!" He was beaming at Matthew.

"It's not that." Matthew looked at Henk's finely chiselled features. "There is something that you don't know about me. Something that might make it difficult for me to be a teacher."

Henk's deep blue eyes were piercing his. "What's wrong, Matthew?"

Matthew couldn't look at him. He closed his eyes, took a deep breath, and said it: "I'm homosexual."

Henk sat there unperturbed, "Jah..."

"What do you mean, jah?" Matthew whined.

"So where is the problem?"

"That's it. Just what I said."

Henk looked dubious. "You are saying that being gay is a problem?"

"*Yes!*" Matthew cried in exasperation. He felt he was beginning to sound silly.

"Why? Any gay people I know have no problems; perhaps it is different in Northern Ireland."

"You *know* gay people?" Matthew asked incredulously.

"Jah. I have a very good friend, Piet, who is gay."

"I've never met another gay person, not really," Matthew complained.

Henk looked at him knowingly. "Ah, I see the problem now. You don't know any other gay people. I shall introduce you to Piet, would you like that?"

Matthew looked at him in amazement, he should have guessed that he couldn't freak Henk. He nodded. "Yes, I would like that."

They cycled further into the Dutch countryside before turning back. Henk led the way, his strong legs pumping the pedals. They flew past the narrow, weedy drainage canals around neat, suburban gardens and their equally pristine Flemish houses. Matthew was having to work hard to keep up with Henk; the saddle was eating into his buttocks and his legs were getting sore. As he cycled he pondered that his friends' reactions to him were becoming predictable. Each time he expected shock and horror but they all seemed to be saying the same thing: there's no big deal in being gay. But Matthew knew that his friends were wrong. He was lucky with them, but they didn't know how hostile some people were and he still couldn't contemplate his family finding out. And what about Henk? Was he or wasn't he? Maybe he was simply tolerant. Maybe he was gay but didn't find Matthew attractive. He hoped Henk was gay and was biding his time with him but that was getting too fanciful. Suddenly Matthew felt ashamed for abusing his friend in his head. He had to stop thinking about him in a sexual way.

Back at Henk's flat, Matthew dragged his sore legs up the steep stairs and flopped onto the couch. As Henk made coffee he talked. "Are you tired?"

"Knackered," Matthew admitted.

"If you lived in Holland this would be a normal afternoon's cycling."

"I'm obviously not cut out to be a Dutchman. My legs are killing me."

"Tomorrow we must cycle again, this will stop your leg muscles becoming stiff," Henk nodded.

"Sure you're Dutch, not German?" Matthew quipped.

"I do not understand."

Matthew put on a stereotyped German accent. "Tomorrow you vill cycle till your legs are falling off!" Then he put two fingers over his top lip and shot his arm out in the Nazi salute.

Henk looked at him with astonishment and Matthew realised he had offended him. He leapt up, grabbed him by his shoulders and shook him affectionately. "Bad joke! Sure we'll go tomorrow.

It'll do me good."

Matthew spotted Henk's serious expression. "Do you still want to meet Piet?"

"Do you mind?" Matthew asked sheepishly; he felt that his slight might have disinclined him.

"Of course not, why should I?"

"I don't know... maybe you are embarrassed to be seen with gays, or something."

Henk frowned. "Why do you think that? Piet is a friend. He's in the same theatre group as I am. Why should I be embarrassed?"

"Well. At Lancaster there was a Gay Soc and everyone avoided its members – no one wanted to be seen with them in case people thought they were gay too."

"That is rather strange, I think. What did you do?"

"I didn't know I was gay. I certainly was nothing like the gays at university, they were so weird. Even if I had thought I was gay, I wouldn't have been seen dead with them."

"So it is true, you have never met gay people?"

"No, I told you so, never."

"I am not gay, but I can imagine that it must be very lonely for you not to know any others. You must be very sad."

Matthew was sad, but Henk couldn't have known that his casual declaration of heterosexuality had caused the greatest sadness. Matthew nodded, "I'm miserable, and I'm frightened too. I can't guess what's ahead of me and it really scares me."

17: Piet Vondel

The theatre group frequented a student bar in the old city. Although not a cellar, it could have been one: dark brick walls were dotted with posters and here and there socially conscious noticeboards bore hand-written cards and leaflets. Subdued lighting and sundry miscellaneous interesting shapes, hanging from the low ceiling, completed the cavern illusion. The barman was sticking up a poster for a South American band as they entered and Henk, on his way for the usual 'twee pils', chatted to him as he finished his task. He returned with the foaming glasses and encouraging news; Piet had been in the bar the previous night and was fully expected tonight.

Henk was trying to tell Matthew about some anti-nuclear activity he was involved with but he wasn't really listening. He was watching everyone who entered, hoping that each beautiful man was Piet. But Piet didn't appear. Matthew was disappointed but didn't want to show it. As they were leaving Henk was accosted by two girls coming in. Matthew stood, politely bored, waiting for him to finish his conversation when he heard the magic word: Piet. When the girls had gone, Henk said, "Piet is in another bar. Would you like to go there?"

Matthew tried not to sound too enthusiastic. "If you want to – sure."

Henk's gorgeous smile split his face. "I think you really do want to meet him," he said conspiratorially. "I can only introduce you; I cannot make him like you – you know this?"

"Yeah, of course I understand. Perhaps we had better not go, if it's such an imposition."

Henk gave his arm a squeeze. "Come along, my friend!" He was a very tactile person; Matthew thought it was a good job he didn't live in Northern Ireland because if he did he would have been labelled queer long ago.

The next bar was long and narrow, with a counter down one side and a wooden staircase leading up to a three-quarter balcony. They pushed their way through the throng towards the far end where there was a pool table protected by a wooden cover. A group of dubious-looking young men were sitting on the table. Some were unshaven, most wore earrings and all were dressed flamboyantly. Henk approached one of them. Unlike his face, the man's taut neck was shaven all the way up to the brim of a black fedora. He wore a bright red silk shirt, a black waistcoat covered in badges, and red and black striped pantaloons tucked into cowboy boots. This was Piet; Matthew was simultaneously terrified and fascinated. Henk spoke briefly to Piet who turned to look at Matthew. His face was small and pinched and his left cheek bore a deep scar. Piet jumped off the table and thrust out his hand. "Piet Vondel," he volunteered formally.

"Matthew Woodhead," Matthew said, "but most people call me Matt." He was stuck for what to say next but blundered on anyway: "You speak English?"

Piet answered falteringly: "Jah, but only if you speak slow for me."

"I'll try my best to speak slowly but stop me if I go too fast for you, won't you?"

Piet smiled an alarmingly seductive smile and said, "Henk said to me that you wish to ask me some questions."

Matthew reddened. "Well," he faltered, "I don't want to pry..."

"Please?"

"I don't want you to think that I am intruding on your per-

for the last phrase, "and the homosexuals had a pink triangle." Piet's face was drawn and serious now; Matthew was conscious of nothing else. Piet grabbed him by the wrist, gripping him tightly as he said, "The pink triangle was a badge of shame; now we are proud to wear it. The pink triangle is telling the world of our defiance. We are saying IT MUST NOT AGAIN HAPPEN."

"It couldn't," Matthew assured him, "Society is far too civilised now. Even in Northern Ireland, where the terrorists have tried the patience of the government to its limits, we still have our civil rights."

Piet looked at him shrewdly, "That is not what we hear. The British government in Ireland is very repressive against the Irish people. The Irish are fighting to free themselves from a colonial power."

Matthew thought to himself that it was lucky he wasn't talking to Willy-John, Alex, or, God forbid, Aaron – they would have floored him on the spot! Even Matthew found Piet's interpretation a bit galling but, in the circumstances, he was reluctant to contradict him. He took a mental deep breath and, trying to sound reasonable, said, "I think you are getting a rather distorted view there."

But Piet was on a roll. "The English are trying to make Ireland part of England by destroying the Irish culture. They do not let them talk in their own language, they will not give the Irish jobs and the Irish are not allowed to work in the government."

Matthew looked at him in bemusement, "Where on earth did you get all that from?"

"In the newspapers and on the television; also I have read some books on these matters. On the television was an actuality film about a town in Ireland that has been completely destroyed by the British army."

Matthew's heart sank. The worst things always seemed to happen when he was away. "When did this happen?" he asked hurriedly.

"Whah. It must have been three or four years."

Matthew was relieved but puzzled. "What town was this? How was it destroyed?"

"It was by bombs," Piet said with certainty. "The name, I am not sure, something like Starvan."

"*Strabane?*" he said incredulously.

"Jah, that is the town, Strabane." Piet beamed at him, nodding in satisfaction.

Matthew chuckled and shook his head in a hopeless gesture. Piet couldn't see what was so funny.

"You certainly have got the wrong end of the stick there," Matthew smiled. "I live only twenty kilometres from Strabane and I assure you the town is still there and, although it is a bit of a mess, it is still thriving. Yes, there have been many bombs there, it is supposed to be the most bombed town but you have it all wrong. It's not the British army that did it; it's the Irish Republican Army, the IRA!" he ended triumphantly.

Piet didn't look the least bit abashed. "I seem to have made a mistake on this," he conceded, "but I am sure that I am correct about the British in Ireland."

Fortunately, at this juncture, one of his odd-looking friends came over and said something. Piet turned his attention back to Matthew. "I'm sorry. I must go now. I don't think you had much opportunity to ask your questions. I am sorry for this."

Matthew's face betrayed his emotions so Piet paused for thought then said, "We should meet again. Somewhere we can talk."

He looked at him gratefully: "Please."

Piet had a gabbled conversation with Henk then said to Matthew, "OK. I see you tomorrow."

They shook hands and Piet followed his gang out. The crowded bar was empty without them. Matthew felt as if he had just been through a violent storm; buffeted and battered but strangely elated.

A hint of sewage wafted on the warm night air as Henk and Matthew strolled through the darkened streets.

"He's very political, isn't he," Matthew ventured.

"Nay, this is normal for Dutch students."

"We hardly talked about homosexuality at all; we got bogged down in Northern Ireland. He probably thinks I am a silly prat."

"I don't think so; he seemed very pleased to meet you again." Henk glanced at him. "I think he likes you," he said slyly.

Matthew looked doubtful. "I hope you are not angry with me for wanting to meet tomorrow," he said.

"No, no," Henk reassured him hastily.

Matthew knew he was at the edge of a precipice. Should he jump into the exciting unknown or should he step back from Piet, into safety?

Piet arrived at Henk's at ten-thirty on the dot. Henk said he had to visit a friend to discuss a project so, after making Piet welcome, he left them alone.

There was an embarrassed vacuum after he'd left which Matthew tried to fill with small talk. "What music do you like?"

"Does Henk have any LPs from Joan Armatrading?"

Matthew flipped through Henk's collection. He had her latest, 'Show Some Emotion' and soon her tortured tones were filling the gap.

Piet wore the same hat and waistcoat but this time with a black cotton shirt, baggy black trousers and sandals. When he flung the fedora onto a chair Matthew was amazed by his tight haircut; he looked like a convict, there was more hair on his face than on his scalp. The previous night Matthew hadn't noticed how thickly accented his English was. Possibly the alcohol had oiled Piet's tongue, Matthew's ears, or both.

Piet looked Matthew up and down and smiled warmly at him. "I was not realising that you are living in Ireland. Where in Ireland do you live?"

"My parents have a farm near Londonderry but I am starting work in Ballycol next September; do you know where that is?"

Piet hadn't a notion where Derry was, never mind Ballycol, but this time there was an atlas to hand so tortuous geographical explanations were not necessary.

"What work are you going to do there?" he enquired.

The conversation drifted on through teaching and generalities about life in Ulster and this time Piet avoided political comment. Eventually he broke the flow. "Jah, jah, my friend," he said, "but I think this is not why you wished to speak to me, to tell me about the life in your country."

Matthew sucked his lips, looked at him and nodded slowly, working his lips between his teeth.

Piet continued, "Henk did not say to me that you are gay, but you are. Is that so?"

Matthew was unreasonably surprised, "How did you know?"

"Whoah," he expired violently, throwing his hands out into a display posture, "if not, why should he be so urgent to introduce you to me? Also, when we were meeting last evening, I could feel it."

"You're very perceptive. Until a year ago I didn't even know it myself!"

"This is often true, but if you look back at your life you can probably see many situations at which your homosexuality was cooking below the top of your thoughts."

"I suppose you're right. There was always someone at school I fancied but I never realised what it was; I thought I was envious of his popularity or his good looks."

Matthew sat in introspection; the pit of his stomach deepened as he cast his mind back to primary school days.

Piet waited patiently.

"This may shock you – it certainly shocks me. At primary school, when I was five, I had a friend. He was beautiful – his red hair glowed – I always wanted to touch it. I expected it to feel cold, like a burnished copper. I fell in love with Daniel. I can see that now, but then I assumed that *all* friends felt like that about each other."

"Perhaps they do," Piet said quietly. "Perhaps society cannot admit that this human emotion exists in a young child. It is possible that young boys love each other in a certain way but when an adult man sees that love he puts his own... what you say, reason."

"Motives? Drives? Desires?" Matthew suggested.

"Jah, desires," Piet nodded. "Many people have a very bad thing with sex; it is of power and control. Many men are ashamed of their own sexuality so when they see it in children they think they must stop it. The feelings you had for your friend are very common; I am sure of this. But boys are told these feelings are wrong. Children have not developed strong sexual desires before puberty. They are not allowed to have independent minds, either, so they play at being heterosexuals until their sexual feelings come, then they want to have sex with women because they have been told that this is the only thing. Most boys do this, I think. We are lucky, my friend, because we keep loving our own sex," he grinned.

"I must ask Danny if he ever felt like that about me," Matthew said wistfully. "You know, I'm still in love with him and I've just realised that I am jealous of his girlfriend. Isn't that terrible?" Piet showed no disapproval. "When I fell in love with him I didn't know he was a Catholic. Everything at school was telling me to despise Catholics but I loved Danny so I didn't. You seem to think that we Ulster Protestants are all evil colonialists but we're not. There are a million Protestants in Ulster and they're mostly very good people. Some were carried along on a tide of prejudice and fear but most kept quiet until it was too late. Now they're afraid to concede anything to the other side; compromise has become impossible." Matthew looked at Piet's gentle, patient face. "I'm sorry, back to Danny. Do you really not think it's a bit odd to have homosexual feelings at the age of five?"

"Not at all," Piet said. "You are falling into the trap I warned you. The feelings you had then are not the same as the homosexual feelings you have now. I will tell you a story which I have not told anyone in Holland."

Piet moved closer to Matthew, sliding his arm along the sofa so that it was brushing Matthew's shoulder. His knee nudged Matthew's thigh. The physical contact was thrilling; Matthew relaxed into him.

"When I was twelve years old," Piet slowly began, "my cousin came to my house when my mother and father went away. He was sixteen and he was very beautiful. I fell in love with him. I wanted to touch him. Do you remember what it was like when you were sixteen, Matthew? Sexual excitement came very easily. Jan was too easy to get excited; I very quickly learned what I must do to get him to do the thing I wanted... What is wrong?"

Matthew had recoiled from him and was looking at the Dutchman in horror.

"It's not right. I mean... he might have harmed you!" Matthew stammered.

Piet tried to control his exasperation: "You see why I tell no one this story? People can not accept that children can have such feelings. This is a bit crazy! Our bodies grow as we get older. Everybody can see this so why can they not see that our sexual feelings grow like this also? We have laws which tell us there is an age when we can do this thing and another age when we can do that thing. Do *you* think our sexual feelings are appearing one day because it is our birthday?"

"That's not it at all!" Matthew exclaimed. "The law is there to protect children from harm."

"Jah, jah. I know this too. But can you not see that all this happened because *I* wanted it to happen; it was *me* that started it and I also stopped it in the end. The law must protect people but it must not destroy the people it tries to protect."

"What happened?" Matthew said more calmly.

"Whoah. I knew that if my father knew we were doing these things, my cousin would have great trouble. I told him that I did not want to do it any more."

"That's all very well for you, you must have been a remarkably independently minded twelve-year-old. But most kids of that age wouldn't have the strength of character to do what you did. If there weren't laws there would be a dreadful danger of adults abusing children."

"Jah, jah," he conceded. "A man who is using his power to force a child into sex is doing much harm to the child. This is not what I want to happen. If we lived in a society where sex had not the same... how do you say, complications of power and selfishness and guilt, it would be possible for a boy to explore his sexuality without being in danger from adults. Is this not so?"

"I suppose so. But it's a terrible risk for a society to take."

"A society that treated children with respect would treat homosexuals better. Jan was not a criminal but I think your British law would have punished him terribly. In Holland, I think, if it became known, we would be visited by our social services but not the police. This is the difference between our two countries."

"I can't see Britain ever getting that liberal," Matthew bemoaned. "What happened to Jan in the end? Is he gay now?"

"No. He is married. He has three children."

"Do you think he was homosexual?"

"No. Just very sexual, I think. Be very careful of young men, Matthew. Do not think that because they have sex with a man, they are gay. If you think this you can be very hurt by these men."

"You're young," he smirked. "So am I!"

Piet hugged him. "This is different. We know for sure that we are gay. We know what we are doing and we are not going to deceive people."

Piet's revelations had profoundly disturbed Matthew. All his upbringing was telling him that Piet was wrong, that kids didn't have sexual feelings, that they were cute little cuddly things that liked toys and sweeties, not devious sexual beings. But nagging at the back of his mind was the knowledge that he had had feelings like that, even at nine or ten. If he'd had the chance, would he have had sex with Daniel? He had loved it when Daniel put his arm round him and he knew he would have liked to have been more physically intimate with him, but was that sex? Then he recalled his earliest erotic fantasies; long, romantic daydreams in which he rescued boys from horrendous danger, thereby earning their eternal gratitude and loyalty. In his dreams he basked in the glow of their adoration but he was sure there had been no thought of sex! Then, much later, when he was fourteen, he learned how to masturbate. He did it a lot; he supposed all boys did, but it was a purely mechanical activity. Orgasm and romantic yearnings were only drawn together by Alex's sexual magnetism. Matthew had been sixteen before it even started to dawn on him that he might be different and even then he was unable to identify that difference as homosexuality. If he'd only had someone like Piet to bring him to his senses he could have had a great time in his late teens instead of moping around trying to ape his friends as they explored the heterosexual world. Suddenly, he was very angry, his face flushed and gore rose in his throat.

Piet noticed. "What is wrong, my friend?"

Matthew looked at him, red-faced, heart thumping. "You're right. I've always been gay and I've been trying to pretend I wasn't. And I've wasted *so* much time!"

They didn't hear Henk coming up the stairs and, to Matthew's horror, he walked in to find them in an embrace. Matthew made to get up but Piet didn't let him go. Henk was so laid back! He behaved as if it was the most normal thing in the world to find two men kissing on his sofa.

They all went out for a drink that evening and, when the bar shut, Piet invited them up to his room. He lived in a university hall of residence; it was uncannily similar to Lancaster's. Henk sprawled in the chair and Matthew lay back on the bed listening to David Bowie's 'Hunky Dory' as they waited for Piet to make some tea. When he joined them, he inserted himself between Matthew and the headboard and cradled his head in his lap. When Henk said he was going, they all assumed that Matthew was staying; and he did.

Matthew's experience with Luc had affected him more than he realised. He desperately wanted to have sex with Piet but he subconsciously dreaded the pain and humiliation it would surely involve. And yet Piet was never threatening, he made Matthew feel it was he that initiated everything. As they caressed, their clothes slipped from them as if they never belonged. In the dark silence of Piet's room Matthew was conscious of the subtle friction of skin against skin, hair against hair and gentle slurps, sucks and sighs as they explored each other. Matthew's fingers, lips and tongue discovered an Aladdin's cave of textures, shapes and temperatures; his knobbly adam's apple with its taut, sandpaper skin; his thighs scattered with coarse hair and the small of his back which was so soft and warm that Matthew wanted to rest his lips there for ever. When Piet did something new he held back a moment, as if to assess Matthew's response. Only if he seemed happy did he continue, so when Piet gently eased their bodies towards intercourse and Matthew stiffened, without a word he changed tack and didn't try again but brought them both to orgasm with his hands. In the warmth of a balmy night Matthew lost all sense of what was him and which was Piet. Entwined as a single entity, they fell into a peaceful sleep; one from which Matthew never wanted to wake.

Matthew's friends back home had unwittingly overwhelmed him with their heterosexuality. Every conversation was about women; their jokes all assumed that straight sex was good and gay sex was bad and everything they wore was intended to attract girls. Their futures were mapped out with wives and families in mind and when they were with women, they mauled them mercilessly. His clique hadn't a clue how pervasive their heterosexuality was; but Matthew knew and he didn't want to subject Henk and his friends to its gay equivalent. Matthew had always been wary of physical contact with other men, especially those he found attractive. People thought him stand-offish, distant even, but he could never risk letting his guard down. So, despite revelling in Piet's affection in the privacy of his room, any intimacy in public places unnerved him. Piet had no such inhibitions. Matthew wouldn't let him hold his hand in public but Piet was constantly reasserting their relationship with a stroke, a squeeze of the hand or a lingering glance, and he wasn't scared to talk openly of gay sex and gay politics. At first Matthew flushed at every reaffirmation, squirmed at each reference to sex, but no one else flinched. Ever so slowly, the numbing frost of Ulster's inhibitions melted in the glow of Dutch tolerance and he was able to enjoy being gay for the first time in his life.

18: Twice Alien

His ten days in Holland became a fortnight and were heading for the three-week mark when the dual call of Strathbeg and lack of finance forced him to head home. Matthew had seen what life should be like and he was filled with hope. Piet was amazed that he didn't know any gay people in Ireland. He asserted that if there were gay discos in Belfast, there must be a gay society, so he gave him the London Gay Switchboard number to ring; Piet said that they would be able to tell him what there was for gay people in Ireland.

The walk down the gangway, onto the dour soil of Harwich, burst his balloon; he was going back to Ulster. Not only that, he was supposed to have spent a week with Danny; he felt guilty that he would only be making a flying visit but he hoped Danny would understand.

Lisa welcomed him warmly and had a pot of tea ready in a trice.

"Where's Danny?" Matthew asked, as he settled down in a comfy chair.

She avoided his eyes for a moment, then, as if she had made a decision, she said, "I don't know, he hasn't been home for over a week; I doubt he'll be back tonight."

Matthew's first emotion was one of disappointment at the thought of not seeing him. But as he digested the import of what she'd said, disappointment turned, through disquiet, to alarm. "Does he do this often?"

"Yes. More and more recently. If he was English, I'd suspect he had another woman, maybe he has, but I'm afraid his affair is with Mr Guinness and Mr Bushmills," she said unhappily.

"He's drinking a lot then?" he asked, knowing the answer.

"When didn't he?" she mourned. "It's getting worse though. It's not working, Matt. The closer I try to get to him, the more he seems to slip away from me. I don't know what's gone wrong."

"I know," he said with emotion. She looked sharply at him. "I mean," he explained, "I've known him a long time and you're right; he's always been difficult to pin down. He's slipped away from me more than once but he's always drifted back brighter and better than before."

"I don't know if I want him to drift back." She shook her head despairingly: "I want to have him back, but as he used to be. I can't stand the uncertainty of living with him as he is." She fixed Matthew in the eye. "Never fall in love with an Irishman, they make great lovers but dreadful partners."

Until that moment, it hadn't dawned on him that Danny might have told her about him.

"Too late," was his reply.

Lisa grinned. "I didn't actually mean it like that, but, now you mention it, I suppose it does apply to you too."

"Have you any idea why he's behaving like this?"

She thought a while. "I suppose it's the difference between our cultural backgrounds. I'm as working-class as he is but I've transcended the restrictions that confined my parents. Don't get me wrong, I'm not ashamed of my roots. But I don't go along with their traditional attitudes, especially to women. I'm my own woman; I do what's right for me and when I settle down it will be with someone who is an equal partner."

"That seems fine to me," Matthew responded.

"That's what Danny says. The trouble is that he doesn't seem to have quite the same concept of equality as I have."

"I can imagine that. He has some pretty traditional views about the family."

"Exactly," she said in exasperation.

"It's funny really, he always says how much he hates Derry, but he's firmly rooted there... You can take the man out of the bog, but you can't take the bog out of the man," he grinned.

She nodded her head in violent agreement. "And the worst thing is that he can't even see it. He thinks he's being terribly trendily liberal and all the time, he's absolutely shackled by his background."

"It's not easy to see your own hang-ups," Matthew explained. "I began to learn a lot about myself this summer."

Lisa's eyes opened wider. "In what way?"

When Matthew had explained how Piet had made him reassess his attitudes to his own sexuality Lisa said, "It's really good that you've begun to see that. I suppose being gay does give you a different perspective on things."

"Aye, but we'll go into that later; what about Danny? Tell me, how did all his secret conservatism sneak up on you?"

"Oh, it was a hundred and one little things. When you were here was typical. His whole attitude about the meal I made and going out with you that night; I wanted to go with you; some chance! A woman's place is in the bed, not the pub." She smiled wistfully: "In spite of everything, he *was* great in bed. It's hard luck on you he's not gay."

A sour look crossed Matthew's face.

"I'm sorry. That wasn't fair," she sympathised. "I know how much you like – can I say love? – him." She was suddenly embarrassed. "That was a bit insensitive, wasn't it?"

A wave of affection welled up in Matthew and he gave her a clumsy hug. He had never felt like doing that to a woman before. Until that moment he had a nebulous concept that the whole of womanhood was 'the enemy'; well, not so much the enemy as 'the competition'. It dawned on him that some women, at least, were on his side.

Danny didn't arrive back that night but Lisa more than compensated for his absence. Matthew learned more about her in one evening than in a whole three years at university. She heard his story and was delighted about him and Piet. He even told her about the agonies he had gone through over Danny and Alex and she took it all in her stride.

It was Matthew's firm contention that British Rail despised the Northern Irish. The train from Carlisle to Stranraer was slow and uncomfortable but the real insults started when you got to the port; the facilities were disgraceful. Passengers were herded into a drafty waiting room with insufficient hard, plastic seats and only a single decrepit coffee machine for sustenance; travel information was rare and vague.

The ferry, which was almost invariably late, crossed a cultural Styx. On board the lounge was dotted with neat, nuclear families, all being terribly normal. Matthew sought out the bar but it was little better; he was just settling in for the crossing when a gang of drunks began to sing sectarian songs. He cringed and buried his nose in his novel. Gay and English, he was truly an alien in Ulster society. He wondered why he was going back and yet he felt stronger than he'd ever felt in his life. He *knew* he was gay. He had just come through the worst phase of the gay experience and, still on a high from being with Piet, he was confident that life couldn't throw anything worse at him. He guessed he would have to fight many battles in the future, but they would be with the straight world, a foe far easier than himself.

19: Onto the Gay Scene

As the summer of 1978 slipped in, it was difficult for Matthew to take in all that had happened and yet he knew that nothing would ever be the same again. Piet had awakened him to the possibility of a gay lifestyle and he had held out the hope that there might be one in Ulster. Matthew postponed contacting the London Gay Switchboard until he knew where he was going to live in Ballycol; practical expedient, he told himself, but he was putting off a momentous step, one which would be an admission he was facing a radically different future.

In mid-August, his father took him to check out some flats. He didn't like the first two but the third address was in Cavanagh Road; a narrow street which started at the Diamond and then widened as it wound up Belle-Vue, a wooded hill to the east of the town where the wealthiest burghers lived. The noble Georgian buildings of the Diamond didn't extend into Cavanagh Road; it was lined with little Victorian two-up, two-down cottages with pebble-dashed fronts. Near the Diamond there was a row of shops which, on closer examination, turned out to be a sprawling emporium. Auchinleck's had begun as a milliner's, expanding into haberdashery and thence into a gents' outfitters, gobbling up neighbouring houses as it went. By 1978 it straggled five frontages and Matthew's flat was to be above the middle of these.

Auchinleck's heavy, hushed, camphor-laden atmosphere was periodically shattered by a whir and crash as the shiny, brass gondola of the antiquated change carrier rocketed along the cobweb of wires on its way to the wood- and glass-panelled gazebo that concealed the cashier. The Woodheads crossed creaking floorboards worn smooth by generations of grey assistants who shuffled about like ageing dormice. The manager's only concession to postwar fashion was a two-piece suit. His half-moon spectacles were fused to a cadaverous nose and when he spoke it was in the obsequious tones of one who has spent a lifetime asking gentlemen on which side they dressed. Weighed down by a great ring of keys, Mr Ellis led them out onto the street. They turned right to an insignificant door which swung open to reveal a dingy staircase.

It was all a boy could want; sparsely furnished, spacious, dry and, best of all, cheap. The front of the flat was taken up by a long, narrow room overlooking the street. There was a cast-iron fireplace at one end and an enormous chest of drawers at the other. Three doors opened into back rooms; a simple kitchen with no hot water but a relatively new cooker; a tiny bedroom with an old wrought-iron bed, and a bathroom with an expanse of cracked linoleum and an Olympic-sized bathtub surmounted by a dodgy-looking electric geyser.

With the prospect of a home of his own, it was time to ring the Gay Switchboard, but he waited until his mother went into town for her weekly shop. Safely in the kitchen, his grandma was unlikely to stray from her favourite chair, so he crept into the office and locked the door.

He dialled the number; zero, the dial crawled back, one, why couldn't they have a faster phone? Three, seven and another seven, three, two and, at last, four. The clicks told him the connection was being made. The beep-beep-beep-beep heralded the unwelcome news that it was engaged.

Matthew was wary of being caught in the house when he should have been working so he made a big point of his desperate need for an unscheduled cup of tea and a fag. Kettle on the hob, he drifted nonchalantly out of the kitchen and flew back to the office. The painfully slow process produced the ringing tone; it seemed an age before it was answered by a sing-song English voice saying, "London Gay Switchboard. Can I help you?"

Matthew was too nervous to speak! Eventually he managed to stutter, "I... I don't know. I hope so."

"How can I help you?" the switchboard operator asked in a friendly tone.

"Well, I live in Northern Ireland," Matthew stammered. "Is there anything here?"

"Oh, I'm sure there is!" came the friendly voice, "Just one moment, I'll check for you. Can you hold on?"

"Yes, thank you."

The phone went silent as the man searched for the information. Eventually his welcome voice returned. "Yes, here we are. It's called Cara, I don't know why, I'm afraid they only operate on three nights; Mondays, Tuesdays and Wednesdays, seven-thirty to ten. You're in luck, you can ring tonight. The number's Belfast two, two, zero, two, three."

Matthew longed to talk but he was afraid of somebody coming in. Reluctantly he bade the operator farewell and went to make his gran her cup of tea.

He didn't dare phone from home that evening so he borrowed the car on the pretext of wanting to visit Billy and found a phone box in Drumahoe. The phone rang a couple of times before being answered. This time the accent was soft Belfast. "Hello, Cara-Friend, gay information and befriending service, how can I help you?"

"You're the gay switchboard?" Matthew enquired stupidly.

"We are. What can I do for you?"

It suddenly dawned on Matthew that he hadn't any real notion of what he expected of them. "I don't know," he said lamely.

The volunteer switched to an ultra-sympathetic tone. "Perhaps I can tell you about Cara-Friend."

"Aye." Matthew wasn't being very forthcoming and he knew it.

"Cara-Friend is run by gay people for gay people. We're a confidential information and befriending service for lesbians, gay men and bisexual women and men. People who think they might be gay can ring us to talk about the way they feel. They can talk freely because we have no way of knowing who they are and there's no danger of what they say going any further because we treat everything in the strictest confidence."

He paused for comment but he got none so he continued: "As I said, most of the people who call us just want to talk to us but some want to meet other gays. We are not a dating agency – we don't put people in contact for sex. You understand that I hope. Two of us meet the caller so we can chat face to face. Then, if they want to we can take them to a gay venue in Belfast."

"What about outside Belfast?" he asked a little too brusquely.

"Unfortunately we can't come out into the province, I'm afraid you would have to come into the city if you wanted to meet us. Where do you live? My name's Brian, by the way, do you mind telling me yours? You don't have to if you don't want to but it would make conversation easier."

He had contemplated lying about his name but when the crunch came, he couldn't bring himself to be dishonest. "My name's Matthew – I live in Londonderry."

"Ah, the Maiden City," the volunteer commented. "Have you rung us because you think you might be gay?"

"I know I am, I think!"

"What makes you say that?"

"Well, I keep falling in love with men and this summer I had a relationship with a man."

"In Londonderry?"

"No, it was in Holland, it was Piet who got me in touch with you, he gave me the London Gay Switchboard number; I rang them this morning and they gave me yours." Matthew was becoming more forthcoming.

"You seem pretty sure that you are gay then?"

"Aye."

"So what can we do for you?"

"Well, I would like to meet some other gay people here. You said that you can meet people but that's only in Belfast?"

"I'm afraid it is, we don't have any befrienders outside Belfast and we can't get out to meet people," he apologised.

"No, no. I understand," Matthew said hurriedly. "I'm about to start work in Ballycol. Are there any gays there?"

"I'm sure there are but I don't know any. Even if I did I couldn't give you their names, it's not our policy to put people in touch like that, I'm afraid."

"What about Enniskillen or Omagh?"

"Same thing; there are bound to be gay people there but they're all in the closet."

"Where?"

"In the closet; it's a term we use for gay people who don't want to admit it."

"I suppose that's me really. I don't want my folks to find out. I've just told a few friends."

"How did they react?"

"It was funny. Most said they'd always known and they didn't mind as long as I kept it to myself, and Henk, my Dutch friend, introduced me to Piet."

"You've already found out that people don't mind as much as you expect them to."

"I suppose so."

"Well, you may find your parents are a lot more understanding than you think."

"Do you think I should tell them?" Matthew said in surprise.

"No, no. That's not what I said," Brian insisted hurriedly. "I only said that *if* you do decide to tell them they *might* react better than you think. We would never suggest that anyone should tell their parents unless they felt they wanted to; it's just up to you to do what you feel is right."

Matthew was just about to speak when the pips went. He fumbled in his pocket and forced another coin into the slot.

"That's my last ten p," he explained.

"OK then. So you think you would like to meet us, do you?" Brian queried.

"It would have to be in Belfast then?"

"I'm afraid so."

"I'd like to, if you don't mind."

"Not at all! When would suit you?"

Matthew decided that he would go up to stay with Willy-John. He wasn't sure how Willy-John was going take it; he was pretty sure that his friend suspected he was gay but Matthew still had a niggling doubt as to how Willy-John would react when he had to face up to fact, as opposed to conjecture.

On the dot of the appointed time Matthew rang the doorbell of the gay centre at number four, University Street; a tall, early Victorian house. As he waited his heart pounded and he nervously glanced around, hoping no one he knew would pass. After an eternity the door was opened by an ordinary-looking man in his thirties.

Paul was of average build with thin, wispy hair worn a little long for his age and a straggly little beard. The sparkle in his eyes belied the lugubrious voice. He led Matthew upstairs to a scruffy room furnished with ancient easy chairs and tatty couches. Unusual posters adorned the walls; one showed a caricature of Ian Paisley holding a petition with the slogan, 'The Ayatollah says, Gays now – who's next?' At the far end of the room a tall, thin man was bending over a Super-Ser. It lit with a whumpph and he turned to meet Matthew. This was Brian and he was the man who was on the door of the gay disco where Willy-John had embarrassed Matthew nine months earlier.

Paul and Brian didn't launch into embarrassing questions but made small talk about the weather and the rush-hour traffic and yet, before Matthew knew it, he was pouring out his all to them. It was such a relief to be able to talk without the fear of freaking them out, although later he worried about how open he had been. They offered to take him to the disco at Queen's University that night.

"I'd like to," he declared, "but I'm staying with my best mate tonight and it might be a bit difficult to get away."

"Well, I'll be on the door," Brian said. "So if you decide to come we'll see you there."

It wasn't far from University Street to the Crescent and his old friend's familiar yellow door. Matthew was still on a high after meeting Brian and Paul and he was almost relishing the prospect of telling Willy-John all about it.

Willy-John was sitting in the kitchen with Symie having a coffee and a smoke. "Well," he said, "This is it! Young Matt starts out into the big wide world, the reality of employment."

"Come on! I'm only going to be a teacher." Matthew grinned, helping himself to a cigarette. "That's not exactly the big wide world, is it?"

"Right enough," his friend said, nodding, "You've just swapped one grove of academe for another."

"Ballycol High's more a copse than a grove, but that's about the height of it."

Willy-John raised his eyebrows. "You're taking it wild and serious; coming up to Belfast just to buy books."

"Got to play the game," Matthew said, not wanting to tell him in front of Symie. "I've got a flat in Ballycol; dead cheap and near the shops."

"Did I tell you I was moving?" Willy-John blurted out.

Matthew shook his head.

"Aye, got a place in South Belfast near Ormeau Park – moving in in September."

"Flat?"

"Nah, I've bought a house. First step on the way to the bourgeois middle class, eh?"

"How much?"

"Sixteen thou – got a mortgage."

"How the hell will you afford that?"

"Dad'll pay until I start work."

"Typical!" Symie chipped in. "The only one of us that is going to be making a mint when he leaves and his dad buys him a house."

Willy-John wrinkled his nose. "There's one drawback."

"Only one?"

"Aye. Allie, she's coming to Queen's and I've got to have her in the house until she's finished. Three years – that's the deal."

"My God! Is she that age already? I still think of her as a wee girl."

"She's not that wee now. I'm going to have to keep my eye on that one!"

Matthew smirked. "Works the other way too. Your wee sister'll be keeping you under surveillance."

"Like hell she will!" he laughed, "Louise's moving in too."

"Bit permanent, isn't it?"

Willy-John glanced at Symie then smiled conspiratorially at Matthew but didn't say anything.

The conversation wallowed aimlessly in the squalor with Symie drifting in and out of the discussions depending on whether they related to Derry or Belfast. At long last Symie went up to his room and Matthew could tell Willy-John his news, but his friend got in first. "Guess what?"

"What?"

"She's goin' to make an honest man of me," he beamed.

Matthew forced himself to smile. "Congratulations!" he exploded. "That's really great; when?"

"She's twenty-one next week; her parents are taking us out for a meal. We're going to announce it then. Don't tell anyone!"

Matthew should have been delighted for him but he felt a buried hurt that he couldn't have explained. So as Willy-John heard Matthew saying, "Congratulations!" his heart was saying, "You bastard, how could you desert me for a woman like this!"

Matthew let the conversation about the engagement wend its way to a natural lull then nonchalantly asked, "What're you doing tonight?"

"Dunno, meeting Louise then prob'ly down the Bot. Why? Any plans?"

He took a breath and launched in. "I haven't been entirely straight with you."

Willy-John was confused. "What're you on about?"

"I didn't come up here to buy books," he confessed, "I came to meet some people."

"People?"

"Em, yeah, er, Cara-Friend... gays." Matthew added.

Willy-John nodded a knowing head.

"Well," Matthew continued, "I met them this afternoon and they've invited me to go to a disco with them tonight."

"You going?" his friend said casually.

"Depends."

"On what?"

"On you. I don't feel quite right coming up to see you then disappearing. It's a bit like using you as a hotel."

"Where is it? The union?"

Matthew nodded.

"I tried to get you to go there once before, remember?" he reproved.

"A lot's happened since then. I want to go now." Matthew felt like a recalcitrant schoolboy in front of his teacher.

"OK, we'll go there then," Willy-John announced.

This Matthew hadn't expected. "Thanks! Em, don't you mind?"

"Nah. I wouldn't offer if I did. Anyway, they're s'posed to be the best discos in the uni but they're impossible to get into. You're our ticket!"

"Alex told you then?" he enquired.

"Told me what?"

"About me being gay."

"Nope, always knew, just wondered when you'd wise up and do something about it," he answered.

There seemed nothing more to say so he let the conversation slide.

Matthew never thought that he would go to his first ever gay disco with Willy-John, never mind his pending fiancée. Brian was on the door so he introduced them and explained the situation, desperately hoping that he wouldn't remember the embarrassing evening the previous December. If Brian remembered he didn't show it, saying he would join him inside.

Matthew had heard that the bar scene at the beginning of *Star Wars* was based on a gay bar so possibly he expected to see exotic aliens. For a moment he thought there had been some terrible mistake and that this wasn't a gay disco at all. There was a throng on the dance floor, bopping away to Gloria Gaynor. It was only when his eyes got used to the light that he realised that most were men dancing with other men. Apart from that, he couldn't see anything unusual about them, they just seemed to be a gang of blokes having a good time. Willy-John soon discovered that the bar was soft drinks only, expressed his disgust and headed up to the union bar with Louise, promising to be back soon. Feeling exposed standing on his own, Matthew found a wall and watched from there.

He was hardly aware of a shadowy figure slotting in beside him until a simpering, effete voice said, "Hello. You're new here, what's your name?"

"Matthew," he replied, looking the newcomer up and down. He was small, pointed and fragile, probably about thirty-five, but he could have been ten years either side. He was standing a little too close to Matthew and proffered a limp, cold hand.

"I'm Doris," he lisped.

Matthew could hardly believe his ears. He couldn't believe that any man would call himself Doris.

"What do you do with yourself when you aren't standing here looking gorgeous?" he pouted emphasising the 'you'.

"I'm a farmer," Matthew lied.

"Ohh!" Doris exclaimed, as if Matthew had just told him he'd won the pools. He put his hand on Matthew's shoulder and ran his fingers down his arm.

"That's where you got all those wonderful muscles!" he simpered. "I'd love a roll in the hay with you, dear."

Panic was welling up inside Matthew; this was exactly what queers were supposed to be like. If it was going to be like this, he did not want to know.

He was rescued by Paul who appeared out of nowhere saying, "I see you've met Doris. Has she asked you to come and see her etchings yet?"

Doris's nostrils flared as he glared at Paul. "Jealous cow," he spat. "Always keep the best to yourself, don't you dear," he added petulantly.

Smiling archly, Doris turned on his heel and floated off.

"She's a vulture, she can spot a bit of chicken from a thousand yards!" Paul confided. "She's harmless really though."

"How did he know I was new? What do you mean, chicken?"

"Chickens are bright, young things and the scene here isn't very big so a new face sticks out a mile," Paul grinned. "Come on, come and meet some people."

Paul led him over to a table occupied by an ordinary bunch of men with names like Rod and Chris.

"Rescued from Doris's clutches I see," one said.

"Just in time," Paul responded, "he was just about to get the Greta Garbo routine."

"What's that?" Matthew laughed.

Paul transformed himself into Doris and said "Dahling, I'm an ector ectually. Did I ever tell you about the time I slept with Sean Connery?"

They all chuckled but Matthew could almost believe that Doris would behave like that and said so.

"It's no joke," Chris said, "he's pulled that one a few times." Chris did *his* Doris impression, "Would you like to sleep in the bed that Steve McQueen slept in?" There followed a bewildering but fascinating conversation of innuendo and abstruse references. For a while Matthew thought that they were discussing girls because names like Flossy, Betty and Prudence were scattered through the conversation but he soon twigged that these were nicknames of gay men, some of whom were in the present company. Matthew found it exciting to hear them talking about each other in such a frivolous way without anyone sneering, but he couldn't join in so was content to sit by and listen.

Most of the group paid scant attention to Matthew. The exception was a laid-back, long-haired being, a bit older than him, called Tim. He asked Matthew out for a dance.

"I'm not very good," he admitted.

"Neither am I," Tim smiled.

He was telling the truth. At least Matthew had some notion of rhythm but Tim jerked and jogged about in front of him like someone trying to keep warm on a cold day. Nevertheless Matthew enjoyed his bop and he was able to freak out to some of his favourites. When they played 'Glad to be Gay' by Tom Robinson everyone seemed to be swaying about on the floor, singing along. After Tim, several guys asked Matthew up to dance and Willy-John and Louise returned to find him weaving off the dance-floor, ears buzzing and dripping with sweat.

The last dance was a smooch and Tim sidled up to Matthew and asked him to dance. As Matthew slipped his arms round Tim he wasn't sure what to do with his hands. At first he rested them primly on Tim's shoulders but Tim's were roaming all over Matthew's back, eventually slipping under the waist-band of his jeans. Tim was rubbing Matthew's crotch with his own. This was turning Matthew on and thoughts of sex flooded into his mind, swamping his common sense. Matthew clutched Tim's buttocks, drawing his thighs into his own so hard that they nearly overbalanced. Tim nuzzled Matthew's neck and kissed the line of his jaw. By the end of the dance the two were snogging in the centre of the dance-floor. As the lights went up Tim said, "Would you like to come back to my place?"

"Do you want me to?" Matthew asked stupidly.

"Would I have asked?"

"Sorry!"

"Don't keep apologising," he insisted, his lips touching Matthew's.

"Sorry," he replied inanely.

Tim's eyebrows shot up and he flashed Matthew a smile.

Matthew smirked at him saying, "I'll have to have a word with Willy-John."

Matthew thought that Willy-John was a bit too accommodating; it wasn't like him not to make some sarcastic comment. "No prob, no prob. What time do you think you'll be back?"

"What time do you get up on a Saturday?" he enquired.

He looked at Louise and pulled a face. "Twelvish?" He wrinkled his nose and Louise grinned.

"OK. I'll be back about twelve then." Matthew hesitated, "You don't mind, do you?"

"Nah," he over-assured him. "Don't do anything I wouldn't do."

"What?"

"Ah yeah. Well, you know what I mean!" Willy-John joked. He put his arm around Louise's shoulder and they climbed the stairs. Matthew thought there was a nice sense of completeness; they were going to have sex and so was he.

The chill of a lost blanket was Matthew's first recollection of Saturday morning. In the cold light of day Tim wasn't quite as attractive as he had appeared the previous night. His unshaven face was greasily spotty and the stubby fingers of the hand resting limply on the stained pillow were yellow with nicotine. A travelling alarm next to an overflowing ashtray told Matthew that it was 6:24; his father would be having breakfast. He imagined what his dad would think if he could see him and felt nauseous. He tried to forget it but thoughts of his parents and safe, comfortable Strathbeg drifted back to plague him. The room was musty and damp, even in August; God knows what it was like in winter. Matthew tried to get back to sleep but he was too cold so he slipped out of the bed and scavenged items of his clothing discarded amongst the debris of Tim's chaotic room. What started as a move to the toilet ended up as an escape from the house. With a note of apology he was free. But what do you do at seven o'clock on a Belfast Saturday morning?

He walked down to the Lagan to watch the ducks. He saw the first Citybuses glide across the Ormeau Bridge, bought a *Guardian* when the shops eventually opened then sat in Ormeau Park reading the paper and watching the city shake itself into life. When it looked awake enough he pottered up to Botanic Avenue to find a cafe and some breakfast then headed into town to waste time in Crane's Bookshop. He would have loved a shower.

20: Ballycol

On a glorious morning late in August Willy-John and Matthew loaded Mr Woodhead's old Landrover and a trailer with mountains of furniture, bed linen, crockery and pots and pans.

"Aw, come on Mum," Matthew complained, "You'll have nothing left in the house!"

"I want you to be comfortable. You know what I think about you going there."

"He'll be fine, Mrs Woodhead," Willy-John laughed. "I hardly had to wipe his nose once in Belfast."

"I know... but he's still my baby, you know," she said.

"Mum!" Matthew whined, "I'm twenty-three years of age! I've looked after myself for the last four years. I'm not going to suddenly become helpless just because I'm going somewhere you don't like."

The two friends drove off down the lane in high spirits; Willy-John was full of his new house and was revelling in the congratulatory air brought about by his engagement. They went via Castlederg and Scraghy. It was a lovely day; the sun was beating down on the bog making it look positively Mediterranean. Just before Ederny they turned off the main road and bounced down a narrow track until they joined the main Omagh to Ballycol road. Despite the Landrover's ailing engine, they were making good time.

There was an army checkpoint about two miles before Ballycol. The soldiers rooted around in his chattels for some twenty minutes before letting them go, but even that couldn't dampen their spirits and they joked and bantered with the squaddies. Willy-John nudged Matthew and pointed to a young soldier prodding his mattress.

"Do you fancy him?" he whispered.

"Not my type!" Matthew sniggered, "Wouldn't mind the sergeant though."

"You'll have to become a soldier doll," Willy-John chortled.

Soon they were rolling up to the security barrier at the top of Ballycol's main street. Beyond the barrier a street as wide as a four-lane highway swept down to the lake which shimmered in the heat of noon. There were no cars and few people other than an army foot patrol dodging from shop door to shop door as they progressed up the street. A policeman heaved on the heavy, red and white pole and the security barrier shuddered into the air. Matthew eased the Landie through, and guided it down the steep street. Two-thirds of the way down, the street widened into a square called the Diamond. He assumed that the remains of the cenotaph in the middle was a notional roundabout and looped around it, turning right into Cavanagh Road.

At about three o'clock the Landrover groaned a sigh of relief and relaxed as its springs recovered. Equally exhausted, the two lads flopped onto the sofa and burst out laughing at each other's dusty, sweat-streaked faces.

"Could murder a pint!" Willy-John gasped.

"Aye. Let's find a bar. Find my local, eh?" Matthew jumped up and made for the door but Willy-John sat on.

"Come on then!" Matthew called.

"I'm not going nowhere with you looking like that!" Willy-John shouted after him. Matthew peered at a half-hidden mirror and saw his point.

Duly cleaned up they embarked on their mission. As they passed the Landie, Matthew ventured, "It'll be alright there. Will it?"

"Should be," Willy-John considered. "No one would nick that thing!"

"What about the police?"

"They wouldn't want it!"

"Ha, ha," Matthew sneered, "It's a controlled zone here. I don't want it blowing up."

Willy-John pulled a face to remind him that he wasn't that stupid. "If you're worried, ask them in the shop to keep an eye on it."

Willy-John had spotted a pub fifty yards up the road and by the time Matthew got out of the shop he was on his way to investigate. He caught him up as he was gingerly pushing the old door open. The pair peered into the indeterminate gloom. The bar was deserted. A cursory glance told them that they were in safe territory; the beer on sale was Bass and Tennant's – Smithwick's and Harp would have implied a Catholic pub – but more significantly, in pride of place over the bar was a portrait of the Queen. Gradually they noticed other loyalist markers: the collecting box on the bar was for the British Legion (not St Vincent de Paul) and on the walls hung tar-stained military photographs and a wonderful shot of the Ballycol Royal Irish Constabulary in front of their new station circa 1910.

The Red Hand Bar was not built for comfort. Simple tubular steel tables and matching chairs were dotted over the worn and cracked lino. A hard, wooden bench ran along the length of the back wall.

Willy-John yoo-hooed and called, "Shop!" until a suspicious old man shuffled out from the back. His chest only just cleared the counter, he was wearing a waistcoat and bow-tie; his shirt sleeves were too long for his arms but elasticated, metal armbands stopped the cuffs drifting over his wrists.

"Yes," he wheezed.

"Two pints of Bass please, boss," Willy-John shot out.

With laboured breathing he gripped the bar top and lowered himself to secure the glasses; this seemed to exhaust him.

"You boys aren't from hereabouts," he gasped as he took their money.

"Nah, Londonderry," smiled Willy-John, simultaneously answering the unvoiced question. "Matthew here's coming to work here," he continued. "Teaching."

"At the High School, would that be?" the barman ventured.

"Yes, that's it," Matthew confirmed.

At this he became a little more friendly but after another pint they left. He didn't really fancy that as a local but Willy-John reasoned that it would liven up at night and, as he pointed out, at least he could go there with Alex if he ever came down to see him.

Willy-John had to head home and Matthew was left to sort the flat out. Once he had the stereo set up he was able to work away to the strains of the LP that Piet had given him, Tom Robinson's 'Power In The Darkness'. After a day he had the flat looking more or less how he wanted it and the next morning he strolled up the steep main street and out along the Omagh Road to the High School.

The sprawling, modern buildings slumbered in the sun, as if gathering strength for the onslaught of September. Helpful signs directed him through a maze of identical corridors to the school office where a beaming, middle-aged lady welcomed him like a long lost son. She introduced herself as Mrs Hammond, the school secretary, and assured him, accurately as it turned out, that the school would grind to a standstill without her. In those first fifteen minutes she found out more about Matthew than most people did in a lifetime. After their cosy chat, he was led out of the office by Mr Wilson, the chief laboratory technician, who took him to the science labs.

Matthew's predecessor had been a chemist who had introduced biology into his repertoire under protest. Matthew was to teach biology to examination classes from form three upward and fill in elsewhere with general science, but no one had thought to leave him syllabuses or anything.

"I could do with a word with my head of department; Mr Richmond, isn't it?" he said to the blasé lab technician.

"You'll be lucky!" he almost sneered. "He's swanning around Greece at the moment. Should be here by Monday though."

"How can I prepare my lessons when I don't even know what I'm going to teach?" Matthew almost whimpered.

"You'll larn!" he smirked.

"I suppose I can make a start on the biology. The last teacher left me a list of what he's covered."

"I wouldn't take too much notice of that," he scoffed. Matthew looked despairingly at the technician. "He spent most of his time discussing racing form," he continued, surveying the sparse lab. "If they passed it was despite him."

Matthew walked back into town with a heavy heart. A playboy head of department, a cynical lab technician and a secretary who appeared to control the school – it didn't bode well for next week.

On the first day of term he was up bright and early and headed up the hill. Even at half past eight the playground was filling with black-blazered kids. Little knots of pristine first-years reminded sonal life," he explained.

"Because I am homosexual, you mean?"

Matthew blushed violently and nodded.

"My friend; I would not be wearing these if I didn't want people to ask me about this thing."

With a flourish Piet flung his fingers, palms outwards, to his chest and gave a little half-bow, beaming impishly. His gesture drew his attention to the colourful array of badges. There was a pink one with GAYS AGAINST THE NAZIS over the arrow of the Anti-Nazi League and a big purple one which bore the white fist of workers' struggle and the logo GAY LIBERATION FRONT. Matthew pointed to a plain, pink, enamel triangle; he was curious as to why that design was repeated on so many of the badges.

"That is most important of all of these." Piet's brows knitted in concentration as he fixed Matthew with his dark eyes. Matthew saw that he was wearing mascara. "In the Second World War the Nazis put many people in concentration camps. Do you know this?" he asked slowly.

"Of course," Matthew chirped.

"But do you know which people were put to these terrible places?"

"Jews, and Poles and political prisoners – communists and the like," he said, proud of those extra categories he had heard of from a Socialist Society member at Lancaster.

"Yes, but did you know homosexuals were also put to concentration camps? Many many thousand homosexuals," he said emotionally.

Matthew shook his head. "No."

"And did you know when the people were freed from the concentration camps everyone was helped except the homosexuals? This was because they said the homosexuals were criminals and they did deserve to be in those places!" There were tears in his eyes.

"*No!*" Matthew exclaimed, "that's terrible!" He was truly shaken; it was the first time it had dawned upon him that a state could actually select gays out for special punishment rather than simple social unacceptability.

"It is the same people who today run our society," said Piet vehemently. "It is the people who would not help the homosexuals who make our laws and run our police. In the concentration camps every sort of prisoner was wearing a badge of identity; the Jews had a yellow star; the political prisoners had a red triangle; the priests had a purple triangle –" Matthew joined in the litany

Matthew of his own first day at school. On the other hand he was daunted by the sight of shabby youths slinking about with casual cigarettes in their mouths; he pretended not to see them.

Mrs Hammond thrust a sheaf of papers into his hands. "There you are my dear," she beamed. "Assembly at nine-fifteen then form teachers to their classes. Giving out books, timetables, attendance registers and filling in personal forms until eleven."

"Am I a form teacher?" he asked in trepidation.

"No, dear. We're not that bad! Next year, if your unlucky. Staff meeting at twelve," she finished, grabbing a hapless pupil.

"Elaine dear. Take Mr Woodhead to the staff room. There's a dear."

Elaine, who was about fourteen, blushed, led him to the hallowed room then fled.

A pall hung over the staff room, a fug of cigarette smoke. The few teachers already there must have been going full steam ahead since their arrival to restore the atmosphere after a pollution-free summer. They all seemed set to ignore him, then a youngish rugger type said, "Which one are you?"

"He's hardly the cookery teacher," another chided.

"And he doesn't look like a PE basher," commented a third.

"Must be biology," said the first. "Woodhouse, isn't it?"

"Er... Woodhead," he nodded, "biology."

"Met Julian yet?" he was asked.

"Who?"

"Julian Richmond. Your head of science."

Matthew shook his head.

The young teacher jumped to his feet, leapt athletically over the coffee table and proffered his hand.

"Robin Young," he announced. "Craft and PE."

He reciprocated: "Matt Woodhead."

"Come on," Robin offered. "We'll go and find Julian."

Their way was blocked by Mrs Hammond. "Matthew, dear. The headmaster would like to see you in his study at nine-thirty."

"Thank you," he blurted as Robin yanked him out of the door.

Julian Richmond had introduced the concept of the gentleman farmer into teaching. About fifty and tanned from his Greek sojourn, he sported a battered tweed jacket and wore a yellow cravat at his open neck. His accent, however, was strong South Donegal or possibly rural Fermanagh. They were soon deep in discussion about his teaching programme. Any worries he had about disorganisation were soon dispelled. It was up to him what he did in biology but general science was delivered through a system of splendid worksheets which Julian had developed.

Assembly was his first view of the kids en masse. A churning sea of adolescent faces were held aloft as the three new teachers were introduced. Miss Moore, domestic science; Mr Pierce, P.E.; and Mr Woodhead, biology.

In the head's study they were introduced to each other and filled in on the general running of the school. Mary was small and competent looking with long, straight hair and a slightly pointed, but otherwise pleasant, face. She dressed with a hint of Laura Ashley. Geoff had strong, angular features softened by youth but accentuated by his severely cropped blond hair. His blue eyes sparkled with the enthusiasm of one who doesn't quite know what's going on but is willing to have a go anyway. With his Scandinavian good looks and his well-honed physique smelling vaguely of embrocation, he was undoubtedly attractive.

After their meeting they adjourned to the staff room to compare notes. Any advantage Geoff's looks afforded him was nullified by his disastrous conversational gambits. "Have you met that Alistair yet?"

Almost imperceptibly, Mary stiffened: "Which one's he?"

"Tall, geeky feller with specs; a real sickener," Geoff continued before Matthew had time to put in his two penn'orth. "First person I met when I got here. A real smarmy being; too nice by half," he insinuated, leaning over to draw him into the conspiracy with a knowing glance. Matthew had an unpleasant feeling that he should have jumped in to defend his former classmate but to do so would have immediately put him into the 'too nice' category in Geoff's eyes. Not that he cared what Geoff thought, but there was the rest of the staff to consider. His guilt was partially assuaged by Mary cutting in with, "You mean he's got some manners! I'm looking forward to meeting him then."

Undaunted, Geoff ploughed on, "You'll probably find he's the other cookery teacher!"

He grinned broadly at this show of wit, displaying his perfect pearly teeth.

Matthew winced. "I think you'll find it's domestic science, not cookery." He mentally patted himself on the back for standing on the side of the angels. At least Mary would be impressed by his ideological soundness.

Without any sign of appreciation, she steam-rollered him, "It's home economics."

Before Geoff had chance to wade in any deeper, Robin arrived, flinging his bundle of papers on the table.

"That man's got something against me!" he almost yelled. "I've got 3Q, the same lot as last year. They're thick as champ, wilfully stupid and thran as mules into the bargain!" He turned to their startled faces. "Agnes was doing life skills with them last term. She was teaching the complex concept of the egg-timer. John Elliot's egg was sitting on the bench. He was peering into the pan... where the timer was merrily boiling away!"

Everyone roared then Robin, with perfect timing, added, "If you think they're bad wait till you get the remedials!"

"There's a lesson for all of us there," Mary said quietly. "We have to make ourselves clear. It's no use using language that they can't understand. We have to tune in to the youngsters if we're going to communicate with them. That's our job," she smiled. "Isn't it?"

Not for the first time that day, Matthew felt humbled. He drew a sigh of relief that he had mostly grammar streams.

Robin introduced himself to Geoff then towed him off to meet the rest of the P.E. department. Mary and Matthew looked at each other.

"I'm sure he's not all that bad," Matthew said.

Mary just snorted, shaking her head despairingly.

They swapped details. She was from Belfast. She had studied at Nottingham intending to go into the food industry. Her mother had died the year she graduated with a degree in food science and she ended up doing teacher training at Queen's whilst looking after her father. She had spent the previous year subbing in Belfast. What she had seen that year had horrified her: "The majority of young people in this country leave school without a notion of good nutritional practice," she declared. "It's no wonder we have the highest level of coronary disease in Europe. The Ulster Fry must cause more deaths every year than the IRA and the UVF put together! By the time I leave this school, every pupil will be getting a firm grounding in practical nutrition."

Such dedication unnerved him. To him, teaching was a matter of going in, imparting a fraction of the syllabus and getting out with body and ego as intact as possible.

The staff meeting held no great surprises, nor did the departmental meeting that followed. All the other teachers were so self-assured; they knew what they were doing and why. Matthew went home that evening marginally less confident about the ordeal to come. He sat up until well after midnight going over the next day's lessons in minute detail. He would be prepared for his debut.

Then there he was. Standing in front of the twenty-eight human beings that constituted 3H. Officially they weren't streamed and the classes were labelled according to their classroom. But everyone knew that 3H was, in effect, 3A. He had practised his opening phrase: "My name's Mr Woodhead and I've come to teach you biology. Now, can anyone tell me what biology is?" At this point he should have seen a forest of eager hands, ready to give him a concise definition. What he got was a sea of blank faces. "Come on," he coaxed. "Surely someone has heard of biology." An innocent boy's hand was tentatively raised. "Yes, what's your name?" He had intended to take all their names before he launched into the lesson proper. First mistake!

"Carl Smyth sir."

"Well Carl, what is biology?"

The cherub launched into his concept of biology: "It's about having it off, isn't it sir?"

Matthew reddened then blanched as the class burst into shrieks of mirth.

"Quiet 3H," he demanded unconvincingly. He raised his voice: "Silence." Nothing happened. "SHUT UP!" he bellowed, slamming a Bunsen burner on the bench; the riot subsided. He was unnerved, he didn't want them to hear next door and what would the head think if he came into the middle of this?

Over the next months that group exploited his inability to dominate anyone by brute force or aggression. Fortunately they were high-spirited but not malicious. They wanted to learn and generally cooperated with him, even if the lessons did periodically erupt into pure mayhem. Each class presented its own personality. Six lower were more interested in discos than school but liked biology so they got along OK. Six upper could be divided into the messers and the sloggers. They were only a few years younger than him and some of the messers were quite charming. Matthew was all too easy to side-track but despairing looks from the sloggers usually brought him back onto the straight and narrow.

In a way, fifth form was his biggest problem. Two years of inadequate teaching had left 5N, the better class, totally demoralised. They had the ability, but hadn't covered the work. The girls were young women and the boys were in that post-pubescent transition from little horrors with big bodies to eligible young men. A few dressed smartly but most were shabby and some smelt distinctly unwashed. 5N at least made a pretence of listening to him but there was a constant undercurrent of shuffling and muttering as they unobtrusively got on with their gossip or pursued vendettas. They didn't make a great racket so he tolerated it, kidding himself that they were taking in his pearls of wisdom. When the class degenerated, as it periodically did, the boys metamorphosed into the Bash Street Kids whilst the girls gossiped unperturbed. The dreadful truth was brought home to him when he gave them an end-of-topic test. The results were dire. They detected his mood as they flooded in for the next lesson. For the first time, they sat in silence as Matthew revealed the depths of their ignorance. Gaining confidence from their acquiescence he embarked upon a diatribe, the bottom line of which was, 'You want to get O-levels and I want you to get them, so let's work together.' Matthew had dropped the me-teacher, you-pupil attitude and it seemed to work. From that point on, he got a fair degree of cooperation from 5N.

By mid-December he was surprised to realise that nearly a whole term had passed and he, like Mary and Geoff, had been thoroughly assimilated into Ballycol High.

21: Finding His Feet

Matthew didn't socialise in Ballycol but, hinting at a romantic entanglement, headed to Belfast practically every weekend where he could be himself, meet interesting people and sleep with them. He was living the double life recognisable to gay people the world over. Sometimes, lying next to a man not much older than his pupils, he mused on what the kids would think if they could see him. He needed sex, but every one-night stand left him feeling emptier and it slowly dawned on him that he needed more than orgasm out of a relationship.

Jeff Dudgeon ran the Northern Ireland Gay Rights Association. He seemed so amazingly self-confident and clear headed; Matthew could never have coped with the humiliation and police harassment that Jeff had taken in his stride. It had all started in late 1975. A gay man was having a relationship with a younger guy; they were also smoking rather a lot of dope. Unfortunately the boy was from an influential provincial family and his mother got wind of her son's lifestyle. She went to the police and their investigation evolved into an anti-gay pogrom. From seized address books they pinpointed other gays and the net was spread ever wider. The RUC applied techniques tried and tested on terrorists to smashing the gay community. For weeks the Belfast gay community lived in fear of the knock on the door, the midnight raid – although as the campaign progressed they became more civilised and began to ring their victims before raiding them. Twenty were arrested but the Director of Public Prosecutions only pursued cases against four, each of them over twenty-one. Three of the four just happened to be the heads of the three gay organisations in Northern Ireland. The police based the gross indecency charge against Jeff and his lover on letters they had found but the Attorney General, Sam Silkin, made an unusual decision and wouldn't allow the cases to proceed. In fact the government had produced a draft order in council to bring the anti-gay laws in Ulster into line with those in the rest of the United Kingdom and it was this that had prompted Ian Paisley's 'Save Ulster From Sodomy' campaign. But the end of the Lib-Lab pact had stopped the law reform. Without the Liberal party the Labour government needed the support of the Unionists to stay in power and the price of this was to abandon homosexual law reform. Jeff had to take the government to the European Court of Human Rights to get the law changed in Northern Ireland. Through Jeff and the others Matthew began to realise that homosexuality was a sexual orientation but gay was a lifestyle statement; he liked the sound of that.

Sometimes he stayed with Willy-John in his new house but more often it was Paul who had the pleasure of his company. Nevertheless he tried to keep Willy-John abreast with news of the gay scene. Perhaps he was being unreasonable in expecting Willy-John to take it all on board but polite interest soon waned to silent disinterest and on to gentle hostility so he learnt to avoid mentioning the subject and their conversations became increasingly superficial. Matthew feared that his friendship with Willy-John was to be the first casualty of his newly discovered sexuality. Sometimes in fits of self-recrimination he wondered if there really was something wrong with being gay but as soon as ideas like that seeped into his head he expelled them. To maintain his own integrity he had to believe that it was Willy-John's problem, not his.

In complete contrast, his friendship with Alex was blossoming. Unheralded, Alex would turn up on his doorstep for a cosy evening in the Red Hand Bar followed by carry-outs in the flat. He never stayed though, always leaving his car at the barracks and driving back to Enniskillen in the wee, small hours. Their conversations, oiled by whiskey and tins of Tennant's, meandered late into the night. He enthralled Matthew with tales of drunken pranks and harrowing experiences in the line of duty. Matthew amused him with tales of life at school but he didn't say too much about Belfast at first. He was afraid of offending Alex with the stories of how his colleagues had behaved with his gay friends but when he did finally tell him he didn't seem at all surprised: "I told you to be careful!" he reminded him. "It is still illegal, so what do you expect?"

"But it's the way they did it!" Matthew complained. "Why had they to be so ignorant about it? They were malicious and vicious. I can't understand it. You wouldn't behave like that, would you?"

"A job's a job!" he stated. "If I was told to, I would. You have to take the rough with the smooth. It's not all helping little old ladies across busy roads and fighting terrorists you know. I wouldn't tell you some of the sick things I've seen."

There was no point arguing. In Alex's eyes homosexuals were practically criminals but that wasn't why Matthew didn't talk to him about his sex life. There was an unspoken agreement not to refer to Matthew's attraction to Alex. Yet sometimes Matthew felt that Alex was almost flirting with him. That's probably the wrong word but he would show little signs of affection, unlike anything Matthew had ever known; his arm around his shoulder; a ruffle of his hair or an almost caressing punch to the jaw. Matthew could not decipher Alex's motives. Was he trying to show him that he wasn't frightened of him? Was it some statement to the effect that Alex tolerated Matthew's criminal persuasion? Or had Matthew somehow missed that this was how all heterosexual men behave with each other and for some reason he had been excluded in the past? He never dared suppose that there was anything more in it even though, or perhaps because, Alex still figured largely in his sexual fantasies. Whatever his motives were, Matthew didn't want to burst the bubble by raising the subject.

22: Simon Montgomery

At school, the frenzy of Christmas festivities had passed Matthew by as he battled with his first-ever set of exam papers. The two great events in the school calendar were the Christmas Pantomime and the sixth form 'formal' at Easter. The formal wasn't technically a school affair as it was entirely organised by the prefects as private individuals. Over the years it had gained the status of a tradition and, even though the head made an annual disclaimer in assembly, it was universally acknowledged as the school's annual do. Coming up to Easter Matthew became aware of a wave of restlessness welling up in the senior school.

"Are you coming to the formal, sir?" This was Julie. Her question threw him in two ways. In the first place, he had just asked her a rather complex question about the electron carrier chain and this wasn't the response he had expected, and secondly he didn't expect to be propositioned in such a way.

Once he had recovered, he said, "It would look a bit odd, wouldn't it? A teacher going to a pupils' dance."

"Oh no, sir!" she protested. "Loads of teachers come. The OK ones anyway."

He was intrigued as to which of his colleagues were ideologically sound in the pupils' eyes. "Who for example?" he demanded.

They were reticent and he thought that he had thwarted them until Julie volunteered, "Well, Mr Young went last year."

She looked mischievous, glancing furtively at her classmates. Sly looks shot across the classroom and Martina sniggered. Soon most were smirking whilst the rest were looking embarrassed.

"What is wrong with you lot?" he asked in half-mock astonishment. He was intrigued to find out what Robin had done to elicit such a reaction but nothing would induce them to tell him. All he could get from them was a cryptic 'Talk to Lynn Maguire', which he had no intention of doing as she was still a pupil.

Bobby continued, "Mr Watson was there the year before last. And Miss Moore might go this year."

"Oh yes, sir!" Julie cried, "Miss Moore. We could ask her to come if you like, sir," she said conspiratorially.

Matthew's heart plummeted as he saw himself being railroaded into a heterosexual trap. He was not going to let his pupils force him into the same sort of situations as his school friends and his bloody sister had.

"Look," he said, tight-lipped. "If I want to go to a dance I don't need you to start matchmaking for me, OK? If I come, it's for your sake, not Miss Moore's!"

The class detected that he was weakening and this was far more interesting than cellular respiration. They warmed to the task of persuading him to go.

"It's great craic, shar," George enthused. "Everyone gets dressed up – the women look great, shar!" (Matthew was never sure whether he finished every sentence with a respectful "sir" or a casual "sure". They both sounded like "shar" to him.)

"Last year George wore a white suit, sir. He looked really neat," Julie declared.

Matthew could believe that. George might be a culchie but tall, slim and dark, he was very handsome in a forties, matinee idol way. "Very suave, George. Where did you get it from?" He beamed with pleasure. Poor George had a wonderful physique but his academic prowess was somewhat lacking and the chance to compliment him was rare indeed.

"Hired it, shar."

"Wasn't that rather expensive?"

"Shar, no shar. Ten notes, shar," the boy drawled.

"It's good to see you're not on a teacher's salary!" Matthew quipped to the usual groans. "I'd love to come but I've no way of getting there and I've nothing to wear and if I did come, what would the other teachers think?"

"Nothing! They'd probably think it was good that you could mix with us, sir."

Matthew wasn't so sure but he liked these kids. They were only four or five years younger than him anyway and the idea of spending an evening with them was quite appealing. Cellular respiration wasn't mentioned again that day and by the time the bell went his sixth-form girls had taken him in hand. Myra, who was in six upper, was brought in to interrogate him on his wardrobe and assess each item. Myra had style so the class decided that his sartorial elegance could be left in her capable hands. He had a distinct feeling of déja vu; it was Willy-John and the Girls' School dance all over again.

He left school that day with a startlingly professional sketch of him in his cricket flannels, his blue blazer and a white shirt. They had toyed with the idea of making him wear a cravat but had decided it would be too poofy and opted for a tie. Myra was to supervise the purchase of the tie after school. They reckoned that, as he wasn't hiring a suit, the least he could do was spend a bit of cash on a decent tie.

His usual Friday routine of dashing for the Belfast express was abandoned the last Friday of term. As he flitted around the flat preparing for the evening, he recalled the excitement of getting ready to go out with his school friends. He skipped into the steamy bathroom and settled into the enormous tub. He luxuriated through the six o'clock news and emerged in time to silence the rubbish that Radio Ulster put out when the rest of Britain was getting comedy shows on Radio Four. He dressed to the strains of 'Outlandos d'Amour', singing along with Sting as he agonised over Roxanne and moaned about being so lonely. He adored Sting's sensuous tones. By 'Archers' time he was ready, resplendent in the red and blue-striped tie that Myra had selected for him. He examined himself; his hair was recovering from its drastic pruning of summer and an unruly blond quiff flopped lazily over his left eye. He experimented with back-combing it but decided that he liked its dissolute affair with his eyebrow. If it hadn't been for the girls, he would never have thought of the flannels. Mum made him bring them in case he needed them for cricket at school. His protestations that cricket was rarely, if ever, played in December around there, had no effect. The plimsolls were a bit impractical for the current miserable weather but they completed the effect beautifully. Myra had revived his grubby pumps with the aid of a tube of whitener and a blue permanent marker hijacked from his overhead projector kit. Matthew looked good and he knew it. He wanted to look attractive but he wasn't sure why. Why the hell was he making the effort? It would be the girls who would be impressed, not the boys. Anyway, they would all be pupils and there was no way he could even flirt with any of them. He couldn't say why, but it did matter and he was enjoying getting dolled up.

The meal was at eight-thirty. His lift was due at seven-fifteen and it was late. Just as the theme music was signalling the end of 'The Archers', the doorbell rang. He grabbed his wallet and keys, flicked the light off and tripped downstairs. When Matthew opened his door his heart leapt on finding an elegant young man awaiting him. About the same height as Matthew, his hair was slightly darker and considerably longer. The newcomer's nose was his most striking feature. It was as beaky as Matthew's was button-like. He wore full evening dress down to the white tie and the silk scarf.

"Ready, sir?" the young Adonis asked cheerfully.

Matthew peered at him myopically. "It's you, Simon!" he exclaimed. "I didn't recognise you in your finery... You look so much older," he added somewhat ruefully. "I thought you were someone's big brother for a minute."

Simon's appearance had momentarily raised his hopes of there being some talent at this do after all. He would have to be careful, he could end up inadvertently chatting up a pupil; Simon was only in form five!

The pupils hadn't brought the car through the barriers so they had to walk up the hill. They must have looked an odd couple, Simon's Fred Astaire looked as out of place as Matthew's 'anyone for tennis?' gear.

Matthew tried to make small talk but Simon cut through it all with, "We're all meeting up at Rodgers'."

"Roger who?" Matthew asked. He couldn't think of any Roger in school.

"The Landsdowne – at the top of the main street. It belongs to Jimmy Rodgers. It's not a bad place."

"Ah!" he said pensively. "A pub."

"What's wrong?" Simon chided. "Don't you drink?"

"Oh I do," he replied.

"Well?"

"Do you?" he asked.

"Course."

Matthew hesitated: "Do your parents know?"

"Aye. Though they probably think I just have a couple of glasses of shandy or something. But they know, surely."

"I suppose that's alright then," the young teacher said, sounding more confident than he was. He should have realised that alcohol would be involved in the evening but he was still a bit daunted at the thought of going into a pub with a fifth-former.

Rodgers' was a typical, soulless modern lounge but that night it was enlivened by the dazzling array of elegantly attired young women and men. Gradually they resolved into individual pupils, most of them from his biology groups.

Jack, the head boy, gracefully rose and welcomed Matthew into the group.

"Can I get you something, sir?"

"Oh, very kind. Pint of Bass please," he said before he had time to think. He should have refused but he was being carried along with the general euphoria. They all looked so different, so much older, it was easy to forget that they were pupils. He was all set for a good night. Matthew hadn't realised that Simon was Myra's brother, nor that she was going with Jack. It made him contemplate how little he knew about his pupils. He tended to ignore the fact that they had lives outside school. What was more, he got the distinct impression that his colleagues felt the same way. But these thoughts were far from his mind as, scrunched next to Simon in the back of Jack's car, they glided down the long, straight road to the Letterdrum Country Club.

The dance was a lot more sophisticated than those terrible school dances in Derry. Myra made sure that Matthew wasn't ignored. If he was sitting for more than one or two dances a female would descend upon him with a "Would you like to dance, sir?" or "Do you like this one, sir?"

Simon filled the gaps between dances with witty and entertaining conversation. In class, he wasn't one of the pupils who stood out. He always answered the questions Matthew asked, he did his homework on time and wasn't one of those boys who considered biology as an extension of break time. He minded his own business and hoped that others didn't mind his. As Matthew watched Simon chatting with a small group of fifth-form boys, he marvelled at his self-assurance; Simon wasn't going to have the hassles he'd had. He enjoyed Simon's easy familiarity and his perverse sense of the ridiculous was reminiscent of his own at that age; Matthew was sure Simon would have appreciated 'I'm Sorry I'll Read That Again'. He combined acute perception of the little foibles he saw around him with incisive wit. As Simon recounted the absurd antics that the youth of Ballycol got up to, both in and out of school, Matthew was drawn into the spirit of the moment, matching him, story for story, from school and university. As he relaxed they empathised ever more and Simon ventured into more risqué fields. Teachers are easy targets. They stand in front of the class for thirty-five hours a week, so pupils can pick up on their tiniest characteristics and habits. Simon excelled at it, delighting Matthew with extraordinary images of his colleagues. His infectious humour enmeshed Matthew and, engrossed in their double act, they fed each other with an easy rapport.

'The Queen' signalled that the evening was drawing to a close. It had been a superb night and his heart sank as he contemplated returning to his lonely flat. He was exhausted but he couldn't sleep; his mind was whirring. Remembering Simon's one-liners warmed his heart and the lingering presence of his personality was almost physical. Matthew found himself looking forwards to seeing him again but he knew he oughtn't expect to mix with the pupils. They had their lives and Matthew had his and besides, they were young and enthusiastically heterosexual; Matthew couldn't possibly fit in. Also he worried that he'd been too free with banter about the other teachers. If any of them knew the way he had been gossiping with Simon, his name would be shit. What if Simon repeated some of the things he'd said? What if one of the youngsters threw something up at him in class? Matthew slipped into an uneasy sleep.

On Saturday evening he was beginning to wish that he'd gone to Belfast, or even home; a long lonely evening stretched before him. By nine-thirty he was restless. He pulled on his coat and clomped down the stairs. He hadn't much of an idea where to go. He half thought of the Red Hand Bar but he found his step carrying him up the hill and on to Rodgers'. Tentatively, he pushed the door open and surveyed the scene; how dull it was without his pupils! He found a gap at the bar and ordered a pint. Just one, he thought, then I'll go home.

Jimmy served him with a friendly hello. "Looking for Jack?" he enquired. "You've just missed him, I'm afraid."

"They're off on the razzle again, are they?" he asked.

"They usually go to the Rugby Club on Saturdays," he was informed.

"Oh." He made a mental note to come earlier in future. There was no one to talk to so Matthew drank up and was about to leave when a couple of vaguely familiar girls came in. They were looking for Jack too; had Matthew seen him? Before he quite knew what was happening, he was in a car on his way to the Rugby

Club.

The club house wasn't nearly as grand as the City of Derry's; a ramshackle wooden pavilion stretched away from a rapidly filling, gravelled car park. The disco console was just in at the door, the bar was at the far end and he could just see Jack at the centre of a little knot of courtiers. Matthew scanned the group in vain for Simon.

As he sidled over to the bar Jack caught his eye and grinned welcomingly. He was seamlessly absorbed into the company and the previous night's revelries were resumed.

Thus began another double life. Months of concealing his gay life had given him ample opportunity to practise deceit. Ballycol began to see more of him at weekends, as did Jack, Myra and, sometimes, Simon. Matthew's flat became a drop-in for a certain set of pupils. It suited them because they could carouse without interference from parents and it suited Matthew because it brought bright, intelligent young people into his lonely life. Everyone played the game with strict adherence to the rules. On Monday morning the conspirators behaved as if they hadn't crossed each other's paths since Friday and as far as the staff knew Matthew was still going up to Belfast every weekend to see his girlfriend.

23: Micky's

Several Loyalist enclaves in Londonderry fed its Protestant schools but it was the farms and small rural communities around that produced most of Ballycol High's pupils. The town itself was socially divided by the main street. To the north, where Matthew lived, was the prosperous Belle-Vue; anyone who was anyone in the town, or thought they were, lived there. The majority were Unionists and most of their town pupils were from there. South of the main street was old Cobblerstown. His flat and the Red Hand Bar really belonged to the old town. It was here that the flavour of old Ballycol lingered, and Protestant and Catholic still lived in relative harmony. Near the tannery were Matthew Street, Mark Street, Luke Street and John Street – The Apostles, an old part of the town which had also been mixed until the troubles came and the Protestants moved out. Between the two old areas were the large modern housing estates which had become Nationalist strongholds. To all intents and purposes the south side of town was a no-go area for their pupils. Geoff lived in Enniskillen, Skintown as he insisted on calling it, in fact most of the teachers commuted from Omagh or Enniskillen. Of the young, single staff living in the town, Alistair, being a Baptist, didn't go to the sort of places that Matthew would choose to frequent, Robin seemed to prefer the rugby fraternity and he thought Mary a bit too prickly to ask out for a drink.

Towards the middle of his first summer term a parents' evening loomed.

"Worry not," joked Robin. "Just bull-shit! Bum their little angels up. Most of 'em are so dense that they can't understand what you're talking about and the rest think their spawn are wonderful."

"That's a bit patronising," Matthew remonstrated.

"Years of practice, my dear Matthew. Umpteen tedious nights of 'Johnny tries his best' or 'Susie isn't stretching herself'," he rejoined. "Anyway. There's one good thing about parents' evenings."

"What's that?" he asked dubiously.

"Getting down the pub after!" Robin triumphed.

Matthew didn't find the parents' evening that bad after all. He was in his best respectable teacher garb and most of the parents seemed more scared of him than he was of them. He tried to give each parent a fair analysis of their offspring's prospects; easy enough for the livelier students but there is a limit to what you can say about an individual who fades into the background and has hardly said a dozen words to you. Much in the way that Robin had predicted, Matthew found himself bluffing about names to which he couldn't match faces. There was one ghastly moment when he was reassuring a timid lady about her daughter. He glanced at the class-list and, to his horror, discovered that her child didn't do biology; he didn't even teach her general science! With a flash of genius, Matthew finished off his exposition with: "Of course. I don't actually teach Sandra *this term*. You really need to talk to Mr Richmond to see how he thinks she will do in science."

By ten, the last satisfied parent had left Matthew's desk and he sauntered over to where Robin was fobbing off a particularly persistent man who seemed to be using him as a marriage guidance counsellor.

"Not away yet?" Robin chirped.

"No. Where does everyone go?"

"Micky's, where else?"

Matthew hadn't a notion where he meant. "Where's that?"

"How long have you been here?" he laughed. "The Lake Prospect Bar; down by the lough. Not been there yet?" he asked incredulously.

"No, why? What's so special about it?"

"Come'n find out," he grinned. And with that they left to find his car.

He hurtled along the desolate road that scythed its way through the industrial estate, towards the tannery. It was a road Matthew wouldn't normally venture down, fringing, as it did, the dreaded Cobblerstown Estate. At the Shore Road he turned right and headed back towards the town centre. The bungalows on the left petered out at the Catholic chapel, beyond which the grey expanse of the lough stretched. On the landward side of the Shore Road dignified, Georgian town houses formed an unbroken line to the main street. Just before the security barrier at the bottom of the main street, Robin pulled over and parked on the promenade. The Lake Prospect Bar was sandwiched between a cafe and a shop that sold fishing tackle; Matthew hadn't even noticed it before.

As the door glided shut, the chilly wind skimming from the lake was replaced by the smoky gloom of a typical Irish town-bar. To his left, a right-angled counter formed a rectangular bar area. The wall beyond resembled a towering Welsh dresser, groaning with bottles of liqueurs and spirits coated in grease and dust; the few shiny bottles testified to the most popular drinks. Between the bar and the window was a wooden screen with frosted glass panels. Later, Matthew was to discover a tiny snug sandwiched between the screen and the front window. Access was from a discreet door in a side lobby. Beyond the bar were three enclosed cubicles in the same wood-and-glass panelling. Further into the gloom, a door led into a bare back room. Opposite the stalls was a welcoming open fire with a couple of cast-iron tables before it. A huge portrait of 'The Monarch of the Glen', hanging over the mantelpiece, dominated the bar. Other than a couple of old chaps drooping over their pints, the bar was deserted. They staked their claim by the fire and waited for their colleagues to arrive. Micky Quinn presided over the bar with the air of an expansive uncle about to carve the Christmas turkey. Ruddy red, apple-pie cheeks were set off by sparkling blue eyes, or rather a sparkling blue eye: the other was glass. Micky's easy bonhomie was deceptive for he was quite capable of manhandling any troublemaker out of the bar.

By eleven o'clock, closing time, the pub was filling up. By half past there were easily thirty customers besides their little group. The head of English, Jack Pollock, had left their company and was deep in conversation with someone perched, like a sack of potatoes, on a tall bar stool. Matthew went up to get the next round in.

"What are you having, Mr Pollock?" he asked respectfully.

"No, no," he growled. "I'm alright as I am, thank you very much."

Matthew didn't know him that well, but he knew he wasn't as grumpy as he seemed. He indicated his companion: "Do you know Mardy?"

Matthew shook his head, held out his hand and introduced himself: "Matthew Woodhead."

"How do you do," Mardy's lilt emphasised the do. He gripped him with a big, soft, warm hand. His accent was definitely not local; it had the soft liquidity of the South.

"Matthew joined us this year. Biology, isn't it Matthew?" Jack queried.

"Aye," he confirmed.

Mardy roared quietly, "Another recruit to the profession of rogues and vagabonds! Good luck to you Matthew. Good luck to you."

"Do you teach too?" he enquired of Mardy.

Mardy declaimed rather than spoke: "I try, I try!" he announced. "I cast historical pearls before the Gadarene swine of Ballycol as they trot from ignorant child to indolent youth."

"Where do you work?" Matthew asked.

"Christian Brothers'."

Ah! he thought; a Catholic. He had heard that CBS was pretty rough. He could understand Mardy's disillusionment.

"And what brought you to this benighted province, young Matthew?"

"Ballycol?"

"The six counties! If I am not mistaken, it's from England that you are. What brings you to the land of saints and scholars? Although I have to admit, that I haven't come across either in my dealings with the youth of this town."

"I suppose I *am* English. But I don't think of myself like that. I've lived in Northern Ireland nearly all my life," Matthew explained.

"And where would your adopted home be?" Mardy wanted to know.

"Londonderry," he replied before he had a chance to check himself. He had committed the cardinal sin; to use the elongated form to a Catholic; he should have said Derry.

Mardy didn't flinch. On the contrary, he burst into song. "In my me-emory, I lo-ong to-o see, The town I-I love a-and know so well..." he crooned, his voice quavering with emotion.

His performance didn't go unnoticed; Micky bustled over: "Please – Mardy. Keep the volume down or I'll have to close up." Well after drinking-up time, Micky was worried that Mardy's keening would attract the attention of a passing RUC patrol.

Mardy resumed his conversation with Jack and Matthew rejoined his colleagues.

162

Robin was the life and soul of the party but Matthew was astounded by Mary; after a few hot whiskeys she was positively frivolous and Geoff was actually amusing. Tomorrow he would see the staff room in a new light. When he returned with the tray of drinks, Geoff was winding up a ribald joke about the nurse and the patient with a tattooed penis: "An' she said, it's not polite, it's Portballintrae!" he finished triumphantly, to hoots of laughter from the assembled intelligentsia.

"What's the definition of passion?" asked Alan.

"Raining very hard in Ballymena!" about four voices chorused; they were coming thick and fast now.

"Did you hear about the brothel in Ahoghill?"

"What about the one about the Jew walking through West Belfast?"

Each teacher jostled to get their joke in next. Matthew could so easily have joined in, just as he used to, but he was afraid that a gay joke was coming soon and he didn't know how he would react.

He decided to test the company with the one about the Donegal farmer trying to chat up an elegant young woman in a Dublin cocktail bar: "After the farmer has bought the woman her third drink, the barman whispers, 'Do you know that that woman is a lesbian?' The farmer seems to take this in his stride and continues to buy her drinks. Eventually he sidles up to her and says, 'And tell me miss, which part of Lesbia are you from?'"

Matthew beamed round the company hoping to be greeted with peals of mirth. He got a wry smile from Mary but the rest didn't find it at all funny.

By three, Micky had had enough of them and politely but firmly declined to serve any more drink. A ragged file of teachers, sniggering like mischievous school kids, crept out of the bar into the cool night air. Geoff made a far from bee-line for his car.

Matthew was genuinely concerned: "You're not driving to Enniskillen tonight?"

"I'll be alright," the P.E. teacher slurred unconvincingly.

"If you've had as much as me, you're not!" Matthew exclaimed. "You'd better stay at my pad tonight. Better safe than sorry, eh?"

The invitation was out of genuine concern for his welfare and he had no ulterior motives. Geoff accepted, so they weaved their way up the main street in a state of benign confusion.

Matthew pointed him to his big bed. "You can sleep there."

"Where're you sleepin'?" he asked.

"I'll take the settee."

"Don't be dopey!" Geoff bleared. "I'm not puttin' nobody out of 'is bed. There's room for two. Unless you don't want to. You don't mind, do you?"

"Course not," Matthew said hastily. It would look suspicious if he refused. Geoff might suspect something if Matthew didn't want to share with him. "I don't mind, if you don't," he said cheerfully. He was beginning to have his doubts but he battered on. Soon, Matthew was lying inches from Geoff's luscious skin. The heavy, sickly-sweet musk of Geoff's after-shave filled Matthew's nostrils and triggered his pheromones. It would have been so easy to make a move and blame it on the booze. Forget it, he told himself as he turned his back on Geoff and fell into a deep sleep.

At the end of May the fifth form and upper sixth were released for their GCEs. All of a sudden Matthew found that he had long stretches of free periods and the school took on a different atmosphere. He found a nice sheltered spot behind the school greenhouse and spent long, lazy afternoons organising his work for the next year.

And suddenly it was summer! The holidays were marked by his singular failure to contact Danny. The two friends had been incommunicado for over a year and neither Danny's family, nor Lisa, seemed able, or possibly willing, to put Matthew in touch with him. Matthew spent a good proportion of his freedom hitching to Vienna, a city he had always wanted to see. His continental jaunt started and ended at Henk's and his reunion with Piet went unexpectedly smoothly. He had written to Piet once but, other than a Christmas card with a distinctly anti-Christian flavour, he'd had no reply, so he thought Piet wasn't interested in keeping in touch. But Henk had informed Piet of Matthew's imminent arrival and shortly after he climbed the narrow stairway, Piet turned up as friendly as before; more so possibly. Henk had told Matthew that he thought Piet had a new boyfriend so Matthew was reluctant to make a move but he needn't have worried. By the end of the first day Matthew was safely in Piet's bed.

"Henk thought you had a lover," Matthew protested weakly.

"I have."

"But won't he...? I mean don't you...? What would he say if....? Well... if he could see us?" Matthew was in a dilemma. He dearly wanted to be with Piet but it went against his sense of fair play to be doing the dirty on him, even if he was the innocent party.

Piet smiled his salacious smile and nibbled Matthew's ear saying, "If Joop was here he would be most jealous. He would wish to be here in the bed with us. But I told him that I wanted to be with you only. You can meet him tomorrow if you want."

That Joop could accept his insertion into their relationship taxed Matthew's comprehension but he was too cosy to worry about it then.

Part Three
DECISIONS

24: Complications

The A-level results were due out on the second Monday of August. By lunchtime Matthew could wait no longer, he left his father and Rodge and headed up to the house to ring the school. He feigned pessimism about the results but in his heart of hearts he was hoping for a miracle. His pessimism was justified but Myra, Jack and the others had done well enough and were heading off to university in October. Matthew wondered what he would do for a social life once they had gone.

He was battling with his electric kettle in his flat when the doorbell rattled out (neither of these electrical devices worked properly). It was Myra and Jack full of their acceptance by Edinburgh University; this brought his impending isolation home to him. Although pleased for them he was sorry to see them go and he said so. Myra gave him an enormous hug: "You'll be alright. Anyway, there's always Simon. You get on OK with him, don't you? And he likes you. He'll look after you."

Matthew's heart warmed. Simon had been so wrapped up in his O-levels that he had hardly seen him outside school since the formal. Then, when they were over, he had gone to his parents' caravan at Rossnowlagh with a gang of his classmates. But now his mates would be in sixth form; they would probably all go out together; Matthew was sure there would be no room for him in Simon's plans. "Oh, he won't want to be seen about with me," he protested.

Myra smiled wryly. "Don't be silly," she drawled. "Look, we've got to go now. See you down the pub?"

Matthew agreed and got back to his battle with the kettle.

Myra may have said something to Simon, because he turned up about two hours later to go for a pint. The months in the sun had worked wonders on him; he was blonder, tanned and less spotty. Even his nose seemed smaller! – maybe his face was longer. He was looking good, Matthew thought with a tinge of guilt. "Congratulations," he said, slapping Simon on his back; his results were better than anticipated.

"Aw, I was lucky," he beamed.

"Lucky nothing! You must have been working your balls off to do so well. I'm proud of you."

Matthew wasn't just proud, he was chuffed that he had made the effort to come round. "Like a coffee? Tea? Or something stronger?"

"Tea please," he shouted to the kitchen, "milk, two sugars."

Simon appeared in the kitchen and regaled Matthew with a blow by blow account of his summer at the caravan. At first the boys had spent all their time at the beach but they soon got bored with soccer and swimming and were glad of any diversion; he was somewhat vague about some of the mischief they had got up to. Then a crowd of girls arrived. Tentative approaches drew scorn and the battle lines were drawn. There was a war of attrition between the two groups which climaxed in a water fight across the caravan site in the early hours of the morning. Next day the owner had the whole lot up to his house and they were told that they would be thrown off the site if there was any more hooliganism. The battle was brought to an abrupt halt and friendly relations were assumed. At this point Simon's attitude to the holiday changed. At first there was good crack with the girls; he even appears to have gone with one of them; whatever he meant by that. But after a few nights he seems to have decided that they were more entertaining as enemies than friends. His friends didn't share his opinion and the girls became permanent fixtures in the company. Luckily for Simon they had to go back to Coleraine and the last few days returned to the anticipated idyll of sun, sea and soccer. He had arrived back in Ballycol after Matthew had gone to Holland and had spent most of July working as a storeman at a grocer's in the town then, after Myra and Jack's results came out, they all headed off down south in Jack's parents' car.

"Weren't you a bit of a gooseberry?" Matthew asked.

He grinned: "That was the whole idea! Mum reckoned that if I was along they couldn't get up to anything. Mum paid me to go along and Jack bribed me to make myself scarce!"

"That can't have been much fun for you."

"What! I found plenty of interesting people. I had great crack! Better than I would have had with those two anyway." He laughed in his open way and winked conspiratorially. After a few suitably vindictive stories about his sister and her doting swain he turned his attention to Matt's holiday. "What did you do anyway, sir?"

"Don't call me sir! It's so... well so... What's the opposite of patronising? Subservient, is it? Or is patronised?"

"Haven't a baldy!"

"Well, don't be it, whatever it is. I don't mind 'sir' in school – don't like it mind you, but I have to put up with it there. But out of school, for God's sake, call me Matt or at least Matthew."

"Sure." He paused then punched Matthew affectionately on his chest: "Matt."

Matthew entertained Simon with his summer adventures,

skilfully weaving his story around Piet to hide the nature of their relationship. Matthew listened for the three cock crows as he made Piet out to be a curious eccentric. He was tempted to test the water by alluding to Piet's sexuality but in the end he didn't, for fear of freaking out Simon.

To Matthew's delight, Simon preferred his company to that of his contemporaries. They were so narrow-minded, he assured him. He liked soccer, women and cars as much as the next man but he didn't want to talk about them ad nauseam. Soon Matthew was seeing more of Simon than he ever saw of Myra and Jack. They would sit long into the night, drinking tea and setting the world to rights. At first he was concerned that Simon's parents would object, after all it could appear that their son was being led astray by a teacher. He worried that if the Montgomerys discovered Matthew was gay and had an inkling of the subversive opinions their son was cultivating they could get very nasty. But Simon's parents thought of teachers as being upstanding stalwarts of the community and were pleased that their son was keeping such 'respectable' company. Simon helped Matt too. Like Alex, Simon loathed smoking so Matt resolved to give up the evil weed.

Visits to Belfast were becoming less frequent but once there, Matthew enjoyed himself, dividing his time equally between Willy-John and Paul. Willy-John had either overcome or managed to suppress his negative attitudes about the gay scene and was being quite his old self. He would make polite, but unrisky gay-related comments and would even draw Matthew's attention to local occurrences which he perceived as having a gay relevance. Louise began to tell him little stories about friends whom she thought might be 'like that'. With Paul he went to gay bars and discos.

He was no longer so interested in scoring as he used to be but it gave him a chance to catch up on what was happening on the gay scene and there was plenty going on politically in both Nothern Ireland and Britain. After the Labour party's disastrous flirtation with the Ulster Unionists, all seemed to be lost; the glimmer of hope for law reform in Northern Ireland had been snuffed out. Then, over this summer of 1979, when Matthew was swanning about Europe, everything had happened at once. Still under the Labour administration, the Home Office had set up a policy advisory committee which reported in June, a month after Margaret Thatcher became prime minister. The report recommended that the age of consent for homosexuals in England and Wales should be reduced to eighteen and a minority even suggested that it should be sixteen, the same as for heterosexuals. Needless to say the Tories ignored the recommendation. Then, in July, a bill was brought in to bring the law in Scotland, which had been the same as Northern Ireland's, into line with English law. It was also in July that the European Commission of Human Rights heard Jeff Dudgeon's case against the British government. Jeff was optimistic; he told Matthew that something like ten thousand cases had been brought to the Commission. Of these only sixty or so had been judged to be in violation of the Convention of Human Rights and twenty-eight had been deemed worthy of taking to the Court of Human Rights. Matthew doubted that Jeff's case could get that far but he was happy enough that it had got to the first hurdle. Matthew used to come out of Jeff's house with a feeling that things were happening. Meeting Jeff recharged his batteries; he made Matthew realise that he wasn't a second-class human being.

It was one Tuesday afternoon in late September. A miserable wind was whipping off the lough, sending sheets of icy rain scything into his face. Matthew arrived home to find Alex sheltering in Auchinleck's doorway; he was half frozen. Matthew bustled him in and soon the Super-Ser was blasting its gassy heat into his living room. Alex was strangely silent as Matthew busied himself with coffee and biscuits.

He had been standing at the door for half an hour and was only wearing a sports jacket. Matt thought it was a wonder he wasn't suffering from hypothermia. "Why didn't you wait in the pub?" he asked.

"I thought you'd be back sooner. Anyway, I wouldn't see you from there, would I?"

"S'pose not," Matthew conceded. "But at least you'd've been dry. You might've been warmer if you hadn't shaved your beard off! Feeling better yet?"

He was, and when, after lighting the fire, Matthew said he was going to the shops to get something to eat Alex insisted on going with him.

As they battled their way up the main street they met a gaggle of sixth-formers coming from rugby practice. Simon was with them.

"See the one with blond hair?" Matthew asked.

"Which one?" asked Alex; in the rain they all looked to have dark hair.

"Big streak of mud down his face," Matt whispered as they approached.

"Hello sir," they chanted in unison.

"Hello," he returned. Then he whispered to Alex, "Did you see him?"

"Aye, what about him?"

"That's Simon. I've got quite friendly with him, you know."

"Pupil?"

"No, a teacher. He just wears school uniform for kicks!"

"Weird friends you have, Matt!"

"Aye, like policemen who stand in the pouring rain for half an hour with no coat!"

Matthew hadn't seen Alex since summer so, as they plucked the ingredients of a spaghetti bolognese off the shelves of Wellworths, Matthew filled him in on the past two months' developments. The account lasted through the meal and into the Red Hand Bar. Matthew thought he would be pleased to hear that he had started to make friends but stories of quiet evenings in Micky's or riotous nights at the rugby club didn't seem to be impressing the young policeman. He looked positively disapproving when Matthew told him how Simon and he would sit for hours in front of his fire. Alex chose his moment and said, "Don't you think it's a bit silly going with one of your pupils?"

A shock of adrenaline burnt through Matt's veins, jolting him into a defensive stance. "You're wrong, Alex! We're just good friends." It sounded so hollow. "Honestly."

"Come off it Matt, I'm not dumb! It's as plain as the nose on your face! And if I know, you can bet others do. It's a wonder no one's said nothin'!"

Matthew floundered: "But it's not true! I like Simon a lot but there's nothin' between us. He doesn't even know about me; no one round here does. Straight up, Alex!"

"I'm not about to turn you in, Matt. But if you get caught they'll throw the book at you – you'll be destroyed. I've seen what they do to people like you. Believe me, most officers hate your lot. If you were even arrested it would be rough; rougher than you could imagine."

"Alex!" he whined. *"I am not having an affair with Simon."* He reddened and looked around to see if anyone had heard, but the bar was practically deserted.

Alex looked long and hard at him. "I just don't understand you, Matthew," he said in exasperation. "If a normal teacher was spending so much time with a sixth-form girl and talked about her as much as you go on about him, it would be a dead cert that he'd be knocking her off."

"Well Simon's not a girl and I'm not a normal teacher. No. Fuck it! I am normal, just not usual. Anyway, no one here knows about me so no one's going to make those assumptions."

"What if someone finds out? What then?"

"How could they?"

"Are you stupid or just wilfully ignorant? You know damn well that you can keep nothin' from nobody in a town like this. One slip and everyone'll know. Then you'll have to really watch yourself."

Matthew looked uncomfortably at the floor. Alex had spoiled everything and he hated him for it.

"There's one thing's for certain," Alex continued gently.

"What's that?"

"You are in love with him, aren't you?"

"Don't be stupid!" Matthew said without conviction. "I'm his teacher; I've my professional integrity. There's no way I could ever contemplate it."

"Maybe that's why you can't see it. You won't let yourself admit it but you *are* in love with Simon. For Christ's sake – be careful."

Alex looked penetratingly at Matthew then smiled. "C'mon. Lets get back to your place."

Matthew stoked up the fire and pulled the couch round so they could bask in the flickering radiance with their backs to the cold expanse of the long room. He rustled up two huge hot whiskeys as Alex selected the music. When he came in Alex had the lights off and was staring into the fire to the strains of Joan Armatrading. He looked indescribably sad.

Matthew handed him his drink and sat next to him. "What's up?" he asked softly.

Alex seemed to think for a moment before slowly saying, "Sorry if I upset you. I'm always doing that, aren't I?"

"Suppose you are. But I should be grateful. You seem to see things that I don't and, what's more important, you tell me. There's no one else who cares enough for me to do that."

Alex held his own neck and gripped it hard shaking his head slowly. Matthew saw the muscles of his friend's strong forearm tensing. "Alex," he coaxed, "what's wrong?"

"Nothing you can do anything about."

"Tell me."

Alex thought for a while and then said almost inaudibly, "Maybe I'm being hard on you 'cos I'm jealous."

Matt's heart skipped a beat. "What do you mean?"

"You and Simon."

"Go on."

"Well. You've found someone to be with. Even if you're not getting it, at least you have someone to share things with."

"Haven't you?" Matthew asked in mild surprise.

174

"'Cept you, no."

"But I thought you had great craic at work. You're always telling me that you get on really well with the others; playing rugby, out on the tear with them all the time. It sounds like a constant round of wine, women and song."

"Yeah – well it is. Wine and song at any rate. The craic is powerful in barracks but we don't get out that much to look for women. When you do you've got to be careful, you never know, do you?"

"How do the other guys manage then?"

"Dunno, they just do. Some have women at home, some go with WPCs and most of 'em seem to be happy screwing some scrubber they meet at a disco and never seeing her again." He fixed Matthew with his sad, brown eyes. "That's not for me, Matt."

"I don't get it," Matt puzzled, "You seemed to manage OK at school."

"We were just kids, finding out if our dicks worked," Alex scoffed. He stared at Matt with that penetrating look again. "You say *I'm* the only one who'll tell you things... Well, *you're* the only one *I* can talk to."

"But you've met loads of girls in the police, haven't you?"
Alex shook his head.

"Wasn't Rosemary a WPC?" Matt asked.

"Aye, but she got fed up with me, she's going with someone else."

"What about the girls we used to know at home?"

"Smart ones went to university and got out. Dopey ones got pregnant and married."

"Sandra's not. Have you seen her lately?"

"You don't have to try and fix me up, Matt!" Alex laughed hollowly, hugging him. He held up his glass. "Any more of this?"

As the bottle of Bushmills steadily emptied Matt heard Alex's hopes and fears for the first time. It was strange to find his long-time ideal of self-assurance leaning on him. Alex's trust thrilled him; for the first time in their relationship he felt that he was being the strong one. He loved Alex for it and told him as much. Alex put his arm round Matthew and drew him to him in a masculine, good mates way: "It's good to have a friend," he croaked. When the record finished Matthew didn't want to get up because he would have to leave the comfort of Alex's arm but Alex rose and made his unsteady way to the record player. He chose Chopin, scraping the needle over the first track as he put it on. "Sorry," he muttered, collapsing back onto the couch. Matthew snuggled up to him and Alex's arm was soon cosily around him again. This time Alex didn't just rest his arm on Matthew's shoulder but cuddled him, massaging his shoulder with his fingers. They chatted in that cosy unity for a while but all too soon Alex got up saying it was time for him to go.

"Don't go," Matthew pleaded.

"Why?" Alex asked lightly, "Getting horny?"

He was, but he would never admit it to Alex and that genuinely wasn't why he didn't want Alex to leave. "You've drunk too much. You can't possibly drive. Kip here and go home tomorrow... Please." Matthew was standing now and gripping Alex's shoulders.

"OK then," he said with hardly a thought. He looked at the brightly glowing fire. "Tell you what. Let's sleep in here. In front of the fire."

They humped the mattress off Matthew's bed and into the space between the fire and the couch. Matthew made up the bed whilst Alex was in the toilet and slipped into his pyjamas.

Alex came back, turned the lights out and stripped in front of the fire. It had been years since Matthew had seen him naked. The body that had thrilled him as a schoolboy had matured into a robustly masculine torso with well defined muscles – an effect only slightly marred by a developing beer gut. Alex's skin tones had mellowed so that his jet black hairs, despite being more abundant, weren't as stark as they had been in his youth. His big penis was not exactly erect but it wasn't dangling as limply as it should have been.

Alex got in next to Matthew. "Come here," he muttered, snuggling up to him.

"Please don't," Matthew whispered hoarsely.

"I thought you fancied me," Alex complained in mock hurt.

"That's why I don't want you to – I'm embarrassed."

But Alex didn't move away. In fact he slipped his arm round Matthew and into the front of his pyjama jacket. "You've got a hairy chest!" he exclaimed.

Matthew couldn't speak.

Alex played with the soft fuzz around Matthew's nipples. "You're very tense. It should be me that's nervous... it's my first time."

Matt's heart leapt a beat and he snorted a tense laugh through his nose.

"Come on; relax," Alex whispered closely. Then Alex 's lips caressed his ear. Matthew's resolve evaporated and he turned to face his big friend. Their lips touched and Matthew murmured, "OK?"

"Mmm," he muttered. "You're really not smoking, are you?"

Matthew was surprised at how relaxed Alex was. He worked Alex's lower lip between his own then explored his delicious big mouth with his tongue. At first he let Matthew make all the moves, as if he didn't know what to do, but he quickly lost his reticence and they began to kiss passionately. As they did, Alex worked Matthew's pyjamas off his shoulders. Matthew progressed to his Alex's angular jaw-line, the stubble hurt the inside of his lips but he didn't mind; Alex tasted wonderful. He sucked Alex's nose and the tip of his tongue felt the tiny hard hairs on its tip. Alex had slipped Matthew's pyjama bottoms off and was massaging his buttocks, pulling Matthew's groin into his own. The sensation of their two hard penises rubbing against each other was quite the most erotic sensation Matthew had ever had; even Piet hadn't been able to do *this* to him! He wanted to eat Alex; be eaten by him. He realised he was digging his nails into Alex's back but it was necessary to keep the wonderful body contact to its maximum. Matthew's mouth found Alex's ear and as he probed with his tongue, Alex's taut body shuddered in ecstasy and he pushed Matthew off. "No," he exhaled, throwing his head back, panting. Matthew looked longingly at the beautiful man and was drawn inexorably to his strong, broad neck. He leaned over and kissed Alex's adam's apple, then his mouth slid down his throat to his broad chest. Matthew licked and chewed at the hairy chest like a cat and Alex rolled onto his back, pulling Matthew on top of him. His great tree-trunk legs curled over Matthew's and his arms embraced him pinning Matthew's body onto his so he couldn't move. The two lay united for several minutes then, suddenly, Alex released him, threw him over and turned the tables on Matthew copying his technique. Matthew writhed as Alex nosed through the pale down on his chest and found his nipple which he sucked and chewed hungrily. Alex was devouring Matthew's neck when he brought him to an ecstatic climax and warm, slippery semen flooded onto their bellies. Matthew went limp and pushed Alex off him.

"Did you come?" Matthew whispered.

"No," Alex said with evident disappointment. He began lubricating his cock with Matthew's semen. Matthew tried to help him but nothing happened.

Matthew kissed him, "I'll go and get a cloth."

Alex lay silently, looking at Matthew affectionately as he wiped the semen from both their stomachs.

Matthew threw the clammy cloth onto the hearth, drew the covers over them and rolled on his side to sleep. But Alex drew Matthew to him, nibbling the nape of his neck. One hand found

Matthew's penis as the other gently probed between Matthew's buttocks. Alex found his hole and started pushing his fingers in; Matthew knew what he was doing but he wasn't afraid. Since Luc he hadn't let anyone near; now he wanted him to do it. Matthew felt Alex's hard, horny fingers replaced by something smooth and hot. Ever so gently he rubbed between Matthew's buttocks with the tip of his cock until it got slippery. Matthew willed him in; he tried to suck him in and slowly and ever so gently, he entered.

"Alright?" he solicited.

"Mmm."

He penetrated Matthew carefully so as not to hurt his friend. After Luc Matthew expected it to be agony but, for Alex, he would tolerate anything. Yet Alex didn't hurt at all. He tightened onto him, wanting to feel every inch of him inside him. Slowly Alex began to thrust, each thrust taking him deeper. Alex's breathing was getting harder and heavier as his control gave way to sheer sexual energy. Now he was clutching Matthew with every sinewy limb, his hard muscles digging into Matthew's flesh. His cock crashed against the base of Matthew's, deep inside his body. Alex shuddered and panted, spending his load inside Matthew and, almost simultaneously, Matthew came again into Alex's hand. Alex let out several short breaths into Matthew's ear and relaxed but he didn't pull out.

And that's how they slept all night, as completely coupled as two men could be.

Then he was gone. A gentle kiss at six-thirty a.m. and a 'see you', and Matthew was alone to get ready for 4P, first period on Wednesday morning – hangover and all.

25: Simon to the Rescue

Alex had waltzed into his life, turned it upside down, and swanned off again. Matthew spent the next few days in a dream and only one thing occupied his mind.

The following Friday, Simon hung back after class.

"Going out tonight?"

"What?" Matthew wasn't listening to him.

"Are – you – go – ing – out – to – night?" he repeated, as if to a half-wit.

The young teacher grinned, snapping out of his reveries. "Cheeky bugger! Probably will. Are you?"

"Hardly would've asked if I weren't."

"Sorry, I was miles away. See you later, OK?"

Puzzled, Simon left.

As soon as Matthew got home he made himself a generous gin and tonic and by nine he had wound down enough to present an acceptable face to Simon.

They made their way down to Micky's. Friday was Micky's busiest night but the Pope was in the South and practically every Catholic in Ballycol had gone to Drogheda or Dublin. Simon joked, "If they close the border now the problem's solved!"

They occupied the two tall bar stools in one of the little cubicles along the counter. On top of the gin, the stout went straight to his head. While Simon rattled on, as only he could, Matthew drifted away into a little world of his own. As they slouched dissolutely over their pints of Guinness, he acknowledged to himself how fond he was of the bright, cheery young man. He fantasised that he was Verlaine to Simon's Rimbaud then he shook the idea from his mind and contemplated his emotional future. He would never win the love of someone as wonderful as Simon. Was he destined to furtive encounters with closet cases like Alex? His eyes filled with tears of self-pity. Simon was trying to tell him about some successful contretemps with his geography teacher when Matthew resolved to tell him.

"Simon."

"What?"

"I've got to tell you something," he declared almost as if it was a duty rather than an indulgence.

Simon was guarded, "Oh yes?"

Matthew hesitated, "I don't quite know how to say this."

"Try," he said perkily.

"There's something about me that you don't know, something important."

"You mean that you're gay?" Simon suggested quietly.

Matthew looked at him in astonishment. "How did you know?"

Simon gave him his most charming smile. "Dunno; just knew." He looked at the extraordinary look on his friend's face and laughed. "Come on Matt. I've known you for ages!"

"It's only about three months actually," he corrected him.

"Aye, but we've spent about a year's worth of time together! In all that time you've never so much as looked at a woman."

"Nor have lots of people," he pointed out.

"Yes, but you're different."

"How?" he frowned.

Simon casually emasculated him. "Well, you're effeminate."

Matthew had endured a lot of blows to his ego in his life but that was the worst thus far. Simon had pulled the plug with that one word. His self-esteem imploded.

"Am I really?" he asked with enough hurt in his voice to force Simon to retract. He didn't.

"Aye," he said as if there was never any doubt on the issue.

Matthew couldn't speak; he couldn't even look at him.

"You're offended now," Simon lamented, looking uncharacteristically serious.

"Na, I'm not," his friend replied unconvincingly.

Simon imitated his teacher's accent and shook him by the arm. "Come on, sir, cheer up! It's not such a bad thing – to be effeminate. There's loads of people admire you for it!" he reassured.

Matthew was incredulous: "For being camp?"

"What's camp?"

"What you seem to think I am. You know, like Larry Grayson – 'shut that *door*'," he simpered. "That's camp."

"I don't mean like that," Simon insisted. "Not really anyway," he added, demolishing the little self-respect he had restored. "It's just little things. A softness in your voice, a lack of something... well... something distinctively masculine."

"Aggression, you mean?"

"Suppose it could be that, yeah. You aren't forceful. Even when you're arguing about something dead important to you – you don't try to win by force. You try to sort of wheedle a win."

"Do you think anyone else suspects?" Matthew asked, hoping above hope for an answer in the negative.

"You're kidding! I get some stick for hanging around with you. Most of the bozos are convinced that we're having it off! I had to threaten McKnight with a kickin' the other week 'cos he called me a fruit. They think I don't go with the women in our class 'cos I'm gay. What they don't realise is that I wouldn't go with yon wee cuties if they were the last women in the world!"

"If you get so much hassle why do you...?"

Simon's eyes shot wide open. "Why do I what? Hang around with you?"

Matthew nodded shamefacedly.

"If you don't know that, you're not the friend I thought you were!"

"Sorry, I should have put my brain in gear before opening my mouth. It's just that I sometimes find it difficult to see why anyone puts up with me."

"God, you are feeling sorry for yourself, aren't you?" he observed. "Hey boy! 'nother?"

They didn't stay long after closing time but headed up to the flat and settled in for a long session over the hot whiskeys. Deep into the night they talked. Once the ice was broken Simon wanted to know what made Matthew tick. When did he first know he was gay? How did he know? Did his family know? Was he worried about them finding out at school? The answers elicited noises of sympathy. Simon was surprised at the depths of Matthew's self-denial, his closetedness. He was scrupulous not to pry into his friend's personal life and steered completely clear of any questions about his sex life. Matthew didn't want to talk about Alex and he didn't suppose that Simon would want to hear.

The conversation was cathartic. Matthew went to his bed that night with a new sense of peace. Simon had gone one step further than any of his other friends, even Alex. Simon accepted his homosexuality as opposed to simply tolerating it. In fact knowing that he was gay seemed to bring them closer together. Even if he had found it difficult to admit it, Alex had been right about one thing; he adored Simon. Matthew loved his company; he didn't go on about women ad nauseam and he never bragged about his sexual conquests and yet, although Simon practically never went out with girls, Matthew knew that he was one hundred percent heterosexual. It was the very fact that he didn't feel the need to make the point that was so conclusive. But Simon *was* his pupil, so he couldn't allow himself the luxury of fantasising. He even told himself that Simon wasn't particularly sexually attractive. He was, of course.

If he had cleared the air with Simon, the opposite was the case with Alex. He needed to talk to him; so many questions were left hanging in the air, the most tantalising one being, was he gay after all? If he was, why had he not contacted him at all since that night? If he wasn't, why had he done it?

By Tuesday, a fortnight after they'd slept together, he could stand it no longer. He had to do something so he sat down and wrote the hardest letter of his life.

> Dear Alex,
> I don't know how to start this letter. I really enjoyed your visit last week. Does that sound too corny? Much as I enjoyed it, I feel that it has opened up all sorts of questions that have to be answered. I don't know the answers and I wonder if you do either? This all sounds most contorted and a letter isn't the way to untwist it all. I really need to talk to you, Alex. Please, if only for my sake, please come to see me as soon as you can.
> Love, Matt.

He sealed the missive, stamped it and rushed to the post-box before he had time to change his mind. He listened to the swish as it fluttered onto the pile of innocent letters and skipped back to the flat with a great feeling that he'd done something decisive.

Alex rang him at school on Thursday; he was subdued, to say the least.

"I'm really sorry, Matt," was all he could say. "I'll get up as soon as I can. I'm sorry. I really am."

"You've no need to apologise," Matthew insisted. "I just want to talk to you, that's all. There's nothing wrong. Really, believe me."

"Yeah, of course," he said warily. "See you soon then."

But he didn't see him soon. It was a full week before he turned up.

"Hello," Matthew said, trying to sound cheerfully casual. "Aren't you coming in?"

Alex peered at his face, as if in it he could divine his next action. He sat down; Matthew had never seen Alex looking so ill at ease.

"Look," he faltered. "I'm really sorry about the other night."

"Alex, there's nothing to be sorry about."

"There is! I've ruined everything."

"You haven't. What are you so worried about?"

"What are *you* so worried about?"

Matthew laughed ruefully, "I'm worried about you. Do you mind if I sit here?" he asked as he slipped next to Alex on the couch.

Alex shook his head. "I'll try and be honest with you." The big policeman looked hunted.

"For God's sake Alex! Don't you trust me?"

He buried his face in his massive hands and shook his head slowly: "I trust you Matt. It's me I don't trust."

"Well I trust you."

They were almost speaking in whispers.

"Listen," Matthew breathed, "I have never let anyone screw me before."

"Don't!" Alex appealed, shaking his head as if to make everything go away.

"It's important – please listen. Remember I told you I was practically raped two years ago; in France?"

Alex nodded.

"Well, it was such an awful experience, I thought I would never trust a man again. I trusted you – and you cherished that trust. You showed me that... I don't know how to put this... I

182

know that if I do find a man who loves me... Well... thanks to you, I know it can work."

They sat silent for what seemed like an age.

"So do you understand what you've done for me then?" Matthew whispered.

"But I hurt you too."

"It didn't hurt at all; it was wonderful!"

"I didn't mean that!" He sounded appalled.

"I know. I'm sorry – joke – bad taste." Matthew paused. "True though."

Alex looked at him, beetle-browed. "You can't cover it up by making a joke about it. You know I'm not," he hesitated, as if it took him all his courage to drag it out of himself, "I'm not gay."

"I never thought you were! Alex – the school stud. Perish the thought!"

Alex gave him a withering look: "You were never that sure, were you? I knew you fancied me at school and I lapped it up. I used to wind you up. God I was a shit! Remember that day I brought the dirty magazine to your house? I was teasing you then. And I got you on the first XV to satisfy some perverse curiosity to see how you would cope. With Willy-John out of the way the lads thought they could have fun at your expense, let's see how poofy little Matthew makes out with real men."

"I never noticed," he breathed.

"But you're a sneaky bastard Matt; know why?"

He shook his head.

"I got to like you. Then I got to respect you for what you were. Then I got to depend on you. Then I fucking used you. I couldn't get a woman – so I used you instead. That's what I did! The worst of it is, I am attracted to you, I think I always was. That time in your bedroom I was getting so horny I wanted to do it with you but I got really scared. That really screws me up 'cos I'm not queer – sorry, gay. Since the other night I've cursed myself for doing it. I kept looking at the other cops and thinking *I've* done it with another man. It could have been him, or him. And my stomach would turn at the thought of it. It's women I fancy. I need a woman. It's different the way I want to be with you. I do like you a lot Matt, but you mustn't think I could ever be your boyfriend or anything like that."

He put his big hand round Matthew's neck. "I hope you get a feller soon Matt."

By this stage Matthew was willing Alex to stay but he knew he wouldn't. If only Alex had been raised in a different culture; one in which he could have reconciled the two aspects of his sexuality. If only.

26: Negative Feedback

A week after their heart-to-heart Alex had called at Strathbeg to go out for a pint but not a word was said about his 'lapse'. The two friends spent a lot of time together over Christmas, culminating in the usual New Year's Eve party at the McIntyre's. Willy-John and the others behaved so normally with him that Matthew almost forgot that he was gay. For all his adult life it had been hanging, curselike, over him. He had always been aware of not quite fitting in. Every social situation had been tainted by that knowledge and he could never let his guard down. Because of this he never had the confidence to assert himself; he had been a wimp! Alex was being inordinately attentive to Sandra and Matthew got the distinct impression that he was trying to make a point. If he was, it was working. Matthew was jealous of his obvious attraction to Sandra but he handled that hiccup and by spring, their relationship was very much back on an even keel.

In Ballycol things were looking up too. Matthew's honesty with Simon had reinforced their friendship and Simon's friends accepted their teacher as one of the crowd. Although they never actually mentioned it, they all took it for granted that he wasn't looking for a woman and he supposed they all assumed that he was looking for a man.

He was teaching upper sixth; past masters at sidetracking him. As none of them liked Simon and didn't associate with him they didn't *officially* know that Matthew was gay so it was alright for them to bring it up in class; they couldn't be accused of compromising him. Their favourite entrée was something like "Did you see 'Spotlight' about the queers in Belfast, last night sir?" or "Did you read about the queer who killed five wee boys?" They knew he would get on his high horse about society's treatment of gay people and they could forget biology for half an hour or so. On this particular day the students had been watching a programme about the Kincora scandal. Several men, among them prominent Loyalists, had been using youths from the Kincora boys' home as prostitutes. Matthew was disgusted that they had used their position and wealth to induce already deprived lads into possibly unwanted sex. He was also angry that they were undoubtably supporters of Ian Paisley's 'Save Ulster From Sodomy' campaign; the hypocrisy of the Loyalist establishment! Unfortunately most Northern Irish people were scandalised in a different way; they saw the affair as one more proof that homosexuals were corrupting and evil and that didn't help the likes of Matthew one bit. The pupils took the 'corrupting homosexuals' stance and before long Matthew was lecturing them on the importance of being tolerant of other people's lifestyles, no matter how strange or different they might seem: "Homosexuals are perfectly ordinary people you know. They have hopes and fears like anyone else. They can't help being the way they are. Society punishes them and forces them to do things that they wouldn't do if their sexual persuasion was accepted."

"Why don't they just behave like everyone else then?" said Mark. "If they're so normal!"

"What do you mean?"

"Well they're pervy, aren't they?"

"Explain," Matthew snapped.

"You know. You're always hearing about them picking wee boys up and things like that. I mean, look at Kincora – dirty old men doing things to orphans."

He had hit a raw nerve and got the response he wanted. "You really believe all that rubbish you read in the papers! All they're doing is titillating the readers with scandal. It's an enormous con. They've created a grotesque caricature of homosexuals that bears no relationship to what gay people are really like. They're scaring Joe Public to death with tales of how dangerous gay people are and then produce horror stories to sell papers. Have you any idea of what that does to someone who *is* homosexual?" Shaking with rage and eyes stinging, he croaked, "What do you think it's like to only ever hear that you are sick and detestable?"

"Is that how you feel?" Mark asked with a glint in his eye.

"What do you mean?"

"Come on sir. Why don't you admit that you're gay?"

Tears welled in his eyes. "OK," he quavered.

"We all knew anyway," his tormentor said. "Now, at least we can all act normally instead of pretending that we don't know."

"I'm sorry. I shouldn't go on so much about it. I'm sure that you're not interested in the least."

Julie disagreed. "It's good to get a different point of view. Wouldn't you like to be cured though, sir."

His gore rose but he couldn't bring himself to chastise her; she was so sincere. "You can't cure something that is part of your character. I can't be cured any more than you could be cured of being short or of having blond hair. Being gay is just part of me."

The oddest thing was, that once he had come out to the class the sidetracking stopped; he had ceased to be fair game. He waited for trouble but it didn't come. None of them had rushed home to tell their parents that 'sir' was gay, or if they had, their parents hadn't thought it significant.

Matthew was feeling particularly lazy one Thursday afternoon. He had the staff room to himself other than a couple of the women who were gossiping in the far corner. His feet were occupying the space on the table normally reserved for the *Times* crossword; the chair was rocking gently on two legs as, eyes closed, he contemplated the forthcoming weekend. He heard the door but didn't stir. Mrs Arbuckle was chattering agitatedly, he caught odd words: 'fist fight... sixth-form study... blood everywhere... caught by Ronnie Knox... headmaster's study... McKnight... Montgomery'.

He was jolted out of his reveries; what had Simon been up to now?

Annaghry was a village about six miles outside Ballycol. Dour houses sported Union flags, the curb stones were painted red, white and blue and slogans declaring 'No Pope Here' and 'Remember 1690' adorned gable ends. Andy McKnight was fairly typical of its inhabitants. He was probably a perfectly decent young man but he was steeped in the ethos of Annaghry, a philosophy of absolute opposition to anything that wasn't strictly in accordance with Ulster Protestant tradition. In fourth year Andy had been in the forefront of a campaign of victimisation against the few Catholic kids in his class and, being friendly with the victims, Simon had complained to his form teacher about the way they were bullied. The headmaster had dismissed Simon as a stirrer until one of the Catholic boys was so thoroughly intimidated that his parents had threatened to remove him to the Christian Brothers' school. By then Simon had been branded a Fenian-lover and he was still very sore about how he was treated, both by his classmates and by the school authorities.

The next bulletin came from Ronnie Knox himself. "Little thugs," he ejaculated as he walked into the room. "Heard a racket in the lower-sixth study... went in, and there was those two going at each other hammer and tongs. Had to drag Montgomery off McKnight. Thumping three shades of shite out of him, he was," he glanced at his female colleagues and put on a posh accent, "Sorry ladies... giving him a jolly good thrashing."

Matthew drifted over. "What did you do?"

"Couldn't do much else, took them both straight up to the boss."

"What'll he do?"

"Probably suspend them – usually does in these cases. They'll have to bring their parents up to see him and apologise to each other in front of them. That's the usual procedure."

Matthew didn't like going up to Simon's house. His folks were always charming but a little too polite for his liking. Matthew's visits always seemed to be a strain for them but he had to go and give Simon some moral support.

Mrs Montgomery opened the door. "Hello Mr Woodhead. Come in. Simon's upstairs in his room, go on up."

He padded up the wide, carpeted stairway and tapped on his door. "Simon. Can I come in?"

The door opened. He was a sorry sight, a bruise was developing under his right eye and his lip was swollen and split; he looked as if he had been crying.

"Are you alright?"

"Aye, no bones broken. You should've seen the other guy," he grinned lopsidedly, then winced.

"What happened?"

He scowled, wrinkling his big nose: "Och! You know what McKnight's like. A mouth. He spouted once too often. I lost the rag, that's all."

"What did he say?"

"Nothin' really, just the usual crap he comes out with."

His stubborn silence drew a veil over that aspect of the affair.

"What'll happen now?" Matthew asked.

"Depends on his folks. Dad says he'll come up with me on Monday to see the boss. If McKnight's are there we'll say we're sorry, get an eatin' from the boss and that'll be the end of it."

"What if his parents don't come tomorrow?"

"I haven't a buckin' clue."

Simon wasn't on form all weekend. He tried to make out that he wasn't worried about Monday but it was preying on his mind. Once back in the flat Matthew did his best to get him to open up about his worries but he was no more successful than he had been on Thursday.

On Monday he collared Simon at break and dragged him into his lab.

"How did it go?"

He looked uncomfortable. "Not too good."

"Go on."

"Well. His dad didn't bother his arse but the boss had us both in front of mine. He asked us what we were fighting about."

"And?"

"The thick bugger wouldn't say anythin'."

"What did you say?"

Simon was evasive. "I told him we'd had a personal disagreement which got a little heated."

"What did he say to that?"

"Nothing. Told us to make up and shake, I offered my hand but he wouldn't. The boss went mad – hey! He asked my dad to go out and he tore strips off McKnight. He told him to get out of his sight and not to come back until he had his parents with him and he had better be prepared to make a full apology to me."

"Oh well, you're out of the shit anyway," Matthew smiled.

"Maybe," Simon said enigmatically.

Andy held out for nearly the whole week. On Friday his father brought him up to school. Matthew was surprised to see that he came in a rather smart looking BMW; he had assumed that as his attitudes were like those of the rough boys from the Carson Estate, his background was similar. Whereas his family was in fact wealthy and, consequently, influential.

He was teaching third form when Simon appeared at the door; Matthew had never seen him so agitated.

"Excuse me, sir. Can I speak to you?"

"Now?" he asked incredulously.

"Please." Simon looked as if he was about to cry.

Matthew told the class to work on and followed Simon into the prep room.

"What on earth's wrong with you?"

"I think we're in shit," he almost spat.

"What are you on about?"

"McKnight, the wee bastard. He was bumming to some of his cronies. He said he told his dad that you and me were... well... you know."

"Friends?"

"More than that."

"Drinking together?"

"God! Do I have to spell it out to you?" Simon glared at him and, after a tense pause, said, "...*lovers!*"

Matthew momentarily lost control of his balance and staggered, grabbing the 'dangerous chemicals' cupboard. "Sheet!" he whistled.

"Do you think he told the boss?"

Simon nodded his head sadly.

"What will he do?"

"How the fuck should I know?"

"I'm sorry. I'd better go and see him."

Leaving Simon watching 3R, he headed over to the head's study without stopping to work out a strategy. He tapped timidly on his door.

"Come!" the head bellowed. His face dropped when he walked in. "Ah, Mr Woodhead. Come in, take a seat."

Matthew hadn't a notion how to begin and the headmaster didn't give him any help. After an awkward silence Matthew started falteringly: "I think there has been some sort of difficulty."

"There has," the head replied gravely.

"Simon Montgomery?"

He nodded.

"I don't know what you've been told."

Mr Wright's tone was casual but compulsive. "You tell me what you think I should know."

Matthew started by mumbling into his hand then, realising that the headmaster couldn't hear a word, he started again: "I'm sorry. Look – I have become friendly with Simon Montgomery and I socialise with him out of school." He paused to give the head space to either show his disapproval or approbation but he remained impassive. "I believe that Andrew McKnight has made some sort of accusation." Again nothing.

"Is that so?" Matthew asked.

"It is."

"About. About the nature of our…" he was going to say 'relationship' but he decided on the safer 'friendship'.

The head assented. At least Matthew had an idea of what he knew and what he didn't. He had to be strong. If he showed doubt in himself Mr Wright would doubt him.

"Did you know that I was homosexual?" he asked.

For the first time the head showed signs of emotion. His voice rose a pitch or so: "Until today I was unaware of this. In fact, until you confirmed it, it was merely a slander against you."

Matthew took his courage in his hands, heart racing, he said, "Well it's true, and I'm not ashamed of what I am. Most of the youngsters seem to know and Simon knows of course. I shouldn't need to say this but I suppose I had better, if only to put any doubt in your mind to rest. I am a teacher and I know that I have responsibilities to the youngsters I teach. It's a responsibility that I carry with me out of school. Simon and I are friends, that is all."

He felt though that more explanation was needed. "Andrew and Simon have been at odds with each other since some trouble lower down the school. Andrew was being malicious when he accused Simon of what he accused him of. He's been needling him for ages and Simon eventually snapped."

The head nodded slowly. "Thank you," he said. "You have been honest with me and I appreciate that. I'm obliged to you for coming to see me. I'm especially grateful to you for being so frank with me. I don't think I have any right to ask you to reveal such personal details but by volunteering so much, you have made things a lot easier for me." He paused and gave Matthew a reassuring smile. "It's true. The allegation has been made. I wasn't inclined to believe the boy, but his father is insisting that I investigate."

"Would it help if I was to ask Simon to talk to you?" Matthew volunteered.

"I hope it won't come to that. It depends on whether or not Mr McKnight makes an official complaint. Unfortunately he's quite prominent in the local DUP. It may suit him politically to make an issue out of this."

"But there's nothing out of which to make an issue," Matthew insisted. "I have not done anything wrong and it's not against the law to *be* homosexual."

"I'm aware of that, but you must know the way the DUP thinks."

Matthew certainly did. With their 'Save Ulster From Sodomy' campaign and their Free Presbyterian schools, they could really use him as a stick to beat Ballycol High.

"I shall do my best for you. You've made an excellent start to your teaching career and good science teachers are hard to come by. Mr McKnight is coming to see me on Wednesday. Because of your openness I can face him confident that I'm in full possession of the facts. Oh! Are you a member of a union?" he added.

"Yes," Matthew replied. "NAS."

"Good. I'm sure you won't need them but it's always useful to have a union on your side.

Actually Matthew wasn't all that sure. He had heard the general secretary of the NAS on the radio saying that he wouldn't want homosexual teachers to join his union so Matthew wasn't too confident of help from that quarter. He wandered back to his lab in a daze.

Simon was hovering just inside. "I had to let them go," he apologised weakly, "the bell went and I couldn't stop them."

"No matter," Matthew smiled. "Well. I did it."

Simon looked apprehensive; his eyes were huge and he sucked his cheeks.

"I told him everything. I told him about how Andy had been hassling you. I explained about you and me... and I told him I was gay."

"What did he say?" Simon's voice was thin with tension.

"He was fine. He thanked me for being honest and I think he said that he would stand by me."

"What do you mean – think?"

"Well, I was kinda freaked out by the whole thing and I didn't take everything in but I got the feeling that he was behind me. He said I was a good teacher and he didn't want to lose me."

The bell rang and Simon looked hunted. "Gotta go," he said, began to leave, hesitated, turned, gave Matthew a quick hug and fled.

As form four filed past him Matthew thanked his lucky stars that they hadn't seen Simon's vote of confidence. He got a few lines on the reflex arc dictated before drifting off into his own little world. What was going to happen next, he wondered as the background hubbub rose to an unruly roar. If he had kept himself to himself, Simon wouldn't be in this mess, neither would he. He wondered what would happen if McKnight pushed it. What if he used his weight to get him the sack? How would the other teachers react when they found out what had been going on? He decided that they wouldn't think much of him consorting with pupils and when they found out he was gay he was sure they would turn against him.

He was brought back by a crash as a glass beaker became victim of the mayhem that was breaking out in Lab Seven. "*Quiet*," he bawled. This was the class who had caused trouble since the first day. "Will you keep quiet!" "Arthur, Colin, John, sit down! Stop doing that, boys. If you don't sit down you will be in real trouble!" Like me, he thought.

After several minutes of yelling and threatening he regained a measure of control over the rabble and concentrated on the job in hand, struggling through to dinner-time.

Matthew wound his way through the seething corridors. The kids didn't seem to be paying undue attention to his passage although he could swear he heard a smart comment from a gaggle of sixth-formers as they brushed past him. He hesitated outside the staff room, took a deep breath and pushed the door before him. The staff acted as if there was nothing amiss. Robin greeted him: "Cheer up Matt. You look like you've lost a pound and found a penny!"

Matthew slumped next to him and tried to smile.

"Anything wrong?" he solicited.

In a low voice, Matthew filled him in with the details.

"Bastards!" Robin exclaimed when Matthew had finished.

He reddened.

"Those narrow-minded shits think they've got it sewn up," Robin went on. "Some of this lot'll be on McKnight's side, you know. The God squad won't want anything to do with you either but I would say the majority of the staff will be behind you. How dare they accuse you of screwing a pupil!"

When Matthew heard it said like that he thought it was a damned cheek. Who the hell did they think they were? "What do you think will happen?" he asked Robin.

"If the boss has any guts he won't entertain him. He should tell McKnight to mind his own bloody business but I'm afraid he won't. You know what he's like: 'Come in any time and discuss any problems with me and my staff.' Parents shouldn't be allowed past those doors."

"So what'll happen then?"

"You've not done anything wrong, have you?"

"No, of course not," Matthew affirmed.

"They can't get rid off you by any legal means. What they might try and do is make life so uncomfortable that you leave."

"What like?"

"The boss could make it tough for you. You know, shitty classes, full timetable, hassling you for detailed lesson plans and so on."

"But he said that he wanted to help me," he protested.

"I'm sure he did. But if they put pressure on him he might have no alternative. You don't know how it all works. A quiet word at the manse or the golf club. Worse still, the old dodgy handshake can work wonders."

"Surely he wouldn't be intimidated by that, would he?"

"Hard to say how sound his principles are. He probably would like to think he'd back you up, but if they started to put the pressure on, he might cave in."

"Cave in?"

"Aye. Be realistic. He has to live in this community. He runs the school so smoothly because he keeps the parents happy. When you think of it, it's remarkable just how much the parents do support us. Anything he wants, he just sends a wee letter out and donations come flooding in. Haven't you ever wondered why there's no bother in this school? Any kid puts a foot wrong and the parents are brought in and they make damn sure it doesn't happen again. He's not going to sacrifice all that for a principle! He could cope with a few awkward parents kicking up a fuss but if they really got the bit between their teeth and got the majority over to their side, he'd be on a hiding to nothing. Imagine, if he couldn't even get the management committee to back him on anything, he couldn't run the school."

Matthew felt sick at the thought. Robin tried to reassure him: "Come on, Matt. We won't let them get away with it. Have you told Julian yet?"

He shook his head, "I've not told anyone."

"We'd better get your version known before the gossip starts. Come on, let's get started."

Surprisingly, everyone to whom he told his story was with him all the way. He got the reassuring feeling that all the staff were on his side. Julian was the only possible exception. "You should have been more careful, young feller." His accent was so soft and artless that he almost missed the tone of his message. "I would have thought you had common sense enough to realise. Knowing you're a homo, they'll suspect your friendship with the children. I'm surprised they don't warn you about that sort of thing at yon college! It's usually the young men and the sixth-form girls, right enough, but in this day and age anything goes, I suppose. Ah well, you'll learn by your mistakes. You'll know not to go gallivanting with the youngsters in future, won't you?"

Matthew didn't exactly go home happy that afternoon but he was marginally reassured. Once home, he had time to brood. What if the head did have trouble from the hardliners? Even if the union did help they would hear at home. He couldn't face his parents; they would be devastated.

Being Friday, he would normally have been buzzing about the flat in preparation for the forthcoming evening's merry-making but that night found him slumped in front of the telly. He hadn't the nerve to face anyone. He wasn't concentrating on the programme; he desperately needed Simon to comfort him but was at the same time afraid of him coming.

When the bell rang, he jumped at its clatter. Heart thumping, he went to let Simon in. He wasn't alone. Behind him was a veritable posse including Julie, Mark and sundry other members of forms six and upper sixth.

"Is it alright if we come in?" Simon asked cautiously.

"Yeah. Sure. Come on up," he said, somewhat taken aback.

The whole contingent trooped to his living room. They stood around listlessly. Big as it was, it felt overcrowded, an impression reinforced by their unwillingness to sit down.

He hesitated to offer them coffee; after all, he only had a limited number of cups.

"All off out somewhere?" he asked awkwardly.

"They turned up at the house," Simon explained. "They wanted to come and talk to you, so here they are."

"What about?"

"Better let them tell you."

Mark was ill at ease. He was shifting from foot to foot, eyes darting between Simon and Matthew. "We thought we'd better come, like."

Julie leapt in. "Aye sir, we know what happened. It's a sin, that's what it is, sir. It's not right."

Matthew cringed. How had they the audacity to come into his home to insult him like this? And with Simon there too. He wasn't going to let them intimidate him, he would come out fighting. "I'm sorry you think like that, Julie, I don't happen to agree with you," he said, his voice hardening. "It happens to be my private business and I don't need comment from you lot, thank you very much."

They all looked uncomfortable. Julie was flustered. "We only wanted to help sir."

"We didn't mean to annoy you."

"Come on," Susie pleaded to the ragged bunch, "We'd better go. Come on."

Simon cut through them all. "Matt, you idiot. They're on our side. It's not *you* Julie meant, it's McKnight!"

Matthew flushed. "Yeah, yeah. Sorry, sorry, sorry." He collapsed into a chair shaking his head. "I should have known. I'm not really with it, you know. It's been a rough day."

"It's OK, sir," Julie reassured him. "It must've been chronic. I bet you're still dead mad, aren't you, sir?"

"You could say that! To be honest I still can't quite believe this is all happening to me. Little did I think, this morning, when I went in, that my sexuality would become public knowledge. And I didn't imagine that I would be having deputations of supportive pupils in my flat."

"Is it true that the boss threatened you with the sack?" Mark asked tentatively.

"No. How did you get that idea?"

"Andy said his dad was going to get rid of you. He said he would tell the boss he had to, like."

Matthew looked askance at him, "And how do you think he could force the headmaster to get rid of me?"

Some quality in his voice alerted Mark, he replied cautiously. "He didn't actually say. His old feller's a real hardliner, like. Black Preceptory and all that. You can't argue with the likes of them. They go on as if they've a hot line to God."

Matthew sniggered nervously.

"Don't laugh," Mark cautioned, "more'n you think go along with them you know. Most don't let on they listen but they do. Look at me old doll. She's dead on most of the time, like, but when Paisley starts you'd think she was Grand Master of the Orange Lodge."

"I know what you mean but not everyone's like that. If it comes down to a fight there's actually nothing they can do. The only way to get rid of a teacher is if he's actually broken the law or if he's been what they call unprofessional. They might not like me being openly gay but it's not against the law."

"Could they get you on the unprofessional bit?" Julie asked.

"No. Being unprofessional is things like having an affair with a pupil or using your position in some other corrupt way. I'm sure they know damn well that Simon and I aren't lovers and I can't be called unprofessional for telling the truth to you lot in class."

"Well if they try we'll go on strike!" said Julie, jutting her chin out defiantly.

Matthew smiled broadly. "That's very sweet of you but I don't think it'll come to that. It's all a storm in a teacup, you wait and see."

He was so convincing that he almost believed it himself. He had right on his side and for the very first time in his life he was discovering that most ordinary people didn't object to him just because he happened to be gay. A long discussion culminated in a massive vote of confidence from them and they all went down to Micky's to celebrate. He was their cause célèbre.

On Monday, he went into school with his heart in his mouth. By then everyone would know about it. How would the youngsters react to him at school? How about the staff?

If he expected to cause a stir as he walked through the doors, he was disappointed. The only comments were a quick word of sympathy from Mrs Hammond, and Robin asking him if there had been any developments. He decided to keep quite about the threatened industrial action by the sixth form. Geoff was strangely reserved; Matthew guessed he was wondering about the night they slept together. Let him wonder, the bastard, he thought.

At lunchtime he was somewhat surprised to see Alistair hovering at the door into his lab.

"What can I do for you?" he cheerily asked.

"I thought that I might do something for you actually," he said cautiously, almost whispering.

"Yes?" Matthew answered, slowly.

"Once, when I was in trouble, you came to me. I suppose I'm returning the gesture."

Matthew didn't say anything but smiled at Alistair in his most encouraging way.

"I thought, perhaps," he was hesitating over every word as if it was an effort to get each one to leave his tongue, "it would help if you could talk to someone." He paused: "Someone who – well – who had been through the same thing."

Matthew did one of his internalised laughs, more of a stifled exhalation really. Alistair was referring to the time when they were pupils and his friend John had committed suicide. Then, half closing his eyes and shaking his head, Matthew replied as kindly as he could: "That's very kind, Alistair. But you know the situation is rather different. In your case the rumour was unfounded." He hesitated, noticing the odd expression on Alistair's face, then guessing that he had taken it the wrong way, he clarified his statement quickly, "You weren't actually gay; I am. And what is more Alistair, I'm not afraid to say that."

He looked at Alistair calmly taking in what he had said. Matthew was sure it would freak him out but he didn't care.

"I can't say I understand you. I don't know anything about homosexuality, other than what I see in the Bible and that isn't a lot. But I believe that you must discover what is right for you." He paused as if to judge the wisdom of the next statement. He proceeded slowly, picking his words. "For me the answer is in Jesus Christ, I know that he has the answer for you too but you have to find him yourself."

Matthew shifted uneasily. All this Jesus crap always made him feel distinctly uncomfortable. It was almost as if he was afraid that somehow he would become infected by it. Saved Christians were so convinced that they were right but he was sure that it was they who were fooling themselves. God was a figment of imaginations which couldn't cope with the brutal fact of the insignificance and mortality of humanity. Despite that he was afraid that one day he would weaken his resolve and be brainwashed into accepting their absurd proposition. Once ensnared he would never get away; never be a free man. He had spent the first twenty-odd years of his life being dictated to by heterosexuals who had no concept that their neat and tidy rules and regulations for a happy life did not apply to him; he wasn't about to let the Christians do the same. Alistair really did seem to want to help, but Matthew wasn't going to let him use this as an excuse to get him hooked on God.

"You know me of old, Alistair – ever the atheist."

"I know that, Matthew. But you are a human being in whom God works, even if you don't know it."

"I thought you once told me that sodomy was an abomination," he challenged.

"I probably did. I had a very simplistic view of life when I was at school. You're not going to hold that against me, are you?"

"Of course not. I am a bit surprised though. I expected you to be breathing hell-fire and damnation at me. That seems to be the Christian attitude to gays."

"Why do you think that? Not because of what I said all those years ago, surely?"

"No, not really. Your man McKnight's a Paisleyite and it's him that's causing all the aggro. Remember Aaron Lindsay?"

"Yes, what about him?"

"He's got heavily into all that too. He doesn't know about me but I got a real sickening from him on morality and teachers. He even tried to get me to help that bloody 'Save Ulster From Sodomy' campaign! They really hate us you know, I think they'd like to see us burn at the stake. Did you know they used to do that? The reason we are called faggots is because they used to burn us. You know, like faggots of wood!"

"Matthew, I hope you aren't confusing the doctrine of Ian Paisley with Christianity."

"They seem to think they're Christians."

"They use the Bible to further their own interests. They select the parts which suit their ends and ignore the bits they don't like. If they were real Christians they would not be preaching hatred for Roman Catholicism. You only need to read the parable of the good Samaritan to know that Christ wouldn't recognise them as true followers."

"I am amazed! We actually agree on something. You don't mind Catholics then?"

"Of course not! The Church of Rome is a corrupt organisation but there are many Catholics who are better Christians than the majority of so-called Protestants. Christianity is a relationship between the individual and Jesus; it's not belonging to this or that church."

"But you can understand why I don't trust Christians, can't you? Did you know that the European Commission of Human Rights heard the case on homosexual law reform here, last year?" he asked.

"No."

"Well they did. And the British government's main evidence for retaining the old law was Paisley's 'Save Ulster From Sodomy' campaign and a letter from Cardinal O'Fiaich. It's ironic, isn't it? The two leading opponents in Ulster's sectarian mess, combining with the government they hate to persecute gays!"

"I can understand why you're wary of some who call themselves Christians," he conceded. "I have been shocked by some of the un-Christian views I've heard in the staff room."

"Yeah. It's great just how much support I've had from the staff," Matthew grinned.

Alistair looked serious. "You don't understand, Matthew. They've been vicious in their criticism of you. Most of them seem to think you've been corrupting the children and you should be sacked – imprisoned even!"

Matthew's mouth dried up. He hadn't heard a single hostile word yet here was Alistair telling him that his colleagues were opposed to him; what an object lesson in hypocrisy! "Who was saying these things then?" he wanted to know.

"I can't say, it wouldn't be fair to reveal that. Just bear in mind that there are a lot who would like to see you out, men and women. Robin Young was the only one I heard standing up for you. Oh, and Mary Moore. She said that they had no right to pass judgment until they knew the facts."

"What do *you* think about gays then?"

"I don't know why God makes someone homosexual but there is a reason. It may be that, through Jesus, a homosexual would cease to be one."

"A leopard can't change its spots you know, Alistair," he objected querulously. "You're either gay or you're not."

"Anything is possible through Jesus," he insisted. "I don't know what Jesus wants of gay people, that's between him and the gay person and it's not my place to comment. All I know is this. When we were at school and I was in great distress, it was you, the one homosexual, and not any of the dozens of heterosexuals, who sought me out to give me comfort. I wish I had known then that you were homosexual. I might have found it easier to talk about what had happened."

Matthew was intrigued, he was dying to know what had happened all those years ago at school but he wasn't sure if this was the time or place to ask. Bugger it, he would risk it. "What did happen?"

"I'm sorry Matthew, I don't know if I can talk about it. It's been on my mind ever since. If I had behaved differently, he might be alive today."

"You can't blame yourself."

"I do though. You see, John was homosexual; I think he was anyway. He told me that he loved me." Alistair faltered.

"Don't if you don't want to," Matthew said.

"I've started so I'll finished," he smiled wryly.

Matthew returned the expression.

"You know we used to get tormented at school – your friends

weren't the worst. It was incessant, humiliating. I shrugged it off. I told myself that they were working for the devil, trying to shake me from my faith. I think I got a kick out of feeling like a martyr."

"Pretty weird!"

"I suppose so. At the time it felt good – me and God against the rest. And then John started. I didn't notice at first. He wanted to be with me all the time. I took it that our faith was the common bond. We became close, really close, and he would be physically close. I still didn't see what was happening. Then he told me." Alistair's eyes were full of pain. "I rejected him. I told him that the devil was twisting his mind. I told him that he had to pray, to get closer to God. He did get closer."

"I'm sorry," Matthew said after a tactful pause. "Truly I am. It wasn't your fault though. It wouldn't have happened if people behaved in a civilised manner. You were both victims of this fucking society."

"No. It's me who should be apologising to you. I came up here thinking I was going to help you and you've turned the tables. What a pathetic case I am. You're in trouble and I unburden my hang-ups on you."

"Don't worry about it, Al. I'm OK actually. I'm confident that these bastards aren't going to get their way. I'm glad you felt you could tell me. That's the greatest honour you could have paid me. Hey! aren't you hungry? If we don't hurry we won't get any lunch." At that they went over to the dining hall and Matthew wasn't in the least bit ashamed to be seen with Alistair.

27: Mary's Sagacity

Matthew was apprehensive about the outcome of Wednesday's meeting. He was teaching until twelve-twenty but Mr McKnight was due to meet the headmaster at eleven. His class knew what was on his mind and urged him to go over to find out what had happened but it was as if to give in to the urge would be to admit that McKnight had him on the run. On the first zing of the bell he shot out, leaving sixth lower to sort themselves out.

In the office, Mary was in conversation with Mrs Hammond. They stopped the moment he walked in, Mary smiled at him and Mrs H. busied herself with some papers.

"Is the headmaster free?" he gasped.

"I'm sorry, dear. He's gone out."

Matthew's voice rose a pitch: "When's he due back?"

"I'm sure I don't know, dear," she said sympathetically. "He didn't say. He shouldn't be long though. He's seeing the Reverend Hamilton at two."

"Will you tell me when he comes back? I'll be in the staff room."

Two minutes later Mary joined him. "I've been in with Mrs Hammond," she smirked.

"So?"

"She can hear everything that goes on in his office. If she *accidentally* leaves the intercom on."

"Ah!"

"Yes," she smiled.

"Go on."

"I just happened to drift in when I saw McKnight go in – she'd forgotten."

A smile fleeted across his frowning face and Mary gave him a hug. "I think it's going to be alright," she reassured him.

He could hardly hold his impatience. "What did you hear?"

She settled down in the comfiest chair in the staffroom and the story unfolded. "The head was impressively formal," she explained. "His stuffy best. 'Mr McKnight,' he said, 'you have made a very serious allegation about a member of my teaching staff. I have made my own enquiries and I am satisfied that it is unfounded.' Then there was an amazing silence. I could imagine him towering over McKnight from his chair – you know, like he does with the kids. After what seemed like an age, he went on, 'However, if you wish to proceed with the complaint your next step would be to make an official submission to the Western Education and Library Board headquarters. If you do that, it will be thoroughly investigated and they will take the appropriate action. I must also warn you that if there is no foundation for your claim, Mr Woodhead's union is likely to advise him to take you to court for slander. Do you understand what I am saying, Mr McKnight? If you intend to proceed I would strongly advise you to seek legal advice.'"

Matthew was stunned. "Phew! What did he say to that?"

"He rambled aimlessly for a bit, then said, 'That man is a sodomite, there's no denying that. I could prove that in court.' The headmaster was really calm, he said, 'Mr Woodhead does not dispute the fact that he is a homosexual.' McKnight nearly had apoplexy! He said, 'Are you telling me that you knew that, that man was a sodomite!' He shouted 'sodomite' like Paisley does, and then he said, 'And you still let him near our children? It's a disgrace! Perverts like that should never be allowed near children. It's a miracle he hasn't corrupted more young minds. You should be ashamed of....' The boss interrupted him and said, 'Mr McKnight!

May I remind you that Mr Woodhead is a trained teacher and as such I have every confidence in his professionalism. I would also remind you that it is neither illegal to be homosexual nor is homosexuality a bar to being a member of the teaching profession.' McKnight blustered incoherently then spat out, 'Wright, you are a disgrace to yourself. A disgrace to Ulster! How dare you sit there and defend that disgusting pervert! Christian, you call yourself! You shame us. You will regret this, mark my words. You haven't heard the last of this.' Then he stormed out slamming the boss's door so hard I thought the ceiling was coming down."

After school, Matthew invited Mary to his flat. It was her first time there and she was impressed by Matthew's little refuge. She told him it was a human room and that it expressed his personality; too many people furnished their homes as they thought people would expect them to. He was surprised to find himself being complimented. He had imagined that, as a home economics teacher, her standards of house pride would be far above his.

He made coffee as Mary browsed through his books. By the time he got back she had reached his meagre selection of gay titles which had started with *Maurice*. She was leafing through *The Front Runner*. "Is this any good?" she asked casually.

"I enjoyed it," he replied, wondering what she would think of the sex scenes between the athlete and his trainer.

"Can I borrow it?"

"Sure, no problem."

"I've never read a gay novel. Big gap in my education," she smiled.

"I hadn't read one until a few years ago," he admitted.

"Where do you buy them?"

"Well, there's Bookworm in Derry but I get most of mine by mail order from *Gay News*."

"This it?" she asked, picking up the latest copy from the table and leafing through its pages. "You're not the only one that gets hassle, I see."

Indeed she was right. Every fortnight there were stories of how gay people were being victimised the length and breadth of Britain.

"Even the bugs seem to be against you!"

"What's that?" he asked.

"It says here that doctors in New York are concerned at a new disease which seems to be singling out homosexuals," she paraphrased.

"Aye, but it's only in America. As far as I can see they're sex maniacs. They've probably caught the clap once too often. Serves 'em right," he joked.

"That's not very nice," she reprimanded. "From what I see here, they get pretty ill and die. You can't make statements like that then complain when people do it to you. Can you now?" she finished gently.

Matthew suddenly felt like a naughty little boy. "It's hard to be charitable," he complained. "I always feel that I'm about to be attacked."

Before he knew it he was telling her his life story. She took it all in, occasionally affirming what he said and drawing him out with little nods and 'mmm, mmm's'.

He learned more about her too. About the time they started teaching, a women's refuge had opened in the town. From this nucleus, a small, but enthusiastic women's group had grown and Mary had been an early recruit. She detested the chauvinism of the men in the school staff room and despised the two-faced backbiting of some of the women. She knew that her views would alienate her colleagues so she reserved them for the women's group; in that respect she was far wiser than Matthew. He was worried about how Mary would take his friendship with the pupils but it turned out that she had her own coterie of girls at school who quietly shared her attitudes to life. As Mary and he grew closer, her pupil friends and his intermingled with a minimum of difficulties.

Simon entertained Matthew, he even comforted him to some degree and yet he couldn't be the rock Matthew needed. From the very start Mary treated him as as a fully valid human being. Never once did she quiz him and yet, when he needed to talk, she was there to bend an uncritical ear.

There were two prevailing attitudes to Matthew in the staff room. Robin typified the first, furious that McKnight should have the temerity to attack one of his colleagues but preferring to ignore Matthew's sexuality; it was a label, a concept, and he never considered the implications for Matthew's lifestyle. The second, and most common, reaction was a tacit refusal to acknowledge the situation. This Matthew interpreted as disapproval.

Had Mary not told him what she did he would have got the impression that the head was on McKnight's side. He got a lecture about the dangers of fraternising with the pupils and a warning to be more careful in the future. He was told that the people of Fermanagh were inherently conservative, asked to consider the local mores, and it was pointed out that if he hoped to get on in Ballycol he mustn't rock the boat. Full of righteous indignation, Matthew described the Head's attitudes to Alex who nodded his agreement with them: "Told you so, didn't I?" he reminded Matt. He hated Alex for being such a prig and he made it worse by talking about Sandra more than necessary. It was with a strangely sinking feeling that Matthew realised he was relieved to see Alex go.

Matthew was nervous next time Alex called on him but by the time they were in the Red Hand, Alex had chipped away at his discomfort with his easy charm. They sat and chortled the evening away and Alex was ready to go before Matthew could so much as hint at a deep conversation. Despite Matthew's protestations that he was too drunk to drive, Alex insisted on going home. Matthew took his courage in his hands and kissed Alex firmly on the lips.

He shook his head and said, "No Matt... I've told you," then bade him a sad goodnight and left.

Matthew comforted himself with the thought that he had prepared the ground for later.

28: Danny Revisited

Matt spent July in Kendal and took a saver return to London. Lisa welcomed him with open arms, tut-tutting and laughing at all the appropriate junctures in the story of his first two years in teaching. He asked about Danny but she'd seen neither hide nor hair of him for eighteen months or more. She didn't know where he was living but suggested contacting him at his work. That's how he ended up waiting at the reception of Xenos Pharmaceuticals. His heart raced in anticipation at seeing his old buddy again; it had been two years, far too long for such close friends to be out of contact.

He knew Danny would have changed but he hadn't expected a woman to greet him. "You're looking for Mr McDaid?" she asked cautiously.

"Aye, where is he?"

"Who *are* you?" she asked suspiciously.

"I'm Matt, his friend from Derry. We were at school and university together," he said, more cheerily than he felt.

On hearing this account of himself, her face cleared then she frowned.

Matt picked up the vibes. "Is something wrong?"

"Probably not," she tried to reassure him.

She looked into his eyes and detected his genuine concern: "He's not been in for three days. We've been covering for him."

"Is he ill?"

She smiled bleakly. "By now, very likely."

"I'm sorry. I don't understand."

"How well *do* you know him? *Really* know him?"

"I was his best mate. It's only since he came to London we lost contact."

"You know he drinks?" she asked carefully.

"Course. Had many a night on the tear. Why?"

"Perhaps I shouldn't be saying this..." She looked hunted. "He disappears. Sometimes for days on end – goes on a binge. It's been happening more recently. He's putting his job in jeopardy."

A pit yawned in Matt's stomach and his face blanched. The woman looked worried. "I shouldn't have told you."

Matt reassured her. "No, no. I'm glad you did. How can I find him?"

"You can't. We've tried going to his digs but he's never there. We just have to hope he makes it back into work before the management starts asking awkward questions."

They left it that Danny should ring Matt when he got back to work. Matt gave Vicky Lisa's number and hoped she wouldn't mind. He also gave his uncle's number in Kendal and his address in Ballycol for good measure.

Danny hadn't phoned by the time he was due to go back up north. He tried ringing him at work but Vicky told him that he hadn't turned up and that he was really in trouble this time.

The following Monday Matt was reading in the garden at Birkholm when his aunt called him to the phone.

The distant voice said, "Matthew? This is Vicky here. He's back, I'll get him to the phone."

There was some background noise then the receiver was lifted. "Hello?" Danny grunted. He was taken by surprise at hearing Matt's voice. "How are you mate?" he cheered.

"Where the hell have you been?" Matt queried. "I've been trying to contact you for over a year."

"Sorry mate, been really busy – you know me."

"Aye, but you could have written or something. I've been really worried."

The conversation went on in a similar vein culminating in Danny promising faithfully to go to Birkholm for the weekend. He would arrive on the first train that left Euston after work that Friday.

In the glorious afternoon sun, Matt strolled into Kendal to check the train times. On Tuesday he rang Danny, and eleven-fifteen p.m. the following Friday found Matt standing at Oxenholme station. The powerful electric locomotive glided precisely into the station and the train disgorged its passengers. Matt peered through the throng for the familiar shock of red hair. He'd just about given up when he saw a familiar form humping a rucksack onto his back. As he started towards him, words of fraternal greetings on the tip of his tongue, he vaguely wondered why he should have brought so much for a weekend. The red-head turned and looked right past Matt – at a female. It wasn't Danny.

"He must have missed the train," Matt explained to his concerned aunt.

"It's funny he didn't ring then."

"Yes," he said pointedly. "It is."

Matt received a letter from Vicky in August. Danny had lost his job. She didn't fill in too many details but assured Matt that Xenos had given him every chance. They had even offered to keep his job for him if he would agree to seek professional advice but at that suggestion he had raged and resigned. She didn't know what he would do next but guessed that he might go home for a while.

Matt finally tracked Danny down at his mother's house in Rosemount. His friend was still in bed despite it being two o'clock in the afternoon so Matt had to wait in the parlour whilst Mrs McDaid went to rouse him. The dishevelled apparition that appeared shocked Matt. For a start, he looked so old. His hair had grown again but it was no longer the vibrant, coppery mop of Lancaster days. Straggly, limp hanks hung over his blotchy skin and his pale blue eyes lacked the brilliance which had once mesmerised Matt. He looked podgy and unfit.

Danny looked at him guiltily. "Sorry I didn't make it up to Kendal. Something came up."

"You could at least have rung."

"I'm sorry, really, but I couldn't." His face creased into an ingratiating smile. "I knew me old mate would understand."

Matt hadn't intended a confrontation but this was shaping into one and he didn't feel like having it in Danny's mother's house.

"Come on," he said. "Let's go somewhere where we can talk."

They drove up to Greenan fort. He didn't know what made him choose that spot but it was exactly right. The reconstructed ring fort was perched on a hill-top overlooking the village of Bridgend. In ancient times, the local farmers would have driven their stock there for protection. The massive, ten-foot high, circular wall was battered by a cold Atlantic wind on even the balmiest day. They parked the Landrover and walked towards the slit-like opening into the enclosure.

Atop the walls they surveyed Inch Island and Lough Swilly

set out before them like a splendid relief map.

"Well?" Danny said after a prolonged silence, "what do you want to talk about?"

Matt examined Danny's bleary face and frowned. "You. Me. Us."

Danny was guarded. "Aye?"

"I feel let down."

"You're not the only one," Danny lamented, "I keep letting myself down too."

"Why do you do it?"

"I don't know, Matty. I just can't help it. I never mean to but, then when it comes to the crunch, I just can't come up with the goods."

"Don't you care about people? The ones you let down?"

"Course I do."

"It doesn't look like it to me. If you cared about me you would have written or something. And you wouldn't have left me standing at Oxenholme station like a prick."

"If you're going to get like that you may as well stop now," Danny growled and started down the steps. Matt followed him as quickly as he could without loosing his footing on the steep descent. Danny hadn't been as careful and was halfway across the enclosure before Matt reached terra firma. He ran after him and grabbed his retreating arm. Danny shook him off but Matt stepped in front of him blocking his escape. He was twice Matt's size and he towered over him. For one dreadful moment Danny looked as if he was going to thump him but he suddenly relaxed and hugged him. "Shit," the big man muttered.

"I'd forgotten anyone cared," he said when they had got back in the Landrover.

"I do. That's why it freaks me to see you like this. It isn't *you*."

Danny stared vacantly through the windscreen. "Maybe it is. Perhaps I've changed."

"No way. You're just a bit low, that's all. Everyone behaves oddly sometimes."

"It's being at me ma's. It drives me spare sometimes."

Matt fell for the line. "Why not come up to Ballycol for a few days?" he suggested. "You can relax and we can get ourselves sorted out."

They arranged to go up to Ballycol for a few days the week before term started. Matt's father even loaned him the Landrover. Danny was at his most charming, although his capacity to drink astonished Matt. Matt was keen to get some hill-walking in but they never seemed to get their act together. Some days they got over to a beach in Donegal and then at night they would head out to the pub – usually to Micky's. After the pub, alone, with Simon or with some of the others, they would head back to Matt's flat to talk the night away. Many a night Matt staggered to his bed at five or six in the morning leaving Danny still supping away on the great sofa chatting to Matt's friends or listening to the stereo alone.

When it came time to take the Landrover back, Danny didn't want to go home: "Is it OK if I stay for another couple of days?"

"Course," Matt smiled with a slight strain. "Great!"

It was all very well sessioning during the holidays but Danny wanted it to go on for ever. At first Matt tried to keep up with him, going to Micky's and then sitting up for a couple of hours drinking before collapsing into his bed. Next morning he would drag himself up at eight to find Danny slumped on the couch instead of on the mattress he'd made up for him in his room. He hated that. The living room stank of stale beer and cigarette smoke and he couldn't sit and listen to 'Today' on Radio Four over his breakfast. Danny's continued presence was becoming increasingly frustrating too. Matt quickly realised that he was still infatuated with Danny. He knew Danny said he wasn't interested in the same way, but he couldn't help thinking how Alex had said he hadn't been either. The longer Danny stayed, the more he featured in Matt's romantic fantasies and the guiltier Matt felt.

The crunch came when he got home from school one afternoon to find Danny well on his way. He was at the stage where he had mellowed enough to be chummy without being so sloshed as to be inactive. He greeted Matt with a large gin and tonic and invited him to join him on the sofa to drink it. His mind was firmly back in college days and he recalled their relationship as having been far more intimate than it ever was in reality. He reminded Matt of the times they slept together 'like brothers' but Matt could only recall sharing a bed with Danny once and that had been pretty harrowing! The gin was making Danny inordinately cosy and affectionate and Matt began to wonder if he was trying to make a pass, albeit very clumsily. Just as the situation was getting interesting, Simon turned up. Matt was appalled when he found himself trying to get Simon out of the way so he could have Danny to himself again but Simon had just had confirmation of his place at university and wanted a good long jaw with Matt. As they became more engrossed in their conversation Danny withdrew, drank more and gradually faded. Finally he grunted a farewell and disappeared unsteadily into the bedroom.

Once Simon had gone Matt went into his room to find that Danny had got as far as getting his jeans off before conking out on Matt's bed. Determined that Danny wasn't going annex his bed, Matt tried to wake him. He shook his face shouting his name but he didn't budge. The feel of Danny's warm skin and stubble awakened Matt's desires. He looked at the inert man on his duvet and recalled the beautiful, vibrant youth that he had been. He kissed Danny's cheek in remembrance of what he used to be and his head lolled back. As Matt watched, a slow smile spread across Danny's lips. He put his lips to Danny's and felt them move invitingly. Not only was Danny not resisting; but he was responding and his tongue gently penetrated Matt's mouth. Otherwise he was unnaturally still.

Matt drew back and looked at his inert friend. He tried to work out what he was up to; just how drunk was he? Was this a come-on or was it simply a drunken reflex? He would try kissing him again, just to see what would happen. This time there were a few positive signals – a slight shift of his body into a more receptive posture, a murmur of pleasure and a reluctance to let his lips free. Matt expected Danny to do something in response; something to encourage or discourage him but he remained passive.

Had Matt been coldly rational he would never have gone so far, but gin and testosterone were too powerful a combination and the bulge in Danny's underpants was beginning to grow.

"Are you awake Danny?" Matt asked.

There was no reply.

Matt pulled the duvet from under him and covered his body – still he didn't stir.

He undressed and climbed in next to his comatose friend. There wasn't much room as Danny had collapsed dead centre of the bed.

"Shift over will you," Matt grumbled, pushing the dead-weight across the bed. The advantage was short-lived because Danny rolled onto his side and occupied the centre again.

Now his hand was resting on Matt's hip – no, not resting – creeping into his jockeys! Matt's heart raced.

He tried kissing him again and Danny slumped closer and gripped Matt's buttock.

As they kissed, Matt unbuttoned Danny's shirt and explored the tight skin and coarse hair on his chest. Gaining confidence, his hand ventured lower and lower, eventually delving into Danny's briefs. His fingers explored the warm, tangle of Danny's pubic area, damp as a tropical jungle. When he connected with the heavy, hardly-flaccid target, Danny shifted a little, settling more comfortably. Not too carefully, Matt undressed the submissive man. There could be no doubt now that Danny was awake but he neither co-operated with nor obstructed Matt's efforts.

Other than when they kissed, Danny was almost totally pas-sive, although he would let out the occasional gasp when Matt hit a particularly erogenous spot. Matt worked him like a sex toy get-ting more and more excited himself. All along he had wished Danny would do something and this he finally did, gripping Matt's but-tocks and rolling on his back, pulling Matt on top of him and forcing their groins together as Matt's body spasmed in pleasure.

When Matt awoke he was lying on top of Danny, pinioned to his body by his huge arm. The duvet had slipped off and there was a slippery film between them. He pulled the duvet over them and snuggled into him, his cheek revelling in the pillow of hair on Danny's chest. He drifted back to sleep anticipating many more blissful nights with his new lover.

Danny didn't move when Matt slid from under his arm at eight. He still hadn't stirred by the time Matt left for school. Drunk as Danny had been, Matt was sure that he was fully aware of what they had done.

His mind wasn't on his work that day, turning the night over in his mind. It was almost as if he had relived that distant night at university but this time, with Danny vulnerable with drink, he had made it go the way he would have liked all those years ago. As he realised this a feeling of dread filled his heart; what the hell had he done? How would Danny take being used like that? He wasn't quite sure what to expect when he got home from school but he needn't have worried; Danny went on as if nothing had happened.

One week passed, then two. Two stretched to three and on to four, all without another such night. Matt's pleasure at having Danny around waned to irritation flecked with guilt. He would prepare a meal expecting Danny to be in for it and when he finally rolled in he would eat it greedily without a word of apology. If he remonstrated, Danny's usual line was to try reasoning with him, but if that didn't work he got churlish and would not say anything for hours. Matt wanted him to leave but if he asked him to go it might seem like he was throwing him out for not sleeping with him again.

Danny had come back with two total strangers at about half past one in the morning. Hearing a noise in the sitting room, Matt got up to see what was going on. Danny grinned at him. "You don't mind if I bring a couple of friends up for a drink, do you?"

"Actually I do, yes," Matt said crossly. "I'm trying to get

some sleep. Some people have to work tomorrow, you know," with heavily laboured sarcasm.

"Och! Matty me old mate," Danny said as he clutched Matt to him. "All them nights we had together at Lancaster. You never minded sessioning till all hours of the morning then, work next day or not. Come on, have a little drink with us."

The other two men, who had been looking a little dubious up till then, joined in. "Do you like wine?" one of them said. Matt's instinct was to say no but he was rather attractive so Matt decided to have a glass.... to be polite, he told himself.

Feargal had an impish face and a mop of curly gingery-blond hair. He had a huge, infectious grin and a gravely voice which was totally incongruous with such a youthful face. He turned out to be an artist and he engaged Matt in conversation about his time at art college. Matt didn't usually enjoy heterosexuals talking about their sexual exploits but Feargal drew him into his world and, before he noticed, he was genuinely caring about his triumphs and disasters. Somehow it wasn't Feargal as a man talking about his conquests of women but Feargal as a person talking about his relationships with people who happened to be female. Other than the gender thing, there seemed few differences between his experiences and Matt's own!

After a genuinely fascinating hour Matt apologised that he had to crash and Feargal made to leave. Danny would hear none of it so Matt went to bed, leaving the party going on next door. It took him ages to get to sleep and they were all still in his living rom when he got up the next morning.

At school Mary noticed how exhausted Matt was and collared him. "What's wrong, Matt?"

"Bit of a night last night, that's all."

"Danny again?"

He nodded.

"Are you sure you're in control there?"

"No, I'm not. But I don't know how to take control."

"What is it that's keeping him here?"

"He likes it."

"It... or you?"

"Me, I think."

She peered into his eyes. "Do you?"

"I don't know."

"How can you find out?" she asked pertinently.

He nodded.

"That's a boy," she confirmed. "Go for it Matthew. It won't be easy but it'll be best for both of you in the long run." She smiled encouragingly. "If you need a bit of moral support, you know where to find me."

"It's talking time," Matt said, shaking Danny as he got in from school.

"Not now," he pleaded, clutching his head.

"Now," Matt insisted.

Danny went into one of his silent sulks. Matt couldn't even be sure if he was hearing him.

"As long as I have known you I have loved you," Matt started.

Danny didn't react at all.

"You know I wouldn't do a thing against you. I asked you here because I wanted to be with *you*. But that's not what I've got! I've got a hybrid between you and alcohol and I don't like it."

He still didn't seem to hear.

Matt kneeled by his bed, staring into Danny's face.

"Do you hear? *I love you.* But I don't like what you become with drink."

He didn't flinch.

He tried again: *"I love you, Daniel."* Then he leaned forward, grabbed Danny's face and kissed him hard on the lips.

Danny still didn't move but a silent tear trickled down his cheek.

Next day, when Matt got home from school, Danny had gone.

"It's just possible," Mary insisted, "that you made him realise what he's doing to himself; and to the people who love him. It may be what he needs to make him snap out of it."

"*Can* you snap out of alcoholism?" Matt asked mournfully.

"I don't think it's as simple as that. The first hurdle is to accept that there's something wrong and I doubt that Danny has; look at the way he surrounds himself with other boozers. He tried to draw you in and when that didn't work, he began to go cut you out. Look how he hurt you were when he went off drinking without you."

"Did it show that much?"

She nodded.

Matt thought of all the times Danny had let him down. "It's funny. I've known him nearly all my life and he's always been the most unreliable person imaginable. When he's with you, you're the most important person in the world but once you're out of sight, you're out of mind. I suppose people would say he's always used me but I don't believe that's true. In his own way he thinks a hell of a lot of me but he can't bear to feel pinned down in any way." He looked at Mary dolefully, "It does make being his friend hard!"

"Anyone else would have given up on him years ago. Possibly he knows that; it might just save him."

"I hope it's not too late," Matt sighed.

"No. You got through to him. He might wise up enough to do something for himself."

"He needs help though; support. Maybe I should go up to Derry and see if I can help him."

"And have a re-run of September? No, he's got to stand up for himself if he's to survive."

Survive! what a final word, Matt thought, but he knew she was right.

29: Turmoil

Spring 1981 saw the hunger strike of Republican prisoners in the Maze prison and feelings were running high. In school the prevailing attitude was, let the bastards die. In Micky's they were brave lads suffering for their country's freedom. Bobby Sands, Matt's MP, died on Tuesday the fifth of May. Everyone was expecting it. The Catholic clergy had asked for calm when he died and Ian Paisley said that the day Sands was buried, he would hold a memorial service for all the innocent victims of terrorism. In Belfast and Derry there were spontaneous Nationalist demonstrations with whistle blowing and bin-lid banging but Ballycol remained unnaturally quiet; the town seemed to be holding its breath in anticipation.

The quiet was illusory. When he got to school on the Wednesday morning the caretaker was scrubbing the front of the building. Thirteen windows had been smashed and someone had scrawled "H BLOCK" in excrement on the wall.

The staff room was buzzing. The previous night a van had been hijacked and burnt on the Pettigo road and there had been rioting in the Apostles. An instruction came to clear out all dangerous chemicals from the labs; apparently a radioactive source had been stolen from a school in Derry and the education board didn't want any more incidents.

The situation deteriorated on the day of the funeral. Sinn Fein had said that everyone should stay off work as a mark of respect. Fortunately for some businesses, Thursday was early closing in Ballycol and many shops didn't open that day anyway, but those that did were very clearly nailing their colours to the mast. To Matt's horror, Auchinleck's, normally closed on Thursdays, opened in defiance. The Convent and the Christian Brothers' schools were closed but the High School tried to carry on as normal.

Being on a hill, the school overlooked the town and at half-eleven Matt saw great columns of black smoke billowing up from the Cobblerstown estate and the Apostles; cars were being burned. Soon parents began to arrive to take their youngsters home. Some had to make long detours to avoid trouble. By lunch-time Mr Wright capitulated to the inevitable and closed the school. Buses were sent for and a few teachers were left supervising the stragglers whilst the rest congregated in the staff room.

Geoff was fuming about the disruption; all Fenians were to blame. Matt tried to reason with him. "Not all Catholics support the IRA, you know. It's worse for them. Can you imagine what it's like to live in Cobblerstown or the Apostles? They must be scared to move out of their front doors!"

Geoff fixed him with a hard glare. "Well why don't you go and join your Republican friends then?" he spat. "See how long you would last there."

The gore rose in Matt's throat but he checked his anger. Staff sympathies would be with Geoff.

The news that night was depressing. Three deaths: a man who had been stoned a few days previously, a policeman shot, and an IRA man who blew himself up. Messages of sympathy had been flooding in from other countries; Iran actually renamed the Teheran street where the British consulate was located 'Bobby Sands Street'! Matt felt a despised minority within a unwanted minority under siege in a hostile world. He longed to have Alex with him but as the security situation had worsened his visits had become less and less frequent, until he had stopped coming to Ballycol altogether.

He needed a drink and some craic; he would go down to Micky's.

The weather reflected the mood of the day. A fine mizzle soaked him as he made his way through the deserted town. On reaching Micky's he couldn't believe his eyes; the ever-open door was shut! He rattled it to make sure but there was no doubt about it; it was locked. He had turned to go when the door opened a fraction and Micky's good eye peered round it.

"Oh, hello Matthew," he gasped.

"Are you open?"

"Oh, couldn't open Matthew, you know what it's like Matthew. You don't know who might be watching. Can't risk any trouble. Best to close you know."

Matt smiled and nodded. "Yeah, yeah. You have to be careful, Micky."

"Troubled times we're living in," Micky said. "Masked men turned children away from school today. Cars on the Shore Road are being given a police escort."

"I'll go then," Matt said. "I'll see you tomorrow... if you're open."

"God willing. God willing. We'll see what it's like tomorrow. Very expensive this; Thursday and Friday are my best nights."

So Matt trudged home in the rain wondering what the hell he was doing in that place.

On Friday night there was rioting and looting in the town and in the early hours of Saturday morning he was awoken by an almighty crash, followed by the burglar alarm. He realised that one of the plate-glass windows in the shop had gone. He was about to try to get back to sleep when it struck him that it could easily be a petrol bomb. Images of Danny being burnt out flashed through his mind. He didn't relish the thought of going out to face an angry mob but neither did he like the idea of being burnt in his bed.

Heart in his mouth, he got dressed and crept down the stairs. He pulled the front door open as quietly as he could but the street was deserted. Cautiously he made his way out and scanned the shop frontage in either direction. On the townward side a concrete slab rested half in and half out of the shattered window and bolts of cloth were tossed into the road. He peered in. There was no sign of smoke but he didn't want to take any chances so he found a phone box and dialled 999.

Even though the unrest went on for the next week or so, the newspapers didn't report anything from Ballycol. Presumably this applied to numerous other towns up and down the province; the situation was worse than people were hearing and in the middle of it all someone tried to kill the Pope. Matt feared that it was some hot-headed Ulster Protestant but thankfully it wasn't.

Eight days after Bobby Sands, Francis Hughes died. Matt expected more trouble in the town but although there was the odd hijacking it didn't seem too bad. The hunger strikes, deaths and riots went on until October and, as always, everyone learnt to live with the situation. It was that June that Willy-John got married.

The wedding was to be in Bangor. All the old clique were invited although, with the security situation, it was unlikely that Alex or Crispy and Jean would be able to make it. They were all to stay in Willy-John's house and Matt supposed that Friday would be the stag night. He arrived in anticipation of a full session but none of the others turned up and Willy-John was determined to stay sober for the next day. The putative stag night ended up with the two of them, plus Symie, having a few tins and reminiscing about old times. Matt expected Willy-John to be nervous about his forthcoming ordeal but he was taking it very much in his stride, a formality that had to be endured.

Billy was already at the church with his girlfriend when Matt arrived. They sat together, the statutory few rows behind the McIntyre's. One by one, the old clique assembled. Alex turned up with Sandra and Helen brought a man. Aaron was next and they were all delighted at the unexpected arrival of Crispy and Jean. Matt hadn't seen either of them for about five years; they were both so English! Matt scanned his erstwhile friends. Each a quarter of a century old, but what had happened to them all? They weren't the fun crowd he used to know. The suited men had short back and sides and the women wore well-cut two-piece suits and matching hats. They didn't look as if they could do anything remotely rebellious; they had all become part of the system.

As the service progressed Matt became increasingly aware how alien it all was. What is all this crap about God ordaining it that man and woman shall have zillions of babies, he wondered. He looked around him at all the smiling couples just waiting for their turn. It wasn't for him: the whole set-up was screaming to him, get out you queer bastard, you don't belong here; we're nice, middle-class heterosexuals.

At long last the service was over; they posed for photographs and then the cortege made its way to the hotel for the booze-up. Perhaps the old crowd will loosen up a bit when they get out of the church, he thought, then we can have a bit of craic, like in the old days.

The wedding breakfast was very formal. Willy-John had made sure the clique were all on the same table and the waiters had been instructed to make sure that they didn't run out of wine. Crispy entertained them with stories of life in the modern army. Everyone seemed envious of his lifestyle but to Matt it sounded like a nightmare. Then Crispy announced his engagement to Jean and asked them all to try to make it over to England for the wedding; it would be a full military wedding and it wouldn't be safe to have it at home.

Symie managed a surprisingly witty best man speech but Willy-John upstaged him with his reply. He toasted Crispy and Jean and trusted that Billy and Alex would be not too long behind. Bastard, Matt thought.

Speeches over, the party moved into a function room where a band was already playing. Aaron had studiously avoided Matt right through the proceedings and at this juncture, to Matt's great relief, he made his apologies to the McIntyres and left. Matt was looking forward to a good bop but when all the couples paired off and took the floor there was no-one left for him to dance with.

After a couple of dances Sandra went off to have a chat with her old school-friends and Alex sat down with Matt. He was looking wonderful. His sharp navy suit and crisp white shirt accentuated his rugged physique. When he turned to watch the others dance Matt watched the nape of his neck with the two vertical lines of closely shaved hair diving into his collar. Just being close to him had a unique effect on Matt. No one else did this to him; the very smell of his body turned him on. The sight of the black hairs on his fingers; the tiny black specks of stubble in his cheek and the deep sultry brown eyes made that V of muscle from his hips to his groin tighten and tingle. But Alex had been insistent that he wasn't gay and he was making a show of his interest in Sandra. He didn't actually ignore Matt but he wasn't exactly communicating either. Matt felt a barrier growing between them but evidently tonight wasn't the night to try dismantling it.

Sandra came back and Alex went off to dance again. Sitting alone at that table Matt concluded that there was no future for him in the heterosexual world that defined his feelings, at best, as not quite right and at worst as sick, perverted and criminal. He was kidding himself if he thought he could pretend to be a part of it. Why bother? It did him no favours. He gulped his drink feeling increasingly sorry for himself. Willy-John and Louise were radiant, dancing an old-time waltz in the midst of his friends. His eyes filled with tears. Willy-John had been his mentor. He was brash and occasionally thoughtless, but he had always been concerned for Matt's welfare; to put it bluntly Willy-John had looked after him. And now he was abandoning him for Louise, she had unwittingly joined the ranks of the enemy.

Then there was a flurry of white and a waft of lavender and Louise was next to him. "Are you alright, Matthew?" she said in genuine concern.

He tried to cover his tears and nodded. "Just feeling a bit maudlin; passing of old times and all that. I'm being a silly old sentimental sod, that's all."

"Come and have a dance," she smiled.

So he got up and put on an excellent show of enjoying himself but resolved to avoid weddings in the future.

30: The Calm Before the Storm

Matt returned to Strathbeg to mope when term finished. Willy-John wouldn't want him interrupting his new-found marital bliss. Alex was apparently seeing Sandra. Danny had disappeared and Simon would be away to university soon. Matt anticipated the bleak and lonely autumn ahead.

The fact that a branch of Cara-Friend had opened in Derry was indicative that there were others who shared his isolation and he resolved to ring the new phone line and see what was going on in Derry. There was also a good piece of news just for him. He got a long letter from Piet relating his activities in Amsterdam, his new home. It wasn't until the very end that he dropped in the welcome news that he was planning to come to Ireland that summer.

On a bright sunny July day Matt drove to Aldergrove to pick the Dutchman up. Piet had the style consistency of a chameleon. At their previous encounter he had sported a mohican – a bright pink, spiked crest of hair with pink triangles dyed into the scalp. Standing in the airport, watching the dowdy businessmen and students in jeans and sweatshirts, Matt dreaded this season's flamboyance. When he appeared he was wearing an electric blue, velvet, three-quarter-length jacket braided and embroidered in yellow and red and festooned with coloured ribbons. Longer on top than at the sides, his hair still showed traces of the mohican but he had it drawn back into a short ponytail decorated with yet more ribbons. Matt recognised his trousers from their first encounter, soft, baggy things in a yellow, satin-like material. As Piet flounced over to him Matt cringed as he noticed that his eyes were lined with mascara. He dodged Matt's offered hand and threw his arms around him, planting a big kiss on his lips; Matt wanted to curl up and die on the spot. Piet noticed. "What is wrong, Matthew? Are you not happy for seeing me?"

"Of course I am. It's just that here, men don't usually kiss in public. It's not even normal to embrace... I'm sorry, I was embarrassed."

"It is not normal in the Netherlands. But we are not normal, are we Matthew?" he grinned.

Oh God! Matt cried inwardly. He had forgotten just how over the top Piet could be. He had forewarned his folks about his flamboyance but how *would* they actually take him?

The drive from Aldergrove to Derry took them over the Sperrin mountains via Glenshane Pass. It wasn't all that special but

Piet was so impressed that Matt took great delight in tantalising him with tales of Donegal.

"Where will we stay?" Piet asked.

"We're going to the farm now. I'll show you round there first then I thought we could go to my flat in Ballycol. We can relax and be ourselves more there."

Piet looked at him suspiciously. "What do you mean, be ourselves?"

"You know. Talk about what we like, do what we want to do... You know."

"Have sex?" Piet grinned.

"If you want to."

"Of course I want to. But why can we not... be ourselves, at the house of your parents?"

"Mum and Dad might find out."

"I don't understand. Do you mean that they would not wish us to love each other in their house?"

Matt pulled the car onto the hard shoulder at the top of Glenshane.

Piet looked at him expectantly. "This is a good place." He smiled as he put his hand round Matt's neck and kissed him.

"That's not why I stopped... I'm not objecting though."

Piet's kiss was a reviving draught in Matt's love drought. Reluctantly, he pushed Piet's yielding body from him. "Come on, Mum's expecting us for lunch." Matt swam in Piet's eyes. "Look. My parents don't know I'm gay. They would *die* if they knew. So *please* don't give the game away."

"You want me to pretend that I am a bloody damn heterosexual?" he said in horror.

"My dear, dear friend, no. Be yourself, only don't let them know I'm *gay*, that's all. *Please*."

Piet planted a gentle kiss on his cheek. "Jah. Of course I understand. In the Netherlands I know gay people who are afraid of their families finding this thing. I think in Northern Ireland the people are less accepting. I believed you were more free. When I read your letter about the troubles you had at school, I was very proud for you."

"Yeah, well. I was really scared that my folks might hear about it but it all came to nothing and, other than people at school, no one knew about it."

He started the engine up and they headed for home.

In deference to Matt's fears, Piet toned down his appearance before entering the house, though he didn't exactly look like the average Derry lad. But Matt need not have worried about him getting on with his family; he was a charmer. Matt's parents immediately took to him, Roger was as gung-ho as usual and Iris was polite. Piet sat for hours by the hearth with Matt's grandmother milking her for tales of life in old Ulster. Matt's main worry was that Jenny might land down to sus Piet out before he got him safely to Ballycol.

Delighted at how Piet had got on with his folks, Matt told him how grateful he was for him making the effort to humour them.

"Matthew, my friend," he said haughtily. "I love your family very much because it is from them that you are. But if I did not like them I would not wish to be speaking to them like this."

Rick was the only one to disapprove of Piet. The moment they met Matt could see he wasn't impressed. Piet looked Rick over appreciatively, and Rick returned the look in ill-disguised disdain. "Quare coat you've got there, sar," Rick drawled. Piet didn't understand a word.

"He's saying that's a nice coat, Piet," Matt paraphrased with a slight, improving inaccuracy.

"Aye," Rick sneered.

"I bought it in a..." Piet hesitated.

"Fancy dress shop?" Rick finished his sentence artlessly.

Matt had to get them apart. "No, I think Piet means a second-hand shop."

"No. It is called The Freak Shop."

"Aye, it would be," Rick interjected.

"It is on Nieuwe Hoogstraat," Piet continued, "in Amsterdam. You remember this shop Matthew; we went there."

Matt remembered the place alright. It was all jellebras, hookers and Indian brassware; a whole shop dedicated to the drugs culture. This was getting dangerous.

Piet ploughed on. "You will have to visit Amsterdam, Rick. You could buy some nice things. There are plants you can buy in Amsterdam which would make you very happy."

He had engaged Rick's attention; he was a bit of a gardener. How could this foreigner know anything about plants? he thought. "What sort of plants would that be then?" he challenged.

"Oh, cannabis sativa; mescal cacti; ipomoea; papaver somnifera," Piet reeled off casually.

"I don't know them fancy names; I call a spade a spade. What're their real names?"

"Hashish, mescaline, LSD, heroin; there are many more, it is such a free city." He smiled beatifically.

"Piet," Matt almost shouted. "He's only joking, Rick. You can't buy things like that there."

"Of course you can," Piet insisted.

"No – you – can – not," Matt said determinedly. "Come on, Piet. We've got to go. Bye, Rick."

As soon as the two friends got round the corner of the barn they collapsed into each other's arms in helpless laughter.

"You bastard," Matt cried. "Now the whole of the UDR will think I'm shacked up with a drug-crazed hippie!"

Between giggles Piet choked, "Did you see his eyes when I said heroin?"

"You shouldn't have done that, you know. He's a bit naïve but he really has a heart of gold."

"I could not help myself. When he looked at my clothing like that I saw the look of a Limburg farmer; they still eat Jews in Limburg."

Later, Rick ran into Matt in the yard: "I'd watch that boy if I was you, Matthew. Don't bend down when he's around. He'll have your arse." With that short, brutal phrase he flung the Ulster mentality full in Matt's face.

Piet wanted to hit the gay scene but Matt hadn't a notion if there *was* one around Derry. So, when Thursday came round, he rang the new Cara-Friend line. The man on the other end was not very encouraging but he offered to meet them on Friday evening and take them to a pub. Matt had intended to head off to Ballycol for Friday night in Micky's but Piet was keen to sample the Derry scene and Matt had to admit he was curious.

Piet took Friday as his opportunity to go overboard in his costume. The electric blue coat was adorned with more decoration, and make-up was judiciously applied. Matt followed him downstairs in grim anticipation of his family's reaction. Piet swished into the room like a superstar. Matt's dad didn't bat an eyelid; his ma gasped, "Oh my! Very impressive! Very Beau Brummel, isn't he dear?"

"Is that what they dress like in Holland these days?" Matt's dad asked incredulously.

"England too," Matt claimed. "Never heard of Adam Ant?"

"Aye," Mr Woodhead mused, "But he was Victorian wasn't he, not Regency."

"Come on, Dad! Adam Ant's a pop singer. You must've seen him on the telly."

"When have you seen your father watching 'Top of the Pops'?" his mother chuckled.

"Right enough," he admitted. "Suppose he hasn't since I lived at home."

"You children think the whole world revolves around you. Jenny's worse. She thinks that we all live in suspended animation when she's away."

Time was getting on, they had to meet Kevin in fifteen minutes and Matt didn't want to be late. "Course, Mum," he said kissing her and making for the door. "Come on, Piet." He glanced back at her; he thought she had an odd, wistful look. "See you later, Mum."

Kevin was waiting by the phone boxes outside the Guildhall. He was a young chap, blond and slightly overweight with an effeminate air. If he was surprised by Piet's appearance, he was careful not to show it.

"It's not a gay bar we're going to, you know," he apologised, "but we all go there. The bar manager doesn't mind."

Piet looked at Matt, who shrugged.

"What doesn't he mind?" Piet asked.

"Us going in his bar."

"Do the other bar-owners mind?"

"Well, not exactly. We would get hassle in a lot of places. You could get a kicking very handy. And no one would lift a finger. This is the place."

They were at a modern door in the blank wall of a much older building. Kevin pushed through and they were in a small, crowded bar. Eyes turned as the outrageous Dutchman made his entrance. Soon they were sitting with a group of half a dozen young men, all of whom were trendily dressed though none nearly approached Piet's style. Matt found it difficult to slot in with the group. He thought they were wound up in their own little world, one to which neither Piet nor he were privy. Kevin made an effort to bring them in. He was building up a picture of Matt and Piet but got the impression that they were an affair and couldn't work out how they managed with Matt in Ballycol and Piet in Amsterdam. Piet draped his arm round Matt and squeezed him, saying, "Our love can cross the miles of ocean," and gave him a big, sloppy kiss.

Kevin looked uncomfortable. "I'd watch it if I was you," he suggested.

"Oh, he's alright," Matt grinned. "It's later that he gets hard to handle."

Kevin elaborated. "John doesn't like us being too obvious. He can get heavy."

Matt shook Piet off in embarrassment, he turned in surprise. "What is wrong, Matthew?"

"Kevin said that the barman doesn't like it."

"I am not kissing the barman!"

"You know what I mean," Matt said crossly. "I have to live here, you know. Some of these people might know me."

Piet didn't look very impressed. "Jah, jah. So you want to pretend to be a heterosexual. You have no self-respect?"

Hurt by Piet's tone, Matt reddened and his body language became isolationist.

Piet softened. "I will buy some more beers. You want the same?"

"Better not. Orange juice and tonic water please," he replied and watched Piet weave his way to the bar. He seemed to be waiting for ages and when he eventually returned he had no drinks.

"What's wrong?" Matt asked.

"I do not know. He said that I could not buy drinks from him."

Matt's heart sank. "I'll go and find out what's wrong."

After standing for a few minutes he attracted the slick young man's attention. "Pint of Harp, pint of Smithwicks and a pure orange and tonic please."

The barman looked uncertain. Before he had the chance to comply with Matt's request an older man came over. "What do *you* want?" he demanded.

"Pint of Harp, pint of Smithwick's and a pure orange and tonic please," he repeated.

"You're barred too, he said. You can leave when you've finished your drinks."

"Why?" he demanded.

"I don't have to give you a reason. You're barred, it's as simple as that. If you don't go now I shall have to make you."

He glared at Matt, defying him to argue. He went back to the table and sat down dejectedly.

"You have no drinks, Matthew?" Piet said with a wry smile.

"You know why!"

"Yes, but I wanted you to experience the same thing."

Matt looked at him miserably; his throat was dry and his voice cracked. "Sorry. It's this fucking country again."

He was aware that Kevin was speaking. "What's happened?"

"Apparently we're barred," Matt mumbled. "Pock-face there told us to get out."

"He must have seen you two at it."

"For fuck's sake, we only kissed."

"I told you they only just tolerated us," Kevin bemoaned.

Piet stood up. "Come Matthew, we will leave." Matt gulped

his beer down and started to follow, but instead of heading for the door Piet walked towards the bar. Before getting there he jumped onto a table and shouted, "Hey, man with the little brain." The conversation lulled. "I come here for a beer with my friend. You send me out because I am a homosexual. You are a fascist, like the Nazis. I spit on you and pity you."

By the time the barman had rushed from behind the bar Piet was stalking out of the bar with dignity, Matt scurrying after him when the barman grabbed him and bundled him out of the door.

"Out! OK?" he shouted. "You'll never get in here again."

"I would not want to," Piet scoffed and off they stalked.

"It is like Holland fifty years ago," Piet raged. "This is not the behaviour of civilised people. This is what the British do to an occupied people."

Matt decided to wait until later to explain that they had been in a Nationalist bar and that 'occupiers' and 'occupied' held gay people in the same contempt.

"Will we have the same problems at Ballycol?" Piet asked.

"If we display our sexuality in public, I'm afraid tonight could seem the height of tolerance."

"*Matthew, Piet,*" someone shouted. Kevin ran up to them breathlessly. "Where are you going?"

"Home, I suppose."

"We're going to McLaughlin's. Are you coming?" he panted.

"Will we get thrown out of there?" was Piet's acid reply.

"No, you'll get the shit kicked out of you if you carry on like that in there!"

"I think we'd better go home," Matt said.

"Come on," Kevin pleaded. "It's not that bad. At least come for one."

McLaughlin's wasn't nearly as crowded. It was a traditional town pub and in one of the stalls most of Kevin's friends from the first pub had assembled.

"We should boycott Johnny's," one said petulantly

"Aye, we'll pass the word round the scene."

"No point. You know most of the queens would go in anyway."

"We could stop them at the door; do a picket! The Socialist Workers would help."

"Honestly, you don't need to, just for us," Matt protested. "We'll be gone tomorrow. Piet'll not be back and I doubt I will."

"Aw, come on," Kevin pleaded, "You've got to come back, Matt. We've barred ourselves from Johnny's now. So you can't desert us, can you now?"

"We'll see. Tomorrow's another day. But you can't deprive yourself of your only pub just because of us."

As the others were excitedly plotting revenge on Johnny, Kevin lowered his voice. "Don't worry about them. They'll never picket the place. It would do them no good anyway and they'd be back in there themselves within the month. Let them have their bitch; that's all it is."

"Have a good night?" Mrs Woodhead asked as they trooped into the kitchen; Matt's dad was engrossed in a film on the television. "Where *did* you go, anyway?" she continued.

Matt hadn't expected her to ask. "Just some pub on the city side," he said as casually as he could.

"What pub?" she asked.

"Don't know its name, it's near the Guildhall," he explained. "Very plush actually, all the arty-farty sorts go there."

"Why did you go there, not the Regal or the Rugby Club?"

"Was meeting a friend there, a friend of Danny's actually."

"How is Danny anyway?" she asked, enabling him to steer the conversation into the safer territory of Danny's problems.

Piet had slipped up to bed whilst Matt was talking to his mum; he wished her goodnight and followed him up. Matt bade Piet goodnight as he passed his room and pushed on his own bedroom door. Cleansed of make-up, Piet was stretched out Matt's bed, naked but for his shorts. "Hello," Matt said, dropping down next to him. "What's the matter?"

He cuddled close to Matt. "I am sorry about tonight."

"Nothing to be sorry about. The guy was an ass'ole."

"Jah!" he whispered, starting to maul Matt.

"No, Piet."

"Why?"

"Not here. Wait till tomorrow. I'll not feel so inhibited there."

Piet flopped back on the bed and shut his eyes: "OK. I am beginning to think you don't like me."

"Aw!" Matt cried as he twisted round, pinning Piet to the bed. Matt pressed his lips to Piet's and convinced him of the fallacy of his last statement.

"Tomorrow," he said at length, prising himself from Piet's arms. "Go on now, please... Or else I won't be able to let you go."

Piet had learnt his lesson. He borrowed some of Matt's things and, to Matt's immense relief, Ballycol never saw his blue coat or his makeup. Safely in Matt's flat, Piet grabbed him: "Now?" he grinned.

Later, Matt took him to the antiquated grocer's where Simon

was working for summer. Piet had been impressed by Auchinleck's Victorian atmosphere, so Matt thought he might find Hasson's interesting. The drowsy town was abnormally quiet for a Saturday, Matt guessed that most of the populace would be enjoying the sun in the grounds of a demolished hotel that served as the town's park. Hasson's was of Auchinleck's era; packets of Ariel and tubs of Pot Noodle looked curiously out of place on the sagging oak shelves. The glorious, heavy smell hit you as you went through the door. It was a wonderful mixture of coffee and spices and fruit. Mr Hasson still sold grains, dried fruit and peel from great tubs and sacks and there was an old bacon slicer from which he would produce dangerous slices of ham. Matt rarely went there; Wellworths supermarket was more convenient. In fact he hardly ever saw anyone in there and he had wondered how Mr Hasson kept going until Simon told him that most of his trade was delivery.

Simon was dealing with the week's orders. He had a box of little notebooks, each bearing a customer's name and address. He was going through one, dropping the appropriate item into a detergent-scented cardboard box as he crossed it out and priced it. "What sort of tea for Mrs Heggarty?" he shouted as they pushed the bell-tinkling door open.

"Amber Glow," came a disembodied shout from the back of the shop.

"Hallo!" Simon beamed. "How's it going?"

"Great, thanks. How's things with you?"

"OK. This must be Piet." Simon turned to him: "I've heard that much about you I feel as if I know you already. How do you do?" he asked, proffering his hand.

Introductions made, they got down to arranging to meet for the evening and left.

Once out on the street, Piet commented, "He is very beautiful!"

"Simon?"

"Yes. He has a tranquillity. I find this very nice. Also, he has a nice face."

"Lay off him! He's as straight as they come, I promise. Did you realise that it was him that all the bother was about? I don't want you seducing him and letting everyone say 'I told you so!'"

"Why should I wish to seduce him when I have you?" Piet said bashfully.

"Because I know you, Meneer van Vondel, that's why!" In a fit of mental aberration Matt grabbed his neck, pulled his head into his shoulder and pushed his lips into his hair. As soon as he realised what he'd done he pushed him away. "You're a *very* dangerous person to have around," Matt complained.

"I will not seduce your friend," Piet solemnly promised.

"I don't mean that. Having you here makes me forget where I'm living. In Ireland you can't grab another man and kiss him in public, you just don't do that sort of thing. I could get into real trouble; that's what I mean."

Saturday night turned into quite a party; Myra and Jack were home as were sundry other former pupils. Then in Micky's they met up with Feargal and some of his friends. Everyone ended up in Matt's flat with bottles of wine and six-packs; the craic was powerful. It was only on Sunday that it dawned on Matt that this was the first time any of them had seen him with another man. Piet and he hadn't been too demonstrative but they were obviously together. He wasn't worried about his close friends seeing him but there were some people there he didn't know so well.

They intended to go to Donegal for the day on Sunday but, as they didn't get up until well after midday, they ended up wandering round the town in the afternoon sun. The glistening lake at the bottom of the main street drew them to its shore. From there the natural route was right, past Richmond Terrace, a row of decaying Georgian town houses gazing balefully across water. Beyond them, the road ended at a great pair of rusting, wrought-iron gates; all that was left of the hotel that once graced the parkland lying between Belle-Vue Hill and the lake. Having survived the earlier troubles, the hotel was one of the first casualties of the recent unrest; it was burnt to the ground in the early seventies. The IRA claimed responsibility but people said that it was a bit too convenient for the near-bankrupt owners.

That afternoon it seemed that all Ballycol was in the park. There wasn't a square yard in which to sit in peace so they wandered along the normally muddy track which threaded its tortuous way between the lough and the salubrious residences of Belle-Vue; this was the short cut to the Creaghmore Forest Park which straddled the border. The best part was next to the shore, where the monotony of conifers was broken by a band of broad-leaf trees. The road entrance was about two and a half miles from the town, but the shoreline track took you there in less than a mile, albeit with muddy feet.

They found a quiet spot and settled down to sun themselves. They lay close with hands and legs touching. A casual observer wouldn't have remarked on their intimacy but both drew quiet comfort from each other's touch. As they dozed to the gentle lapping of the lake and an occasional, desultory chaffinch chirp, the heavy tang of pine and hum of insects drifted down the hill. Even there, the peace was periodically disturbed by dog walkers and adventurous kids. "Tomorrow," Matt vowed, "we'll have to get to Donegal. I hate crowds like this."

"You think this is a crowded place! You do not know the Netherlands!" Piet declared. "In a place as beautiful as this you would not be possible to find such peace! Even on a raining day!"

By a miracle, they managed to tear themselves from each other early enough to make a start on Monday. It was the twelfth of July, the day the Orangemen marched, and Matt wanted to be well away from Ballycol before they started. Their first stop was the ruins of Donegal Priory. The town's cemetery was in its grounds where masses of ox-eye daisies combined with shattered walls and gravestones to make an interesting foreground to spectacular views of the muddy estuary with its mysteriously tree-cloaked islets. From Killybegs, they wound their way to Carrick along a tortuous road which threaded its way along the rugged coastline. Across Donegal Bay, Benbulben thrust its angular back into the shimmering sky; below them, Atlantic rollers broke over shoals and skerries before crashing onto the rocky beach. Rounding a tight headland the view changed. Here the estuary of the River Glen stretched inland. The community of Glen was sprinkled over a patchwork quilt of fields and beyond, the grey bulk of Slieve League loomed like a great bear slumbering under its counterpane. Soon they were creeping up the steep, crumbling road over the seaward paw of Slieve League. Piet was exhilarated; at times the road clung so closely to the cliff edge that there was nothing between them and the foaming sea, hundreds of feet below. The track ended at Bunglass, where the cliff top gave a stunning view of the shattered flank of Slieve League; a great sweep of cliff, scree and boulder-strewn slopes tumbling from the mountain's two-thousand foot summit down to the turbulent sea. A path wound its way along the cliff-top towards the summit some two miles away. Although they were already five hundred feet above the sea, with all the ups and downs it was far more than a fifteen-hundred foot ascent. They weren't shod for the walk but Matt hardly demurred when Piet started along the track.

After an hour of toiling through the long heather they were both stripped to the waist and the cool sea breeze was whisking the moisture from their sweating bodies. "Hold on," Matt gasped, flopping down at a particularly spectacular spot.

"It's so beautiful!" Piet cried, flinging his arms into the air and throwing back his head as if to drink in the sun and wind. "I want to have this always!" he shouted.

Matt smirked contentedly and reclined into the springy heather. The sun beat down on his eyelids.

"Come, Matt! This is wonderful," Piet called.

He sat up, startled to see Piet in the same stance but stark naked. He put him in mind of a Mucha poster. His dyed blond hair streamed in the Atlantic breeze and his spindly, pale body was rigid, chest thrust forward in adulation of the elements.

"For God's sake Piet, put your clothes on. You'll catch your death of cold!"

"Come, Matt. Join me. It is like orgasm!"

"Someone might come."

Piet ignored him and began a strange, slow-motion dance, pirouetting across the heather and stabbing the air with well-controlled jabs of arms and legs reminiscent of Tai Chi. With a balletic leap he landed astride Matt's prone body and lowered himself to a crouch, his genitals dangling over Matt's chest. He beckoned Matt to join him with slow hand movements but sprang out of reach when he tried to grab him. "Come," he enjoined, "join the wind and the sun and me."

"You're crazy!" Matt laughed.

"I am free!" he yelled, swivelling on one foot. "Take off your chains and be free too!"

Matt was transfixed by his choreography, horribly aware that someone might come along any moment. At last Piet flopped down next to him like a rag doll. Matt kissed his cool forehead and he opened his eyes and smiled indulgently. "You're not free yet Matt, not free."

"Get dressed," Matt replied. "We'd better be getting back."

31: Exposure

Disaster struck at ten-thirty on the morning of Wednesday, July the fourteenth. They were still in bed when the doorbell rang. Matt pulled on his jeans and stumbled downstairs, trying unsuccessfully to pull on his tee-shirt as he went. Vaguely, in the back of his mind, he feared the police (all homosexual activity was still illegal in Northern Ireland) but what met his eyes was infinitely worse.

"Hello, Matthew," his sister breezed, "I've come to see your Dutch friend. I've heard so much about him from Mummy I thought I'd come and see for myself. She says he's a nice lad. Are you only just up? You lazy so-and-so."

Jennifer swept up the stairs past him and was searching the

flat by the time he caught up with her.

"Who was it?" Piet demanded as Jennifer pushed through the door. " Come back to bed."

He sat upright, gloriously naked, and smiled at her saying, "Hello, my name is Piet, how do you do?" As Matt walked in he added, "This was the correct introduction, Matt?"

"Perfect... just perfect," he murmured.

"I'm Jennifer, Matthew's sister," she said haughtily. "Matthew, you go and get my things from the car and I'll make a pot of tea while he gets up."

Matt tried to make small talk with her as they waited for Piet to finish in the bathroom but she never was one for beating around the bush.

"So," she started, "there's more than meets the eye to your *Dutch friend.*"

"You could say that," Matt replied sullenly.

"I certainly could! Now *what* is going on?"

He tried to be defiant. "I don't see that it's any of your business."

"Don't you now? Don't you?" she snapped. "It seems to me that it is a lot of my business. What do you think Mummy and Daddy would say if they knew what's being going on? You silly, silly boy!"

"Nothing's been *going on,*" he said pathetically.

"Grow... up... Matthew! I come in, find you half dressed and him stark naked in your bed, shouting for you to come back to him. Do you think I was born yesterday?"

Inexplicably, Matt started to cry. He wasn't listening to her blistering words, a sniffle became a sob and the sobs became uncontrolled weeping.

Piet breezed in and stopped, stunned by the scene before him. "What is wrong?"

Matt couldn't reply.

Piet rushed over to Matt and, enveloping him in his warm arms, he turned to Jennifer. "What has happened?" then slowly, "has somebody... died?"

"No," Matt choked, "unless you count my reputation with my family."

"Here, have a cup of tea and stop snivelling," Jennifer said more gently.

Piet didn't move or speak as Matt sipped at the tea. Jennifer had put sugar in and he hated sugar.

"Look," she went on in the same tone, "I didn't mean to be so rough on you. You've been a bit silly, that's all. As long as you wise up and neither of you say anything about this childish episode, no one need know. You're only young fellers, all boys mess about. You've just left it a bit late, that's all," she said in a dismissive tone.

"What does she mean?" Piet whispered.

"She's giving us the chance to say that we were just *experimenting*, that we're not really homosexual. She thinks we are silly little boys playing games."

"Jah?"

Matt braced himself. "Jennifer. You've made one big mistake."

She smiled, self-indulgently.

"We weren't *experimenting*. We don't need to *experiment*, we're both very experienced. Piet and I have been lovers for three years. And he's not the only one." Piet's grip tightened in approval.

Matt watched Jennifer pale as his revelation sank in. "I shouldn't have hidden it; I've known for years. Piet has helped me to come to terms with my sexuality. You may not like the idea but it is me; the way I am... I was about to say, I can't help it, but that makes me sound like a victim. I'm not, and I don't think I would want to be, any different; I am what I am, and I like me as I am. Maybe it causes problems but they are not *my* problems. It's everyone else that makes a big deal of the way I was born. For years I have been terrified of what would happen if X or Y found out. Well everybody, from A to Z, can fucking well know, and if they don't like it, they can bloody well lump it."

Jennifer swallowed and sounded shaken for the first time. "You're being very selfish Matthew. You can't tell Mummy and Daddy, they would take it badly."

"Why?" he spat. "Their own flesh and blood being honest to them for the first time in his life? Can you imagine what it has been like all these years, pretending to be something I'm not? Can you imagine the barriers it's created? Do you realise that I don't even *know* my own parents? And they don't have a clue what goes on inside my head. And it's all because I have always been told that I have something to hide, something to be afraid of. But I haven't. I love Piet. I love him and he has shown me that there is nothing to be ashamed of. If I have any shame, it is for this bloody country for being full of cruel, arrogant hypocrites."

Jennifer sat and gaped at him, as he launched back into his diatribe. "Now I know I *will* tell Mum and Dad. If they throw me out and never want to see me again that's better than living in this house of cards. 'Cos that's what it is. This pretence of *normality*; that's what you call it anyway. It's not normal to me, it's a perversion of the real me!" He paused but she didn't react. Noticing an hysterical edge creeping into his voice, he calmed down a bit. "I love you all, you know. I'm not doing this to hurt anybody. Please understand. I have to do what is right for me."

She shook her head slowly. "I've never heard you talk like that. I always thought of you as a silly, inconsequential little boy. I don't know what to say."

"Just say you understand."

"I don't. But you are my brother so I suppose I'll have to, won't I?" she said begrudgingly.

She'd intended to stay for the whole day but, after a tense lunch at an hotel in Kesh, they parted company and she headed back to Strathbeg.

"You are very quiet," Piet observed.

Matt nodded. "That was some set-to."

"How are you feeling about it?"

"I'm still a bit stunned. I never expected it to happen like this. I'm quite relieved actually. By the time I get home she'll have told Mum and Dad everything. I suppose it'll make it easier than if I had to find a way of breaking it to them myself."

"You might find that they already know," he said quietly.

"Why?" Matt snapped. "Have you said something to them?"

"No," he faltered, "nothing to your parents."

"What do you mean? Who *have* you been talking to?"

"Your grandmother."

"What have you told her?" Matt yelped.

"I told her that I was gay. I didn't wish to but I could not prevent it. She was asking me about the Netherlands and about my life there and she asked me if I had a girl there."

"But you didn't tell her about you and me?"

"No. She said it; she asked me if I had a man?"

"And you said me."

"No. I told her the truth. I said that I did not have one special man-friend."

Matt took a deep breath and beseeched heaven. What on earth would Grandma have made of that?

Piet continued. "She said that I should maybe get a nice young man. She suggested you."

"*What?*"

"Your grandmother thinks that you and I should be lovers," he grinned.

"Come on, you're having me on... aren't you?"

"No. She knows you are gay, I am certain of this. And not only this, she wants you to be happy. If your grandmother has worked it out I think your mother and father will also know this too."

He was stunned by Piet's casual outing of him but decided to put the forthcoming confrontation to the back of his mind and enjoy the rest of his stay.

He hadn't imagined how sorry he would be to see Piet go. As he watched his blue jacket disappearing through the departure gate a wave of emptiness swept over him. He felt impossibly alone; all his friends had gone and Ballycol would never be the same again without Piet.

The moment he arrived home Jenny struck. "Matthew. Roger and I want a word with you."

"What about?"

"You know very well what about."

"Yeah," he sneered.

"We're only trying to help," she said in a haughty, hurt tone.

Matt waited in the parlour. Out of bounds to him when he was little, it was a mausoleum to the Edwardian era. He eyed the yellowing antimacassars, the embroidered screen that hid the grate and the gigantic aspidistra glowering in the gloom of heavy lace curtains. It wasn't just anticipation of what was to come that made him profoundly uncomfortable. Since his grandfather had ailed and died in that room, he had hated the place.

It was almost a relief when his siblings finally came in. Roger looked as unhappy as Matt about the impending confrontation. He shut the door deliberately and turned to face him. "Hi Matthew," he said, with little conviction.

"Well, go on," Jennifer urged.

Roger scowled at her. "Jenny er... told me about the other day."

"I thought she might," Matt said cynically.

"Is it true?"

"Depends on what she said."

He knew Roger was hating this but he wasn't about to make it easy for him.

"She told me what happened."

Jenny interjected: "I told him that you and Pansy Pants were in bed together and I told him you were going to tell Mummy and Daddy."

Matt stood up and, eyes narrowed, he said, "There's no need to insult Piet. If you're going to adopt that attitude you can just piss off." He made to leave but Roger grabbed his arm.

"There's no need to use foul language!" Roger said angrily.

Then, softening, he said, "Hold on. She's a bit upset."

"She's upset! How do you think I feel? She's insulting the only person in the world that really cares for me."

"We care for you," he insisted.

Matt's temper flared. "Why are you treating me like a criminal then?"

"Calm down, Matthew," Jenny soothed. "We know it's not your fault. You've been blinded by him, that's all. He has a very strong personality. I can see how he might have impressed you but we know that it's only a phase you're going through."

Matt reddened and spluttered. "God. You really don't have any respect for me, do you? You're as narrow- minded as the rest. I thought that you would have picked up a splinter of decency at university but no! You..."

"Stop it you two," Roger pleaded as he physically restrained his furious sister. "If he's a homo that's his business not ours. What is our business is Mummy and Daddy. What'll happen if they find out?"

"When they find out," Matt insisted.

"They mustn't," Jenny shouted.

"It's my bloody life, not yours."

"Matthew!" Roger cut in. "Did you know that Daddy's been in hospital?"

"Yes. So what?"

"Do you know what for?"

"Not exactly. Mum said it was a check-up."

"It wasn't. He's getting on, you know. He's got a dickey heart. He had a slight attack; just a fright but next time it could be more serious."

Matt's stomach sank.

"You see now why you can't tell them," Jenny smiled snidely. "It could kill Daddy!"

Without Piet around there seemed no point in going back to Ballycol so he stayed at home. In the back of his mind he was hoping that Alex might turn up. Not being expected to do so much on the farm anymore he moped around the house. He was miserable without Piet, and Jenny had made it worse. His mother didn't take long to realise that something was wrong. He was sitting at the kitchen table, staring dejectedly into a cooling cup of tea when she broached the subject. "You're missing him, aren't you love?"

"Who?" he gulped.

"Piet... You're really fond of him."

Tightly pursing his lips, he hid a tearful pout as he nodded his head. "Mum?"

"Mmm?"

"Nothing."

She sat down opposite him and took his hands in hers. "Come on, love."

"Mum?" he murmured. "Did you like Piet?"

"He's a bit of an oddball, but he's a lovely young man."

"He's not like other people, you know."

"You obviously think he's a bit special."

"I don't mean that... he's gay."

"I thought so," she smiled.

"And you don't mind?"

"Why should I, love?"

"I didn't think you would approve."

"Is it important that I do?"

"Why should it be?"

"You tell me."

"You know, don't you?"

"Tell me," she said quietly.

It was so hard to actually say it: "I'm the same as Piet," he mumbled.

"Oh, love," she sighed.

"I'm sorry, Mummy. I can't help it, I've tried not to be, I really have, but I just am."

"If anyone's to blame it's us. If your father had spent more time with you when you were little. If we had found more friends for you to play with..."

"Mum!" Matt shouted. "It's nobody's fault. It's just chance, just the way the genes fell when you produced me. From the moment I was conceived the die was cast; this was inevitable. I'm not worried for myself, the only thing I'm sorry about is you and Dad. You expected me to marry and have grandchildren and be a respectable member of society who you can talk about to your friends and relations. Instead I'm always going to be the one you don't talk about. You must feel I've let you down."

"I can't pretend that I'm overjoyed. But I think we've always known, deep down. We've watched you grow up and we've seen your friendships. We never heard about girls, did we now?"

"Was it that transparent?"

"No, but we always had a sneaking suspicion."

Matt's voice had become child-like. "Jenny and Rodge told me I hadn't to tell you. I didn't know Daddy had a bad heart; they said the shock would kill him. Has he had a coronary?"

His mother nodded. "A mild one. He didn't want to worry

234

any of you but I told Roger."

"And the swines used that to put the frighteners on me."

"They obviously don't know us very well. Ah! Children, children, children," she declared, shaking her head.

"So I can tell Daddy then?"

"Of course you can. He will be pleased that you felt you could. It's sad that you've had to keep something so important from us all these years."

They talked for the whole afternoon. He got the distinct impression that she thought that being gay was really just like being straight except you married a man instead. In her mind was a picture of the future with Roger and Iris, Jenny and her husband and him with his man, making up one big happy family. They didn't discuss sex, of course, but other than that his mother was slowly introduced to a whole side of his life which she hadn't even suspected existed. She said that he should bring any boyfriends home although she did point out that she wouldn't treat them any differently from Jenny and Roger's boyfriends and girlfriends; that was, they would get separate bedrooms.

When his father came in his reaction was even more laid-back. His main concern was that Matthew shouldn't suffer at the hands of prejudice. As he pointed out, if they could do so many evil things to each other with the excuse of religious differences, what might they do to him for being as he was? That night he and his father talked for the first time in their lives.

32: Synthesis

Matt wrote a long letter to Piet to tell him all that had happened. As he wrote, he realised how much everyone in his life had changed. His grammar school clique hadn't really surprised him. Willy-John seemed to have been born with a route map of his life etched on his heart and he hadn't deviated from it one jot. Aaron's attitude had always been selfish and critical and although there had been no hints of his rabid fundamentalism at school his final stance hardly surprised Matt. Crispy in the army and Billy in a building society; no surprises there either. But when he thought about his two primary school pals he realised just how much the tables had turned. At Dungiven Road he had been absolutely dominated by Danny and Alex. At six and seven they had been so sure of themselves – so powerful, so in control. Now his two rôle models were floundering; each wallowng in his own confusion. Matt couldn't have imagined that they would eventually need him to be the strong one. He put down his founatin pen (a present from Piet) and formulated a plan.

Next Sunday, after lunch, he arrived at the McDaids'. Danny was watching soccer with his brother but Chris left as soon as Matt came in.

"Come on Danny," Matt ordered.

"What are you talking about," he asked, bewildered.

"I've got dad's car. Let's do that walk we'd been meaning to do."

Before Danny had time to object he was in the car and Mrs McDaid was told he would be back the next day. On the way down to Ballycol Matt enthused about the hike he'd done with Piet. Danny could never work out how Matt did it, but by the time they were in Ballycol he was quite looking forwards to the walk the next day. At the flat Matt busied himself putting a camp bed up as Danny found himself in the kitchen peeling a mound of spuds. He searched the fridge for Matt's beer supply but there wasn't a can to be found. After dinner Danny prepared to go out but Matt stopped him: "There's nowhere open – it's Sunday."

"There's a hotel isn't there?" he complained.

"Aye but it's miles away and I'm not drinking and driving. Besides you have to get a good night's sleep, you've got to get up early tomorrow. Want a cup of tea?" Somehow Danny hadn't the energy to object and after watching a film they crashed at midnight.

Danny and Matt battled against the wind as they slowly ascended Slieve League; the day wasn't nearly as nice as the last time but the wild buffeting made it more real somehow; more rugged and wild. They got to Piet's dance arena and found a sheltered spot. "Look," Matt shouted, pointing to a tattered flock of choughs reeling in the gusts. "An English bird-watcher would give his right arm to see this. Really rare in England, they are!" An eerie mew pierced the wind and a shape scythed through the air. "He's going for the chough!" Matt said excitedly, "Look at him go!"

Despite himself Danny was caught up in the drama: "They're too fast for him, aren't they?"

"For a peregrine? No way. Fastest bird in the world that," Matt laughed as the frightened crows darted for the safety of the cliffs.

"Damn," Danny exclaimed as the peregrine disappeared over the cliff edge. "Do you reckon he got one?"

"Wait and see. It should come up with its catch if it gets one."

They waited for a good fifteen minutes but the protagonists

didn't reappear so they went on to the top. "Well, what do think?" Matt asked when they finally reached the summit. Danny took a deep breath: "Fantastic!"

"Glad you came?"

Danny threw his arm round Matt. "You know I am," he smiled, chubbing Matt's cheeks.

"Thanks for a fab day," Danny said getting out of the car that evening. "I'd never have thought I could enjoy a day out with a friend so much! I still can't work out what's with you, you know Matty. You're different. I'd like to meet this Piet, he must be some feller to have that effect on you!"

Matt smiled what he hoped would be an enigmatic smile.

"What did make you drag me out like this today?" Danny demanded.

Matt practised that smile again as he let the handbrake out.

"Matt?" Danny said, as his friend leaned over to pull the passenger door closed.

Matt looked at him, foot poised on the clutch. "Yes?"

Danny knew he had to say something important but he wasn't sure what. It was an idea in the recesses of his brain but, like a patch of blue sky obscured by shifting clouds, it was infuriatingly elusive. "Matt... I... "

Matt turned off the ignition and looked expectantly at his befuddled friend. "Yes?"

"Matt... I'm sorry."

"What for?"

A rare moment of clarity told Danny what he had to say. "I've fucked you about, Matt." He looked embarrassed and fixed his eyes on the car seat. "I don't know why I do it," he said shaking his head as he spoke. "I don't mean to but there's a monster in me that takes over and I just behave like a bastard." He looked straight at Matt with a serious expression. "I'm sorry Matt, I really am!"

Matt examined his friend's face. "Yes," he said. "Yes. For the first time I really think you are!"

A smile broke over Danny's face. "Right! I am! I'm fucking sorry Matt! Fucking sorry!" He closed the door. "Look. I'll see you mate. OK?"

"Yeah," Matt said. "I'll see you," and with that he started the car and drove off feeling sure that he had at long last got through to his friend. The rest was up to Danny.

Part two came together the following Thursday.

"What's up Matt?" Alex inquired querulously as he joined

him in the lounge of the hotel in Enniskillen. "You've never rung me at work before, it must be important."

Matt had been perfecting his enigmatic smile and gave it without a second's thought: "Nothing! Just wanted to spend some time with you. You said this was your first night off and you'd nothing planned."

Alex was a bit thrown by that one. "Oh, right. Well. Nice to see you Matt. Em. Er. How are things with you?"

"Great. I feel on top of the world. You'll never guess what happened when Piet came over..."

And so Alex heard the whole story. As Matt took Alex through the highs and lows his face betrayed nothing of his emotions but as Matt finished triumphantly he couldn't conceal a sick feeling in the pit of his stomach. "Well?" Matt demanded. "What do you think?"

"About what?"

"About me coming out to Mum and Dad!"

"That's great Matt..."

"But?" Matt added.

"But nothing."

"Come on, Alex. I know you, There's something up with you."

Alex smiled, tight-lipped: "It's all so easy for you isn't it? All so cut and dried..."

"What do you mean?"

"Well. You decide you're gay. You meet Piet. You have uncomplicated sex with him and you both go your own ways as happy as Larry. Life's not that simple for the rest of us. Having a girlfriend involves responsibilities, commitments."

"Alex!" Matt complained. "If I meet someone I want to be with I'll have responsibilities and commitments to him! If you and I had got it together that's how it would have been," he added softly.

"But it's different with a woman. There's different rules. There's pregnancy to worry about and then you've got to think of the families and marriage and everything. It's not so easy."

"That was your choice, wasn't it?" Matt said tartly.

"Listen to you!" Alex objected. "If I'd said that being gay was a choice you would have gone down my throat!"

"Yeah. Because I'm being true to my nature but you're denying yours!"

Alex reddened.

"Sorry, sorry, sorry," Matt garbled. "I shouldn't have said

that. I was out of order."

Alex stood up. "Where are you going?" Matt demanded.

"To the bog," Alex announced, turning his back on Matt.

Matt sat biting his lip wondering where Alex had got to. His coat was still on his seat. Surely he wouln't go off and leave it but he was taking an awful long time.

Outside the hotel Alex paced the lakeside path collecting his thoughts. It was easy to feel heterosexual when he was with Sandra or his colleagues but as soon as he was with Matt, rogue emotions surfaced. Now Matt was challenging him like he had never done before and he didn't know how to handle it. Pull yourself together man, he thought. I'm not a randy teenager any more. I have to start behaving like an adult. There's no reason why I can't have a mature, normal friendship with Matt and still have a girlfriend. Matt'll be wondering where I am. I mustn't let him know he's fazed me. I'd better get back.

"Got lost?" Matt asked as Alex returned.

"Met a colleague in the foyer. Got chatting," he said airily. "Did you say you'd seen Danny? How is the old bastard then?"

By closing time they were both relaxed and chatting like old times.

"How are you getting back?" Alex suddenly demanded. "You've had a few and you never drink and drive. What're you going to do?"

Matt waved a set of hotel keys in his face.

"Bloody hell, Matt! This place costs a fortune!"

"Yeah but the rooms are lovely, want to see?"

Alex admired the plush room. "You really went out of your way, didn't you?"

"You're worth it, Alex. You know how important you are to me. I felt we were slipping apart. I had to do something."

Alex stared at the striking, beautiful man facing him. It was as if he'd seen Matthew for the first time in his life. This wasn't the frightened child he was used to. He felt decidedly strange. He had never felt like this before; his heart was racing and a clogging sensation filled his throat. "I'll always need you, Matt," he said, not clearly knowing what he meant but the moment he'd uttered it he was terrified and elated. Alex looked at Matt in a way that sent thrills down his sides. Matt felt like a rabbit caught in the blaze of those huge, liquid brown eyes.

"Want a nightcap?" Matt stammered. "Room service is supposed to be very good here."

"Oh. I don't think we want to be disturbed tonight, do you Matt?" Alex murmured.

"I reckon not," Matt concurred, smiling happily. Game, set and match, he thought as he sank into Alex's arms.

— THE END —

Also in the new GMP series:

Teleny *by Oscar Wilde*
The only complete edition of this erotic tale

First published in 1893, this outrageous novel of homosexual love has been attributed to Oscar Wilde with varying degrees of certainty. This edition, carefully prepared from original sources in the British Library archives, is the only one on sale annotated and unabridged. Ahead of its time in its celebration of uninhibited sensual passion between men.

"It is a bizarre book, alternating porn with florid purple passages, a hymn to sodomy with an angry attack on notions of the 'natural'" New Statesman.

price - £9.95

ISBN : 1 902852 00 1

Foolish Fire *by Guy Willard*
The first in a new trilogy of an all-american teenager's sexual adventures.

Guy willard is your all-American boy, a good-looking, popular teenager with only one hidden secret... a flaming desire for other boys. This first book in a trilogy of his sexual adventures is set at Freedom High School, where he inches his way out of the closet through a series of humerous and poignant episodes. From "Physical Education" to "Technically a Virgin", Guy's personal story is thoroughly true to life: always sexy, but very human.

price - £8.95

ISBN : 1 902852 02 8

All the Queen's Men *by Nick Elwood*

A revealing account of fourteen years as an openly gay man in the British Army.

"Out for most of my career as a cavalry bandsman, I discovered a gay military world where many squaddies were partial to a bit of cock fun. I indulged in numerous flirtations and affairs. There were no threats and rarely any hostility. Encounters with the Military Police, at first invasive grew into an irrepressible reckless defiance. We banded together, protected by peers and senior ranks alike.

I became engaged to a 16-year-old civilian, lithe and brown eyed Andreas, the summer soulmate of my dreams. Working up through the ranks to Trumpet Major I experienced much during my army career, pride in my sexuality, elation and loss. What a bummer it is to be in love."

price - £9.95

ISBN : 1 902852 03 6

Banged Up *by Jack Dickson*

Detective Jas Anderson, the hero of "Freeform" is imprisoned and fighting for his life in this new adventure.

Detective-Sergeant Jas Anderson, the violent anti-hero of Freeform, ended that story being expelled from the Glasgow police force. Banged Up starts with Jas being framed by his ex-colleagues, and remanded to Barlinnie prison. Soon he is forced to share a cell with Steve McStay, sentenced for Aggravated Assault on two gay men. In this all-male enviroment, inmates don't divide into gay and staight, rather into who fucks and who gets fucked. But resilient as ever, Jas forms an unlikely partnership with Steve in his fight survival.

price - £9.95

ISBN : 1 902852 04 4

Growing Pains *by Mike Seabrook*

The sequel to this author's most popular novel "out of bounds".

Mike Seabrook's many fans will remember Stephen Hill, the dashing young cricketer from Out of Bounds, his teacher and lover Graham, and his clever schoolfriend Richard. Two years after Stephen was forced to leave home, Graham dies in a plane crash, and Steven comes into an unexpected legacy, including a large country pub in Sussex. But as well as the strains this new fortune places on his relationship with friend Richard, the pair have to confront the homophobia of a group of the villagers, resentful of the changes Steven and Richard bring into their lives. Things finally come to a head when a young boy is brutally raped and left for dead.

price - £9.95

ISBN : 1 902852 05 2